*'I came across the dress by c...
It was my mother's, wasn't i... ...
she wore it! Was it when she met my father?
Aunty, you simply must tell me!'*

M ONA AND HER AUNT LIVE IN A LITTLE
cottage on the edge of the Somerset estate, where
her aunt sews dresses for the lady of the house. Mona
never knew her mother or father, but Aunty has always
looked after her – and Mona knows she can always talk
to her mum where she lies in the village graveyard.

When Lady Somerset dies and a new member of
the Somerset family inherits the house, things begin
to change for Mona. She has never really fitted in
anywhere, but the new Bohemian atmosphere at the
house offers opportunities for her to shine – and to find
new friends. Dancing at fancy costume balls and trips to
decadent 1920s London are wonderfully exciting – but
new experiences sometimes bring revelations and Mona
discovers there are secrets in her past she can't dance
away from.

ABOUT THE AUTHOR

JACQUELINE WILSON wrote her first novel when she was nine years old, and she has been writing ever since. She is now one of Britain's bestselling and most beloved children's authors. She has written over 100 books and is the creator of characters such as Tracy Beaker and Hetty Feather. More than forty million copies of her books have been sold.

As well as winning many awards for her books, including the Children's Book of the Year, Jacqueline is a former Children's Laureate, and in 2008 she was appointed a Dame.

Jacqueline is also a great reader, and has amassed over twenty thousand books, along with her famous collection of silver rings.

Find out more about Jacqueline and her books at www.jacquelinewilson.co.uk

Jacqueline Wilson

Illustrated by Nick Sharratt

DANCING THE CHARLESTON

CORGI YEARLING

CORGI YEARLING

UK | USA | Canada | Ireland | Australia
India | New Zealand | South Africa

Corgi Yearling is part of the Penguin Random House group of companies
whose addresses can be found at global.penguinrandomhouse.com.

www.penguin.co.uk
www.puffin.co.uk
www.ladybird.co.uk

First published 2019

001

Text copyright © Jacqueline Wilson, 2019
Illustrations copyright © Nick Sharratt, 2019

The moral right of the author and illustrator has been asserted

Set in 10.56/14.09pt New Century Schoolbook LT Pro by Becky Chilcott
Printed and bound in Great Britain by Clays Ltd, Elcograf S.p.A.

A CIP catalogue record for this book is available from the British Library

PAPERBACK ISBN: 978–0–440–87167–5

All correspondence to:
Corgi Yearling
Penguin Random House Children's
80 Strand, London WC2R 0RL

MIX
Paper from
responsible sources
FSC
www.fsc.org   FSC® C018179

Penguin Random House is committed to a
sustainable future for our business, our readers
and our planet. This book is made from Forest
Stewardship Council® certified paper.

To Ed and Jolyon of
Pickering and Chatto

I think you've been dreaming, girl.

1

MAGGIE WAS QUEEN OF THE PLAYGROUND on Monday, showing all the girls how to do this new dance, the Charleston. Her big sister went to Hailbury Town Hall on Saturday nights and came back with all the latest crazes.

'You flap your arms around and kick up your legs and pull this silly face while you're doing it,' said Maggie, demonstrating.

We all tried to copy her, while the boys jeered. I knew I was hopeless at dancing and probably looked like a demented hen as I flapped away, but I saw Peter Robinson watching me. He was smiling.

When Maggie and I walked out of school arm in arm, he was watching again. We tapped and kicked our way down School Lane, and he whistled after us. We both tossed our heads and didn't look round, though my cheeks were burning and I knew I'd gone candyfloss pink.

'Peter Robinson's sweet on you,' said Maggie.

'No, you're the one he likes,' I said, though I was secretly sure he was whistling at *me*.

I didn't know whether I liked him or not. Aunty would say he was a bit of a lout, with his home-cut hair and his frayed shirt and his clumsy boots, but then she'd say that about nearly all the boys at our school. She would also say it was nonsense to start liking boys at my age. I tended to agree with her – but Peter Robinson did have a nice smile.

When Maggie and I turned the corner I glanced round quickly and gave him a little wave.

'Mona!' said Maggie as we went up Market Street. 'You're just encouraging him.'

We walked like soldiers: a charge past Mr Samson the butcher's shop because we hated seeing the rows of dead birds hanging above his door, their beaks dripping blood; a quick march past Mr Thomas the greengrocer and Mr Slade the ironmonger and Old Molly's general stores because they didn't interest us; then a sudden halt outside Mr Berner's toyshop.

He sold many other things too – tobacco and newspapers and all kinds of basic household goods that Old Molly forgot to stock nowadays – and on the shelves behind his counter he kept jars of sweets, though we rarely had a penny between us for two ounces of fruit drops or sherbet lemons or banana toffees.

It was the toys in his window that always made us pause. It wasn't a patch on his glorious Christmas selection, when he stocked dolls as big as real babies with their own cots, and prams you could push along, and a Noah's Ark with a lift-off lid and pair after pair of wooden animals – elephants the size of our fists, all the way down to a couple of minute ladybirds with black dots on their glossy red backs.

Still, today there was a toy yacht to sail across the village pond, a spinning top all the colours of the rainbow, a skipping rope with red handles, net bags of marbles, and two dolls in floral dresses, one with yellow hair, one with brown.

Maggie and I spent a good five minutes discussing the merits of the dolls, and whether we preferred the blonde one or the dark one, though our chances of buying either were nil. Maggie didn't have any proper dolls, just a very grubby bolster that she insisted was her baby, Mary-Ann. She had to fight to maintain maternal rights over Mary-Ann because she had younger sisters who wanted to share her.

'You're soft in the head, Maggie Higgins,' said her mother. 'A great girl of ten playing with dollies! If you fancy doing a bit of mothering, then lug your baby brother around and feed and change the little beast.'

She didn't actually say *beast*, she said an incredibly rude word that made my eyes pop. Aunty says Mrs Higgins is rough and common and she wishes I wouldn't play with her Maggie all the time. I like Mrs Higgins. She shouts at all her children and calls them rude names, but she gives them lots of cuddles too, and she tosses the little ones in the air and makes them squeal in delight.

As always, when we got to Maggie's tumbledown cottage at the end of Rook Green, I stopped off to say hello to Mrs Higgins. She gave me a big kiss on the cheek as well as Maggie, and cut us generous slices of bread and dripping.

We rarely had such a treat at home – we didn't have roasts on Sundays to make the dripping from. Aunty said it wasn't worth it just for the two of us. Besides, she said bread and dripping was common, just for cottage folk. We lived in a cottage too, but when I said this to Aunty she gave me a slap and told me off for cheeking her.

She'd have liked a niece like Curly Locks, sitting on a cushion and sewing a fine seam, working alongside her but only speaking when spoken to. I've got coal-black hair that won't hold a curl, no matter how often Aunty twists it up with rags. I can't sit still for five minutes indoors – not unless I've got a book to read, and Aunty thinks reading stories a waste of time.

I hate sewing, which exasperates Aunty no end. She's a dressmaker and sews exquisitely. All kinds of grand ladies wore Aunty's dresses, even Minor Royalty. I don't know who Minor Royalty is, but she makes Aunty very proud: she whispers her name the way people murmur *Jesus Christ* in church.

Nowadays Aunty sews garments for elderly folk because the fashions have changed. She disapproves of the short skirts that show off the young ladies' ankles – sometimes even their knees. 'Call themselves ladies!' she says, sniffing.

She's running out of old ladies now – they keep getting ill and dying. She mostly sews for Lady Somerset, who doesn't pay very much for her clothes because we live rent-free on her estate. Aunty and I don't have roasts – we don't have steak pies or chicken or chops either. I'm only sent to Mr Samson's for half a pound of his cheapest mince, or a little bit of liver or, worst of all, tripe.

If Lady Somerset is late paying her bill, Aunty makes me go and ask Mr Samson if he has any bones for our dog, when any fool knows we don't have a dog, much as I'd love one. Aunty makes soup by boiling up the bones with a few onions and carrots and some pearl barley. It tastes quite good, but it makes the whole cottage smell, and Aunty worries that the reek will get into all the fine materials stored on shelves in her workroom. We have to have the windows wide open on soup days, even in winter.

The Higgins family don't have much money for food either, especially as there are so many of them, but they always have bacon because they keep a pig in their back garden, and fresh eggs from their chickens. They sometimes have pheasant and rabbit and trout too, as Mr Higgins and Maggie's oldest brother, Tom, sneak up to the estate late at night. I'd never mention this to Aunty in a million years in case she told on them to Lady Somerset and they got nabbed for poaching.

It's quite hard for me to keep secrets. My teacher, Miss Nelson, says I'm a terrible chatterbox. I know I drive Aunty daft with my questions. She made me work on a cross-stitch sampler with the motto *Silence Is Golden*. No wonder it's called cross-stitch. It makes me terribly cross as I stitch. I keep poking my fingers with the needle, and then I get little red dots on the material. I can't understand how Aunty can bear to stitch-stitch-stitch all day long – and once, when Lady Somerset wasn't happy with her new evening gown for the Hunt Ball and demanded a substitute, half the night too.

My mother didn't stitch ball gowns, she *wore* them. One day, when I was hiding at the back of Aunty's wardrobe, I found a beautiful dress. (Aunty discovered I'd been secretly helping myself to the raspberry jam in the store cupboard and looked ready to give me a good slap.) I felt the slippery satin and the strange bobbles of the beads brushing my head as I crouched down. I risked opening the door a crack to see what it looked like. The satin was the palest pink with elaborate silver beading, the most beautiful dress I'd ever seen.

It couldn't have belonged to Aunty. She's plain and pinched and wears fierce glasses, and her dark frocks have high necks and long sleeves. The pink dress had little puff sleeves, and such a low neck it must have shown a lot of bosom. Aunty hardly has any chest at all. I held the pink dress close, rubbing it against my cheeks, even though the beading scraped uncomfortably, and breathed in the faint scent of rose.

After I'd been discovered and given the slap I asked if the pink dress had belonged to my mother, even though any mention of Mother makes Aunty agitated.

'How dare you go in my wardrobe and mess about with my clothes, Mona!' she said.

'I'm sorry, Aunty. I came across the dress by accident. It's so beautiful. It *was* my mother's, wasn't it? *Please* tell me when she wore it! Was it when she met my father?

Aunty, you simply *must* tell me! Please, please, please!'
I begged.

But it was useless. Aunty was as uncommunicative as the dressmaker's dummy in her workroom.

'That's enough, Mona. Don't work yourself up into one of your states,' she said, and she wouldn't tell me a single thing I wanted to know.

On Saturday night, when she was in the kitchen having her weekly bath in the tin tub, I crept upstairs and looked in her wardrobe again. I couldn't find the pink dress. I opened the door wide and searched all the way through Aunty's dark serges and cottons, and even felt around the bottom of the wardrobe in case the pink dress had slipped off its hanger. But it wasn't there.

I waited until after I'd had my own bath, and then, while Aunty was brushing my wet hair, I said as casually as I could, 'Please may I have another peep at that lovely pink dress with the silver beads, Aunty?'

'Which dress?' she said. 'Don't be silly, Mona. I don't have any dresses like that.'

'Yes you do. I found it at the back of your wardrobe. It *was* my mother's dress, wasn't it?' I pressed her.

'I think you've been dreaming, girl. A pink dress with silver beads! Even Lady Somerset in her heyday would never have worn such an outfit. There, your hair's nearly dry now. Up the little wooden stairs to Bedfordshire, if you please,' she said, giving me a light tap on the shoulder with the hairbrush.

That's the trouble with Aunty. She's as slippery as the pink satin dress. She'll never answer properly. But I've found that, if I listen carefully enough, Mother herself answers.

Today, when I left Maggie's cottage I decided to go and visit her, even though I'd already lingered too long – Aunty liked me to come straight home from school.

Still, Mother didn't live too far away. I ran down Church Lane, through the old lychgate and up the path, nodding at the ancient yew trees on either side and muttering, 'Pleased to meet yew,' giggling at my own silly joke. I greeted a lot of the gravestones too, reading their names and saying how do you do. The Somersets had a lot of very grand graves. Sir William had a big marble tomb like a little house. I wondered if Lady Somerset would be stuffed inside when her time came.

Mother was round the back, half hidden in the shade, at the end of a long row of gravestones covered in lichen. It was much nicer for her there, away from the recent raw graves with their withered wreaths.

I made sure that Mother had flowers too. I didn't have any money to buy them, but now that it was spring I could pick buttercups and daisies and cowslips and bluebells, and I sometimes stole a hothouse rose or two from someone else's wreath. I didn't think they'd mind too much. I once seized a large bunch of lilies and arranged them in a holy cross over Mother's grave, but then I had a nightmare: the newly dead person had struggled up through the muddy earth to grab their lilies back. I didn't dare go back to the churchyard for days after that.

Aunty never went to visit Mother. I couldn't understand why. She'd taken me to see the grave when I was four, and about to start at the village school.

'There you are, Mona, do you see?' she said, pointing

to the green mound at the end. It looked very plain without a headstone.

I felt sorry for Mother, and when I'd learned to write properly I tried carving her one myself. I found a bit of old fencing and etched *Sylvia Mona Smith* slowly and laboriously with Aunty's sewing scissors. I was named after her. I rather wished she'd called me Sylvia too, because it was much prettier than Mona. I carried on carving, but gave up after *Beloved Mother* because it was such hard work. I'd already blunted Aunty's scissors and she was furious, but I didn't care. I needed Mother's grave to look special.

'So where's Father's grave? Why doesn't he have a bed beside Mother?' I wondered.

'It's a grave, Mona, not a bed. Don't be fanciful. He's buried where he fell in France,' Aunty said.

I didn't know about the war then. I took her literally and worried that I might die each time I fell over. I tumbled frequently because Aunty bought my shoes a size too big so she didn't have to replace them too often.

Once I'd seen the grave I wanted Aunty to take me to visit Mother regularly, but she said it was morbid. I didn't know what that meant, but then I often didn't understand her. When I was trusted to get to and from school by myself, I started taking a detour and wandering around the churchyard on my way home.

If it hadn't rained for a while I'd look around furtively to make sure no one was watching, and then lie full length on top of Mother's rectangle of grass. I pictured her underneath, smiling up at me. I refused to believe that she had turned into a skeleton: she would be perfectly preserved, her skin still fair, her black hair neatly brushed, lying in her white nightgown with her arms crossed piously over her chest.

Today I lay with my head pressed against the grass and my eyes open, trying to see down through the earth.

'Hello, Mother. I've picked you cowslips. I hope you like them. They don't really smell much, but they look pretty. Mrs Higgins gave me some bread and dripping. I like her making a fuss of me. At home I just get a malted milk biscuit and they don't really taste of much, though I like the picture of the cow. I wonder what you'd have given me when I got home from school.'

I waited. I could hear Mother laughing softly. She said she'd have given me a hug and a slice of cherry cake. Then she asked how I'd got on at school.

'I got ten out of ten for my story about a rainy day,' I said proudly. I didn't tell her I'd only got two out of ten for my arithmetic test. She didn't need to know that.

Mother told me that I was her bright girl and she was proud of me.

'I wish Aunty would say that!' I said wistfully.

'But she's not your mother,' she replied. 'You're *my* girl, Mona.'

She always said that, and she was always such a comfort. I wanted to stay lying on her grave for ages, but I heard footsteps coming round the side of the church. I scrambled up, cursing inside my head.

'Are you all right, child?' It was the vicar in his long church dress. 'Did you trip?'

'I just felt like lying down, Mr Vicar,' I said, brushing

grass off my dress. I didn't know his proper name. Aunty and I weren't churchgoers. She said she didn't hold with it, though I didn't know why.

'On a *grave*?' he said. 'Oh dear, you mustn't do that! It's not respectful.'

'Yes it is,' I said. 'I'm always very respectful to Mother.'

The vicar blinked at me. 'Don't answer back!' he snapped.

'I shall if I want,' I said, and then I ran off quick. I hoped he didn't know who I was. I'd be for it if he reported me to Miss Nelson.

I ran all the way along Church Lane, then down the alley and over the stile and across the meadow. There were several skippy calves butting at their mothers' sides. You weren't meant to go too near the cows when the calves were young in case they charged at you, but their faces looked kind, their long-lashed eyes gentle.

'You won't hurt me, will you?' I called. 'I'm Mona. I'm your friend.'

They munched tranquilly, and several nodded their heads as if they understood. Animals seemed to like me. I wished Aunty would let me have a pet. Maybe I could help Mr Thompson, the vet, when I was older. I'd begged him to take me on his rounds during the school holidays, but he insisted I wasn't old enough. Perhaps he was alarmed at the thought of my seeing baby animals being born.

I expect he thought I still believed in storks and gooseberry bushes. Aunty had fed me such nonsense, but when the last baby Higgins arrived Maggie had had to help her mother. She told me about it in detail, and swore she was telling the truth. We both resolved there and then never, ever to have babies ourselves.

I dodged the cowpats in the meadow, and then crossed the road and went through the great gates of Somerset Manor. There was a deer on top of each one, and when they were closed, it looked as if they were about to clash antlers. Aunty told me that many years ago there were real deer in the grounds. I wished they were still here now. I'd have loved to see little fawns. I always looked around carefully when I wandered in the woods just in case one or two still lurked there.

Our cottage was tucked just inside the entrance. It was the old gatekeeper's cottage. Lady Somerset didn't have a gatekeeper any more. Sam, the head gardener, opened and closed the gates when he could be bothered. He used to have ten men under him, Aunty told me, but now he just had Poor Fred, who was simple, and Geoffrey, who had only just left school. He seemed a little simple too – he'd had to repeat a year to get his leaving certificate.

When I got home Aunty was usually in her workroom (which was originally the front parlour), stitching away, her mouth full of pins. I could never work out how she managed not to swallow any. However, today she was standing on the doorstep, dressed in her Sunday black, looking agitated.

'Where have you *been*, Mona? School finished an hour ago! Look at the state of you! You've got your frock all creased! And what's that down the front? Is it grass stains? What have you been *doing*?' She seized hold of me, pulled me into the kitchen and whipped my dress right off before I realized what she was up to.

❦ 12 ❦

'Aunty! Don't!' I protested as she wet a corner of the tea towel and started scrubbing my face. 'I can wash myself, for heaven's sake! What's all the fuss?'

'We're going to see Lady Somerset,' she said.

I could see her lying beneath the bedcovers.

2

I WAS ASTONISHED. AUNTY WENT TO SEE LADY
Somerset to fit a new dress or repair a rip or replace
buttons, but I only ever went on Boxing Day, when Lady
Somerset held a special party for all the village children.

It wasn't the sort of party you read about in children's
books, with fairy lights and jelly and ice cream, and
strange-sounding games like Blind Man's Buff and Squeak
Piggy Squeak. I rather dreaded it, because we had to
wear our Sunday best and file into the grand hall and,
unless you were lucky enough to be standing right by
the fire, it was freezing cold.

We didn't play any games at all. We had to have a sing-
song, with Lady Somerset's daughter-in-law, Barbara,
playing the piano. We sniggered at her in secret because
she looked so weird. She didn't wear smart clothes.

She wore odd bright velvets and trailing scarves and mad shoes, with her hair hanging loose down her back.

She played carols, and we joined in half-heartedly, often forgetting the words. Miss Nelson would have been ashamed of us. The Somerset children sang loudly and confidently, holding their fair heads high. Aunty whispered their fancy names as if it was a magic spell: Esmeralda, Roland, Marcella and Bruno. She seemed especially impressed by them, though she winced at their scruffy clothes. They had long hair too, even the boys, which made my classmates nudge each other and whisper rude remarks. I actually preferred their long tangled locks to the bristles and raw red necks of the village boys.

Barbara's husband, Mr Frederick Somerset, the eldest brother, had died of influenza just after the war, but she had a new husband now – an artist called Stanley Barber. He was supposed to be famous, but no one in Rook Green had ever heard of him. He didn't even bother to try to sing. He looked a bit of a ragbag too. He didn't count as a proper Somerset.

There was a second Somerset brother, Mr Eric, but he had died in battle right at the beginning of the war, like my father. Aunty said Sir William and Lady Somerset had never got over losing their two elder sons. Sir William died of a seizure a year or so later, which made it worse. However, she still had her two younger sons.

The third brother, Mr George, sang in a hearty baritone, opening his mouth wide in a comical fashion. His wife, Mary, was the opposite of Barbara, stiff and proper in her tailored clothes. She kept dabbing at her eyes with a lace handkerchief and looked mournful, though Aunty said she'd never got on with Lady Somerset. They had two children, a pug-faced boy, Cedric, and a little girl called Ada who looked like a Kewpie doll.

I liked the youngest brother, Mr Benjamin, best. He sang too, but he sometimes copied Mr George's singing, or Barbara's habit of tossing her long waves, which had us all in fits. Mr Benjamin was dark, with a curly cap of black hair, and he wore the most exquisite clothes. Aunty sighed over the fine stitching on his shirts and the style of his suits, though she didn't approve of his jewellery. He wore several big rings on his smooth white hands, just like a lady.

After the sing-song we had tea, and that was a jolly affair – hundreds and thousands on thin bread and butter, iced buns and ginger pop. We were only given one slice of bread and the buns were small but, if we gobbled them down quickly, there was a chance of seconds.

Then came the best part: the presents off the tall Christmas tree at the end of the hall. We had to line up in age order – boy, girl, boy, girl – while Mr George and Mr Benjamin climbed a ladder and unhooked parcels from the prickly green branches. They handed them to Barbara, who in turn gave them to Lady Somerset, sitting in a big gilt armchair like a throne. Several of the girls curtsied to her as they were given their presents.

The wrapping paper was colour-coded: pale pink and blue for little children, red and navy for older ones. I'm still very small for my age, so last Christmas I was still given a pink parcel. It contained a white felt mouse with pink bead eyes. It didn't even squeak. I'd have loved a *real* mouse to tame and feed on titbits. The older girls were given necklaces or bottles of violet scent or storybooks, all of which I'd have preferred. Maggie was a big, hefty girl, and was given a book called *The Madcap of the Fourth*. She wasn't much of a reader, so she agreed to swap with me. Aunty saw us furtively exchanging gifts in the corner and was furious because she said it looked ungrateful.

The *Madcap* book wasn't particularly exciting anyway – just a story about some silly pranks played by posh girls at boarding school. They didn't seem to do any lessons and spent their time playing a strange sport called lacrosse, which didn't interest me at all.

'Is Lady Somerset going to give me a present?' I asked Aunty now.

'Of course not!' she said, shocked. 'What a thing to say! Poor Lady Somerset is very ill.'

How was I to know that? I badgered Aunty with questions as she threw my best daisy dress over my head and tidied my plaits. Aunty was proud of her embroidery, but I felt it was much too fancy.

'Does Lady Somerset have measles?' I asked. It was the only real illness I'd ever had and it had been awful. I'd had to stay in bed in a darkened room even when the rash had disappeared, and I wasn't allowed to read in case it strained my eyes. I had never been so bored and fidgety in all my life. Aunty dutifully read to me for twenty minutes or so after lunch, and I knew she was doing her best, but she read in such a mono-tone that she even managed to make *A Little Princess* sound dull.

'No, she doesn't have measles, silly,' said Aunty. She lowered her voice meaningfully. 'She has pneumonia.'

I'd never heard the word before. 'What's that, Aunty?'

'It's like influenza, but worse,' she said, shaking her head in concern.

'Won't we catch this pneumonia if we go and see her?'

'It's a condition that elderly folk get,' said Aunty. 'Ella said she was very poorly.'

Ella was the lady's maid at Somerset Manor. She and Aunty were friends. They didn't walk around arm in arm and tell each other jokes like Maggie and me, but they had cups of tea together, and chatted about the doings of the Somerset family. Ella sometimes slipped Aunty half a sponge cake or a plate of iced biscuits left over from afternoon tea at the manor, and every year Aunty made Ella a new dress and rejigged her hat with silk roses.

I wondered if Ella would have to nurse Lady Somerset. But why had Aunty been summoned? She could hardly be wanting to order a new dress if she was very ill. And why *me*?

'We're going to pay our respects,' said Aunty. 'Now, you're to be very quiet and well behaved. No fidgeting. And don't lean on Lady Somerset's bed.'

I assured her that the very idea horrified me. 'Is she going to die?' I asked.

Aunty nodded meaningfully.

'But she won't die in front of us, will she?' I persisted.

'Of course she won't!' she exclaimed, as if I'd suggested that Lady Somerset might spend a penny in front of us. 'Now promise not to show me up, Mona!'

The moment we were outside she took my hand as if I was a baby. I tried to wriggle free but she squeezed it tightly.

'You'll only forget yourself and skip or run. We must act solemn and dignified at a time like this,' she said.

'But it's not as if Lady Somerset's family,' I protested. 'I don't think she even likes us.'

Aunty quivered. 'Don't talk nonsense, Mona! She's been very kind to us.'

She might have been kind, giving Aunty her custom for years and letting us have the cottage for free, but I was sure I was right. Lady Somerset had never said more to me than 'Merry Christmas' when she handed me a present, and she did so gingerly, making sure that her pale veiny hands didn't brush against mine. She treated Aunty in the same manner. Out on the estate Lady Somerset always stalked past as if she didn't even know her – yet every few months she stood in her bust bodice and knee-length knickers so that Aunty could pin her dresses into place.

The image was so bizarre that I couldn't help grinning.

Aunty saw, and gave my arm a tug. 'Take that smile off your face, Mona!' she hissed. 'Hurry up now – and don't scuff your shoes like that, you'll get them all over dust.'

We entered Somerset Manor through the back door by the kitchen garden. We walked along the narrow, dark passageway leading to the servants' quarters.

'So are you a sort of servant, Aunty?' I whispered.

'No, I'm an independent lady,' she said proudly. 'But I don't use the front entrance because I'm Trade. Trade is when you sell things. I sell my dressmaking services to Lady Somerset.'

Aunty took all these distinctions very seriously, and seemed to think them right and proper. I preferred the Higginses' attitude. The girls might curtsy and the boys tug their forelocks if forced to, but they joked about the gentry in private, mocking their manners and plum-in-the-mouth voices. Maggie called Lady Somerset Lady Somersausage, which made us both squeal with laughter, though it wasn't really funny.

We turned a corner and came across the Somersets' butler, an ancient stooped gentleman in tails, who glared at us.

'What on earth are you doing here?' he asked.

'We've come to pay our respects, Mr Marchant,' said Aunty.

'That's nonsense! Her ladyship won't want to be concerned with the likes of you just now,' he said brusquely.

I frowned at him. How dare he talk like that to Aunty as if she was dirt!

'Her ladyship has sent for me,' said Aunty.

'A likely story!' he said. 'She would have asked me to contact you if that was so.'

'She wishes to see me about a very personal matter,' Aunty persisted. 'She told her lady's maid to contact me. Ask Ella if you won't believe me.'

Mr Marchant winced a little at the word *personal*. Then he twitched his shoulders. 'Very well,' he said, and turned his back on us.

Aunty pulled my hand, whisking me on down the corridors. 'Pompous old fool,' she muttered. 'I'm not taking any notice of him. Come along now, Mona.'

She led me up a narrow wooden flight of stairs. These were clearly the servants' stairs, because the ones leading off the big hall were wide and softly carpeted, with gold stair rods and an imposing carved banister. I'd eyed it wistfully, wondering what it would feel like to slide all the way down.

We went through a door – and there was the carpet, and a landing lined with dark paintings of old people and bleak landscapes. Aunty's friend Ella was peeping round a door right at the end, subdued in her uniform, her cap pulled down to her eyebrows.

'There you are!' she mouthed to Aunty. Then she stared at me. 'Heavens, Flo! You've brought *Mona*?'

'Yes, I have.'

'But it's not right! You can't take a child into a sickroom!' said Ella.

'Yes I can,' Aunty replied.

'I'll be the one in trouble,' Ella said wretchedly.

'I need Lady Somerset to see her,' said Aunty, but when Ella reluctantly let us into her ladyship's bedroom, Aunty told me to stand in the corner, out of the way.

I was happy to do as I was told. I wanted to be as far away from Lady Somerset as possible. The curtains were closed and it was very dark and gloomy in the room, but I could see her lying beneath the bedcovers, her craggy old face as white as her pillowcase. Her eyes were closed and her mouth was open, giving her a long witch chin. If it hadn't been for her heavy breathing, I'd have thought her dead already.

There was a sour smell in the room, and I wished

someone would open the windows. Ella approached the foot of the bed and murmured something to Lady Somerset.

'What?' she said irritably, opening her eyes.

'I said Miss Watson is here, Lady Somerset,' Ella repeated.

'Who?' she asked. Her voice cracked. 'Water, girl, water!'

Ella poured water from a blue carafe into a glass, and then awkwardly slipped her arm round Lady Somerset's shoulders to help her sit up. The old lady still had her own teeth – they clanked against the glass – but she slurped inexpertly, like a toddler. Water dribbled down her chin and onto her chest. Ella dabbed at it with a cloth until her hand was slapped away.

'Leave it, girl! Stop flapping at me!' Lady Somerset lay back on her pillows with a great sigh.

'Remember Miss Watson is here. You asked to see her,' Ella said.

But Lady Somerset closed her eyes and didn't respond.

Ella shook her head at Aunty. 'Better leave now,' she whispered. 'She's gone back to sleep.'

Aunty took no notice. She went right up to the bed and bent her head low, near Lady Somerset's ear. 'Good afternoon, your ladyship. It's Florence Watson here. How are you feeling?' she said.

Lady Somerset's eyes opened again. 'How do you think I'm feeling?' she rasped. 'I'm dying, woman. Has that wretched dressmaker come yet?'

'I'm your dressmaker, Lady Somerset. I'm Miss Watson. How can I help you?' Aunty asked.

'Ah! At last. It's the matter of a shroud,' she replied.

Ella gasped and looked at me anxiously. I wasn't quite sure what a shroud was. Was it some kind of sheet thing you wore in your coffin?

'You mustn't trouble your head about such matters, your ladyship,' Ella said hurriedly. 'I'm sure the undertakers will take care of things in due course.'

'I don't want them to! I wish to take matters into my own hands!' Lady Somerset insisted. Her breathing was harsher now, and she had to take great gulps of air when she spoke. I was desperate to get out of this horrible sickroom. I pressed myself against the wall behind me, wishing I could slide straight through it.

Clutching her sheets, Lady Somerset tried to speak. The veins on her forehead stood out.

'The shroud?' Aunty persisted.

'Don't want one!' the old lady burst out.

'But – but you have to have one, your ladyship,' said Ella. She shook her head at Aunty, tapping her temple, indicating that Lady Somerset must have lost her mind.

But Aunty suddenly understood. 'Do you want me to make you an alternative, Lady Somerset?' she asked.

'Yes! Yes! Can't stand shrouds – dreadful things. And I don't want a nightgown either – silly floppety nonsense, and too many buttons. I want something simple but stylish.' Lady Somerset was making a huge effort, running her words together to get them all out while her breath lasted.

'I think a gown might be more suitable, your ladyship,' said Aunty. 'Something *regal*. A white brocade embroidered with gold thread, and lined with white silk. Very loose and comfortable – no buttons at all, but with enough material for you to look suitably modest in your repose.'

'Dear Lord, she'll look like the Archbishop of Canterbury!' Ella murmured, and I had to cover my nose and mouth to stop myself snorting with nervous laughter.

Lady Somerset seemed thrilled by Aunty's suggestion. 'Excellent!' she declared. 'Exactly the sort of thing! But how soon could you make it? I haven't got long, you know. Even that fool of a doctor has to admit I'm on my way out.'

'I'll be as quick as I can, Lady Somerset. Within twenty-four hours,' said Aunty.

Ella and I stared at her in astonishment. She would have to buy the material, do the embroidery, stitch it together and then line it. How could she possibly manage such a feat?

Lady Somerset nodded, taking it for granted that Aunty wouldn't let her down. 'You're a good sort, Florence Watson,' she said, breathing more easily. Her eyelids started flickering.

Aunty had gone very pink. She opened and closed her mouth several times, and then suddenly blurted, 'There's just one thing, Lady Somerset.'

'Yes, yes, I'll see you're properly rewarded for the task. If it's a regal robe, I shall pay you royally,' she said, and wheezed with laughter at her own joke.

'Thank you very much, your ladyship, but it's more a matter of reassurance than reward,' said Aunty.

Lady Somerset's eyes were closed now, but Aunty laid a hand on her shoulder and shook it. 'Lady Somerset?

Can you promise me that I will be able to stay on at the cottage after – after your demise? It's not so much for *my* sake – it's for the child,' she said.

'Child?' Lady Somerset murmured.

'Mona! Come over here!' Aunty commanded.

For a moment I couldn't move. I didn't want to go anywhere near that bed. But Aunty glared at me, eyes popping, and I had to. I approached tentatively, going to stand right behind her.

'Don't hide behind me! Let Lady Somerset have a good look at you,' said Aunty, pulling me in front of her. 'Nearer, now. Her eyesight's not very good.'

She propelled me forward until my tummy was pressed against the side of the bed. Lady Somerset looked worse close up, and I couldn't help grimacing.

'You!' she said sharply. 'Why are you pulling a face?'

I didn't know what to say.

'Mona!' Aunty hissed. 'Speak to Lady Somerset!'

I couldn't possibly say that I thought she looked a fright. 'I've got a pain,' I lied.

'*You've* got a pain?' said Lady Somerset. '*I'm* the one on the brink of death!'

A teardrop suddenly rolled from her eye. I think it was simply watering – but perhaps she was crying because she didn't want to die. It made me stop being scared of her and feel sorry instead. It must be awful knowing that you're going to die. Had my mother known? Had she been frightened? Had she lain on her back, dishevelled and distraught like Lady Somerset?

I found I was crying too, in sympathy.

'What are you crying for?' asked Lady Somerset.

'Take the kiddy away, Flo. I knew it would be too much for her,' Ella said.

But Aunty kept me pinned by the bed. 'She's crying because she's sorry you're ill, your ladyship,' she said. 'That's right, isn't it, Mona?'

I nodded.

'Odd little thing,' said Lady Somerset, but she looked rather pleased.

'She's a good girl. A dear, clever little girl, top of her class at school. A girl to be proud of,' said Aunty. I was amazed – she never praised me like that in case it made me big-headed. I felt myself going hot with embarrassment. Lady Somerset screwed up her eyes, perhaps to focus better.

'So could I have your word that we may keep the cottage, your ladyship?' Aunty persisted.

Lady Somerset nodded, her chin grazing her chest.

'Thank you,' Aunty breathed. 'Thank you so much. And if you could see fit to provide for her in any way—'

'Flo!' Ella hissed, horrified.

Lady Somerset looked over my head at Aunty. She was frowning now. Aunty's fingers were digging into my shoulders.

The old lady opened her mouth, ready to say something – but then she coughed. It was a bad cough and she couldn't seem to stop, her face going an ugly red with the effort.

Ella ran over to help her sit up. 'You must go now!' she said. 'You're upsetting her, can't you see! I'm calling for the nurse.'

At last Aunty loosened her grip on me and we backed away, Lady Somerset still coughing and coughing.

'Oh dear Lord,' Aunty whispered.

The nurse came running into the room in her stockinged feet, a large slice of cherry cake still in her hand.

'That's it, lift her up higher. There now, Lady S. Take a spoonful of your medicine if you can,' she said, dropping the cake on the floor.

I couldn't help staring at it, though I knew I couldn't possibly snatch it up for myself. Lady Somerset's coughing fit subsided and she lay back on her pillows, exhausted. Her eyes closed and she fell asleep immediately, starting to snore.

'Thanks so much, Nurse,' said Ella. 'Sorry to drag you away from your tea break, but I was scared she was really going this time.'

She turned and saw that we were still in the room. 'Buzz off, Flo, and take the kiddy with you. You've got a cheek, I must say, asking for favours like that,' she said. 'Not that it'll get you anywhere. She's in no fit state to call for a lawyer and change her will, if that's what you were angling for.'

'She asked for me,' said Aunty.

'And I was the mug who passed the message on,' said Ella indignantly. 'Why couldn't you have put in a good word for me too! *I'm* the one who feeds her and washes her and wipes her! What's going to happen to *me* when she goes?'

'I wasn't begging favours for myself. I have to think of Mona,' said Aunty, tight-lipped.

'Well, what's *she* got to do with it? Her ladyship's barely set eyes on her, and she's never had a soft spot for children, apart from her own boys. *I've* been here since I was scarcely older than your Mona, and I'm pretty certain she won't be making any provision for me. What am I going to do, eh? At least you can do dressmaking till your eyes give out. Who's going to employ me as a lady's maid now? They'll want a girl half my age. I haven't any savings to speak of. Where will I go?' Ella's voice was getting higher and higher.

'You could stay with us at the cottage until you find a place,' Aunty said.

'Oh, stop that nonsense! You'll be turned out quick as a wink when Lady Somerset dies. We're all in the soup, Flo – you and the kiddy, me, old Mr Marchant, the other maids, even the gardeners. Likely they'll have a clean sweep and bring in their own staff,' said Ella.

'Then we'll all keep each other company in the workhouse,' Aunty snapped, and she dragged me down the stairs, along the corridors, past Mr Marchant and out of the back door.

We hurried through the grounds at such a pace I could hardly keep up. 'Slow down, Aunty, I've got a stitch!' I panted.

'I've got a lot to do,' she said, pulling me into the cottage and then bolting the door behind us, as if she thought the bailiffs were coming any minute. 'You put the kettle on to boil and bring a cup of strong tea to my workroom. I've got a marathon task ahead.'

I did as I was told. I cut us both a slice of bread and jam too. It didn't look as if there was going to be any proper supper. I divided Aunty's portion into tiny bite-sized chunks. When I took them in, she was crouching over her big chest of materials, dragging out a roll of white and gold brocade!

'You've got the right stuff already, Aunty!' I gasped.

'Of course I have. I thought of it the moment she said the word *robe*. It's curtain material, and it weighs a ton, but she won't be walking around in it, will she? It'll be a bally nuisance lining it with silk, but I'll manage,' she said, heaving the bolt onto her cutting table. 'Watch where you put that tea, Mona!'

'There's bread and jam too, Aunty. I've cut yours into little pieces. I could pop one into your mouth every now and then so you don't get jam on the material,' I suggested.

'Thank you, dear,' she said. 'Very thoughtful.'

She spread out the brocade and then fetched her big, sharp cutting scissors. After trying to engrave the headstone for Mother I'd been forbidden to touch them. Aunty said if she ever caught me with them again she'd cut off my fingers with the sharpened blades. I knew she wouldn't *really*, but I still kept well away from the scissors, and their *crick-crick* cutting noise made me shiver.

'Aunty?' I said, tucking my hands into my armpits. 'Aren't you and Ella friends any more?'

'Oh, I dare say we are. She's just worried, that's all,' she replied.

'*Will* we all end up in the workhouse?' I asked. I hated even saying the word. It was a terrible building at the end of Rook Green. I always ran past it. The windows were so high up I couldn't see inside, but once I heard a terrible scream, long and loud and utterly despairing. It echoed in my head for weeks afterwards.

'We're not ending up in the blooming workhouse,' said Aunty. She usually spoke like a genteel lady, but now her voice sounded much harsher. 'Lady Somerset will be so pleased with her robe that she'll see us right, you mark my words.' Her knuckles were white as she cut into the brocade.

Ella came bursting through our door,

red and breathless with running.

3

AUNTY WAS STILL IN HER WORKROOM WHEN I woke up in the morning. She looked grey, and behind her glasses her eyelids kept twitching, but her hands didn't pause: stitch-stitch-stitch.

'Have you been up all night, Aunty?' I asked.

'No, I went to sleep, and the needle and thread stitched all by themselves,' she said.

'Hadn't you better go to bed now?' I suggested. 'You look awful, Aunty.'

'Any compliments gratefully received,' she said grimly. 'Go and make a pot of tea, Mona, and then get yourself off to school.'

I boiled the kettle and searched in the pantry for something to give Aunty for breakfast. There was just the heel of the loaf left, one egg, an onion and a few potatoes and carrots. I boiled the egg, toasted the bread, made the tea, and set it all on a tray.

'Here you are, Aunty!' I said, nudging the door open. I hoped she'd be pleased with me.

Aunty was sitting bolt upright, but her head was nodding, her eyes closed.

'Aunty? Are you asleep?'

She shook herself awake. 'I was just resting my eyes,' she said. 'Dear Lord, they ache! Oh, Mona, what have you done? That egg was put by for your tea! What a waste!'

'I was only trying to be helpful,' I protested. 'You've been up all night and you look so tired.'

'I'm used to going without sleep,' Aunty snapped. 'Here, you'd better have the egg now, and the toast. You can't go to school on an empty stomach.'

'I made it for *you*,' I said. 'I thought it would be a lovely surprise. I'm not touching it.'

I flounced off to my room, got dressed in my school frock, polished my dusty shoes with yesterday's socks, plaited my hair and marched out, banging the front door. I didn't say goodbye to Aunty.

I didn't go hungry. I called for Maggie, and Mrs Higgins gave me a potato cake, piping hot from the pan.

'I wish I lived with you, Mrs Higgins,' I said.

'There now, child – your aunty looks after you beautifully. You're always so perfectly turned out. You put my scruffy lot to shame,' she said.

'She never makes me potato cakes. And she's always cross with me,' I said.

'It's because she's so busy making all them lovely frocks. I dare say she's a bit particular, but it must be hard for her, bringing you up by herself,' said Mrs Higgins.

'It's hard for *me*!' I said, but I was starting to feel guilty.

I kept thinking about Aunty's grey, pinched face as Maggie and I skipped to school. I wondered what would have happened if Aunty hadn't taken me on when Mother died. I would have had to go to an orphanage. Maggie and I used to play orphanages with ha'penny dolls and a shoebox, taking it in turns to be a fierce matron who beat the orphans if they misbehaved. I was good at inventing dire punishments that made us both snort with laughter. What if that sort of thing happened in real orphanages? Maybe they were as bad as the workhouse – or worse.

My lovely potato cake turned into a hard lump in my stomach. I wanted to run all the way home again, but we were at the school gate now, and Miss Nelson was ringing the bell. I had to go in, but I couldn't concentrate, and for once I didn't get all my spellings right.

'Really, Mona Smith, what's up with you this morning?' said Miss Nelson.

I mumbled that I wasn't feeling very well.

'You do look pale,' she said. 'Come here and let's feel your forehead.'

I hoped she might send me home and then I could make it up with Aunty, but she said I didn't have a temperature. My head might be cool outside, but inside it was boiling with a hundred and one worries. At lunch break I felt too on edge to sit in a corner of the playground and play Five Stones with Maggie. Instead I joined the boys in their running games so I didn't have to think so much.

'Let's play Kiss Chase!' said Martin Bellamy, a big ugly lad who I couldn't bear.

'Don't play, Mona!' Maggie warned.

But he and the other boys would jeer and call me chicken, and I wasn't having that.

'Yes, good idea!' I said.

I had to run like the wind to avoid Martin. The thought of his big rubbery lips on mine made me feel sick. I darted past Peter Robinson instead and let him catch the hem of my dress. All the boys yelled at Peter to kiss me. He went very red and hesitated for a second too long. I whisked my dress away and dashed for the girls' toilets, where he couldn't follow me.

'Honestly, Mona, you are a tease!' said Maggie disapprovingly when Miss Nelson rang the bell for afternoon lessons.

The girls had needlework last lesson, while the boys did woodwork with Mr Granger, the village corn merchant.

'I wish *we* could do woodwork,' I said, sighing. 'I hate sewing.'

'But you're quite good at it!' said Maggie.

I knew how to do the different stitches, and I could hem and do buttonholes because I'd been brought up by Aunty, but I didn't have the patience to do it neatly. It made me feel guiltier than ever. If my hands ached and my neck hurt and my eyes itched after half an hour's hemming, how on earth must Aunty feel after stitching all night long.

I was so glad to get out of school at the end of the day. I shot out of the classroom the moment we'd finished singing our goodbye prayer.

'Wait for me, Mona!' Maggie called crossly. 'Why are you acting so odd today?'

'I just need to get home early, that's all,' I said. 'Come on, Mags, hurry!'

We walked off smartly, but at the end of School Lane someone suddenly ran up behind me and seized me by the arm. I turned round, startled, and Peter Robinson gave me a quick kiss on the cheek.

'There you are! You owed me that kiss,' he said, and then ran off again before I could remonstrate with him.

'I *told* you he was sweet on you!' said Maggie. 'And you like him too – you've gone all pink.'

'No I haven't,' I insisted. 'And I *don't* like him. I don't like any of the boys. Still, I'm glad it was Peter who kissed me, not Martin Bellamy.'

'Urgh, yes! Imagine!'

We giggled in disgust, and then suddenly we were friends again.

'I'm not supposed to tell, but Lady Somerset's very ill – she's going to die any day now,' I confided. 'Aunty's sewing this dress thing for her to wear in her coffin.'

Maggie shuddered. 'I don't want one of them coffin things – they give me the creeps. When I die I want to fly straight up to Jesus.'

She went to Sunday school every week and tried to be very holy.

'But wouldn't you want to stay in your coffin in the graveyard? Then your mother and father and all your brothers and sisters could come and talk to you,' I said.

'But by then they'll be dead too, so we'll talk to each other up in heaven,' said Maggie. 'We'll have a cottage together – like ours, but bigger – and it'll be newly thatched so we won't need buckets in the bedrooms, and we'll have our pig, but we won't ever have to kill it because we'll eat heavenly manna instead. We'll wear our Sunday best every day, and it'll never wear out or get too small, and our boots won't pinch. It will be lovely.'

It *did* sound lovely, if unlikely. Perhaps Mother would wait for me in the churchyard until it was time for me to die too, and then we could ascend to heaven together. We might be able to meet up with my father, though I wasn't so keen on that idea as I didn't know anything about him, apart from the fact that he'd fought in the war. I thought of Mr Bellamy, Martin's father, who had come back with only one leg. His wooden one hurt him a lot, so he was always shouting at his family. Then there was the butcher's son, Michael, who had all his limbs but had lost his senses, and suffered from such bad nightmares he woke all the neighbours. I knew it was very bad of me, but I didn't mind not having a father.

What about Aunty? Deep down I just wanted to live with Mother in heaven, but everyone said that Aunty had been good to take me in. She *was* good – but she wasn't much fun. She'd be forever nagging me to curtsy to Jesus and all the saints, and telling me off for eating my heavenly manna with my mouth open. Perhaps Mother and I could live together in one cottage and Aunty could live down the street somewhere, and we'd invite her to tea once a week . . .

I tried to convince myself that she wouldn't mind, but I knew she would, dreadfully. I felt even more guilty about Aunty now. When Maggie asked if I wanted to call in at her cottage on the way home, I shook my head.

'No thanks, I've got to get back to Aunty,' I said, and ran off, though I badly wanted a hug from Mrs Higgins – and a slice of bread and dripping.

I took a very brief detour into the churchyard, picked a few primroses for Mother's grave, and then knelt beside her, asking if she'd pray that Aunty and I could stay in our cottage and not have to go to the workhouse. Mother promised to pray her hardest. I told her that I felt bad about Aunty, and Mother suggested I take the primroses to *her* instead.

I thanked her for the suggestion, gathered the primroses into a bunch and hurried home.

'Aunty! I'm back!' I called as I ran in the door.

Aunty didn't answer. I went to her workroom. She wasn't there. Perhaps she was having a much-needed nap . . . No, she wasn't in her bedroom either. Not in my room, or the kitchen. She wasn't outside in the lavvy. She wasn't anywhere.

I stood clutching the primroses, my heart thumping. Aunty was *always* there. Where could she have gone?

'Aunty? Aunty?' I called, though I knew perfectly well that she wasn't in the cottage. I felt so panicky I was nearly crying.

'*Pull yourself together, Mona!*' I said, in Aunty's voice. '*She'll be back in a minute. Now put the kettle on for a cup of tea and arrange those primroses in a little vase – they're wilting already.*'

I did as I told myself and set the tea brewing in the pot, covering it with the patchwork cosy to keep it warm. The cosy was made of little pieces from long-ago dresses –

velvet and grosgrain and cambric for customers, serviceable serge from Aunty's clothes and cotton from mine. There was even a patch from my favourite Viyella nightgown: red roses and sprays of blue forget-me-nots on a pale blue background. Aunty had made a tiny matching nightgown for my toy dog, Archibald, with a special hole for his tail to poke through. He obviously didn't grow any bigger, so he was still wearing them.

Then I heard footsteps outside – I ran to the door, and there was Aunty holding a brown paper parcel. She looked ghostly pale and her eyes behind her glasses were bloodshot.

'Oh, Aunty!' I said, and I threw myself at her and hugged her hard.

'Careful, Mona! You'll have us both over!' she said. 'What's all this about, eh?'

'I was so worried! I didn't know where you were,' I wailed.

'Don't be so silly! I was up at the manor, delivering Lady Somerset's robe, of course. I promised I'd finish it in twenty-four hours, and I have! I thought I'd be back before you got home from school, but you're early today.'

'I didn't stop at Maggie's. I wanted to get back,' I said. 'I'm sorry I banged out of the cottage this morning and didn't even say goodbye, Aunty!'

'Well, I dare say I was a bit snappy with you. I was pretty exhausted. Still am! I think I'll go to bed as soon as we've had a bite to eat,' she said, sitting down at the table. 'You've made a pot of tea. That was thoughtful, dear. And such pretty flowers too.'

'I could start supper too. Is it vegetable stew or jacket potatoes?' I asked, glowing.

'Neither!' said Aunty. 'Look!' She unwrapped the paper parcel. There was a loaf of bread, a slab of butter keeping cool in a dock leaf, a big wedge of cheese, two thick slices of pink ham, half an apple tart and two ginger parkins!

'It's a feast!' I said, round-eyed.

'It is indeed. Lady Somerset rallied a little when she saw the robe. She liked it, Mona! She said it was the best gown I'd ever made for her – and for once she realized how hard I'd worked. She told Ella to take me downstairs and make sure Cook gave me a hearty meal because I'd earned it. So I asked if I could take it home with me instead, and no one minded. She paid royally for the gown too – and she said she'd make sure we stayed here in the cottage for as long as we wished. Oh, Mona!' Aunty's sore eyes were brimming with tears now. 'The relief!'

I fetched some plates and we started our feast, washing it down with cups of tea.

'This is the best meal ever!' I said. 'And you're the best aunty.'

She tutted and told me not to be such a soppy ha'p'orth, but I think she was pleased. She didn't eat very much – just a sliver of ham, a slice of bread and half a parkin, but she let me tuck in until my stomach was gloriously full. There was still a big spread left for tomorrow, which I tidied away in the pantry.

Then I massaged the cramps out of Aunty's aching hands, and did my best to ease her shoulders too. Her head was nodding already, and she went to bed telling me I was a good girl. I went to bed too, and read

The Story of the Treasure Seekers from start to finish. I'd borrowed it from Old Molly's penny lending library, though I'd read it twice already. Old Molly didn't charge me because I kept the books in order and counted up everyone else's pennies and recorded the borrowings in her red account book.

The Story of the Treasure Seekers was one of my favourites. I loved the part where Oswald explains that his mother is dead, and they all miss her terribly though they don't often mention it. I loved it when the children tried to make their fortune too. Sadly none of them seemed at all sensible, and they were forever getting into scrapes. Albert-next-door's uncle had to keep coming to the rescue.

We didn't have a next door, and I wouldn't have wanted an Albert for a friend, but I'd have dearly loved his uncle. Uncles seemed far more jolly than aunties. I'd once asked Aunty if she'd never wanted to get married, and she said it wasn't the sort of question you should ever ask a lady. I suppose that meant she'd have liked to, but no one had asked her. I tried to imagine her with a husband and a handful of children like Mrs Higgins, but it was impossible.

If Mother hadn't died and Father had come back from the war, I wondered if they would have had more children. I wished I had a sister or a brother. I was very good at imagining, and I was rarely bored so long as I had a book to read, but I often felt lonely.

I was feeling lonely now. I was starting to picture Lady Somerset lying on her back in the manor, gasping for breath all night long, with death creeping nearer and nearer. I longed to have a sister to cuddle. If she woke up in the middle of the night with a pain, Maggie would slip into bed with her mother and father. I couldn't imagine getting into bed with Aunty. She was always so private. She didn't like me seeing her in her nightgown, with her hair plaited and her teeth missing, and she was so thin and bony she wouldn't have been very comfortable to cuddle anyway.

I didn't fall asleep until two or three in the morning. Aunty shook me awake at eight, and gave me a ham sandwich for my breakfast, which was delicious. She put a ginger parkin wrapped in paper in my school bag.

'You can share it with Maggie. I know Mrs Higgins is always giving you bites, so now we've a chance to give her Maggie a little treat,' she said.

At break time Peter Robinson wanted me to play Kiss Chase again, but I sat demurely with Maggie, and we shared our parkin, nibbling it in turns so that it lasted a long time.

'Oh my, don't it taste good!' said Maggie, licking the crumbs off her fingers. 'Sometimes Mum makes ginger cake for a special treat, but it's not as good as this. Did your aunty make it?'

'No, Aunty never has time for baking. They were from the manor,' I said. 'They've got a special cook.'

'How I'd like to be the lady of the manor!' said Maggie. 'I'd have parkin for breakfast, parkin for dinner, parkin for tea, nothing but parkin.'

'You wouldn't want to be Lady Somerset – she's past eating anything,' I said.

'So who will be the new Lady Somerset?' Maggie asked.

'There won't be another Lady Somerset – she only had the title because of Sir William,' I told her. Aunty had filled me in on all the details. 'Roland will probably inherit as his father was the eldest son, but of course he's not much older than us. Maybe he'll come and live at the manor, with Barbara looking after him.'

'I lose track of them all. Which one's Barbara?'

'You know – the loopy lady with the funny clothes and the long fair hair,' I said.

'Oh, *that* one. Well, it won't be her – Mr Frederick's dead now. I bet it'll be the boot-faced one who gets the manor. Mr George's wife. Do you think she'll want your aunty making her clothes?'

'Aunty says she gets her clothes made in London,' I said.

'Then your aunty better find herself some new customers quick,' said Maggie.

Where could she find them? I wondered. No one in Rook Green needed fine clothes, and they couldn't afford them anyway.

I clasped my hands round my knees and held on tight, trying to think what she could do. Maybe I could help out with my own job? Old Molly was getting more and more in a muddle, and she was so stooped she couldn't reach the top shelves. Perhaps she could take me on part time and pay me a proper wage. Then, when Old Molly got even older, I could take over the shop. But I didn't really want to become Old Mona. What else could I do when I was grown up? I definitely didn't want to be a dressmaker like Aunty.

'Maggie, what do you want to be when you're grown up?' I asked.

'I told you, I want to be the lady of the manor and eat lots of parkin. Come on, Miss Nelson's ringing the bell,' she said, searching for one last crumb in the paper.

'No, really,' I said.

Maggie shrugged. '*I* don't know. I don't want to be a dairymaid like our Mabel – she gets cow dung all over her shoes. I suppose I might go into service like our Sarah-Jane, though she doesn't like it much. She has to work so hard. I hope I can just stay at home and help Mother.'

'What, until you're an old lady?'

'No, stupid! I'll find a sweetheart and get married,' said Maggie.

I pulled a face.

'Don't you want to get married, Mona?'

I tried imagining settling down with someone. Not Martin Bellamy with his big rubbery lips, obviously. Someone nice, like Peter Robinson. It wasn't such a terrible idea. And I suppose we could always have Aunty come and live with us. She could make clothes for our children.

'Mona Smith, Maggie Higgins! Stop daydreaming and come into school this instant!' Miss Nelson called.

I didn't dawdle on the way home – ten minutes with Mrs Higgins and a quick murmur to Mother – and then I ran all the way back to the cottage.

Aunty was in her workroom, sketching in the special notebook she used for her designs.

'Hello, dear,' she said, sounding absorbed.

I went to look over her shoulder. She'd drawn a row of little girls in short dresses with sunhats to match, both with a daisy trim. There were a couple of little boys too, wearing shorts and shirts with a chain-stitch train on the pocket.

'My, Aunty, that's so weird! I was just thinking that you'd be able to make clothes for my children one day – and now you're designing them!' I said.

'I'll be happy to make clothes for your children, but that's a long way in the future! I thought I might mock up a few samples and take them to the big draper's in Hailbury. They have a few ready-made gowns in their window, but nothing for kiddies. I know most mothers make their own, but not this sort of quality. What do you think?' Aunty asked.

'I think it's a brilliant idea,' I said.

'Hardly brilliant,' she replied. 'They're a bit of a come-down after making ball gowns, but they might earn us a few pennies. Put the kettle on, Mona, and set the table, there's a good girl.' She started sketching again, a bigger girl this time, in a frock with three frills. She drew a matching pair of frilly knickers too.

I made tea hoping with all my heart that Aunty wouldn't make *me* wear frilly knickers. Imagine what would happen if the boys at school pulled my dress up! They'd start calling me Mona Frilly-Bum and make my life hell.

This tea was a feast too, because there was still plenty left from yesterday. Aunty ate more heartily, but still nowhere near as much as me.

'You don't eat enough, Aunty,' I said, looking at her

pinched face and bony wrists and flat chest. 'You're too thin.'

'I haven't always been thin, you know,' she said, delicately nibbling her tiny slice of apple tart. Her eyes were dreamy, the way she always looked when she'd been designing. 'As a matter of fact, when I was a young girl I was quite curvy.'

'Really?' It was hard to imagine. 'Was Mother curvy too?'

'Yes, your mother was beautiful,' said Aunty. 'Here, Mona, I can't quite finish this.' She put the rest of her slice of tart on my plate.

'I *wish* I had a photograph of her,' I said. 'And you too, Aunty,' I added, so she didn't feel left out. 'Why don't we have any photos at all?'

'There was an album, but it got lost long ago,' said Aunty. She was looking out of the window. 'There's Ella! And in such a hurry too!'

Ella came bursting through our door, red and breathless with running. 'Her ladyship's gone!' she panted.

For a moment I thought she meant that Lady Somerset had heaved herself out of bed and staggered off somewhere in her nightgown – but then I realized that it was a genteel way of saying she'd died.

'Sit yourself down, Ella. There's still a cup of tea in the pot,' said Aunty. 'Oh dear, you look done in!'

'I know it's daft, but it's such a shock that she's gone at last,' said Ella.

'Mona, that tea looks stewed. Go and put the kettle on for a fresh pot.' Aunty lowered her voice. 'Did she go easily?'

'It was a real struggle – she had a little fit near the

end and couldn't get her words out. She kept trying to talk. It was very upsetting. Even after she passed she had this look of outrage on her face,' said Ella. 'She don't look peaceful at all.'

'Ssh now, not in front of the child,' said Aunty. 'Have the family been told?'

'Mr George and his wife are arriving this evening. I've no idea whether they're bringing their kiddies or not. Mr Marchant sent a telegram to Barbara and her husband in France. Beats me why they want to live in such a rum place. I hope they can book a ferry. I can't keep Lady Somerset looking fresh for ever. She looks very grand in that robe you made her. Mr Benjamin admired it no end!'

'Did he really?' said Aunty eagerly. 'So he's here already then?'

'He's been a brick, bless him,' said Ella. 'He came down from London yesterday evening, when Mr Marchant telegrammed to say her ladyship was on her way out. He'd been going to some party and was all dressed up in a cream suit with a sash, did you ever! But he sat up with his mother half the night and sang to her, would you believe.'

'He *sang*?' I asked.

'Pipe down, Mona, we're talking,' said Aunty.

'He sang all sorts,' Ella said. 'Her ladyship's favourite hymns, and Christmas carols, and concert songs, and little bits of opera in Eye-tal-ian, and sea shanties, and even bawdy songs from the music hall. He held her hand all the while, tapping it in time to the music. It really wasn't proper at all, but it was touching all the same. Her ladyship's always had a soft spot for

Mr Benjamin, seeing as he's her youngest. He's never quite grown up in her eyes. Well, in *anybody's* eyes. He's not a boy any more, he's back from the varsity, and yet he larks around without a care in the world. Except for now, of course. When her ladyship breathed her last, he started crying his eyes out, blubbing like a baby.'

Ella drank her fresh cup of tea in three gulps and then put her cup down. 'I'd better get back. I've got the bedrooms to prepare for Mr George's family, and Barbara's brood, and then there'll be a hundred and one things to plan for the funeral. Goodness knows how many people will be coming to the wake. Cook will have to get a couple of girls from the village to help her.'

'I suppose I could come and help out,' said Aunty.

'Best not,' said Ella. 'Mr Marchant didn't like you coming the other day, even though you was sent for.'

She rushed off, and Aunty went straight to her workroom. I found her pulling a roll of black crêpe down from her material shelf.

'What's that for?' I asked.

'Come on, Mona, you're supposed to be bright!' she said. 'It's for our funeral outfits. You don't need to go completely in black, so I'll put a black ribbon round your Sunday hat and you can wear a black armband – but I'll need a new black dress. We must look smart and show proper respect.'

'Will we be invited to the funeral then?' I asked.

'You don't need to be invited,' said Aunty. 'And we're going. Definitely.'

Four fair tousled heads peered down at me.

4

THE FUNERAL WAS ON THE FOLLOWING Saturday. Half the village turned up outside the church to gawp. Maggie was there, with all her brothers and sisters and Mrs Higgins. They weren't wearing black, but quite a few of the older villagers wore black armbands like the one sewn onto my cream Sunday coat, and Old Molly wore black from top to toe.

'I like a good funeral,' she said. 'Wouldn't miss it for the world.'

Her funeral outfit was at least forty years old, and it trailed on the ground because she'd shrunk as she aged, but she stepped out proudly. Aunty looked the finest of us all in her black crêpe dress with matching jacket. She'd trimmed her hat with black roses, and she'd attached one black rose to my summer straw too.

We all waited while the church bell tolled solemnly. It was an unusually hot day. My straw hat prickled and my dress stuck to my back. The little children fidgeted and whined, wanting to run off into the woods to play, but their mothers hung onto them fiercely.

Then we heard a clopping of hooves, and the crowd looked along the lane expectantly. There was the big black funeral carriage, gleaming in the sunshine, drawn by two sleek black horses that looked like they'd been polished for the occasion. Two solemn men in black top hats and frock coats marched in front of the carriage, with another two behind.

The rest of the family travelled in Daimlers, processing slowly behind the carriage. It seemed fitting that Lady Somerset should lead the way in her usual commanding manner. The village men took off their caps, and the women bowed their heads. Old Molly crossed herself. A small boy started crying and was hushed by his mother.

'Bow your head,' Aunty hissed at me.

I did as I was told, but still stared hard, peering up through my fringe. Mr George and his wife got out of the first car, dressed in black from top to toe. She even wore a veil. The children were in black too – tailored coats with brass buttons. Cedric had a little black cap and Ada wore a black satin ribbon in her wispy blonde hair.

The crowd murmured approvingly. They gasped when Barbara and her husband and their four children got out of the second Daimler. Aunty quivered. Barbara wore a cream linen jacket over a black beaded dress that was far too fancy, and her hat was navy rather than black, though she had at least tied up her flowing hair. Stanley wore a black velvet jacket, green trousers and brown shoes. The boys wore grey winter suits. They still hadn't had a haircut and were as tanned as tramps. The two girls were in white summer dresses with black sashes, and black dancing shoes.

The crowd were indignant. *Why aren't they in proper mourning clothes? Talk about disrespect! It isn't as if they're short of a bob or two. They might not have had time to have funeral outfits made, but surely they should have had the sense to be prepared. What sort of example is it to the village?*

Aunty, resolutely tight-lipped, didn't join in the whispers, but she looked horrified. As the family processed into the church, people peered expectantly at the third Daimler. Mr Benjamin was well-known for his flamboyant friends and outrageous outfits, but the two men getting out of the car looked very dignified.

Aunty breathed in as if she was smelling perfume. Mr Benjamin's friend was tall and broad-shouldered and handsome in his morning suit. Mr Benjamin looked imposing, though he was small and slender. His black suit was exquisitely tailored, his shirt dazzling white, his black satin tie secured with a pearl pin, his dark curls tamed with pomade.

The crowd nodded approvingly, on the verge of applause. There were two more Daimlers full of elderly posh folk, and the household staff walked along behind, all in severe black, even the little kitchen maid who was not much older than me. Ella raised her eyebrows at Aunty as she passed.

Aunty gripped my hand. 'Come along, Mona,' she said, pulling at me to follow the servants into the church.

'But we can't go in, Aunty! All the village folk are staying outside!' I said, horrified.

'We're not village folk,' she said, and pulled harder.

I had to follow her, cringing when I heard the murmurs behind us. The church was only half full, so there was plenty of room in the pews, but Aunty didn't quite have the courage to go and sit in the rows directly behind the chief mourners. We sat right at the back, in the shadows. I fervently hoped no one would spot us if they looked round.

The deep sad sound of the church organ made me quiver. Lady Somerset's coffin stood in front of the altar, taking pride of place. The vicar started the service, his voice slow and solemn like the music. I hunched down in case he recognized me as the girl who'd cheeked him.

Next there was a hymn. Mr George and his wife didn't sing at all, and neither did Stanley, but Mr Benjamin sang beautifully, and Barbara threw her head back and drowned out everyone else. Aunty didn't sing, thank goodness, but she mouthed the words, pointing along the lines in her hymn book.

The vicar started talking about Lady Somerset, saying how respected she had been in the local community. The village children had loved the splendid treats she laid on at Christmas time. He spoke as if she'd made all the buns herself and wrapped every present, and gone down on her knees and played with each and every one of us.

After a while I grew bored and started going through

the hymn book for something to read. Aunty glared at me when I flicked the thin pages, though I hardly made a sound. Barbara's children were fidgeting and whispering now, but they weren't being told off at all. Mr George's children sat stolidly, scarcely moving, though Cedric picked his nose when he thought his mother wasn't watching.

At last the service was over and there was another sombre tune on the organ while the undertakers and Mr George and Mr Benjamin carried Lady Somerset out again. They took her over to Sir William's large tomb. I was glad she wasn't being buried near Mother – Lady Somerset would have been a very grim companion.

Aunty and I hung back, watching as her coffin was awkwardly levered inside. I couldn't help thinking it was a terrible waste of the white-and-gold brocade robe. I wondered if Aunty thought so too, but knew she'd be shocked if I asked her.

When they closed the tomb again, Mr Benjamin placed white lilies against it in an artistic way. Barbara had picked some cow parsley, and all four of her children sprinkled it around the tomb. Aunty sniffed disapprovingly. Unlike Mr Benjamin's beautiful lilies, cow parsley was a common weed. Even Stanley looked embarrassed, and Mr George sighed impatiently. His wife told Cedric and Ada to bow their heads in respect, and then led them away.

The youngest child hung onto a big cow parsley stem, twirling it round like an umbrella. Mr Benjamin shook his head, took it away and tapped it lightly on the little boy's head.

'Monkey!' he said fondly. Then he looked up, saw us lurking behind a big tombstone and nodded in a friendly manner.

'Hello, Miss Watson. Hello, Mona.'

I was thrilled that he knew my name, and bobbed him a curtsy.

'My, don't you both look smart! Thank you so much for coming. I know just how much my mother relied on you, Miss Watson,' said Mr Benjamin. 'It was wonderful of you to make her that splendid robe in such a short space of time.'

He smiled at us both, while his handsome friend looked at us curiously.

'I am so sorry that you've lost your mother,' Aunty murmured. 'I don't know how we'll all manage without dear Lady Somerset.'

'Thank you. I dare say there will be changes now,' said Mr Benjamin. 'And, of course, there will be someone new at the manor.'

He glanced at his sister-in-law, Mary, holding her children's hands as she picked her way delicately through the tufty grass.

Mr Benjamin raised an eyebrow, and then joined his friend. Mr George was the only one left beside the tomb now, his eyes closed in prayer. Aunty hovered. When at last he blew his nose fiercely and walked away, she took a step forward.

'Don't, Aunty! He's not friendly like Mr Benjamin,' I hissed, but she didn't listen.

'I'm so sorry about your mother, Mr George,' she said, bowing her head.

He looked at her, frowning.

'I'm Miss Watson, sir, Lady Somerset's dressmaker,' she said. 'And this is my niece, Mona. We live in Gatekeeper's Cottage.'

'Yes, I know you do,' said Mr George. He hadn't wiped his nose properly and it looked most unpleasant.

'It was your dear mother's dying wish that we should stay there,' Aunty went on.

Mr George gave her such a dreadful look that I felt sick. 'So you say,' he said curtly.

Aunty flushed. 'It was in front of witnesses, sir.'

'Well, we shall have to wait and see,' he snapped. 'This is hardly the time or place to discuss such matters, but I would start making plans for the future, Miss Watson. We shall have to wait until my mother's will is read, but I very much doubt that there will be any mention of you or your charge.' And he walked off briskly.

Aunty put her hand to her chest. Her eyes were screwed shut, as if she was in terrible pain.

'Are you all right, Aunty? Don't trouble yourself about him. He's a horrible pig. And did you see his snotty nose?'

'Mona!' Aunty said faintly.

'Don't take on so. Mr Benjamin likes us. *He'll* let us stay,' I said, squeezing her hand.

'Yes, but he's not the one who'll inherit the estate. If it doesn't go to Roland, then it'll be Mr George – and now I've put his back up! Oh Lord, why did I go and accost him? You were right to warn me, Mona,' said Aunty. 'Now he'll turn us out just to make a point.'

'He can't do that. Lady Somerset agreed we could stay. In front of witnesses, like you said.'

'In front of Ella. He'll never take the word of a maid,' said Aunty, looking desperate.

I had to take her arm and help her out of the churchyard as if she was an old lady.

Mrs Higgins was gathering up her children. 'We're going home for a spot of tea, Miss Watson,' she said. 'Somehow funerals always make you hungry, don't they? Would you and Mona care to join us? We've got nothing fancy, but I've made a big lardy cake.'

I held my breath. Mrs Higgins's lardy cake was amazing – rich and curranty and liberally sprinkled with sugar, light in the mouth but wonderfully heavy in the stomach, keeping you full for hours.

'That's very kind, Mrs Higgins, but I'm afraid we have to get home,' said Aunty.

'Oh!' I said, unable to help myself.

She hesitated. 'Well, I have to get back to my work – but I dare say Mona could stay a little while, if you don't mind having her.'

'Of course we don't. She's a dear little thing, and such lovely manners. She puts my kiddies to shame,' said Mrs Higgins cheerily. 'She's a credit to you, Miss Watson.'

Aunty nodded awkwardly and then darted off. I watched her scurry away like a little black beetle, and I knew I should give up on the lardy cake and go with her. She was very worried now. I wondered if we really *would* be turfed out of the cottage, but I couldn't bear to think about it just yet. I wanted to lark around and have fun, and so I went and joined the Higgins family.

I had a big slice of lardy cake while we all discussed the funeral, solemn when talking about Lady Somerset, but shrieking with laughter at Barbara and her shabby artist and all her wild children. I gave an imitation of Mr George, making him snort like a pig, and Mrs Higgins said I had him spot on, and I was a right card.

Maggie's smallest sister, Bertha, had taken a shine to me. She climbed onto my lap and I held her tight and rubbed my head against her fat rosy cheeks and wished I could swap places with Maggie and live there for ever. But after an hour or so Mrs Higgins looked at the clock ticking on the mantelpiece between the two white china dogs and shook her head regretfully.

'I think you'd better be hopping off home, Mona dearie. I don't want your aunty fretting. Here – I'll wrap up a slice of the lardy cake for her. Or perhaps she doesn't eat cake . . . She's as thin as a pin. I wish I could say the same for myself!' She patted her broad hips cheerfully. 'I'm a walking lardy cake myself!'

'I think you look lovely,' I said shyly, taking the cake. I thanked her, said goodbye to everyone and kissed little Bertha.

I wanted to talk to Mother, but I hated the idea of going back into the churchyard and seeing Lady Somerset's tomb. I walked straight home instead.

Aunty was in her workroom, wearing her old olive-green dress and checked overall. She was arranging paper patterns on a remnant of candy-striped material she'd bought from Hailbury market. She juggled the pieces around to get them to fit.

'I'll have to make do with a lace collar and manage without pockets,' she murmured to herself. 'And I wanted matching knickers, but the material won't stretch to that. I've got the right shade of pink though – that might work. And I could always add pink pockets to the frock as a contrast – with a white daisy in satin stitch on each one.'

Then she looked up and her eyes focused. I saw her face tighten with worry as she looked at me. Sewing was Aunty's way of soothing herself. If she fussed about shapes and stitches, she could stop thinking about anything else.

'Hello, Aunty,' I said softly. I held out my little parcel. 'I've brought you a slice of lardy cake from Mrs Higgins.'

'That was kind of her, though you'll have to eat it. Lardy cake always gives me indigestion,' she said. 'But you can make me a cup of tea.'

I did as I was told. The milk was on the turn because it was so hot, but I fished out the little white lumps on the surface.

Aunty pulled a little face as she drank. 'I should have scalded the milk this morning, but I had other things on my mind,' she said.

I nodded, looking at the paper shapes pinned onto the candy-stripe material. I was used to constructing them inside my head and pictured the finished frock.

'It will look pretty,' I said. 'It's the sort of dress little Ada would wear.'

'That's what I'm aiming for,' said Aunty.

'Just so long as I never have to wear that dinky kind of frock!'

'You'd get the candy-stripe crumpled in two minutes,' said Aunty. 'Now run along and let me concentrate.'

She worked until well after dark, screwing up her

eyes in the dim gaslight. We only had the one lamp, so I took a candle up to bed. I was reading one of Old Molly's library books called *Rags and Tatters*. It had a pretty green cover with a picture of two little golden-haired children perching on the edge of a pavement, arms round each other. Rags was a girl and Tatters a little boy, and their mother had died from a fever. I liked books about children with dead mothers, so I read on eagerly. Rags and Tatters had a father, but in his grief he turned to the demon drink and beat them mercilessly.

The children didn't have an aunty to come and care for them, so they ran away to fend for themselves on the streets of London. This wasn't the fairy-tale London with streets paved with gold. It was a bleak world of grimy alleyways and tumbledown tenements. Rags and Tatters had to beg for food and often went hungry. Tatters started stealing fruit from market stalls, which seemed sensible enough to me, but it worried Rags terribly because the Bible says, *Thou shalt not steal.*

I sensed Tatters would come to a bad end – it was that kind of book – and, sure enough, he got run over by a horse and cart while trying to escape an angry stallholder. Rags was distraught at his death, and wandered around weeping, eventually taking refuge in a great tall building with pretty coloured-glass windows.

It was a church, of course, and the vicar took pity on her and brought her home to his wife, and by the end of the story Rags had become their own little girl. Every night she said a prayer for her brother, and begged that he might be forgiven and allowed to live with the angels up in heaven.

I read right to the end, using up a whole candle, which would annoy Aunty when she found out. I couldn't sleep afterwards, worrying that Aunty and I might be reduced to living on the streets of London. I knew Aunty would never beg, let alone steal – I'd have to be the one to do it – but I didn't want to end up under a horse and cart.

By this time Aunty had gone to bed, but I heard her springs creaking every now and then as she turned over, and I guessed she was still awake. I lay listening for a long time, and then I pattered across the landing and opened her door.

'Aunty?' I whispered into the dark.

'Go back to bed, Mona!' she said. Her voice was muffled because she had her teeth out.

'I can't sleep.'

'Try counting sheep,' she suggested.

'But that's so boring,' I said.

'That's the point.'

'Can't I come into your bed seeing as we're both awake?'

'I'm not starting those games. Now off you hop.'

I tried hopping, thudding across the uneven floorboards on one foot and setting Aunty's soap dish and tooth mug jingling on her washstand.

'Mona! Stop clowning around and go to *bed*!'

I stomped off. 'If Mother was alive, I know she'd let me cuddle up with her!' I muttered.

I heard Aunty sniff, but she didn't say anything more. I got back into bed and lay down, feeling cross and miserable. I tried sheep-counting, herding each woolly creature one by one through a gate. I imagined them so vividly I could hear the silly things baaing, but they didn't make me feel any sleepier. I switched to pigs instead, all grunting away, with Mr George's pink face and smeary nostrils. My bedroom started reeking of pig and I had to bury my nose in the pillow.

I suppose I must have gone to sleep after all – because when I lifted my head it was daylight.

It was a long, long, long day, and Aunty spent most of it in her workroom, even though it was Sunday. She made us a proper cooked lunch, with roast potatoes and carrots, but the only meat we had was the leftover ham, though she baked it in the oven so it tasted like pork.

When we'd eaten she went straight back to her sewing, so I washed up the dishes and then wandered off for a walk. I wanted to visit the Higginses, but that wasn't an option on Sunday afternoons. Maggie and her brothers and sisters were sent off to Sunday school while Mr and Mrs Higgins had a little lie-down. Instead I trailed around the estate, keeping to the woods because I wasn't supposed to go anywhere near the manor.

Then something landed right on my head with a *thwack*. It was a stick.

I yelled and looked up. Four fair tousled heads peered down at me from a big oak. The Somerset children! They were crammed into a rudimentary treehouse.

'Clear off, trespasser!' the smallest one yelled.

'Shut up, Bruno. He hasn't hurt you, has he?' the younger girl called anxiously.

'Yes, he has!' I said indignantly. I rubbed the top of my head. 'I'm bleeding!'

'Oh Lord!' said the older girl, and started climbing

down towards me. 'Let me see.' She jumped the last couple of feet and landed neatly beside me. She was much bigger than me, her fair hair even longer than her mother's.

This was the eldest, Esmeralda, who was about fourteen. Her sister, Marcella, was only a little younger than me. She wasn't very pretty, and she had a gap between her front teeth, but she looked more friendly. The youngest one, Bruno, looked anything but – he was waving another stick at me.

'I'm going to spear you now!' he shouted, climbing down.

I wasn't going to let a little kid of seven or so threaten me, especially a posh one with a silly name.

'No you're not!' I said, and I snatched the stick and snapped it in two.

Bruno looked outraged and started trying to beat me with his fists. He was smaller than me and not very strong, so it was easy enough to pin his arms to his sides and whirl him about, though I hoped the others didn't join in or I'd have to run for it.

Bruno squealed like a stuck pig, utterly furious. His big brother, Roland, peered down from the tree at us, laughing.

'Do shut up, Bruno,' said Esmeralda. She appealed to me. 'Would you mind putting him down? He'll shriek even more if you don't. I'll make sure he doesn't hit you again.'

'*I'll* make sure,' I said, but I dropped him.

He landed on the grass. He wasn't hurt, but he cried determinedly, though no one took any notice.

'Is your head bleeding badly?' Marcella asked anxiously.

'Yes!' I said, waving my bloody finger at her.

'Let me see,' said Esmeralda. She peered at the top of my head. 'It's only a scratch. I think it's stopped bleeding now.'

Marcella stood on tiptoe, trying to see. 'It must be very sore all the same.'

I shrugged, wanting them to think me brave, but it *was* sore. My whole head had started thumping.

Roland climbed down from the tree, leaping the last six feet. He was about a year younger than Esmeralda, and just as good looking.

'Let me look too,' he said. 'Gosh, the cut's quite deep. And you're not making any fuss either. Unlike some.' He shook his head at his brother. 'Stow it, Bruno!'

'I won't! Why are you taking the side of a beastly village girl?' he replied indignantly, wiping his nose with the back of his hand.'

'I'm not a village girl,' I said.

'I rather think you are,' said Marcella gently. 'We're not supposed to play with village children, but you do seem very nice all the same.'

'I live here, on the estate,' I said, sticking my chin out. 'With my aunty.'

'*Aunty*?' said Esmeralda, mimicking the way I said it.

I flushed, feeling ridiculous.

'I know who you are!' said Roland. 'You're the dressmaker's niece. Mother told me about you. You live in Gatekeeper's Cottage.'

'We do now,' I said, 'but maybe we won't any more. Aunty – *Aunt* – asked your uncle George if we could stay, but he wouldn't talk about it. And we don't have anywhere else to go. We'll have to live on the streets and end up in the workhouse,' I declared dramatically.

I didn't really believe it. Aunty might sell enough of her children's clothes to rent a room for us in Hailbury. And at breakfast she had suggested that, as a last resort, she could always be a housekeeper to some kindly gentleman – perhaps a vicar – who might allow me to live in his house too.

The Somerset children looked shocked when I said the word *workhouse*.

'That's terrible!' said Marcella.

'Yes, it is,' I said. 'Especially when your grandmother promised my aunt we could stay. She did, truly. But I don't think your uncle believed us.'

'I'm sure our father would have let you stay – he was a very honourable man,' said Roland. 'But he died of that beastly influenza, and now we have a horrible stepfather. We don't know who's going to be living at the manor. Grandmother was very secretive about her will, though Uncle George is confident of getting the estate.'

'It should be Rupert,' said Marcella. 'Only Grandmother disapproves of us and says we live like gypsies. I wish we did! I'd love to live in a caravan.'

'We won't be living here anyway,' said Esmeralda. 'We've already got a house in France. I tell you what, I think Uncle George is rather fond of me. He's always patting my back and calling me Goldilocks. I shall ask him if you can stay as a special favour to me.'

'Would you?' I asked.

'I'm sure Bruno's sorry he hit you. He just gets carried away,' said Marcella.

Bruno frowned, but didn't contradict her.

'I shall go and ask him right this minute,' said Esmeralda, and she sauntered off, tossing her long golden hair.

'Perhaps you'd better ask your aunt to wash your head and put iodine on your cut,' Marcella suggested. 'It stings, but it makes the cut better.' She turned and walked off too, taking Bruno by the hand.

'I hope your head stops hurting soon,' said Roland.

'Thank you,' I said.

Roland nodded and followed the others. Then he turned. 'I'm Roland, by the way.'

'I'm Mona.'

'Sorry about everything,' he said. 'I'll try persuading Uncle George to let you stay too.'

Then he ran off.

'Stop! Stop the car!' she shouted.

5

I TOLD AUNTY THAT ROLAND AND ESMERALDA were going to speak to their uncle George on our behalf. I thought she would be pleased with me, but she wrung her hands at the thought.

'It will only make him more determined to get rid of us,' she said. 'And what were you doing, talking to Roland and Esmeralda? You mustn't approach the Somerset children!'

'*They* approached *me*! That nasty little Bruno dropped a stick on me – look! It jolly well hurt.' I bent my head and showed Aunty my wound.

She tutted as if it was somehow my fault, though she did clean it carefully. We didn't have any iodine, but Aunty kept a small bottle of brandy for medicinal purposes, so she poured a drop or two onto cotton wool and dabbed with that. It stung and I protested.

'Stop whining!' she said sharply. 'And count yourself lucky I'm not swigging the whole bottle myself. This constant fretting is enough to make me take to drink.'

We tried to carry on as normal. Aunty sketched and sewed constantly, making enough dresses and shirts and shorts and rompers for a small kindergarten class. I went to school, played with Maggie, visited the Higginses, whispered to Mother in the churchyard, and went home again, day after day.

Every lunchtime the boys invited me to play Kiss Chase, but I refused. I sat with Maggie and we played Treasures. Maggie had an old chocolate box containing a blue bead necklace without a clasp, a black pebble that she swore was jet, a little pot of rouge with a smidgen of red still inside, a lace hankie she'd found in the street, a matchbox containing a long-dead butterfly, and a four-leafed clover – though it looked as if it had been doctored.

I had a soap box that still smelled of lavender if you sniffed hard, a skein of jade-green embroidery thread, a set of doll's chairs made of conkers with pin legs, a stick of pink chalk, a few pressed rose petals and a farthing china doll half the size of my thumb.

We handled our treasures lovingly and told stories about them and occasionally swapped them. Maggie was keen to own my little doll, and offered in exchange her best treasure, the blue bead necklace. I was very tempted – I thought Aunty could make a new clasp for it – but I loved little Farthing and decided she was worth far more to me than any jewellery. So we reached stalemate and got bored with our game. We realized we were getting too old for it now: our so-called treasures were of value to no one but ourselves.

On Thursday Peter Robinson came over and sat beside us.

'What are you doing, Peter? This is a girls' game. Clear off,' said Maggie.

'I can sit anywhere I want,' he said. 'And anyone can play that game. I've got my own box of treasures at home. I've got a postage stamp from India, and six cigarette cards of cricketers, and a whopping great green glass marble.'

We yawned to show we weren't impressed, though I liked the sound of the marble.

Peter sensed this. 'Why don't you come home with me after school, Mona, and I'll show you?' he said.

'She comes home with me,' said Maggie.

'Well, she could come home with me just this once,' Peter insisted. 'We could swap stuff, Mona. I could even give you the marble for nothing, if you really liked it.'

'Maybe I'll come some other time,' I said. I didn't want to hurt his feelings. He was really quite a nice boy. He couldn't help his short hair, which made his ears look big. His feet seemed too big too, clumsy in their rough boots. I couldn't help thinking of Roland Somerset, with his long tangled mane and easy grace.

'That told him,' said Maggie as we walked home together, our treasure boxes clutched to our chests.

'Poor Peter,' I said.

'You don't *like* him, do you?' she asked.

'No, of course not.'

'I think you do.'

'I don't like any boys,' I insisted. 'Not even Roland Somerset.' I hadn't meant to mention him. The words just slipped out because I'd been thinking about him.

'Roland Somerset!' said Maggie, and she spluttered with laughter. She nudged me as if I'd made a joke. 'Didn't the family look *awful* at the funeral. Even Mum said it was a disgrace, and she never speaks ill of anyone. The boys look like *girls*! Their hair! They couldn't even go to the barber's for their grandma's funeral!'

She paused, expecting me to join in. So I did, just to keep her happy. In some ways it was enjoyable ridiculing the Somersets. Roland and Esmeralda made me feel so shy and awkward. So we skipped along laughing at their looks, their clothes, their loud ringing voices, their ragbag mother, their shabby stepfather. We did the Charleston together in the middle of the lane, and every time we took a step it was as if we were stamping on the Somersets.

I stopped off at Maggie's cottage, and Mrs Higgins gave me my usual slice of bread and dripping.

'Did your aunty like the lardy cake?' she asked eagerly.

'Oh, yes, thank you, she said it was absolutely delicious,' I lied. 'And very kind of you.'

'I'll make sure she has a big slice next time I make one,' said Mrs Higgins. 'She looks as if she needs feeding up, your aunty. She's so neat and nicely dressed, always the proper lady, but so *thin*. And you're such a little scrap too, Mona, compared with my Maggie.' She paused, nibbling at her lip. 'You two don't stint yourself on food, do you?'

I wondered what to say. Aunty and I *didn't* get enough to eat. If I admitted it, then Mrs Higgins might give us the odd slice of pie or suet pudding, eggs from their hens, a few rashers from their previous pig. The Higginses were poor, but they always had enough to eat even though there were so many of them. Mr Higgins was head dairyman up at the farm and earned a reasonable wage.

However, I knew that Aunty would die if I said we'd be grateful for any spare food. She could accept charity leftovers from the manor, but not kindness from the Higginses. She acknowledged that they were good people, but she still thought them very rough and ready.

'We have lots to eat, Mrs Higgins,' I fibbed. 'Aunty's just got a small appetite. And we're naturally thin, both of us.'

I don't know if she believed me or not, but she didn't press me further – though when I left to go home she gave me another slice of bread and dripping, saying she'd spread one too many by mistake. I think she was fibbing too.

I went to see Mother – I wasn't so bothered by Lady Somerset's tomb now, telling myself she'd be happy to be reunited with her husband. In fact, I pinched three of Mr Benjamin's lilies and arranged them on Mother's grave, where they looked beautiful. I imagined one lily in Mother's long hair, one pinned to her bodice and one in her hand. She wouldn't wear an awful shroud. She wouldn't wear a stiff brocade robe either. She'd wear a soft ivy-green velvet dress and look absolutely beautiful.

I wished I had just one photograph of her. I decided to borrow Aunty's sketching pencil and attempt a portrait. When I got home Aunty was standing in the doorway of the cottage, peering out anxiously.

'Hey, Aunty! I'm not late, am I?' I said.

'No more than usual,' she replied. 'I'm watching out for the cars. It's been action stations all day. A big Daimler came through the gates just before eleven this morning, and I'm pretty certain it was the lawyer come to read the will. I've been keeping watch on and off ever since. He left around two – he must have dined with the family. Not long afterwards, Barbara and that awful artist fellow and the four children left in their dreadful muddy car – no chauffeur, Barbara herself at the wheel, would you believe.'

I felt devastated to find that they'd gone already.

'Mr George and his wife are still up at the manor. I wish I knew what he's going to do. Will he give us a chance to find a new place to live or will he turn us out straight away?' said Aunty, clutching her chest. 'Oh, how my heart's banging!' She looked down fearfully, as if she expected her heart to thump right out of her skin.

'Don't fret so, Aunty,' I said, scared. 'Mr George might let us stay. Esmeralda said she'd try to get him to change his mind.'

Aunty shook her head. 'As if she could make any difference!' she said. 'And I told you, they've gone.'

'I wish they hadn't,' I said, sighing.

'I keep hoping Ella will slip down and let us know what's going on—' said Aunty. 'Wait a minute! I can hear another car! If it's Mr Benjamin, shall I ask if he can help us? He's always been so kind.'

The car swung round the corner, but it wasn't Mr Benjamin's cream Lagonda. It was Mr George's Daimler.

He was sitting in the front with his chauffeur, looking very grim. His wife was in the back, with Cedric beside her and Ada on her lap.

'Oh my Lord!' said Aunty. 'Well, best get it over with.' She swallowed hard and then stepped out onto the drive, standing up straight, chin up, waiting for the car to slow down.

However, it drove straight past her. Mr George didn't even glance in her direction, and neither did his wife, though the children stared.

'Hasn't he even got the guts to tell me to my face?' said Aunty.

She chased after the car. 'Mr George! Stop! Stop the car!' she shouted.

The chauffeur braked, and Aunty rushed up, putting her foot on the running board so the car couldn't move off.

'Mr George, please tell me, what are you going to do? Are you really going to put us out of our home, even though your mother promised we could stay?' she panted.

'Get down, woman! Get off my car!' he protested.

'Please, sir! Please, madam,' said Aunty, appealing to his wife too.

'You're making a spectacle of yourself!' she replied. 'Stop it! You're frightening the children.' I saw that Cedric and Ada were starting to snivel.

'*You're* a mother. You want to protect your children. I have to look after my little niece. Please could we stay just for the summer, to give me a chance to find somewhere to go,' Aunty begged.

'How dare you address my wife in such a way! Get off

my car or you'll find yourself on the ground. Drive on, man! And be sharp about it!' Mr George commanded.

The chauffeur did as he was told. Aunty clung on for a few seconds, but then had to jump off. She landed awkwardly, nearly toppling, and sank to her knees. Mr George didn't even look round.

'You hateful pig!' I shouted after him.

'Mona!' Aunty murmured.

'Well, he *is* a pig, treating you like that! Have you hurt yourself, Aunty? Oh dear, you're getting your skirt all dusty.'

She heaved herself up and brushed her skirt down. 'She's right, I suppose. I *have* made a spectacle of myself – and all for nothing. He's never going to let us stay now. He'll be calling the bailiffs in to do his dirty work. We'd better start packing, Mona. We don't want all our possessions flung out onto the driveway. Oh dear Lord, what are we going to do? Where will we go?'

I pictured us trudging off, lugging our shabby suitcase and the big shopping bag and the laundry sack. What about Aunty's sewing machine and all her bolts of material and her dressmaker's dummy and her special iron? How could she make a living without them? We'd have to hire a horse and cart from Rook Green. Maybe Mr Higgins would help. I thought of saying goodbye to Maggie, my best friend in all the world, and little Bertha – and dear Mrs Higgins, who had been like a mother to me.

What about my own mother? If Aunty and I had to move far away, how could I go and see her every day? Would she think I didn't care about her any more?

I started shivering. Somehow, up until now, I hadn't

believed it would really happen. I took hold of Aunty's hand. She held it tight. She was shaking too.

'Well, whatever happens, we've still got each other,' I said.

She stared at me, and then her face crumpled, her eyes filling with tears.

'Oh, Aunty, I'm sorry. I didn't mean to make you cry,' I said, panicking.

'You're a dear girl, Mona,' she mumbled. 'A dear brave girl. Come on then, let us get organized. Pick out one book and one toy and your best dress and a jumper and a clean nightie and spare underwear and your washing things, and see if they'll fit in my old carpet bag. Best dress on top, with tissue paper in the folds, so it won't crease.'

One book, *one* toy? I went and looked at the books on my window sill – all my birthday and Christmas presents. I stood there, running my fingers up and down the dear familiar spines, unable to choose. Then I looked up – and saw Mr Benjamin strolling down the driveway, immaculate in a fashionably cut black suit, with a black silk scarf in a bow at his neck, and black patent boots as shiny as satin. He paused when he got to our cottage, and then walked up the path. He was coming to see us! There was a gentle knock at the door.

'Aunty!' I called, running to fetch her. 'Aunty, it's Mr Benjamin!'

Aunty came out of her workroom, carrying an armful of dresses and shorts and romper suits as carefully as if they were real children. 'I didn't hear a car,' she said.

'He walked here. What does he want? *He's* not come to turn us out, has he?' I asked.

There was another knock. Aunty looked down helplessly at the children's clothes in her arms. 'Answer it then, Mona!' she hissed at me.

I opened the door and stared at Mr Benjamin fearfully.

'Hello, Mona,' he said. 'Don't look so frightened! I'm not that dreadful, am I? Could I pop in for a moment and have a little word with your aunt?'

I nodded and stood back to let him in. He wafted past me, smelling beautifully flowery. All the other men I knew smelled of sweat on weekdays and carbolic soap on Sundays. Aunty was standing in the kitchen, staring at him, so unnerved that her arms slackened and the clothes fell to the floor in a flutter of pink and blue.

'Oh my goodness, what exquisite little garments!' said Mr Benjamin, bending to rescue them. 'Did *you* make them, Miss Watson? Marvellous little stitches – just like Miss Potter's magical mice!' he said. 'Have you read *The Tailor of Gloucester*, Mona? I think it has to be my favourite little book in all the world.'

I remembered the little white books at the end of Old Molly's children's shelf. 'I'd have thought *The Tale of Benjamin Bunny* would have been your favourite,' I said.

'Mona! Don't be impertinent!' said Aunty. 'May I offer you a cup of tea, Mr Benjamin? I'm afraid I can't take you into the parlour – I use it as a workroom.'

'A cup of tea would be most refreshing, Miss Watson. It's only a ten-minute walk from the manor, but somehow I feel exhausted! It doesn't help that I'm wearing new boots. Oh dear, just look at them!' he said, sitting down on a rickety chair, quite at ease. 'Dusty all over! I shall have to get myself some proper countryman's shoes –

those conker-brown affairs with little holes in. And I dare say a stout walking stick would set them off a treat, don't you think?'

Aunty looked at him uncertainly, not sure whether he was serious.

'Could you put the kettle on, Mona,' she said. She lowered her voice. 'Best cups.'

We only had two rose-patterned, gold-rimmed china teacups with matching saucers. We used our plain green tea set for every day, and most of the cups had chips or cracks. They were good enough for Ella, but Mr Benjamin must only have the best – even if he was here to throw us out.

I set the tea tray with the two rose cups and the nicest of the green cups for me. Mr Benjamin and Aunty didn't say much, just murmured something about the funeral. Mr Benjamin talked about the hymns, saying he'd helped Lady Somerset choose them.

'Mummy was always very particular, though I'm sure I don't need to tell *you* that, Miss Watson! It annoyed her that she couldn't write the sermon! I kept expecting her to tap on the coffin lid in irritation when the vicar came out with the usual platitudes. Still, at least she was dressed in style. She was extremely pleased with her robe. And no wonder! I've a mind to put in an order for one right this minute, just in case I drop down dead tomorrow. I shall follow Lord Baden-Powell's motto for his little boy scouts. "Be prepared!"'

Aunty smiled weakly.

'Are you all right, Miss Watson? You look very pale. Am I upsetting you, talking so frivolously? You must forgive me. It's just my way. I'm truly grieving. Mummy was very dear to me. I loved the old darling, even though she could try the patience of a saint. I know you were fond of her too. Has her death come as a great shock?' Mr Benjamin asked gently.

'Yes, it has,' Aunty murmured. 'Especially as . . .'

'Especially as . . . ?' he repeated.

'As we have to leave the cottage!' Aunty sobbed, unable to hold back any longer. 'Oh, Mr Benjamin, what are we going to do?'

I dashed over and patted her heaving shoulders. She was crying like a child, her mouth square, all attempt at dignity gone.

'Oh good Lord, I'm so sorry! I didn't mean to upset your aunt, Mona. I prattle on so,' said Mr Benjamin. 'What's all this talk of leaving the cottage?'

'Mr George says we can't stay,' I said.

'Even though your mother promised we could!' Aunty wailed, tears rolling down her cheeks.

'Here, dear Miss Watson,' said Mr Benjamin, offering her his immaculate white handkerchief. 'Why does George have any say in this?'

Aunty and I exchanged glances. Was Mr Benjamin playing some kind of game with us? Or was he a bit simple, for all his way with words?

'As Mr George is now in charge of the Somerset estate, he has the right to put us out on the street,' said Aunty, dabbing at her wet face.

'And he won't listen to Aunty, and practically accused her of being a liar!' I said indignantly.

'Then my brother is no gentleman,' said Mr Benjamin.

'And he's also been issuing idle threats. He has no power whatsoever to uproot you from your home.'

'Did Lady Somerset put in her will that we can stay in the cottage?' Aunty gasped.

'Unfortunately not, though I'm sure the intention was there,' said Mr Benjamin, fiddling with one pearl cufflink. He paused, gazing down at it, and then looked up with a beautiful smile on his face. 'But my mother's will said very firmly and clearly that my brother George should *not* inherit the estate.'

'So she's left it to young Roland?' Aunty gasped.

'Rather to everyone's surprise, she has left it to *me* – though I view myself as a caretaker for the boy. But as I'm now in charge of the estate, I have the right to decide who lives in this cottage. I promise you it is yours, rent free, for however long you wish to live here.'

'Oh my Lord!' said Aunty, and started crying all over again.

'I hope you were addressing our father up in heaven! I'm no lord and I'd love you to carry on calling me Mr Benjamin. It sounds far more friendly than Mr Somerset,' he said. 'I wonder, could we possibly have that tea now?'

I turned to finish making it. I heard Mr Benjamin whispering to Aunty, and when I set the tray down before them he was actually patting her hand.

I poured the tea without spilling a drop, and handed round the cups. I offered a small plate of biscuits too. We kept a few plain digestives for emergencies. We'd had them for months, and they were very stale, but Mr Benjamin bravely swallowed his down.

'You're a very competent girl for your age, Mona,' he

said. 'You put my nephews and nieces to shame. As soon as my renovations to the manor are complete, I shall be inviting Barbara's wild quartet to come and stay. I hope you will come and play with them.'

'That's too kind of you, Mr Benjamin, but I don't think it would be quite proper,' said Aunty. 'I'm not sure your sister-in-law would like it.'

'Oh, Barbara's very relaxed about the social niceties, bless her,' said Mr Benjamin. 'Unlike my other sister-in-law! I shall issue invitations to George and his family too, but I'm not sure they'll want to come. George is very angry – and Mary accused me of inducing my mother to change her will. Can you believe it! You know my mother, Miss Watson. She was her own woman right to the end, utterly indomitable.'

Aunty blew her nose on Mr Benjamin's handkerchief as delicately as she could. 'Why do you think your mother made her decision, Mr Benjamin?' she asked.

'Oh, Aunty, it's obvious – Mr Benjamin is *much* nicer than Mr George,' I blurted out.

'Mona! Hold your tongue!' she said.

Mr Benjamin laughed. 'I hope you're right, Mona! But I rather think it was Mary who upset her own apple cart. Mother once discovered her making lists of all the paintings with a view to getting them valued – they wanted to sell them when George inherited the manor. Imagine! Mother couldn't bear her – she felt that Mary had got George wrapped round her little finger. She wasn't too keen on little Cedric and Ada either – she thought them very mealy-mouthed.'

I giggled, and Aunty shot me a look.

'What's got into you, Mona? Mind your manners. Giggling like a simpleton when poor Lady Somerset has been buried for less than a week,' she said sternly. 'And here's Mr Benjamin in full mourning clothes.'

'Oh, I'm only dressed like a crow today for the benefit of the lawyers and the family. If I appeared in my normal togs, I dare say Mary would contest the will. She thinks I'm a degenerate, unfit to inherit. I expect she and George will be plotting against me, but Mother took care to make her will watertight. She changed it a month or so before she died, and took me into her confidence. It's been such a lark this past week, hearing George and Mary making grandiose plans for the future. But as soon as I get back to my London flat I shall be putting my black suit right at the back of the wardrobe. In fact, if the weather stays sunny, I might well wear my new white suit. I have a divine panama hat too. Perhaps you might care to trim it for me, Miss Watson? I fancy silk flowers – maybe a twist of honeysuckle around the brim so I look like a country cottage.'

'With pleasure, Mr Benjamin,' said Aunty, though she looked a little startled. I wondered if he was teasing her. Surely gentlemen didn't really have their hats trimmed like that, even in London!

'I'm sure I'll be able to put some business your way, though I can't think of any friends with little children. Your exquisite outfits would be wasted on Barbara's wild offspring. They'd suit Cedric and Ada to a tee, but I think we'd better not approach Mary just yet.'

'I thought I might see if the big draper's in Hailbury would consider stocking them,' Aunty said shyly.

'I should aim a little higher, Miss Watson. Try London! How about Harrods? I think they'd jump at the chance of selling them.'

'You're too kind, Mr Benjamin,' she said.

'And of course you will have Mona's allowance to ease your financial situation a little,' said Mr Benjamin.

'My allowance?' I asked.

'I told your aunty about it while you were making this excellent pot of tea. My mother took such a shine to you that she decided to give you a little monetary gift each year,' said Mr Benjamin. 'Well, I must rush back to the manor and supervise my packing. Mother's lady's maid is very sweet, but she has *no* idea how to fold a shirt, bless her. I shall be able to have a proper valet now, praise the Lord!'

Aunty stiffened. 'I don't quite know how to say this, Mr Benjamin, especially as you've been so exceptionally kind and generous, and Mona and I will never, ever be able to thank you enough, but could I just . . .'

'Could you just what, Miss Watson?' said Mr Benjamin. He seemed amused rather than irritated.

'Could I just mention that Ella, Lady Somerset's maid, is very good and willing, and I'm sure she could still serve you in a useful way. And perhaps, in the fullness of time, she might prove her worth looking after your future wife,' said Aunty in a rush. She looked agitated. 'Please don't take offence, Mr Benjamin. You must do as you think fit. It's certainly not my place to offer advice. I think I must sound very impertinent.'

'On the contrary, Miss Watson, you sound sweetly concerned. Don't worry, I shall have a little chat with

Ella and see if we can come to some mutually agreeable arrangement – though I will be very surprised if that includes a bride for me,' he said. 'But rest assured, for the moment I shall be retaining all the staff. I'll be rushing backwards and forwards from London, keeping an eye on my refurbishments. I intend to be in full residence by midsummer.'

'Then that will be a pleasure for all of us,' said Aunty, clasping his hand and thanking him again and again for a full two minutes.

When he'd sauntered off with a cheery wave, Aunty gave me a kiss on both cheeks, kicked off her black shoes and danced around the living room in her stockinged feet. I laughed at her incredulously, and started dancing too.

'Look, Aunty! This is the Charleston. Maggie showed me. It's all the rage,' I said, demonstrating.

'Dear goodness – give me an old-fashioned waltz any day,' said Aunty. 'Oh, I can't believe everything's going to turn out all right! No wonder Mr George had a face like thunder when he drove past!'

'Mr Benjamin's so lovely,' I said. 'And he said I was getting an allowance . . . How much is it, Aunty?'

I was thinking it might be a pound. Perhaps five pounds . . . I thought of all the wonders in Mr Berner's toyshop. I could take my pick – and buy Maggie and Bertha and the other little Higginses a present too. I might even buy Peter Robinson another glass marble.

'It's a whole hundred pounds a year!' said Aunty.

'Two whole pounds for a little girl like you?'

6

I HAD SO MANY PLANS FOR THAT MONEY. WHEN the cheque arrived, we both marvelled at it, reading the amount over and over again.

'We'll take it straight to the bank,' said Aunty. 'We'll open up a special account just for you, Mona.'

'And then they'll give me the money? Imagine one hundred pound notes! Or perhaps I could have it in half-crowns – then it would look so much more! Or even thruppenny bits – I could keep them in a big wooden chest and pretend they were gold,' I gabbled excitedly.

'Don't be silly, dear,' said Aunty. 'You're to keep it all safely in the bank.'

'But how can I spend it then?'

'You're not going to spend a penny of it! Not unless there's some dire emergency. You can save it until you're twenty-one – then you'll have one thousand, one hundred pounds – more than that, with interest added on. What a wonderful amount! You'll be an independent young woman of means, Mona. You'll be able to buy your very own cottage. You'll dress in the finest clothes, dine in the best restaurants. You'll lead the life of a lady, not needing to work unless you choose to,' Aunty marvelled.

'But I don't particularly *want* to be a lady, all la-di-da like Mr George's wife or loopy like Barbara. I don't want to eat fancy food, and you can make my dresses, and I don't want my own cottage, I want to live here in Gatekeeper's Cottage with you,' I said. 'Mr Benjamin says we can live here for ever and ever, and so we shall.'

Aunty looked touched by my declaration, but she was adamant. 'It's your future security, Mona. You don't realize how valuable that is. I won't let you fritter away your inheritance on toys and trinkets,' she said firmly.

'Can't I even buy you a present with my own money?' I said. 'I'd like to get you some new spectacles – you strain your eyes so with all that stitching. And how about some new shoes – pretty ones with straps and little heels – and some new silk stockings so you can throw your old darned lisle ones away.'

'Dear Lord, you'd have me kitted out like a chorus girl!' said Aunty. 'No, the entire hundred pounds is going in that bank and staying there. And don't you go telling Maggie or anyone else about it either.'

'But I want to!'

'I dare say you do, but it's to be a secret. I don't want anyone gossiping about you. Do you hear me, Mona? Promise me you won't say a word to a living soul.' Aunty took hold of me, cupping my face so I had to look her in the eye. 'Promise now!'

'I promise,' I said, sighing.

It was a great sacrifice: I was so excited about the money I felt ready to burst. Still, I could tell someone – because she wasn't a living soul any more. I lay on Mother's grave and whispered into the grass and thought I felt her stirring happily beneath me.

Then I forced myself to go round to the front of the church and approach Lady Somerset's tomb. Her flowers had withered, but I rearranged them as decoratively as I could. Then I knelt down in front of the tomb, getting my knees muddy. I spoke loudly, hoping my voice would penetrate the marble.

'Thank you very much for the money, Lady Somerset. I'm ever so grateful, and so is Aunty. She won't let me spend any of it though. I don't know why you took a shine to me – I didn't say much, and I'm not pretty like Esmeralda or kind like Marcella, though I'm definitely not mealy-mouthed. I hope you're comfortable in Aunty's robe. I'm sure no one else in this graveyard has one like it.' I couldn't think of anything else, so I finished by saying, 'Rest in peace,' very solemnly, and then stood up.

I'd got the hem of my dress muddy as well as my knees, and Aunty was cross when she saw, but she stopped fussing when I explained that I'd been to visit Lady Somerset.

'I suppose it's only right and proper, if a bit morbid. Graveyards aren't really a place for little girls,' she said, her head bent over her sewing.

I wondered what she'd say if she knew I went there every day to talk to Mother. Did Aunty ever go to see her sister? It was usually a forbidden subject, but Aunty had been in such a good mood since Mr Benjamin's visit that I decided to risk it.

'Do you ever go to see my mother?' I asked.

There was a little pause. Aunty's head was bent so I couldn't see her face.

'Do you go on her birthday? Or – or on her deathday?' I persisted.

'No! Sylvia's gone, Mona,' she said shortly.

'Don't you miss her?' I sighed. 'I miss her terribly.'

'That's silly. You didn't even know her.'

'I do so still miss her,' I said. 'And I miss my father too, though not as much. What sort of a man was he, Aunty? You must have met him.'

'Ssh now, I have to concentrate. Satin stitch on silk is very tricky.'

I looked at the material. It was a rich purple, soft and slippery. I was puzzled. Aunty was making children's clothes now, using up all her long-hoarded fine cottons and voiles. They were cream and pink and pale blue. Purple was surely too bold a colour for a small child.

I reached out and stroked it.

'I hope your hands aren't as mucky as your knees!' Aunty snapped. 'Go and have a wash.'

'They're practically spotless!' I said, showing her. 'Is the purple for a little girl or a little boy?'

'Don't be silly, Mona. These are pyjamas for a gentleman,' she said.

I blinked at her. I'd seen pictures of men wearing

pyjamas in her pattern books, but they were always blue-and-white striped affairs, serviceable and boring. These pyjamas were beautiful and exotic. I couldn't imagine any man wearing them – apart from one . . .

'Oh, Aunty, are they for Mr Benjamin?'

'What do you think?' she said, and she held out the soft pocket, showing me the white monogram: a very fancy B and then half an S.

'Benjamin Somerset!' I said.

'Well, it's going to be Benjamin Sebastian Claude Somerset when I've done,' said Aunty. 'That's his full name.'

'How on earth do you know, Aunty?'

'I know everything about the Somersets,' she said. 'Do you think he'll like his pyjamas? I'd never make anything else for Mr Benjamin – he's very particular about his clothes and goes to Savile Row for his suits, and I can't attempt a shirt because I don't know his exact measurements – but pyjamas are loose.'

'I think he'll love them!'

'I wanted to make him a present because he's been so kind to us. You don't think pyjamas are too . . . intimate?' Aunty asked.

'Not at all,' I said, though if Mr Benjamin were inside his purple pyjamas right that minute, his head would be cradled against Aunty's chest. I stifled a giggle.

'Do you think my father would have liked purple silk pyjamas?' I asked.

'What sort of a question's that!' said Aunty.

'Well, what sort of a man *was* he? Was he like Mr Benjamin, funny and chatty and particular about his clothes?'

'No, dear.'

'Was he like Mr George, very pompous and proper?'

'No, he was . . . quieter,' said Aunty, her face suddenly dreamy.

This was promising. She'd never given me so much as a hint about his personality before.

I tried to think of a quiet man. There was only Maggie's father, who came home from the farm tired out, and fell asleep with the children crawling all over him.

'Like Mr Higgins?' I asked.

'No! Your father was a gentleman!' said Aunty.

'A gentleman?' I asked, astonished. 'So was Mother a lady?'

'How you do run on, Mona! Now go and scrub those knees this minute and put that grubby dress to soak. Dear goodness!' Aunty exclaimed.

I couldn't get another word out of her. I washed and plunged my dress in the tub, and then lay on my bed in my vest and knickers and socks, thinking about my father. Had he really been a gentleman? I liked the idea enormously.

I wished he had a grave in the churchyard too so that I could feel close to him. I knew he was buried somewhere in France, with lots of other soldiers. I had a sudden astonishing thought. When I was older I would have enough money to take a ship to France and visit his grave. One thousand one hundred pounds plus interest! I could go anywhere I wanted.

I took my little china doll out of my treasure box and balanced her on the back of my hand. Then I steered her across the waves of my blue eiderdown, taking her to France, to Italy, all the way to America – to all the faraway lands in Miss Nelson's atlas of the world.

'Sail away, little Farthing,' I said, and she waved her tiny china arm and slid all the way down the Niagara Falls of my leg.

She wore a wisp of a dress, just crumpled muslin, so as soon as Aunty had finished the four-letter monogram I begged her to make my doll a new purple silk party frock out of a scrap left over from Mr Benjamin's pyjamas.

'I've got too much to do, sewing all the children's clothes,' said Aunty. 'I shouldn't have spent all today sewing the silk pyjamas, but I wanted to have them ready for when Mr Benjamin next visits.'

'Haven't you got enough little clothes now to take them to one of the big department stores in London? Mr Benjamin said to try Harrods,' I reminded her.

'I'm not sure he was serious. Harrods is a tip-top department store,' said Aunty, 'and London is a very big city. It isn't just a matter of getting the train. I'll have to take an omnibus too, and it's all so noisy and confusing, and I'll be lugging the suitcase full of clothes and getting so flustered I'll hardly be able to say my own name, let alone persuade the buyer of the children's department to take my little garments. It's making my heart flutter just thinking about it.'

'I'll come with you, Aunty,' I said.

'Don't be silly, Mona. I'm not having you missing school.'

'We could go on Saturday. Oh, please let's. It will be such an adventure!'

'I can't afford the fare for me, let alone for you,' said Aunty.

'*I* can afford our fares,' I said grandly. 'We can go to the bank and draw out some of my money.'

'I told you, we're not touching a penny of it,' she said.

'You said we wouldn't spend it unless there was a dire emergency. And it is, sort of,' I said. 'You need to sell the clothes and get orders for more.'

'I'll go to Hailbury and sell them there,' said Aunty.

'They won't want quality stuff in Hailbury. Mr Benjamin said you'd be better off trying in London,' I insisted.

'Yes, well, it's easy for Mr Benjamin to say that when all he has to do is call up his chauffeur and get driven wherever he wants,' said Aunty.

'We could ask him to take us in his car,' I suggested.

'Don't be so silly, Mona!'

'But he's our friend now.'

'Yes, but not so that we can ask him for any more favours! For goodness' sake, child, we have to know our place,' said Aunty.

That was the trouble. We didn't seem to *have* any place in society. We weren't villagers. We weren't gentry. We didn't have our own gentleman to look after us.

'I wish we weren't always the odd ones out,' I said.

'So do I,' said Aunty. She kneaded her forehead, frowning.

'Have you got a headache?'

'It's nothing, child,' she said, but she looked very pale.

I ran to the kitchen, held the tea towel under the cold tap, and then wrung it out carefully.

'Here, Aunty,' I said, and I made her sit back in her chair while I stood behind her and pressed the cold towel to her forehead. 'Is that nice?'

'Yes. Lovely,' Aunty murmured. 'You're a good girl, Mona. Bless you, dear.'

'And we'll go to London on Saturday, you and me?' I begged. 'I'll run home from school quick as quick tomorrow, and we'll go to see Mr Freeman at the bank in the village and take out the money for our fares.'

'No, Mona!'

'Yes, Aunty! Yes, yes, yes!' I insisted.

I went on saying yes, emphasizing the last letter so that I hissed like a snake, and eventually Aunty gave in. She really needed to sell the clothes and she could see that Mr Benjamin's idea made sense. She seemed scared of going to London though. It wasn't just because it was a big city. She didn't really like going out anywhere, not even down to Rook Green. She always sent me to do the shopping or run errands. After we'd been to the bank with the cheque she had to have a lie-down. She always thought people were staring at her, even when they barely gave her a second glance.

Poor old Aunty, I thought. I'd look after her when we went to London. I'd help her carry the case and we'd find our way to Harrods. If Aunty got tongue-tied, I'd speak up. We'd sell all those dinky little dresses and Aunty would be thrilled.

The next day, the minute we were let out of school I started running.

'Hey, Mona, wait for me!' Maggie called indignantly.

'Well, get a move on. I'm in a hurry,' I said.

'Why? Where are you going?' she demanded.

'Somewhere,' I said. I couldn't tell her about going to the bank because I'd promised Aunty not to talk about my inheritance. And I didn't really *want* to tell her any more, even though she was my best friend. She was starting to get on my nerves a bit.

'Tell me!'

I held my nose and wiggled it in reply, indicating that she was being a nosy parker.

'Don't be horrid,' said Maggie. She ran faster and caught hold of my arm. 'Are you meeting up with Peter Robinson?'

'No! Are you mad?'

'Then are you seeing that fancy-pantsy Mr Benjamin?'

'Don't call him that!'

'Well, he *is*. We all think he looks a right sissy in them clothes. I don't know why you think he's so wonderful.'

'You just don't understand fine clothes,' I said, sniffing.

'Oh, shut up, you swanky mare,' said Maggie.

I had to stop running because I was out of breath, but I walked as quickly as I could. Maggie kept pace with me, but we didn't say another word until we got to her cottage. Bertha was tethered to the doorknob, toddling barefoot through the grass. When she saw me she shouted happily and held up her arms.

'No, sorry, Bertha, I've got to run home,' I said.

'Aren't you even coming in for your bread and dripping?' Maggie asked.

'Not today,' I told her.

Maggie flounced off, and went to pick Bertha up herself.

I shifted from one foot to the other, wondering if I should try to make up with her. Then I thought of spending Saturday in London, and ran on without even saying goodbye.

I was worried that Aunty would pretend she'd forgotten all about going to the bank. I was all prepared to drag her out of her workroom – but she was standing at the door waiting for me, wearing her coat and hat.

'Wipe your face and get changed quick, dear,' she said.

I did as I was told, putting on my hat and my little white gloves too. Visiting the bank was as solemn a thing as going to church. We walked back down into Rook Green, Aunty scarcely glancing to left and right to avoid making eye contact with anyone. If someone greeted her, she gave them a quick nod but walked rapidly past. Most village women stood and had a natter whenever they met, but not Aunty.

Old Molly was sitting in the doorway of her shop, her eyes still bright in her old wrinkled face. 'Afternoon, Miss Watson,' she said.

Aunty nodded.

'Where are you two going then, all dressed up to the nines?' Old Molly asked.

'I'm on business,' Aunty answered curtly, and tried to hustle me past.

Old Molly hooted with laughter. 'On *biz-niz*! Who do you think you are, Miss High and Mighty?'

Aunty walked on, pretending she hadn't heard.

'You might talk with a plum in your mouth like gentry, but you're no better than you ought to be – *I* know,' said Old Molly, cackling.

Aunty flushed. 'Hurry!' she hissed at me, practically running. I had to take extra little skips to keep up with her.

'What did Old Molly mean, Aunty?' I asked.

'I've no idea. She's just a horrible, vulgar old woman,' she said.

'Why is she so nasty to you though?'

'It's just her nature,' said Aunty. 'I don't want you going to her shop any more.'

'But I get my library books from her!'

'You've got your own books. Old Molly's books are cheap and nasty and none too clean. I don't want you catching a disease from those greasy pages. Now stop arguing!'

We hurried on down the street to the bank. I was looking forward to seeing Mr Freeman again. He had told me I was a lucky young lady and had shaken my hand as if I was a grown-up. But when we went into the cool green room and stood at the mahogany counter and asked the young lady for Mr Freeman, she shook her head.

'I'm afraid you can't, he's at a meeting,' she said.

'Then we'll wait,' said Aunty.

'No, dear, he's away at head office, and won't be back today.'

Aunty flinched. She hates anyone calling her dear. I don't know why – they're only being friendly. And I sensed she'd taken an instant dislike to this lady: her cheeks were very pink, and Aunty disapproves of rouge. She smelled of perfume too, a heavy, musky scent, not at all like Mr Benjamin's heavenly cologne.

'Then we will have to come back tomorrow,' said Aunty.

'We can't, Aunty! It's *Saturday* tomorrow,' I cried.

'And we're not open anyway, not at the weekend. But Mr Freeman's left me in charge. I'm fully trained. I'm sure I can help you, dear,' said the lady.

Aunty's smile tightened at the second *dear*. 'I think we'll wait to see Mr Freeman next week,' she murmured.

'Oh no!' I said. 'Please let's take my money out now!' I stood on tiptoe and peered over the counter at the lady. 'My name is Mona Smith and I have my own account at this bank. Could I take two pounds out please?'

'No, no, Mona. We can make do with one,' Aunty protested.

'*Two*,' I insisted. 'Just in case.'

'Two whole pounds for a little girl like you?' said the lady, raising her thin eyebrows.

'Aunty and I are going to Harrods in London tomorrow!' I explained.

'Mona! No need to tell everyone our private affairs!' Aunty said, looking mortified.

'Oh, I say! Two whole pounds! That's going to be a shopping trip and a half! You have to fill in a form for your money and then sign it. Write neatly, dear.' She nodded at Aunty. 'You have to sign too as she's a minor.'

I was trembling with excitement so my signature was a little wobbly. I added a couple of fancy flourishes at the end to make it look more grown-up. I glanced at Aunty, wondering if she'd tell me off, but she was looking up at the ceiling, biting her lip, her own cheeks red though she hadn't gone near a rouge pot in her life.

'My, my!' said the lady when she consulted the big red book and saw how much I had in my account. '*You're* a lucky girl!' When Mr Freeman had said exactly the same thing it had sounded pleasant, but when she said it I felt a little squirmy, and Aunty was clearly dying of embarrassment.

The lady went over to the cash box, counted out two pound notes and put them in an envelope. 'There you are, dear,' she said, handing it to me.

'I'll look after it for you, Mona,' Aunty said faintly, putting the envelope in her bag.

'Well, enjoy Harrods,' said the lady. 'You've certainly done all right for yourselves, haven't you!'

Aunty took me by the hand and marched us out of the bank.

'Why was that lady acting so weirdly, Aunty? Sort of nice and nasty all at the same time?'

'Because she's a sow,' Aunty murmured.

'*What* did you say?' I said, stunned.

'I didn't say anything.' She clasped her bag tight under her arm all the way home, as if thieves were about to dart out of the hedgerows to snatch it. When we got back we had a cup of tea, and then Aunty opened her bag and carefully unpeeled the envelope and laid out the two green notes as if she was dealing cards.

We stared at them in awe.

'We needn't go to London, you know,' said Aunty. 'We might do just as well in Hailbury. I've enough change in my purse to get us there and back. We don't have to touch your money. We can take it back to the bank on Monday, and then you'll have your full hundred pounds in your account.'

'Mr Benjamin says you should go to Harrods. We have to try. And I want to go to London so much. Please let's, Aunty,' I begged.

'I don't know what to do for the best!' she wailed. Then she stood up and went to the sideboard. She brought out the little bottle of medicinal brandy, poured a few drops into a clean teacup, and then put it to her lips and swallowed. She shuddered, and I wondered if she'd spit it straight out as it obviously tasted horrid. But she swigged the last dreg and then set the teacup down resolutely.

'There!' she said defiantly. 'All right, then. We'll go up to London first thing tomorrow.'

'It's like a ride at the Whit Fair!'

7

WHEN I WOKE UP ON SATURDAY, I SAW MY
little doll, Farthing, lying beside me on the pillow,
wearing a beautiful purple party dress. She even had
little gossamer wings stitched onto the back so she could
pretend to be a fairy.

'Oh, Aunty, you angel!' I cried, making Farthing fly
through the air.

Aunty must have been up half the night. She'd not
only made Farthing's fairy frock, she'd washed my white
socks and my white gloves and my white knickers in
a blue rinse, and now they looked like a soap-powder
advertisement. She'd pressed all the creases out of
my daisy dress, and even ironed my pink satin hair
ribbons. She'd polished my shoes until they looked brand
new, and hammered Blakeys into the worn soles and

heels so that I sounded like a tap dancer when I slipped them on.

She'd polished her own shoes too, and sponged and ironed her clothes and turned up the hem of her best black frock a couple of inches, so that it was very nearly calf length!

'Oh, I say, Aunty, you're showing your legs!' I said.

'I don't look vulgar, do I? I hate short skirts, but I was worried they'd think me dowdy in Harrods,' she confessed.

'How could they possibly? You're always the smartest lady in the village. You knock spots off Mr George's wife!' I paused wickedly. 'Of course, Barbara's a different matter. She's absolutely the queen of elegance.'

Aunty stared at me, astounded, and then burst out laughing. 'You bad girl! You shouldn't mock your betters,' she said. 'And she has a certain Bohemian style all of her own.'

'Oh come on, Aunty. She looks like a scarecrow,' I said.

'You're such a saucebox. I don't know where you get it from,' said Aunty.

'Was Mother a saucebox too?' I asked hopefully.

'I dare say she had her moments. Now eat your breakfast quick – and tuck the tea towel into the neck of your dress just in case. I've made porridge to sustain us for the journey.'

Aunty's porridge was usually a grim affair, a grey mess of watery oats, but this time she'd added milk and even allowed me a spoonful of syrup. I wanted to take my time, pouring a yellow M on top of my porridge and savouring every sweet mouthful, but Aunty ate hers standing up, urging me to hurry.

'The bus goes from the market square at seven. We need to catch the ten-to-eight train, so I hope it isn't late,' said Aunty. 'Wipe your mouth now, and then pay a visit. Heaven knows when we'll next find a lavvy.'

I did as I was told, and then we walked down to the market square as smartly as we could, Aunty carrying the suitcase, me holding the carpet bag. Mine wasn't really heavy – it just contained the surplus children's clothes and a lot of tissue paper – so I felt free to tap a little dance in my reinforced shoes.

'Stop that now! You'll get them all dusty,' Aunty remonstrated.

I walked sedately, but I took Farthing out of my pocket and made her swoop through the air, perching on pussy willow and swinging on catkins.

'You're such a funny kid,' said Aunty, shaking her head at me. 'You talk like a little old woman half the time, and yet you still play all your daft baby games.'

We were in the market square by five to seven. There was already a long queue at the bus stop. Aunty started worrying that we wouldn't get onto the bus. As the church clock struck seven there was still no sign of it.

'Oh Lord, what if it's been held up somewhere? We'll miss our train and it's an hour till the next!' said Aunty, and chewed at her bottom lip anxiously.

Then we heard the chug of the motor, and the green bus appeared round the corner. There were people in all the window seats, and Aunty shifted from one foot to the other in agony. However, we managed to squeeze on, although I had to sit on Aunty's lap, with the case by our side and the bag clutched in my arms.

The driver fussed about the case, saying it was an obstruction, and insisted that it should be stowed in the cubbyhole.

'Anyone could make off with it,' Aunty argued, but he was adamant. 'All right then – let's get going. We're late enough as it is,' she snapped.

'For pity's sake, the church clock's only just struck the hour. We arrived dead on time! You're the one holding us up with all this extra luggage,' said the driver, but he set off again.

Aunty peered at her pocket watch whenever people got on and off at each stop. 'We're going to miss the train, I just know it,' she kept muttering.

'Then we'll get the next one,' I said.

'It's a bad omen,' said Aunty. 'This whole journey is just a waste of money. *Your* money, Mona. I feel dreadful about it. Once we get to Hailbury we should turn round and go straight home. We'll put the money back in your bank account on Monday – I can pay the bus fares out of my own money.'

'Oh, do stop worrying, Aunty,' I said. 'We're going up to London and that's that. We'll be like Dick Whittington and make our fortune. We'll *both* have heaps of money, and we'll live like ladies and have roasts every Sunday and cake for tea every single day.'

We got to the railway station with five minutes to spare. Aunty bought our return tickets, wincing at the expense, arguing that I should go free because I could sit on her lap. I protested – I'd felt such a fool on the bus – but then the train came roaring into the station and we had to scramble over the bridge to the other platform.

The third-class carriages were at the end, and it was a long way up. Aunty went first, showing more than her calves in her shortened dress. She dragged the big case up behind her, and then reached out to grab hold of me. The guard blew his whistle before I was safely inside, and for one terrible moment I thought the train was going to start while I was still dangling there helplessly, but I jumped up, and Aunty got the door shut behind me just in time.

We collapsed onto the dusty seats, breathing heavily, both of us in a fluster.

'First time on a train, ladies?' said a lad sitting opposite us. He was wearing his cloth cap on backwards and had a checked handkerchief tied around his neck. He tipped his cap to us and gave us both a cheery grin.

'Yes, and we're going all the way to London!' I said.

'What are you going to see?' he asked.

'Harrods!'

'There's no need to tell everyone our business, Mona,' Aunty said primly.

I knew she wouldn't approve of any lad wearing his cap like that, especially when he didn't even bother with a tie. I wished she wasn't so narrow-minded. And I suddenly realized why the lady in the bank had mocked her when she said the word *business*. She said it in such a prissy, pinched-nose way. She was trying to sound like the Somersets, but not succeeding.

'Mona,' said the lad. 'Pretty name. Unusual.'

'It was my mother's middle name,' I said.

He looked at Aunty.

'Oh, she's not my mother, she's my aunt. Mother died

when I was born,' I said, widening my eyes and using the hallowed tone that usually made people feel sorry for me.

It worked too. 'You poor little mite. Still, nice of your aunty to look after you,' he said, giving her a nod.

She sniffed, scarcely acknowledging it.

'I'm Arty,' he went on. 'Short for Arthur.'

'How do you do,' I said politely.

Aunty frowned. 'Please be quiet now, Mona. Have a little nap. You were up early. I shall do the same.' She looked at Arty. 'Please excuse us,' she said curtly.

Arty pulled a sympathetic face at me. Aunty nudged me, so I closed my eyes. I opened them after a minute or so. Aunty had her own eyes closed, her lips pressed together. Arty winked at me. I did my best to wink back, though I'd never quite mastered the art. I must have pulled a weird lopsided face because he spluttered with laughter.

'That's enough now!' said Aunty, opening her eyes. She bent towards my ear. 'We'll get out at the next station and find another carriage, away from this lout,' she whispered.

However, she must have weighed up the time it would take to get out of the carriage with her suitcase, my bag and me, and worried that we wouldn't have time to go through the whole performance in reverse, so she didn't risk it. I was glad, because Arty was funny and friendly and I didn't want to hurt his feelings.

'Have you ever been to Harrods?' I asked him, though Aunty glared at me for starting another conversation.

'Oh, many a time,' he said. 'I get all my clothes there,

naturally – and all the furniture in my humble abode is Harrods' finest.'

'Really?' I said, impressed.

'He's talking nonsense,' Aunty hissed.

'Course I am,' Arty said cheerily. 'The likes of me don't even get in the front door. They have these military chaps in green uniform who turf you out if they think you're not out the top drawer.'

'They don't!' I said, thinking he was still having me on.

However, this time Aunty looked anxious, and I wondered if he might be right. 'As if you'd know,' she said, trying to reassure herself.

'I *do* know,' said Arty. 'I've got a mate lives in London, works up Billingsgate fish market, and after his shift we play this dare game, see. Nothing too wicked – just schoolboy stuff like tipping the bowler hat off of a business gent or singing a daft song at the tops of our voices. Anyways, he suggests we go to Knightsbridge, where all the toffs do their shopping, and we bowl into Harrods, talking all fruity voiced, but this huge chap in green grabs hold of us and escorts us out the store.'

'My goodness! Just because he didn't like the way you look?' I asked.

'Well, in my mate's case it was maybe because he always reeks to high heaven,' said Arty, laughing.

'Of course you wouldn't be allowed into a place like Harrods,' Aunty sniffed.

'Will they let *us* in, Aunty?' I asked.

'Don't be ridiculous, Mona, of course they will,' she said, though she didn't sound certain.

'Are you going to see your mate today?' I asked Arty.

'No, I'm going on a recce,' he said. 'I'm going to have a look-see at some jewellery.'

'In Harrods?'

'Well, they're supposed to have the finest gems, but it would be a tad out of my league,' he said cheerily. 'Likewise Hatton Garden. But my mate's tipped me off there's some bargains to be had at Portobello Market, so I'll try my luck there.'

The only market I'd ever been to was in Hailbury, where they sold carrots and cabbages and apples, and chickens in cages that pecked you through the bars if you didn't watch out. I wondered if Arty was joking again. Half the time he seemed to be talking a different language.

'I'm getting this ring,' he said, rubbing the third finger of his left hand. 'For my girl,' he added when I still looked blank. 'I've been going out with this young lady for six months or more and it's getting serious. I'm thinking of popping the question – you know, will she marry me?'

'And will she?'

'Not if she's got any sense,' Aunty murmured.

'Don't be like that,' said Arty. 'I've a feeling she'll be thrilled, but I need a ring, see. No use taking her up west with me and finding I can't afford a proper sparkler. I want to have one tucked in my pocket, ready. So what kind do you think she'd like, ladies?' He looked at Aunty. 'If some gent was to ask you to marry him, what kind of engagement ring would you fancy?'

'I wouldn't fancy any kind,' said Aunty. 'I've never wanted to marry.'

I wondered if she was telling the truth. She'd

never had any gentleman followers, and always spoke disparagingly of the men in Rook Green – of all men, apart from the Somersets. I'd often been told that I had a vivid imagination but, try as I might, I couldn't conjure up any vision of Aunty tenderly courting.

I wasn't sure romance would ever happen to me either – though I did have a soft spot for Peter Robinson. And Roland Somerset, but he was unlikely to speak to me again, let alone propose.

'That's a shame,' said Arty. 'A lovely lady like you shouldn't end up single. I bet you were a saucy minx back in the war.'

He was obviously teasing now. Aunty should have laughed it off or said something crushing, but she went pink and bent her head.

'No offence meant,' Arty added.

Aunty carried on staring into her lap. Arty pulled a face at me and didn't say any more. After ten minutes or so his eyes closed and he fell asleep, his snores making it clear that he wasn't pretending. Aunty winced.

I stared out of the window. We were still in the countryside, but these were new hills, new trees, new hedges. I hadn't realized how huge the country was. I remembered lisping 'Tom, Tom, the Piper's Son' when I was little, loving the last line – *Over the hills and far away* – but I was now far, far, far away and I blinked through the grubby window, fascinated.

Every time we stopped at a station Aunty peered out, looking for the name, and then subsided back against her seat, rubbing her fingers one by one. She did this at the end of the day to ease their soreness after sewing, but it was a habit now and she did it whenever she was anxious. She moved her lips, sometimes even muttering under her breath. I wondered if she was rehearsing what she was going to say to the children's buyer at Harrods.

The train went through such a big town that I was sure we must be in London at last, but it chugged on and on, and my own head started nodding. Then, at last, Aunty was shaking me awake, and I realized that the train had stopped and we were in a vast railway station. Doors banged violently and trains sent explosions of steam and soot across the platforms. It was all so different, so strange, that I cowered in my seat while Aunty struggled with the case.

'Here, let me,' said Arty, springing into action.

Aunty hung onto the case for a moment, as if she thought he might run off with it, but there were people pushing to get off, and she had to accept his help. He took my bag too, and accompanied us along the teeming platform.

When we reached the ticket collector, Aunty fumbled frantically in her purse, but then found our tickets in her pocket.

'There we go!' Arty said cheerily. 'Shall I see you two ladies into a taxi cab like a true gent?'

'No, that won't be necessary,' said Aunty hurriedly. 'We prefer to walk.'

'It's quite a step to Harrods! Why not travel in the Underground train?' said Arty.

'Under the ground?' I said. 'Really?'

'Really, truly. In special tunnels. Follow me!' he said, grinning.

'No, I don't think so,' said Aunty. 'We'll catch an omnibus instead.'

'Oh, please let's go in the Underground train, Aunty!' I begged. I had no idea that trains could go underground. Were they travelling through tunnels right beneath my feet? I thought of my fairy-tale book at home, and the eerie picture of the seven dwarfs trekking through a dark tunnel, holding their lamps high. The oldest went first, with his beard hanging right down to his ankles, and then came all the others in varying shapes and sizes, with a sweet little boy dwarf right at the end, so small that I reckoned he'd only come up to my kneecaps. I loved those kind, cheery little men. If I were Snow White I'd have waved the handsome prince goodbye and settled down in the cottage with seven special playmates.

I was too old to believe in fairy-tale dwarfs now, but I was still fascinated by the idea of tunnels, and decided I'd keep my eyes peeled, just in case I saw the glow of little lamps.

Aunty didn't look keen on the idea, but when she stopped a porter wheeling a trolley of suitcases and asked if he could tell her where to get an omnibus to Knightsbridge, he shrugged rudely.

'Haven't got a clue,' he puffed. 'I'm paid to know the trains, not the buses. Can you move out the way, please – I've got to load these onto the train and it's going in two minutes.'

There didn't seem to be anyone else for Aunty to accost, so she followed Arty. There was a great crowd of people pushing to get through the entrance to the Underground.

'Keep close and follow me,' said Arty, diving in.

Aunty had to do as she was told because he was still carrying our luggage. She held my hand tightly, and then gave a little squeak as we found ourselves teetering at the top of a long moving staircase. 'We're not setting foot on that!' she protested, but the crowd behind us pushed forward and there was no way to turn back. We stepped on and started sailing downwards.

'Oh my Lord!' Aunty gasped.

'It's like a ride at the Whit Fair!' I said. 'No, it's better! It's such fun! Don't be scared, Aunty.'

'I'm not scared, you silly girl,' she said, but I could feel the dampness of her hand through our thin white gloves.

When we were on firm ground again, Arty led us this way and that, helping us to buy a ticket and taking us to the right platform. I peered down at the tracks below us, and was surprised to see a little black mouse darting about.

'Look, a mouse!' I said.

Aunty didn't like mice, but living in the country she was used to them. Two ladies in short, shapeless coats saw where I was pointing and clutched each other, squealing. Then a sudden gust of wind nearly blew our hats away and Aunty clutched me fiercely. There was a great rumbling, and then a strange train without a proper engine rattled along the tracks.

'Here you are. I'll hand in your luggage,' said Arty.

'Aren't you coming with us?' asked Aunty.

'No, it's the wrong line for me. Quick – in you get. Don't want to get shut in those sliding doors, do you!'

'Well, thank you so much for your help,' said Aunty. 'I'm much obliged.'

'Goodbye, Arty. Thank you! I hope you find a lovely cheap ring for your girl!' I called.

He pushed the case and the bag through the open door, and we jumped after them just in time. The train drew out of the platform so quickly I didn't get time to wave to him. There were lights in the train, but it was pitch black outside.

'We're really in a tunnel!' I shouted above the roar.

'What a horrible way to travel,' Aunty shouted back. 'The noise!'

The train stopped at station after station.

'Where do we get out, Aunty?' I asked.

'How do I know?' she said.

I turned to the young lady next to me. 'Is this the stop for Harrods?' I gabbled.

'Yes,' she told us. 'Though you'd better be quick.'

But we weren't quick enough: the alarming doors closed with sudden spite and the train went on.

'You can get off at the next stop, South Kensington, and take a train back to Knightsbridge,' said the young lady.

This time we managed to get off, and then blundered around the different tunnels. Aunty decided she'd had enough. She put down the suitcase, her hand on her chest. She was breathing heavily.

'I can't face going in another of those awful trains,' she said weakly. 'I've got to get some air.'

This was the best time I'd had in years – and yet my heart was thumping too, and I knew how Aunty felt. She had to screw up all her courage to step onto another electric staircase, stabbing at the moving stair with a wary foot and then withdrawing it before wobbling on properly. I stepped on behind her, helping to balance the suitcase, and at last we emerged into the daylight.

'Breathe deeply,' said Aunty, doing so herself. She leaned against some railings and took off her gloves to blow her nose. 'Oh Lord, look at them – they're grey with dust! Come here, Mona, let's see. Dear goodness, smuts all over your face!'

Aunty's snuffly nose had to wait while she spat on her hankie and wiped my nose and cheeks, and then took out her pocket mirror and cleaned her own face. She straightened her hat and mine, and gave me a determined smile. 'There now. That wasn't such a terrible ordeal, was it?' she said.

She was the one who'd been terrified, not me, but I knew it wasn't wise to point this out. We asked directions, and set off for the Brompton Road, which wasn't too far away. We passed such an impressive building that I wondered if it was Buckingham Palace, where the King and Queen lived, but apparently it was the Victoria and Albert Museum.

'Then *that's* Buckingham Palace,' I said, pointing to a vast, domed red-brick building in the distance. 'It must be *someone's* palace, even if it doesn't belong to the King.'

'Unless . . . unless it's Harrods,' said Aunty.

'Oh, Aunty, don't be silly, that's not a *shop*,' I said.

But she was right. It *was* Harrods. It said so in gold lettering. It rose six storeys high, not counting the central dome, with twenty-one windows shining in the sunlight on every floor. I stood on the opposite side of the road, counting them. We crossed the street, dodging motorcars, and looked at the window displays.

Aunty breathed in sharply, her face transfixed. 'Oh!' she whispered. 'Such style! Such elegance!'

'No wonder Mr Benjamin shops here,' I said.

There were lots of entrances, all guarded by large men in green uniform, just as Arty had said. And there were *dogs* chained at the door – splendid creatures, totally different from the rough collies and terriers in our village. These were fancy London dogs: poodles with bizarre hairstyles, snuffly Pekinese, little pugs with anxious expressions, tiny Yorkshire terriers with ribbons in their hair.

'Hello, you lovely little things,' I said, squatting down and patting them.

'Mind your fingers, miss – that little hairy one can be a bit snappy,' said the doorman.

'No, he likes me, look!' I said, stroking his beautiful fur. 'He's so sweet! Are these dogs for sale? Oh, Aunty, can I buy this one with the little ribbon?'

'Don't be so silly, Mona,' she said. 'Harrods isn't a pet shop. They don't sell animals!'

'I'm happy to say that we do sell animals, madam. Dogs and cats and parrots, and even exotic breeds. I dare say we'd find you an elephant if you ordered one specially,' said the doorman.

I giggled delightedly.

'But I'm afraid these particular animals aren't for sale. They belong to customers. They leave their little doggies in our safe care while they shop at their leisure inside our emporium,' he explained. 'The snappy one belongs to a devoted dowager who frequently carries him in her handbag. And on the subject of bags – I'm afraid you will have to leave your suitcase with me if you wish to go into the store.'

Aunty stared at him. 'I can't possibly do that,' she said.

'Rest assured, I will guard it with my life. I'll even give you a numbered ticket so that you can reclaim it,' he told her.

'But I need to take my case inside,' Aunty insisted.

'I'm sure you have good reason to do so, madam, but it's against the rules. Obviously you're a perfect lady and have no sinister intentions, but we get all sorts trying to gain access with big bags and cases, even trunks. Then, when they think the staff are distracted, they appropriate sundry items and stow them in their luggage.'

'Are you suggesting that I'm a thief?' Aunty asked.

'Of course I'm not, madam. I'm simply explaining why we have this rule about luggage.' The doorman was still smiling, but his voice was firm.

He took a step forward, barring her way. He was very tall, at least six foot, and very wide too. Aunty was a foot shorter, very slight, and she'd started to stoop because she sat bent over her sewing ten hours a day. But now she drew herself up as straight as she could and raised her chin.

'I'll have you know that I have an appointment with the buyer of the children's outfitters. He is keen to see the garment samples currently packed in my suitcase,' Aunty fibbed. 'Now please get out of my way.' She sounded as imperious as Lady Somerset herself, but to no avail.

'I don't care if you have an appointment with Sir Woodman Burbidge, our esteemed managing director, himself. Rules are rules. You cannot take that suitcase inside,' said the doorman.

'What about my carpet bag?' I asked.

He looked it up and down. 'I would say that just about qualifies as a handbag, if a large one. Of course, we would never part a lady from her handbag, miss.'

'Then it's easy, Aunty! Let's unpack all the clothes from the suitcase and put them in my bag. I'm sure we can squeeze them in somehow,' I said eagerly.

'But they'll get horribly creased! I've packed them in tissue paper.' She turned to the doorman. 'If I show you the items, perhaps you will understand and make an exception.'

'I can make no exceptions, madam. I thought I'd made that clear,' he said implacably.

So, at the entrance to the most famous and exclusive department store in the country, we had to crouch down over the suitcase and transfer every little frock and shirt and romper suit to the carpet bag, while the dogs barked excitedly and the doorman stood over us, arms folded, shaking his head. However, at last he summoned a pageboy to remove the suitcase, seized the gold handle of the door, and opened it wide for us.

We were in!

Most astonishing of all were the ladies.

8

I T WAS LIKE STEPPING INTO A FAIRY PALACE.
There were glittering glass display cases, marble
columns, chandeliers with lights like glass flowers
shining over us, and a rich red carpet beneath our feet.
It was so spectacular I wouldn't have been surprised if
pairs of hands had come to offer us fruit and wine, as
they did in 'Beauty and the Beast'. But there were no
beasts here, only beauties – slim young ladies standing
discreetly to attention, while fashionable customers in
velvet cloaks and fur stoles drifted languidly, pointing
and beckoning.

Aunty and I wandered from department to
department, dazed. We almost forgot why we were there.
We found ourselves surrounded by silverware, then
handbags, and then astonishing jewellery with shining

stones, white and red and green and deep blue.

'Are they *real* jewels, Aunty?' I whispered.

'I think they must be,' she whispered back.

Even the food departments were like treasure troves, with tall palm trees and shiny tiled floors. There was a vast fish display, with a little fountain refreshing the gleaming scales, and fruit piled into pyramids, each apple polished to perfection, and hothouse peaches and grapes blooming on silver salvers. There were cakes of every kind and shape – tiny fancies decorated with sugared roses and delicate whirls of cream, fruit tarts and almond macaroons, sponge cakes and Swiss rolls, and gateaux and layer cakes, with their flavours listed: orange, chocolate, pineapple, strawberry, coffee, walnut and maraschino.

'What's maraschino, Aunty?' I asked.

'I think it might be cherry,' she said.

The confectionery department was even more dazzling. There were glass bottles of boiled sweets – tangerine balls, acid drops, barley-sugar nibs, butterscotch cubes – but I was familiar with these from the jars in Mr Berner's shop. I concentrated on the chocolate displays. I gazed at a shelf of chocolate animals – glossy brown cats and dogs, and even three little bears: Father Bear, Mother Bear and Baby Bear. I ached to own those bears – but how could I ever *eat* them? And how terrible it would be in the summer, when their ears and snouts started melting and their legs buckled in the heat!

I moved on to the chocolate selections instead.

There were splendid big boxes with pictures painted on the lids, chocolates nestling in neat rows inside. Their rich smell filled the room and I could almost taste them on my tongue. It was a long time since I'd had my porridge.

'Could we buy a box of chocolates, Aunty?' I begged. 'With my money?'

She shook her head.

'It wouldn't be a waste, because we'd have a lovely box for hankies or ribbons when we'd eaten all the chocolates,' I said earnestly.

'Mona, look at the prices,' Aunty whispered in my ear.

I looked. The sweetmeat cabinet was ten whole shillings! The princess chocolate assortment, in a box edged with lace and tied with a blue ribbon, was a whole pound! The biggest Japanese lacquer box painted with storks cost two guineas!

I felt dizzy.

A gentleman in a white apron and a neat moustache was looking at us sympathetically. 'Perhaps the little girl might like to sample a chocolate?' he suggested.

'That's very kind, but I'm afraid we won't be buying a box,' said Aunty.

'That doesn't matter. Why don't you try one, dear?' he said, nodding at me.

I looked at Aunty pleadingly.

'Very well,' she said.

'Choose which one you want then,' he said, smiling.

It was almost impossible. I went along the vast glass

cabinet twice, trying to decide. All the flavours were labelled: Raspberry Cream, Chocolate Peppermint, Hazelnut Whirl, Orange Royale, Seville Dessert, Mocha Walnut . . .

'Hurry up!' Aunty hissed.

'Let her take her time,' said the lovely man with the moustache.

I chose the Raspberry Cream. It was dimpled like a real raspberry, and when I bit into it, the cream inside was deep red. I stood still, eyes closed, savouring it.

'Say thank you, Mona!'

I opened my eyes and gazed gratefully at the man. 'Thank you ever so, ever so much,' I said. 'I've never eaten anything so wonderful in my entire life.'

Then Aunty whisked me away, though I wanted to go on gazing at the beautiful chocolates, learning each flavour.

'He'll think you're angling for more! It was so kind of him to give you a sample. I hope he won't get into trouble,' she said, getting out her hankie.

I shied away from it.

'But you've got chocolate round your mouth!'

'I'll lick it off. I don't want to waste a single drop.'

'Well, lick quickly and don't let anyone see. Come on then, Mona! Let's find the children's department.'

A woman behind the bread counter heard what she'd said and leaned forward. 'It's on the first floor, madam. You'll find the staircase past the next department,' she said.

We found the staircase – but it was another electric one, moving upwards all by itself!

'Oh my Lord!' said Aunty. 'The whole of London's been electrified! What a nightmare! I'm not sure I can face it again.'

Another doorman smiled at her reassuringly. 'Don't worry, madam, we have proper staircases at the other end,' he said, and he even came with us to make sure we didn't get lost.

It was the grandest staircase I'd ever seen, much more splendid than the one in Somerset Manor. The steps were wide and spacious, and soared upwards in a graceful curve, with a carved banister to hold onto. Aunty and I walked up together. Aunty was carrying the carpet bag now, so I was free to do a little dance on each step.

'Stop showing off, Mona! And watch you don't trip and fall,' said Aunty.

We found the ladies' costume department first, though it was hard to believe it was actually part of a shop. It was like Cinderella's ballroom, with gilding on the white ceiling, red-and-white striped chairs, and elegant sofas set at an angle, ornate looking glasses reflecting everything so that the huge room seemed twice its actual size. But most astonishing of all were the ladies: very tall, slender ladies with shiny bobbed hair who glided around, an arm in the air, occasionally pausing with a pointed toe. They were dressed in a variety of clothes, some in sleeveless frocks with bangles clinking on their white arms, some in beaded evening gowns, some in costumes with cloche hats.

'Are those grand ladies customers, Aunty?' I whispered.

She was staring at them too. They all towered above her and made her look sadly dowdy, even though she was wearing her best outfit with its newly shortened skirt. She watched their strange progress backwards and forwards across the room, not speaking to anyone, not even making eye contact.

'I think they're models!' she whispered back. 'They're just here to display the gowns. And aren't the clothes beautiful – but so indecently short!'

We wandered on through the ladies' coat and mantle department, and the misses' costume department, and at last reached the actual children's outfitters. I'd been hoping that there would be real children there too, skipping about in their Harrods outfits, but there were just models of girls and boys, all with eerie eyes and grinning mouths.

However, we saw a real grizzling baby with a mottled face. It was being dandled by a nurse while its mother selected day gowns and nightgowns and petticoats galore: they wouldn't even have fitted into the big wardrobe at home. She had all the attention of a young assistant and a boot-faced woman who was clearly in charge of the department.

This gave Aunty and me a chance to look around, peering at the clothes on the mannequins. There was a little blue linen suit, and another in crêpe de Chine, a cotton baby's romper suit with a contrasting collar, and a white haircord dress with coloured smocking. Aunty bent to examine the detail and sniffed.

'Yours are much nicer, aren't they, Aunty?' I whispered.

Aunty nodded. 'They're not very special at all,' she murmured. 'I've seen better in Hailbury at half the price.' She was flushed with excitement.

We waited while the baby wailed incessantly. I pulled a face. 'Did I sound like that when I was little?' I asked.

'Sometimes,' said Aunty. 'And you didn't sleep through the night till you were two. You were a real shocker.'

I realized that I must have turned her life upside down when she took me on. I hadn't really thought about it before. I suddenly squeezed her hand.

'Can I help you, madam?' It was the young assistant speaking. Her superior had started wrapping all the little outfits in swathes of tissue paper, tying each parcel with a pink bow.

'I'd like to speak to the buyer of this department, please,' said Aunty, trying to sound brisk and matter-of-fact.

'The buyer?' the girl said, startled. 'Well, that's Mr Brisby, but he doesn't come in on a Saturday.'

'Are you sure?' said Aunty, looking devastated.

'He won't miss his golf,' the girl mouthed, glancing over her shoulder to make sure the boot-faced lady hadn't heard.

'Then who is in charge of the department on Saturdays?' Aunty asked, though it was obvious.

The girl nodded behind her. 'Miss Shaw,' she said.

'Then I'll wait to see Miss Shaw,' said Aunty.

'Well, she told me to come and serve you, madam. Are you sure I can't be of help?'

'Quite sure. But thank you very much.'

The assistant backed away and we stood there, waiting. And waiting and waiting. At last the final small garment was neatly packaged, the woman paid, and she and the nurse and the baby left the department. We could hear the baby crying all the way to the staircase.

Miss Bootface Shaw didn't even glance in our direction. Aunty coughed several times. Finally she got up the courage to approach her.

'Excuse me,' she said.

'My young assistant will help you,' said Bootface, busying herself writing in an accounts book.

'But I need to see you,' Aunty persisted. She took a deep breath. 'I had an appointment with your buyer, Mr Brisby, but I forgot he doesn't come in to work on Saturdays. Still, I'm sure he won't mind if I do business with you. I have some beautiful quality children's clothes to show you.'

'I'm afraid we don't do business that way in Harrods,' said Bootface disdainfully.

'Yes, and it shows,' said Aunty. 'You have magnificent clothes in the ladies' salons, fit to rival the finest gowns from Paris. But your children's clothes don't have that extra finish – the stylish embellishment and fine embroidery one would expect. Please let me show you a sample of my work.'

'No, thank you. We have our own in-house dressmakers,' said Bootface, but Aunty was already delving into the bag and spreading out her little dresses higgledy-piggledy over the top of a display case. They looked sadly crushed. Aunty gave a little moan.

'Please put them back in your bag!' said Bootface, flicking a dress as if it was an old duster.

'I know they're a little creased,' said Aunty. 'I had them beautifully laid out in a proper suitcase, but the doorman wouldn't let me bring it into the store.'

'I should think not! Now, take yourself and your clothes and your gawping child out of my department immediately, or I shall call security and have you physically removed,' she said.

'Won't you just look at the stitching, the embroidery?' Aunty pleaded.

'I'll do no such thing. Take them away!' Bootface swept half the little clothes off the cabinet onto the carpet.

Aunty gave a little sob and started putting them back in the bag. I helped, feeling so sorry for her. The young assistant was shaking her head. New customers were pointing. The child mannequins were staring.

Aunty stuffed the last little garment into the bag, grabbed my hand, and we fled. In our confusion we ran the wrong way, through the lace department, and haberdashery and ironmongery, unable to find any staircase, electric or otherwise. Aunty blindly pushed through a door – and we found ourselves in a dark corridor that didn't look like part of the store at all.

We peered around helplessly.

'Where are we now?' I asked.

Aunty shook her head. 'I suppose this is the office part. Oh dear Lord!' She peeped inside the stuffed carpet bag and automatically smoothed the topmost dress. 'All that hard work,' she said mournfully.

'They'll be right as rain once you've given them an iron, Aunty. And then you can take them to the draper's at Hailbury, and I know he'll think them splendid,' I said, trying to be comforting.

'I dare say he'll send me packing too,' said Aunty. 'Oh dear, Mona, why is everything such a wretched struggle?'

'Come on, Aunty. Chin up! Shall we go back to that lovely man with the moustache in the confectionery department. He might give *you* a free chocolate this time!'

'Mona! Oh dear, I don't think I can face going back through all those departments with everyone staring at us. I just want to get out onto the street! There must be a back entrance for the office staff. Let's see if we can find it,' she said.

'Are we allowed in here though?'

'I don't know and I don't care,' said Aunty. 'A fire exit will do. Come *along*, child.'

I hung onto her coat as she blundered down the corridor. There were doors to the left and right, but no one peered out at us.

We turned a corner and found ourselves in another, grander corridor, with green pendant ceiling lights and big mahogany doors. The one right at the end had gilt lettering on it:

SIR WOODMAN BURBIDGE
CHAIRMAN AND MANAGING DIRECTOR

'Look, Aunty!' I said, pointing. I had a sudden mad idea. 'Let's go and show *him* your clothes!'

'Don't be silly, Mona! You can't barge in on a managing director!' she protested.

'Yes we can,' I said, and I knocked boldly on the grand door.

I didn't really think anyone would answer. None of the office staff seemed to be around. I was practically certain Sir Woodman Burbidge would be off playing golf somewhere, like the children's department buyer.

It was a terrible shock when someone called, 'Come in!'

Aunty put her hand over her mouth. 'Oh my Lord,' she whispered behind her fingers. 'Quick – let's make a run for it!'

I wanted to run too, but something made me open the door and walk right in, so of course Aunty had to follow. A balding man sat behind an enormous desk, his chin resting on his wing collar as he bent to write a letter. He glanced up at us and blinked in surprise.

'Oh my goodness, I rather think you're lost, ladies. I take it you're customers at Harrods?' he said politely. 'Allow me to show you the way back into the store.'

His kindly tone gave me courage.

'We're not customers, Sir Woodman Burbidge, sir. We've come specially to see you. My aunty wants to show you the children's clothes she's made,' I said.

'Does she?' he said. 'Perhaps it might be better to go to the children's outfitters, though I'm afraid we employ our own dressmakers.'

'I know, the lady there told us that – but if I may take the liberty, sir, I feel that my custom-made clothes could add a little extra to your range,' said Aunty, finding her tongue. 'They are unfortunately crumpled, because I was not allowed to bring their display case into the store, but I'm sure you can ignore a few paltry creases and see the fine stitching and extraordinary finish. I'm not an amateur needlewoman, sir. I started my training at the age of fifteen. I design all my own clothes, and my ladies' gowns have been taken for Parisian *haute couture*. However, fashions change, and the little shifts young ladies prefer nowadays don't demand much skill, so I've started a children's range for the discerning mother who wants the very best. Allow me . . .'

Aunty had been talking at top speed, worried he might stop her before she was through. She now delved into the bulging carpet bag and drew out a little frock. She shook it vigorously and then held it up by the tiny shoulders.

'Do you see the fine smocking? The embroidered flower on the white collar, and the two little pockets? Please examine the seams. They are strong enough to stand the most vigorous use, and yet the stitches are scarcely visible.'

'Like the mouse stitches in *The Tailor of Gloucester*,'

I chimed in, wanting to add my two penn'orth.

'That's my little goddaughter's favourite book,' said Sir Woodman, nodding at me.

'Then I could make her a dress with little mice on the pockets, or dancing round the hem,' said Aunty. 'That's the point of my clothing. Each item can be individually designed to suit a particular child. I know many mothers sew their own children's clothes from patterns nowadays, and make a fine job of it too – but not with my flair and skill, though I beg pardon if I sound immodest.'

'What about little boys?' asked Sir Woodman.

'Oh, I have a romper suit here . . . somewhere.' She rummaged further into the bag. 'Yes, here it is – my little check number, blue and white, but with bright red trains embellishing the pockets. And here's a shirt-and-shorts combination, also in blue, with a yellow bear on the breast pocket. Do you see, I've made a tiny toy bear that slips neatly into the pocket and made sure it doesn't spoil the line of the little trousers.'

Sir Woodman took hold of the shorts and examined the bear.

'The bear's jointed so that he can sit up and wave his arms,' said Aunty, showing him.

He actually chuckled. 'You're a lucky girl to have an aunt who can make you such fine novelty clothing,' he told me.

I'd always been embarrassed by Aunty's fancy little frocks, wishing like anything I could wear plain cotton like Maggie and all the other girls in the village – but now I nodded proudly as I leaned on his desk.

❦ 133 ❦

'Stand up properly, Mona, and take off your coat to show your frock off properly,' Aunty commanded.

I did as I was told, though I felt foolish. I even did a twirl to show that the daisy chain on my coral bodice went all the way round and tied itself into a mock bow in the middle of my back.

'Goodness,' said Sir Woodman. 'My goddaughter would love a pretty party dress like that.'

Aunty stared at him, holding her breath.

'What is your name, madam?' he asked.

'Miss Florence Watson, sir. And this is my niece, Mona.'

Sir Woodman wrote our names down on a piece of paper. 'And your address?'

'We live in Gatekeeper's Cottage, Somerset Manor, Rook Green, Hailbury,' said Aunty. 'I was Lady Somerset's personal dressmaker, but she's sadly passed away recently.'

'Hence your trip to Harrods,' said Sir Woodman. 'I wonder if you're aware of my motto for Harrods, Miss Watson?'

'I'm afraid not, sir.'

'It's *Imagination, Enterprise and Courage*,' he said. He looked at me. 'What did I just say, Miss Mona?'

'*Imagination, Enterprise and Courage*,' I parroted.

'Well done! And these are the very qualities your aunt has shown, my dear. So I shall personally order the daisy-chain frock, and the shirt and shorts with the toy bear – four of each, in ages two, four, six and eight. You will make a display card with your details set out clearly, saying you are willing to make a bespoke outfit after a consultation with any Harrods customer,' he said.

'Oh, Sir Woodman! That is too kind!' Aunty gasped.

'It's not kindness at all, it's shrewd business sense. We will see how it goes. If you get any orders, you will have to be available for fittings – once a week, say. Travel to London won't be a problem, will it?' he asked.

'Oh no, sir. I pop up to London regularly,' Aunty lied airily, as if she jumped on trains and ran up and down electric staircases all the time. She paused. 'I will need to carry the eight outfits suitably protected. Is it possible for you to have a word with your doormen?'

'You may come into the store via the staff entrance at the back,' he said, writing swiftly on an embossed card. 'Here, Miss Watson – simply show this and you will be ushered in without any problems.'

He saw that Aunty was still hesitating and put his head on one side enquiringly.

'When I've brought the outfits in, plus the card with all my details, will they actually be displayed in children's outfitting? I'm not absolutely certain that they're to the taste of the staff who work there,' she said, struggling to put it tactfully.

Sir Woodman Burbidge smiled. 'I shall give my orders, Miss Watson. I hope I am a fair and benign employer, but I assure you that my staff do exactly as I say.'

'I'm sure they do, Sir Woodman. Well, thank you so very, very much. I shall have everything ready within a fortnight,' Aunty promised, folding all her clothes back into the carpet bag.

'You will need to consult with Mr Brisby, the buyer for children's outfitting, about pricing and payment. I am sure you will be able to come to an arrangement that is agreeable to you. We pride ourselves on our fairness at Harrods,' said Sir Woodman.

'It's the best store in the whole world,' I said.

'Yes, it is, Miss Mona,' he said, smiling complacently.

He shook Aunty's hand – and then my hand too. The moment we were outside I gave a great whoop of triumph.

'Ssh, Mona, he'll hear you!' Aunty hissed – but when we were a little distance away she gave a whoop too. Then we went through the door, back into the bright lights of the store, and walked boldly through all the departments, directly to children's outfitting.

'Where do you think they'll display your clothes, Aunty?' I asked.

'Ideally I'd like them right beside the counter, on little girl and boy mannequins,' said Aunty. 'With a rack beside them showing the different sizes. But we shall see.'

Bootface was glaring over at us.

'Let's say, *Ya, boo, sucks to you*,' I suggested.

'Don't be vulgar, Mona!' said Aunty. She smiled pleasantly in Bootface's direction. 'Good day,' she called, and swept past.

'We mustn't forget to collect the suitcase, Aunty!' I said as we went down the stairs.

'Quite. But we have one little call to make first,' she said.

She took me to the confectionery department and

bought us a small box of assorted chocolates: Raspberry Cream, Chocolate Peppermint, Hazelnut Whirl, Orange Royale, Seville Dessert and Mocha Walnut. We ate them on the train home.

He tossed it in the air and I caught it, quick as a wink.

9

AUNTY WAS INCREDIBLY BUSY NOW. WELL, she'd always been busy, but in an exhausted kind of way. Now I heard her humming to herself above the whir of her machine. She sang *'Daisy, Daisy, give me your answer, do,'* while she was chain-stitching the daisy chain around each coral bodice.

Sometimes I stood in the doorway of her workroom watching her. She was so absorbed she didn't even know I was there. She only stopped sewing on Saturday morning, when a large shiny motorcar came through the gates.

'It's Mr Benjamin on his way to the manor! Quick, Mona, stop him! We must thank him!' Aunty called urgently.

But Mr Benjamin was coming to call on us anyway! His hand – in a pearly grey kid glove – was raised to knock as I opened the door.

'Hello, little Mona! My, you look bonnie this morning. I thought I'd come and see how you and your aunt are getting on,' he said, smiling.

'We're getting on simply splendidly!' I said.

'Ask him *in*,' Aunty called from her workroom. I knew that she was struggling out of the old overall she wore over her dress when she was sewing.

'Please come in, Mr Benjamin,' I said. 'We're so pleased to see you.' I found I was bobbing a wobbly curtsy at him again.

'You only need to curtsy if you meet the King, Mona – and if you do, make it a grand gesture, like so!' He held out an imaginary skirt and swept the most beautiful curtsy, head up, back straight, one black-and-white shoe stretching forward.

I saw the chauffeur in the parked car shaking his head fondly – Mr Benjamin was such a card! I tried to copy the curtsy, and nearly fell over.

'Whoops!' said Mr Benjamin. 'Well, never mind, Mona. I'm sure you have many other accomplishments.'

I wasn't quite sure what these might be, but was pleased that he thought I might have them. I ushered him inside and took him into the kitchen. I knew Aunty was mortified that we didn't have a proper parlour – but there wasn't anywhere else. Mr Benjamin must have been used to grand drawing rooms with elegant furniture, but he sat down happily on a rickety wooden chair and crossed his legs, totally at ease.

'I'll put the kettle on,' I said. 'And I know it's best china for visitors, especially when it's you.'

'I'm honoured,' he said.

Luckily we had milk for his tea, and there were fresh custard creams in the tin. I set them out in a circle on my favourite bluebird plate.

'How pretty,' said Mr Benjamin. 'I love custard creams. Nanny always gave me one with my glass of milk at bedtime.'

Aunty came hurtling into the kitchen, overall discarded, wearing her good shoes instead of her comfy checked slippers. She'd managed to dislodge her bun, and little wisps were escaping at the back, but I couldn't tell her because it would have embarrassed her so. It made her look much younger, like a schoolgirl putting up her hair for the first time. She was clutching a soft parcel of pale mauve tissue paper tied with a maroon ribbon.

'Hello, Miss Watson. You look in the pink, if I may say so,' said Mr Benjamin.

'I'm so very happy, sir!' said Aunty. 'I took your advice. We went to Harrods. And at first we got nowhere, and the mean old stick in children's outfitting turned up her nose at my garments, but then Mona and I found ourselves in the offices, and Mona here only went and knocked on the managing director's door!'

'Oh, my! You're a very bold girl, Mona,' said Mr Benjamin, shaking his head at me.

'I just about died – but Sir Woodman is a true

gentleman, so kind, and he didn't seem to mind us barging into his grand study. He likes my kiddies' clothes, Mr Benjamin!' said Aunty, eyes shining behind her spectacles. 'He's going to try out two of my lines, and if they're successful he'll want more. I can't believe I have such a golden opportunity! And it's all down to you.'

'And Mona,' he said. 'And your own talent and flair, dear Miss Watson.'

'Well, anyway, I've made you a little present to say thank you. I do hope you won't think I've taken a liberty,' said Aunty, holding out her parcel.

'Oh, I love presents!' said Mr Benjamin. 'May I open it now?'

'Please do,' said Aunty. She bit her lip anxiously as he carefully untied the ribbon and opened up the tissue wrapping. He held up the slippery silk pyjamas, looking delighted.

'They're wonderful! With my very own monogram, and so beautifully stitched! They're the most splendid pyjamas ever. You're so kind, Miss Watson. I can't wait for bedtime now!' he said enthusiastically.

Aunty blushed, but she was clearly delighted. 'Are you staying at the manor tonight, Mr Benjamin?' she asked.

'No, not this trip. It still seems very much my mother's house!' he said, pulling a face.

'But I'm sure the staff have kept several bedrooms prepared, sir. They'll be keeping the entire manor spick and span, ready for you to move in,' said Aunty.

'I dare say, and it's very good of them – but now that all the paperwork is completed and the manor is at last mine, I can start on the renovations before I actually move in. Mother might have worn exquisite clothes, courtesy of you, Miss Watson, but her taste went seriously awry when it came to furnishings. I am here to have a wander around the rooms and make plans.'

'You're redecorating, sir?' Aunty asked, surprised. 'But Lady Somerset had all the main rooms repapered three or four years ago, I remember.'

'With those hilarious floral wallpapers – roses like cabbages, mid-Victorian style!' said Mr Benjamin. 'I've a good mind to start ripping them off personally! And I have to get rid of all that hideous furniture – so brown and shiny and formidable, requiring buckets of beeswax every week. It's a wonder the maids aren't worn to a thread having to use so much elbow grease!'

Aunty smiled uncertainly. 'I think you must be joking, Mr Benjamin!'

'I'm deadly serious, Miss Watson. Don't look so anxious! I adore interior decoration. I've designed the London houses of several of my friends, and they're utterly thrilled with the results. Wait and see! I shall send a team of willing workers to the house next week and, by the time I move in this summer, Somerset Manor will be transformed,' he declared.

He was as good as his word. As I set off to school I saw motor-vans chugging through the gates of the estate – and when I came home Aunty and Ella were having a cup of tea together in the kitchen. Ella looked very pale, with beads of sweat on her forehead.

'I can't believe it! You should see the drawing room, Flo. It's utterly destroyed! They've even taken away the Venetian chandelier. Poor Lady Somerset will be turning in her grave. It's sheer vandalism! Mr B's gone stark staring mad!'

'Mr Benjamin is going to transform the manor,' said Aunty, sticking up for him because he was our hero now.

'I'll say! He's transforming that beautiful historic house into a rubbish tip, that's what he's doing. Mr Marchant literally fainted when he saw what they were doing. Fell to the floor right in front of us! We thought he was dead. He's recovered now, but he was so incensed he's handed in his notice. We're all considering following his example. How can we stay on there with the dust swirling all around us? Mr Benjamin was just a little boy when I came to work here, as pretty as a girl with all those dark curls, and such winning ways. I lost my heart to him there and then, but now I'm starting to think he's the devil incarnate. How can he tear the house down when his mother's scarcely cold in her grave?'

'Hush, Ella! Stop talking of graves in front of the child,' said Aunty.

I didn't mind. I'd only just come from the graveyard. I'd had a long conversation with Mother, and then I'd had another look at Lady Somerset's tomb. I'd put my ear to the cold marble to see if she was muttering away inside.

'Well, I can't stand it. Look!' said Ella, holding out her shaking hand. 'See – my nerves are shot to pieces.'

'I'll give you a tot of brandy, dear. Don't worry, it's only medicinal,' said Aunty, going to the sideboard for the precious bottle. 'Mr Benjamin told us he's moving into the house in the summer, so everything will be tickety-boo in a few weeks' time.'

She was very reassuring, but when we went to have a peep at Somerset Manor we were both shocked. The outside still looked the same – serene grey stone with mullioned windows – but there was a deafening crash and clatter inside, and when we slipped through the open door we stared in disbelief. The grand entrance hall had been stripped back to its bones, the rich patterned carpet like a giant Swiss roll in one corner, the red-and-white-striped chairs upturned, waving their spindly gilt legs in the air. The ancestral paintings that had hung over the staircase were all gone, leaving large rectangular shadows.

We dodged workmen and went along the corridor. Lady Somerset's drawing room no longer existed. Every chair, table and trinket was crowded against one wall while workmen prised the nails out of the pink and cream paisley-patterned carpet and tugged it back to expose ugly bare floorboards.

'The Turkish carpet!' Aunty gasped. 'It was Lady Somerset's pride and joy. She insisted that all her visitors change into slippers so the carpet wouldn't be marked. I can't bear it!'

'Let's go home, Aunty,' I said, tugging at her.

However, she had to see one more room: Lady

Somerset's bedchamber. There were workmen in here too, dismantling the large four-poster bed. The pillows that had propped up Lady Somerset's head had been tossed into a corner. The doors of her huge wardrobe hung open, her clothes spilling out onto the floor.

'It's a desecration,' Aunty whispered, tears pouring down her face. Then her lips tightened and she went over to the wardrobe. She reached out a hand and fingered the stiff, dark beaded frocks and scalloped-edged mantles that she had stitched so carefully.

'You should wrap these clothes in tissue paper and store them in suitable trunks,' she said to the workman nearest her.

'There's no need for that, madam. The young master's given his orders. He doesn't want any of it kept. *Out with the old, in with the new* – that's what he says. We've been told we can help ourselves to anything we fancy, but my missus wouldn't want any of the old girl's clothes, it would give her the creeps.'

Aunty swallowed. 'Then can I have them?' she asked.

'You?' said the workman, looking at her with his head on one side. 'But they'd swamp you, madam. You're half Lady Somerset's size.'

'I don't intend to wear them. Please may I have a selection?' Aunty persisted.

'All right, help yourself. Though I don't think even a second-hand shop would want such old-fashioned clothes. Here, wrap what you want in a dust sheet – we've got plenty,' he said cheerily, and went back to struggle with the bed.

I knew I should help Aunty gather up the clothes

and pile them onto the dust sheet, but I agreed with the workman's wife. The clothes smelled musty and sour, and I couldn't bring myself to touch them. I watched the workmen dismantling the bed instead. They were unscrewing the bottom now.

'Hello, what's this? A hidden stash of money!' the man said.

I peered over – but it was just a silver sixpence.

'I wonder if she got it out of a Christmas plum pudding long ago?' he said. 'Here, nipper!'

He tossed it in the air and I caught it, quick as a wink, and popped it in my pocket.

'Thanks very much,' I said, thrilled. I might have ninety-eight whole pounds in the bank, but it wasn't really much use if Aunty wouldn't let me spend it. Sixpence was a fortune in our village.

Aunty was too upset about Lady Somerset's clothes to tell me off and make me give it back. I helped her lug the bulging dust sheet all the way back to the cottage. She shook out each garment carefully and then hung it on the special hangers suspended from the picture rail. When she was finished, there were head-less ghosts of Lady Somerset all around us. It was very unnerving.

'You're not going to keep them all, are you, Aunty?' I asked.

'I don't know.'

'Are you going to try to sell them?'

'I wouldn't do any such thing!' she snapped.

'Then what do you want them for?' I said. 'They're hideous.'

Aunty blinked, and I realized how tactless I'd been.

'They're beautifully made, of course,' I said hastily. 'But they're so old-fashioned.'

'Of *course* they're old-fashioned. I've been making Lady Somerset's clothes for many years. And she *liked* them like that,' said Aunty. She ran her fingers down the skirt of a dark evening gown decorated with shiny black bead flowers, then snatched her hand away when she saw me staring. 'It took me days and days to stitch all that jet,' she murmured.

'Well, why not just keep that one then,' I said, 'and throw out the others.'

'It would seem so disrespectful. And the materials are good quality. Perhaps I could rework them in some way . . .'

'But the colours are all wrong. You're making children's clothes now. They can't wear black and brown and navy,' I pointed out. 'Besides, they all smell of old lady.'

'I could hang them up outside in the fresh air,' said Aunty obstinately.

In the end she repacked them carefully in the dust sheet and tacked it together at both ends. It looked like the shroud of a very, very large person. She made me help her carry it up the ladder to the attic and lay it on the unboarded slats. Then she went back to stitching blue shorts and tiny teddies, while I sat fingering the sixpence in my pocket, planning how to spend it.

I took it to school with me and showed it to Maggie at break time.

'Oh, my! A whole sixpence. What are you going to

buy, Mona?' she asked. 'You could get a whole pound of chocolate drops from Mr Berner's.'

I wasn't sure I fancied his manky old chocolate when I'd recently eaten the heavenly Harrods selection. Instead I thought about fruit drops, or sherbet lemons, or maybe liquorice bootlaces. I couldn't eat them all myself, but I could share them with Maggie. She was looking at me eagerly.

But then, I thought, in an hour or so they'd be gone, and I'd have nothing to show for my sixpence. I considered buying a toy instead: little friends for Farthing and an India rubber ball. Or a net bag of marbles. Or the tiny ship in a bottle in the window!

I dithered, but in the end I didn't buy any of them. Coming out of school, I saw Old Molly's nephew, Big Alf, lumbering down the lane, his pockets bulging and emitting high-pitched yowls.

'What you got there, Alf?' I asked.

'Mind your own business,' he said. He didn't like children. He didn't seem to like anybody much.

'Look, it's a kitten!' said Peter Robinson, pointing to a tiny face peeping out of Big Alf's pocket.

'Oh, how lovely!' I said. 'Is there a kitten in your other pocket too, Alf? Oh, do let's see!'

'Come on, show us, Alf,' said Maggie, trying to get at his pockets.

'You get your pesky hands off,' he said, slapping her away.

'The kittens can't be very comfy in your pockets, Alf,' I said. 'And they look ever so young. Can't you take them back to their mother?'

'My boss told me to get rid of them. Their cat had three kittens and they don't want no more cats about the house,' said Big Alf. 'Now leave us alone, I've got business to do.'

'But what are you going to do with them?' I asked.

'Never you mind, Miss Longnose,' said Big Alf.

'You're going to drown them!' Peter realized.

'So what if I am? The boss said to get rid of all three, so I've got to, haven't I?'

'How could you possibly drown such dear little kittens?' I asked, horrified.

'I drowns them in a bucket of water, don't I?' said Big Alf.

'You mustn't! Give them to me,' said Maggie. 'My mum won't mind. She likes cats. And it will tickle our Bertha.'

'Could I have one?' asked Peter.

'And me!' I suddenly longed for a kitten with all my heart. 'There you are, Alf. You don't have to go to the bother of drowning them, which must be horrible. We'll look after them for you.'

Big Alf narrowed his eyes. 'How much will you give me for them?'

'You were going to drown them!' I said indignantly. 'You can't suddenly start asking for money.'

'Oh yes I can!' Big Alf wasn't as daft as he seemed. 'How much?'

'You're very mean asking children for money,' said Maggie. 'You know we haven't got any money. Well, you keep your kittens then.'

'Ain't you got no money, any of you?' he said in disgust.

'*I* have!' said Peter, feeling in the pocket of his

shorts. He brought out a handful of toffee wrappers and stubby pencils and his famous green glass marble – and a penny. 'Here!'

'A penny? That's not nearly enough for three dear fluffy little kittens,' said Big Alf.

'Just one kitten then.' Peter nodded at me. 'She can have it. She wants it badly.'

'So do I!' said Maggie indignantly.

'Well, none of you can have even one. A penny's not enough. Tuppence it is. And that's cheap for a kitten,' said Big Alf, nodding authoritatively. 'Well, suit yourselves. I'll go and drown 'em. And it'll be *your* fault.'

'No! Wait! Look, I've got sixpence,' I said. I knew he was conning us. I knew the kittens were very little, too young to be taken from their mother. They might only live a day or two. I knew Aunty would be very cross if I brought one home, but I couldn't help it. 'Sixpence for the three of them,' I said, holding out my money.

'No, it's more than that,' said Big Alf quickly. 'A shilling for all three! That's what they're worth.'

'No it's not! You said tuppence for one kitten. And three twos are six, and that means sixpence for the three. So you give them to us now and I'll give you this sixpence,' I said, holding it out.

'And if you don't, you'll be going back on your word, and I'll tell my dad on you,' said Maggie.

'Oh, have the darned things then,' said Big Alf, snatching my sixpence.

We had to delve in his horrible greasy pockets to get the kittens. Maggie found a black-and-white one, Peter scooped up a little ginger one, and I got a tiny coal-black kitten, even smaller than the other two, but utterly perfect, with a heart-shaped face and pointy ears and preposterously long whiskers.

Big Alf shambled away, pocketing my sixpence.

'Can we really have one each?' said Maggie. 'Can I keep this one with its pretty white face and white paws? It's the best one! I shall call it Mittens.'

'Would you sooner have the ginger one, Mona?' asked Peter. 'It's the boy, and it's the biggest. *He's* the best.'

'Thank you, but no, I want mine. I love it ever so much. I'll call it Sixpence,' I said.

'You always give your precious things money names,' Maggie giggled, holding Mittens up to her face and rubbing noses with it. 'You call your little doll Farthing and your kitten Sixpence. If you get a little dog, will you call it Shilling? If you get a great big dog, will you call it Half-Crown? And if you get a donkey, will you call it One Pound Note?'

'*You're* the donkey,' I said. 'What are you going to call your kitten, Peter?'

'Ginger,' he said. It wasn't a very imaginative choice, but he'd been willing to buy a kitten for me, so I said that was a perfect name.

Peter blushed until his ears glowed.

Maggie sniffed. 'Mittens is a perfect name too – it looks as if my kitten is wearing little white mittens on each of her paws, *and* it rhymes. Look – she's much the prettiest.'

'You should have let Mona have first pick of the kittens seeing as it was her money,' said Peter.

'I'd have picked Sixpence anyway,' I said. 'I love her.

Or him.' I squinted hard at Sixpence's nether regions but couldn't see anything. I decided she had to be a girl because she was so dainty.

'What'll your aunty say?' Maggie asked.

'She'll love her too,' I declared. I knew this was highly unlikely. Aunty wasn't very fond of animals because they made a mess. And she'd be shocked to the core when she found out that I'd given my precious sixpence to Big Alf.

I wasn't too keen to get home, so I lingered at Maggie's house while Mrs Higgins exclaimed over both kittens, and spread jam from her last precious pot of raspberry on my slice of bread in thanks. She found an old hankie for me to wrap Sixpence in on my way home.

'You need to keep her warm as she's very small,' she said.

I left Maggie making a special bed for Mittens in an old pie dish lined with rags, and wandered on my way, whispering softly in Sixpence's small furry ears. I took her to see Mother, letting her scamper over the grassy mound. Her furry legs weren't very strong yet, so I soon wrapped her up in the hankie again.

'This is Mother, Sixpence,' I said. I'm sure she loved animals, especially kittens. 'But now I suppose I'd better take you home to Aunty. Try and look as sweet as possible when you see her.'

Aunty was humming as she sewed, a good sign. I stood in the doorway to her workroom, holding Sixpence in my cupped hands.

Aunty peered over the top of her glasses. 'What's that you've got there? It's not a baby rabbit, is it? Put it back in the grass!'

'It's not a baby rabbit, Aunty! It's my kitten – look. Isn't she lovely?' I said, holding out my hands.

'Oh Lord, Mona, what will you do next?' said Aunty. 'We can't have a kitten! Imagine if it got into my sewing silks! And I'll be spending a day a week in London. You can't leave a small kitten alone all day long.'

'I forgot,' I said. 'I'll have to take her to school on your London days.'

'As if that Miss Nelson would let a kitten run amok in her classroom! See sense, Mona. Give it back to whoever gave it you.'

'I can't! It was Big Alf, and he was going to drown her, and Mittens and Ginger,' I wailed.

'You're not telling me there are more!'

'I gave one to Maggie and one to Peter Robinson,' I said. 'And I've got Sixpence.'

Aunty blinked, putting two and two together. Two and two and two.

'You've never given that oaf your sixpence!' she said.

'I had to, Aunty. I couldn't let him drown them. And I wanted a kitten so much. *This* kitten.'

She came over and peered at Sixpence. She lay quietly in my hands, quivering a little. 'Oh, Mona, I don't think she'll even last the night,' said Aunty wearily.

My eyes prickled. Sixpence went blurry as the tears ran down my cheeks. 'Do you really think so?' I wept.

Aunty sighed. 'Well, we'll have to see,' she said. 'Keep her wrapped up for now. I'll warm a little milk in the saucepan and we'll see if she can drink it.'

Sixpence didn't know how to lap from a saucer yet. I tried dipping my finger in the milk and holding it to her mouth. She managed to suck a little, but her mouth wasn't very strong.

'She's going to die, isn't she, Aunty?' I sobbed.

Aunty's mouth was pinched, as if she was still holding pins in it. 'We'll do our best to keep her going,' she said. 'Wipe that runny nose, Mona. I reared you when you were scarcely bigger than that kitten, and it looked like you wouldn't last the night either. We'll just have to wait and see.'

I looked up and saw Peter standing at his front window.

10

WE TOOK IT IN TURNS TRYING TO GET
Sixpence to lap some more milk. By two in the
morning I was so tired that I fell into a deep sleep, and
then suddenly it was morning. Aunty was standing over
me with a breakfast tray of porridge and tea.

'Here, dear, get this down you. You're still going to be
late for school, but you were sleeping like a baby so it
seemed a shame to wake you. Eat up now. You've got a
sprinkle of sugar on your porridge,' she said.

She was being so kind to me my heart started
thumping. I tried a spoonful of porridge but I couldn't
swallow.

'Aunty?'

'Mm? Don't talk with your mouth full!'

'Did Sixpence die in the night?' I whispered.

'No, she didn't. I've managed to get more milk down her, and she knows how to suck now, but she's still as weak as . . . as a kitten!'

'Oh, let me see her!' I said, jumping out of bed.

Aunty had made her a special little nest of scraps of material. Sixpence lay curled up, her eyes closed, though her small chest was rising and falling miraculously.

'You've saved her!' I said.

'I don't think she's out of the woods yet. Don't get too attached to her,' Aunty warned.

But it was too late. I already adored my little cat – and, as I watched Aunty stroke her and murmur to her, I knew that she did too. When I was at school she went to Mr Berner's and bought a doll's bottle with a tiny rubber teat, and when I came home she showed me how to feed her. It was the most wonderful thing in the world, holding Sixpence in the palm of my hand and seeing her small mouth suck and suck. After a week I stopped worrying that she was going to die. After another week she was pattering around the room on her tiny paws. Aunty had to keep all her threads out of her reach and hang every garment as high as she could.

Before long Sixpence learned to climb, and thought Aunty's shelves of material her own personal ladder. She could scamper right up to the ceiling in seconds, and would then mew plaintively, unable to get down again. Aunty had to keep leaving her sewing to rescue her.

'That dratted cat,' she declared a dozen times a day,

but she smiled fondly when she said it.

On her Harrods day I took Sixpence in her little patchwork travelling bag to stay with Mrs Higgins. After school I had tea there. Maggie and I played with our kittens until Aunty came wearily home to collect me. Mittens was still much bigger than Sixpence, but not as bold. She was still pretty, with her white face and paws, and much less fidgety than her small sister, content to sit on Maggie's lap for hours, but privately I thought her rather a boring little thing.

Sixpence was much sharper when we played games, able to pounce on a toy mouse on a string with deadly accuracy and chase a little ball about the room. Bertha was enchanted by both kittens, but we had to teach her not to grab at them or pull their tails. Mittens mostly put up with it, but Sixpence was indignant and hissed at Bertha in a hilarious way.

'Now then, Sixpence, don't be a naughty girl. Bertha's only a baby, she didn't mean to upset you,' I said, though I was secretly proud that she knew how to stick up for herself.

'Mittens has a lovely placid nature, doesn't she?' said Maggie.

'Hark at you two!' said Mrs Higgins, laughing. 'You sound like a pair of little mothers!'

We couldn't take the kittens to school of course, but we talked about them all day long.

'Isn't it lovely that we're best friends, and now Mittens and Sixpence are best friends too,' said Maggie as we walked around the playground with linked arms.

Peter Robinson was hovering. 'It's not fair that Ginger doesn't get to see his sisters,' he said. 'He's being left out.'

'He's just a ginger tom,' said Maggie. 'There's two of them in the barn at the farm – I've seen them. They prowl and yowl about the place, and my dad says they'll scratch you soon as look at you. Your Ginger can go and play with them when he's a bit bigger. Gingers are farmyard animals. He's not like Mittens and Sixpence. They're proper pets.'

'You're talking rubbish,' said Peter. 'Ginger's *my* pet. Anyway, he probably wouldn't *want* to play with your cat, Maggie Higgins, not if she's as mean as you.' And he stalked off, whistling like he didn't care.

'Good riddance!' Maggie shouted after him, and squeezed my arm. 'He's a right nuisance, isn't he, that Peter Robinson? Always hanging around!'

I didn't know what to say. Maggie was being really mean. She was probably making it up about the ginger toms. She just wanted Peter to leave us alone. I didn't know why he annoyed her so. He was really quite a nice boy. I knew I should have stuck up for him, but then Maggie would have been annoyed, and maybe she'd have stopped being friends with me.

I needed her as a friend. None of the other girls at school liked me much. They said I sounded snobby, and whenever I came top of the class in our weekly tests they all groaned and muttered 'teacher's pet'. Maggie had palled up with me last September, when Miss Nelson sat us next to each other. At last I had someone to go around with at break time. And, of course, it wasn't just

Maggie – it was also Mrs Higgins and little Bertha and the bread and dripping . . .

I tried not to mind about Peter Robinson, but my tummy clenched, and it got worse every time I looked over at his bent head. I started to think about Ginger too. I knew it was daft, but I pictured him moping in a corner with no one to play with. It didn't matter if he grew up into a prowly-yowly tom cat. Just now he was still a little kitten, and Peter was quite right – he was probably missing cuddling up with his sisters. And missing his mother too.

It wasn't Aunty's trip-to-Harrods day, so I didn't linger at the Higginses' cottage very long. I went to see my mother. I'd been so eager to see Sixpence recently that I'd simply stopped to pat the grass on her grave three times, meaning *I Love You*, and then rushed off home. This time I lay down flat and begged Mother to make me feel better.

She was as gentle with me as ever – but not very comforting. 'Poor Peter,' she murmured. 'Poor Ginger.'

'But Peter's not my actual friend,' I said.

'He'd like to be,' said Mother.

'Well, I can't help that,' I replied sulkily.

'Mona,' she said softly. 'You're my good kind girl. You know what you're going to do.'

I sighed, scrambling up and brushing the grass off my school dress. I could easily disobey Aunty when she snapped at me, but I couldn't resist Mother's gentle suggestions. I left the graveyard and doubled back on myself. I went down the narrow alleyway behind the cottages in case Maggie was playing in her garden.

I headed for the pink-washed cottage at the other end of the street, where the Robinsons lived.

It was one of the prettiest cottages, with roses round the white door and a garden full of flowers, with never a weed in sight. Mrs Robinson had time on her hands because she only had the one child, Peter. She didn't have to work like Aunty. She had Mr Robinson, who was a train driver, and earned a good wage. Almost all the boys at school wanted to be train drivers when they grew up – they begged Mr Robinson to take them up into the engine with him. It made Peter very popular.

I hovered for a minute or so, pretending to myself that I was simply admiring the flowers. I was feeling nervous. I knew that Peter liked me, but I wasn't sure his mother would. Then I looked up and saw him standing at his front window, his forehead against the glass. He looked comically surprised.

I gave him an airy wave, then went to the front door and knocked politely – Aunty had trained me never to bang hard. I hoped Peter himself would come running, but it was his mother, in a dress as floral as her garden, without an apron.

'Yes, dear?' she said. Her voice was as refined as Aunty's.

'How do you do, Mrs Robinson?' I said, holding out my hand.

She shook it, disconcerted. 'And you are . . . ?'

She knew perfectly well who I was. Everyone knew who I was. I was *that girl who lives with her aunt in the cottage on the estate.*

'I'm Mona Smith,' I said.

'She's in my class at school, Mother,' said Peter, coming to the door too, cradling Ginger. 'Hello, Mona!'

'Hello, Peter. Oh, Ginger's grown! He's much bigger than Sixpence, but he's still very sweet. I was wondering – would you like to come round to my house with him so he can play with Sixpence?'

'Yes, please!' said Peter, going painfully red. 'Can I, Mother?'

'But I'm just making your tea! I thought you said you were starving!'

'I'm not hungry any more. Oh, please!' he begged.

'Won't your aunt mind?' she asked me.

There! She *did* know me.

'Peter could have tea at my place,' I said.

We had much nicer food now that Aunty had a contract with Harrods. We had ham or corned-beef salad, or cheese on toast, or egg and beans – really tasty food that filled you up but didn't need much cooking. (Aunty was busier than ever, sewing and sewing until her hands stiffened and her sight blurred. Still, she didn't seem to mind too much. She held out the skirts of her little dresses, checked the white collars and puffed sleeves, examined the embroidery, and then gave them a little pat, as if there was a real child wearing them.)

'*Please*, Mother,' said Peter.

'Oh, very well then. But don't outstay your welcome. Come back home after half an hour like a good boy,' she said. 'Let me look at you.' She ran a comb though his short hair and then spat on her hankie and wiped round his mouth. Peter wriggled uncomfortably.

'I wish she wouldn't *do* that,' he said as we set off.

'My aunty does it too,' I said. 'I expect the kittens' mother licked them clean too.'

'I keep wondering if Ginger is missing her,' said Peter, rubbing his cheek against the bright furry head.

'I keep thinking that too!'

'Do you miss your mother, Mona?' Peter asked. 'Oh, sorry. I shouldn't have asked that.'

'It's all right. She died when I was born, but I sometimes go to the graveyard and talk to her,' I said. I'd never told anyone that before, not even Maggie, because I knew she'd think it weird.

Peter stopped in his tracks, looking interested. '*How* do you talk to her? Is it like saying prayers?'

'Not really. I just lie down beside her – well, *on* her, actually – and whisper stuff down to her,' I said.

'You mean you lie on her *grave*? Isn't it a bit scary?' Peter asked.

'Not in the slightest,' I said. 'And she talks back to me.'

Peter must have squeezed Ginger quite hard in surprise, because the kitten gave a little protesting mew.

'Sorry, Ginger! She doesn't really *talk*, does she? Like a ghost?'

'She's not a ghost, she's my mother, and she still loves me and wants to look after me, even though she's dead and buried,' I said.

'Cripes!' said Peter. He stood there, stroking Ginger. 'Are you going to talk to her now?'

'No, I've already done it. She told me to invite you

back to my house so that our kittens could play together,'
I told him.

He blinked. 'That was nice of her,' he said. He paused.
'Did she tell you to invite Maggie too?'

'No, she didn't actually.'

Mother didn't seem to think much of Maggie. I'd told
her all the secret things we whispered about sometimes,
and Mother had been shocked. She hadn't scolded me –
she never did that – but she did murmur that it wasn't
very nice for little girls to talk about such things.

'Though I do understand that it's lovely for you to
have a special friend, dear,' she added comfortingly.

Aunty didn't mince her words. She didn't know about
Maggie's surprising knowledge or her rude jokes (she'd
have been utterly horrified by them), but she didn't think
much of her manners. The one time I'd invited Maggie
to tea she'd wiped the crumbs off her face with the back
of her hand, and once she'd even wiped her runny nose.
Maggie had got down from the table without asking, and
when she peeped into Aunty's workroom she'd whooped
at the sight of the sewing machine.

'Let me have a go!' she demanded, sitting down on
Aunty's chair and touching the machine's gold lettering
with her sticky fingers.

'Oh no, dear, it's not for little girls,' said Aunty, giving
her a steely smile.

She sighed deeply when Maggie went home. 'Well!'
she said. She didn't say any more. She didn't need to.
I knew she wouldn't want me to invite Maggie back,
though it was a little awkward when kind Mrs Higgins
minded me once a week now.

I worried that Aunty wouldn't take to Peter either, but when we got to the cottage he was very polite.

'I won't outstay my welcome, Miss Watson,' he said, quaintly quoting his mother. 'I'd just like to let my kitten Ginger meet up with Sixpence again. I think it would be good for them.'

'Sixpence has been a very naughty girl today,' said Aunty, shaking her head. 'She's just knocked my box of embroidery silks off the shelf and got them into a terrible tangle!'

'Oh dear!' said Peter. 'Shall we help you untangle them?'

Aunty had vowed never to let any more visiting children into her workroom, but surprisingly she agreed. We shut Sixpence and Ginger in the kitchen together, and then sat cross-legged on Aunty's lino floor, winding each different skein of silk. Aunty sat on her little chair, unpicking knots in a totally mangled thread, nodding at Peter approvingly.

'You've got nimble fingers for a boy, Peter Robinson,' she said.

'They're not a patch on yours!' he replied. 'I love that little shirt thing you're making. My mother makes my shirts, but they're not a bit like that. She gets Simplicity fashion patterns. Are they what you use, Miss Watson?'

Aunty was always scathing about patterns, but she simply shook her head. 'No, dear, I create my own designs.'

'Aunty makes children's clothes for Harrods,' I said proudly.

'What's Harrods?' Peter asked.

'It's the biggest, best department store in the world,' I said. 'It's up in London, and I've been there with Aunty, and it's astonishing – like a palace, with marble pillars and soft carpets and those huge bright sparkly lights.'

'Chandeliers,' said Aunty.

'And you've really been there, Mona?'

'Yes, and Aunty bought us a box of Harrods chocolates, which were incredibly expensive. I'd have offered you one, but we ate them all. I've still got the box though. I'll fetch it,' I told him.

I'd turned it into a house for Farthing. The bottom drawer was her kitchen. I'd made her a little cardboard stove and baked her some miniature jam tarts when Aunty was making pastry. I'd even put a dab of jam in each tart. I'd made them as small as I possibly could, but Farthing could have used each tart as a large sofa, only then she'd have got her dress sticky.

The middle drawer was her living room, with a lot of conker chairs in case she had visitors. I'd made her a book to read too, and written the title with a pin carefully dipped in the ink bottle: *Thumbelina*.

The top drawer was Farthing's bedroom. I wanted to copy the fairy story and give her a walnut-shell bed, but I didn't have any walnuts, so I had to make do with a matchbox, which wasn't anywhere near as pretty, though I did give her silky bedding from Aunty's bag of scraps. I put the top from a little medicine bottle beside the bed in case Farthing needed a potty in the night.

I kept the drawers firmly shut while I showed Peter,

but he asked if he could open one to see if he could still smell the chocolates.

'Well, just a peep,' I said reluctantly, worrying that he would laugh at me for being such a baby.

He had more than a peep. He peered at each drawer in turn, smiling, but only in admiration.

'You've made a little house for your doll!' he said. 'I love all her furniture! And you *can* still smell the chocolate!' he said, breathing in deeply. 'Your doll's so lucky living in a house that smells like the best chocolate in the world!'

'I've always liked the bit in "Hansel and Gretel" where they find the gingerbread cottage, and the tiles on the roof are slabs of chocolate!' I said.

'And the door knocker's made of barley sugar! If I had a house like that, I'd eat it all up,' said Peter.

'Is that a hint that you two would like some tea?' Aunty wondered.

'Yes please!' said Peter, who had clearly got his appetite back.

We all went into the kitchen, and Peter and I did our best to keep the kittens amused while Aunty started cooking. Peter got out a little India rubber ball and bounced it into a corner. Sixpence and Ginger raced across the room to pounce on it. Sixpence was slightly faster, even though her legs were shorter, but Ginger was stronger. They tussled for it, rolling over and over, play-fighting. Then they ran around in circles, dashing this way and that, so fast we couldn't catch them. Suddenly Sixpence was exhausted: she flopped down on the rag rug and put her head on her paws. She was asleep in seconds. Ginger looked disappointed, made a circuit of the room by himself, and then lay down beside Sixpence.

'Aah!' we exclaimed simultaneously, and then laughed.

Aunty made us a good tea – poached eggs on toast and then treacle tart. The tart was a little stale now, but still very good heated up and served with cream from the top of the milk.

'This is spiffing food!' said Peter. He talked with his mouth full, but Aunty didn't seem to mind.

'The tart's from the manor,' I explained.

'Mona!' said Aunty. It was meant to be a deadly secret that Ella sometimes slipped us leftover food. Aunty worried she might get into trouble – but Mr Marchant had gone now, and he hadn't been replaced yet.

After we'd had our tea the kittens woke up again. We fed them too, and then sat with them cuddled on our laps. It was very peaceful in the kitchen, with just the ticking of the clock and the whir of the sewing machine from Aunty's workroom.

'I do like it at your house,' said Peter. 'Ginger likes it here too.' He looked up at the clock and sighed. 'I've been here an hour and a half!'

'But you haven't outstayed your welcome,' I told him.

'Really? Still, Mother will be worrying. I suppose I'd better go,' he said, tucking Ginger down his shirt front.

He said goodbye to Aunty and thanked her for having him. I went to the front door with him.

'Thank you very much too, Mona,' said Peter. 'Could I come again?'

'Yes, of course.'

'Just Ginger and me, like today?'

I nodded. We didn't need to spell it out: we had to keep this a secret from Maggie.

It wasn't easy at school. I went around with Maggie all the time. I didn't speak to Peter much, though we sometimes caught each other's eye. I'd nod and he'd wink.

Maggie caught him once, and was outraged. 'Peter Robinson winked at you!' she said.

I shrugged. 'So what?' I said, though I could feel myself going pink.

'And you had a silly smile on your face like you didn't mind!'

'Oh, Maggie, do shut up about it,' I said.

She went off in a huff, and my tummy clenched, wondering if she was going to break up with me. She joined some of the other girls in their skipping game, and ignored me. I sat by myself, pretending I didn't care. Peter hovered, looking anxious.

'Go away,' I muttered, and after a while he did.

I sat with my head on my hands, wondering if I'd lost both friends now, but when it was time to go home Maggie linked arms with me and we went back to her house, same as always.

I didn't go calling for Peter straight away, but when I dodged back to his house a few days later he seemed thrilled. I was invited in for tea, but it wasn't quite the same. I didn't have Sixpence with me so the kittens couldn't play together, and Peter and I couldn't play properly either, because his mother stayed with us all the time. In fact, she insisted on playing too. She liked card games. The three of us played Snap and Happy Families and Old Maid.

I'd played Snap with Maggie, but after five minutes it became boring. I found Happy Families quite enjoyable because I liked the pictures on the cards and it was fun getting to know each family in turn. I detested Old Maid right from the start. I was left with a card showing a grotesque old woman, and Peter and Mrs Robinson pointed at me and shouted, 'Old Maid, Old Maid!' in mocking voices. I knew it was simply part of the game, but I didn't like it at all.

'Why are you doing that? What does it mean?' I asked, ashamed to find that I was nearly in tears.

'We're not being horrid,' Peter said quickly. 'You have to shout whenever someone's left with the Old Maid card. I expect it will be me next time, and then you can shout at me.'

'But why do you shout *Old Maid*? Why does she look so horrible?'

'Because it *is* horrible to be left a sad old maid. It means that no one wants to marry you,' said Mrs Robinson, twisting the wedding ring on her finger. Then she looked at me and suddenly went red. 'But it *is* rather a silly game, Mona. Shall we have a change and play Spillikins?'

She'd remembered that Aunty was an old maid. No one had ever wanted to marry Aunty. Was she sad about it? Was that why people weren't always very nice to her, and whispered behind her back? I wanted to stab Mrs Robinson with her own spillikins.

'I don't think I'd better play any more. I have to get home. Thank you for having me,' I gabbled, and then headed for the door.

Peter came running after me. 'Are you upset, Mona?' he asked anxiously. 'Mother didn't mean to say that. You will come again, won't you?'

I shrugged, not wanting to now.

Peter came nearer so his breath tickled my ear. 'I can still come to yours, can't I? With Ginger? It's ever so much nicer at your house.'

I nodded, and then very quickly he kissed me on the cheek. We both sprang apart and I ran off down the street. When I got to the corner I looked back, and he was still standing at his front door, waving. I waved back. I supposed he was my sweetheart now. I wasn't sure I was keen on the idea, even though I liked him. It might mean that I would never have to be an old maid – but was that really so dreadful?

Aunty stopped working and made me a cup of cocoa when I got home. She made herself one too, but didn't take it into her workroom in case she got a brown drip on the delicate cream silk she was sewing. We sat together in the kitchen, sipping away.

'Aunty, do you mind not being married?' I blurted out.

She looked startled. 'Has someone been saying something to you about me?' she asked.

'No, no! I just wondered, that's all,' I said quickly.

'I'm perfectly happy as I am,' she told me.

'You don't ever get lonely?'

'Well, I've got you to keep me company, haven't I?'

'That's right,' I said, relieved. 'There's you, me and Sixpence.'

I decided we were a Happy Family too.

He took a daisy out of his hair and stuck it behind my ear.

11

'YOU SHOULD SEE WHAT'S BEEN HAPPENING up at the manor now!' said Ella. 'Oh, Flo, it's breaking my heart! He's had all the paper ripped off, and the walls painted the most bizarre colours you've ever seen. You'll never guess what colour the drawing room is. Pink! Bright pink! Pink as a stick of seaside rock! And now the new furniture is arriving, and it's all as rum as anything – hideous pale wood, and ever such funny shapes. It's meant to be some art style, but it don't look the slightest bit artistic to me, and it's dead uncomfortable into the bargain.

'And the art itself – well, it makes you boggle, it really does. All the fine family portraits have been stored in the attic and replaced by the most hideous paintings.

Most aren't even fit for a lady's eyes. There's one true shocker – a stark naked man not even trying to cover himself – and they've hung it bang above the mantelpiece so you can't blooming miss it!'

Ella only paused for breath to sip her tea. Aunty was so absorbed in the conversation that she didn't notice I was listening at the door, otherwise I'm sure she'd have sent me away. The more Ella went on about the refurbishment, the more I was desperate to see it. Mr Benjamin had such style and elegance – he couldn't seriously wreck the house, could he?

Aunty and I tried going for a walk up to the manor the next day, wanting to see for ourselves – but the cheery workmen were gone, and a bossy man in a beret and smock fluttered his fingers at us when he saw us approaching.

'Shoo, shoo!' he said, as if we were riff-raff. 'I don't want any gawpers here. This is private property!'

'We're friends of Mr Benjamin!' I said indignantly.

'A likely story,' he said.

I was all set to argue, but Aunty pulled me away.

'We're not going where we're not wanted, Mona,' she hissed to me. 'I'm not having that creature telling tales about us to Mr Benjamin. We'll simply have to wait until we get a proper invitation.'

I couldn't wait. I woke early on Sunday morning, before Aunty was stirring. I was pretty certain that no one would be working at the manor at the weekend. I decided to go and have a look by myself. I scrambled into my clothes and ran off.

The grounds seemed so silent without the roar of

the lorries and the shouts of the workmen. I stole up the gravel driveway, blinking at the flower borders. Before, they had been planted in straight rows, all the blooms standing to attention like soldiers. The beds were empty now, apart from a few broken stalks and scattered petals, as if giant badgers had been digging there all night.

I stood there, shaking my head, when I heard light footsteps coming round the side of the house. I turned on my heel and started running.

'Mona! Is that you? Come back, sweetheart!'

It was Mr Benjamin, wearing an old-fashioned nightshirt that was much too large for him. His feet were bare and he had a couple of ox-eye daisies stuck decoratively in his black curls. I gawped at him. He smiled back, unabashed.

I bobbed him an awkward curtsy. He laughed merrily and curtsied back, holding out his nightshirt.

'I'm so sorry, Mr Benjamin, sir. I didn't know you were going to be here this weekend,' I said, hanging my head.

'I didn't know myself until three in the morning,' he replied. 'I was at the most utterly boring soirée, and then I went on to a nightclub and danced until my ears were ringing and my poor feet ached. I suddenly longed for the peaceful delights of the manor, so I drove down and let myself in the back door with my own key. I don't think the servants have a clue I'm here yet. My delightful new silk pyjamas are at my London flat, so I had to dig out one of my father's old night-shirts. Isn't it a scream! Still, it's rather a lark wearing such voluminous skirts. Do you think it suits me, Mona?'

'I think anything suits you, Mr Benjamin,' I said. I did think he looked wonderful, though if he was spotted by the village lads they'd shriek with laughter.

He happily accepted my compliment. 'However, I have to admit I'm becoming a little chilly. The wind does rather blow up one's nightgown, and although I enjoyed the feel of soft grass underfoot, my poor toes are now blue with cold.' He wriggled them at me and I giggled.

'I think I had better go back inside,' he continued. 'Would you care to accompany me?'

I hesitated. 'I don't think I'm allowed inside, Mr Benjamin.'

He raised his eyebrows at me. 'Who owns the inside of Somerset Manor, Mona?'

'Well – you do.'

'Precisely. And I take great delight in allowing you there. In fact, when I move in – pray God, only a matter of a week or so now – you are very welcome to come calling at any time.'

We walked back towards the manor, Mr Benjamin keeping to the grass beside the empty flower beds and avoiding the sharp gravel.

'Did all your flowers die, Mr Benjamin?' I asked.

'I had them all dug up. I can't stand formal gardens. I intend to have cottage flowers running riot, and wild meadows full of these delightful daisies.' He picked one out of his hair and stuck it behind my ear.

We reached the large wooden front door. 'Ah!'

said Mr Benjamin. 'My key is in the pocket of my trousers. Oh well, I shall have to bother the servants after all.'

He knocked loudly. We heard a scurrying behind the door, and then thumps and muffled cursing as someone struggled with the bolts. The door opened, and there was Ella in her cap and apron, eyes goggling at the two of us.

'Mr Benjamin! Oh my goodness, we didn't even know you were here!' She turned away, going pink at the sight of his nightgown, though he didn't seem at all embarrassed himself. 'And what are *you* doing here, Mona? I'm so sorry, Mr Benjamin. I'll send her home immediately.'

'No, no, Ella. Mona is my guest. We will take a light breakfast and then I will give her a guided tour of the house. I can't wait to show off my refurbishments,' said Mr Benjamin.

Ella gave me a sidelong glance, but rushed off to order breakfast. I wasn't quite sure what a *light* breakfast was. I hoped it might be more than a cup of tea and a biscuit. I was feeling really hungry, but for once I forgot about my empty tummy. I was amazed by the house.

Somerset Manor had always been such a gloomy place, with thick damask curtains at the windows, shaded lights, and huge, dark brown pieces of furniture looming everywhere. There had been dozens of occasional tables cluttered with wax flowers in glass domes, and ornate vases, and fancy pillboxes, and little silver knick-knacks, and photographs of Somersets past and present in elaborate frames. The wallpaper pattern had been obscured by portraits of older

Somersets looking plain and grim, with not a smile between them.

Mr Benjamin had swept all these away, and installed a huge light shaped like a sun in the hallway. It shone a golden glow on the high white ceiling, and the primrose-yellow painted walls echoed the sunny effect.

'What do you think?' asked Mr Benjamin, taking a cloak from the coat stand and wrapping it around himself like a dressing gown.

'It's beautiful,' I said. 'The most beautiful room ever.'

'Ah, wait till you see the drawing room. Come, come!'

It was pink – but not the bright, sugary shade I'd pictured from Ella's description. It was painted a wonderfully subtle, deep rose, with cream curtains patterned with pink and blue circles. The two sofas and the armchairs were a soft blue, and the rugs were cream, so pristine that I walked round them carefully just in case I marked them. And there was the painting of the naked man, so huge it was almost life size! It was a back view, so you only saw his bottom. He was pink and cream, with blue shadowing, perfect for the room's colour scheme.

'You're right, Mr Benjamin! *This* is the most beautiful room ever!' I declared.

'Oh, Mona, you're a little treasure,' he said delightedly. 'You have an artistic soul.'

I felt very proud. I sat on the edge of a blue armchair, crossing my legs in what I hoped was an artistic manner. Ella sniffed at me when she put her head round the door to say that breakfast was served.

Mr Benjamin had worked wonders in the dining room too. It was painted apple green, with huge paintings of apples and pears and flowers on the walls. At one end there was a big yellow dresser with carefully arranged willow-pattern plates, and a long table with a yellow cloth, set with orange and blue and green patterned plates.

'I wanted it to have a workaday country cottage look,' said Mr Benjamin.

I thought of the Higginses' home. It certainly didn't look anything like this. The room was palatial by comparison, and the so-called breakfast set out on platters was palatial too. There were scrambled eggs and bacon, a plate of toast and another of muffins, a dish of butter, a jar of honey, a jar of strawberry jam, and a big green bowl of purple grapes. A yellow pot of tea stood on a stand, with a blue milk jug and a glass jug of orange juice.

'Shall I serve you, sir?' Ella asked.

'I think we can serve ourselves, thank you, Ella,' said Mr Benjamin.

'Yes, thank you, Ella,' I said, in as grand a voice as I could manage.

'Don't you come all grand with me, missy!' Ella hissed, and flounced away.

'Right, tuck in, Mona,' said Mr Benjamin.

So I tucked in for all I was worth. I had orange juice and two cups of tea, scrambled eggs and two rashers of bacon, toast and honey, a muffin with jam, and then looked in awe at the grapes. I'd never seen the purple sort before – I wasn't sure if they were part of our breakfast or a table decoration.

'Here,' said Mr Benjamin, picking me a little bunch and putting them on my plate. I put a large one in my mouth and bit into it. The sweet juice squirted over my tongue. I chewed the soft flesh, and then swallowed something small and gritty. I clutched my throat in alarm.

'Have you swallowed the pip?' asked Mr Benjamin. 'Nanny always used to tell me I'd have a whole grapevine growing inside me if I ever swallowed one!'

'That couldn't happen, could it?' I asked.

'Of course not. She just liked frightening me. She was actually a bit of a tyrant, but she made a fuss of me because I was the youngest. She'd always hankered after a little girl to dress up, and I was the next best thing! Though she was strict with Frederick – and very proud of him too for being such a brave little man. She had a soft spot for poor Eric as well – he was very kind and gentle – but she was positively ferocious to George. He was a bumptious little beast even then, and Nanny saw it as her duty to put him in his place. She used to beat him with her hairbrush, bristle side up.'

'Good!' I said. 'Mr George was horrid to Aunty and me.'

'Well, I will never let him be horrid to either of you ever again, I promise,' said Mr Benjamin. 'He's turned down my invitation to come and stay here for the summer. I hoped Mary might let Cedric and Ada come with their nanny while Barbara's lot are here, but that's a no-go too. I'd have liked all the cousins to run wild together. The manor's been like a tomb for the last few years while Mother's health declined. It's time for fun and merriment. I intend to have my London pals to stay too. I'm sending for a gramophone and a stack of records so we can all dance. Do you dance, Mona?'

'I can do the Charleston,' I said proudly.

'Oh, my! You little flapper girl! You'll be telling me you have a boyfriend next!'

I stuck out my chin. 'I do,' I said.

'Goodness! And what's the young gentleman's name?'

'He's called Peter.'

'And do you love him?'

'I don't think so. But I think he loves me just a little bit,' I said.

'That's the right way round, sweetheart,' said Mr Benjamin. 'You're a remarkably mature young lady for ten.'

'That's my exact age!' I said.

'I'm very good at keeping up with ages. I remember the birthdays of all my nieces and nephews. I'm only hazy about my own age. I've resolved to stay twenty-one for ever. Don't you think that a good plan?' he asked.

I nodded as I nibbled my way through my grapes. Then I had one more muffin, thickly spread with jam. I'd have liked to sit at the long table all day, but I remembered Peter's mother's warning.

I made myself stand up. 'I think I'd better be going now, Mr Benjamin. Thank you very much for having me,' I said.

'Oh dear, are you starting to get bored?' he asked.

'Not at all! But I don't want to outstay my welcome.'

'You could never do that, Mona,' said Mr Benjamin. 'You must come calling any time you fancy. You will *always* be welcome.'

I skipped home singing, '*You will always be welcome*,' over and over again.

'Someone sounds cheerful,' said Aunty. 'Where have you been, eh? You little monkey!' She was in the kitchen for once, and there was a wonderful rich smell that made my mouth water, even though I'd just eaten such a splendid breakfast. Aunty was holding the big pudding bowl with one hand, and whisking something energetically with the other. I peered hopefully at the pale yellow liquid.

'Are you making pudding, Aunty?'

'*Yorkshire* pudding,' she said. 'And there's a joint of beef roasting in the oven.'

'Beef!'

'Only a very small one, and it'll have to stretch out all week, in cottage pie and cold cuts, as it was still a shocking price. I said so to that butcher,' Aunty declared with spirit.

She must have gone into Rook Green yesterday while I was with Maggie. She'd become a lot bolder recently, and more inclined to buy us treats. Mr Brisby at Harrods was delighted with Aunty's outfits. She had lots of orders now, mostly for party frocks. Each dress took ages to complete because they all had elaborate hand-smocking, and special lace-trimmed petticoats and knickers to go underneath, so Aunty was stitching first thing in the morning to last thing at night – though after a dizzy turn she had started taking several breaks during the day, and sleeping in on Sundays.

Perhaps it was the extra rest or better food, but Aunty was starting to look almost pretty. Her face was plumper and her cheeks were pinker, and she walked with a spring in her step. She didn't scold me so much either – though she was horrified when I told her I'd been up to the manor.

She stopped beating the batter mixture. 'You did *what*?' she said, and she gripped the whisk tight. For a moment I was scared she'd beat me with it.

'It was all right, Aunty, I promise. Mr Benjamin invited me. I just bumped into him in the grounds. He looked ever so funny – he was wearing an old nightie.'

That distracted her. 'He was wearing a *nightgown*?'

'But he said he much preferred the pyjamas you made him. He'd left his clothes at his London place. He'd been to a party,' I explained.

'Oh, that Mr Benjamin!' said Aunty, shaking her head. She paused. 'You don't mean to say he was wearing one of *Lady Somerset's* nightgowns?'

'No, Aunty! It was one his father used to wear. He wouldn't wear a lady's nightie!' I said, spluttering with laughter.

'I wouldn't put anything past Mr Benjamin,' said Aunty. 'Mona, are you sure he invited you in? You weren't too forward? You haven't let me down?'

'Aunty, Mr Benjamin *likes* me,' I said, a little huffily. 'He showed me his drawing room.'

'And is it a total horror, like Ella said?'

'No, it's absolutely beautiful. Ella doesn't know what she's talking about,' I declared. 'It's the loveliest shade of pink, and the sofas and chairs are blue. It's so pretty.'

Aunty looked doubtful. 'It sounds more like a lady's bedroom,' she said. 'Pink and blue are very odd colours for a gentleman's drawing room. Still, I suppose

Mr Benjamin is a little odd himself, bless him.' She paused. 'And did you happen to notice any paintings?' she asked casually.

I knew she was wondering if Mr Benjamin really *did* have a picture of a naked man hanging on his wall. I feared she might think this a step too far.

'I didn't notice any in particular,' I said, and changed the subject.

I couldn't wait to show off to Maggie at school the next day. I told her I'd bumped into Mr Benjamin in the grounds and he'd only been wearing a nightshirt. I edited out the flowers in his hair – I thought she might laugh, though she laughed at the nightshirt anyway, and kept repeating, 'In his *nightshirt*!' until I felt like slapping her.

'It wasn't *his* nightshirt. He'd had to borrow it,' I said. 'Anyway, he invited me in and gave me a lovely breakfast – eggs and bacon and muffins and all sorts, even black grapes.'

But Maggie wouldn't leave the nightshirt alone. 'Didn't he put his trousers on? So he was sitting with you in just a nightshirt? That's rude! Calls himself a gentleman!'

'Of course he's a gentleman. Gentlemen don't bother with silly rules. They're above that sort of thing,' I said airily. 'Mr Benjamin's got a very big painting of a naked man over the mantelpiece and it's not rude at all, it's just modern art.'

'He's got a picture of a totally bare man hanging in his living room?' Maggie gasped.

'It's his *drawing* room,' I said, feeling superior because I knew the difference.

'So he drew it himself?' Maggie screwed up her face in disgust.

'No, no, you don't draw in a drawing room. You just sit there,' I said.

'And stare at a great big dirty picture!'

'It's not dirty!' I snapped, getting irritated with her. 'It's beautiful.'

Maggie burst out laughing. 'Beautiful!' she spluttered. 'Give me strength! You think a bloke's dangly bits are *beautiful*?'

'You can't see them in the picture. He's got his back turned,' I said.

'So what's beautiful then? His bum? You're a dirty little whatsit, Mona Smith.' She poked me in the chest, which made Peter Robinson come running over.

'What are you doing to Mona?' he demanded. 'Don't poke her like that, Maggie Higgins.'

'Oh, trust you to come shoving your oar in. You think your precious Mona is so pure and goody-goody. Wait till you hear this. She's been hanging around that snooty fancy-pants Mr Benjamin Somerset – the one who's inherited the manor – and she's seen his living room and thinks his painting of a completely naked man is *beautiful*.'

Peter blinked. Then he took a deep breath. 'So what?' he said. 'There are lots of paintings of naked ladies in art galleries. I saw one in my mother's magazine. Well, she wasn't completely naked, but she just had a little wisp of a thing around her. Mona's right – it is beautiful if it's art.'

I decided I might love him quite a lot now.

'Naked men aren't art, they're just disgusting,' said Maggie.

'What about Jesus?' I asked, suddenly inspired. 'Think of the statue of him in church! He's just got a loincloth and you can't possibly say he's disgusting, or the hand of God will reach down out of the clouds and smite you dead.'

That shut her up, but only for a moment.

'Anyway, Mr Benjamin's disgusting too, talking to you when he's just wearing his nightshirt,' she said.

'I keep *telling* you, it was a borrowed nightshirt because he'd been out at a party.'

Peter's expression changed. 'What? He was just wearing a nightshirt when he was with you?'

'Yes. Don't look like that. It was perfectly decent. The nightshirt came right down to the ground so he was completely covered up, and he wore a cloak over it too,' I said.

'Even so. Gentlemen shouldn't prance about in their nightclothes in front of ladies,' said Peter.

'He wasn't *prancing*. And I'm not a lady, I'm just a girl. Stop it – you're making it sound horrible and it wasn't a bit like that,' I said, getting cross.

'It still sounds wrong. And you know it is, because you're blushing,' said Peter.

'No I'm not!'

'Yes you are, you're bright red,' Maggie taunted me.

'Just shut up, both of you,' I said.

'It's not your fault, Mona – I'm just saying, he shouldn't have done that. You stay away from him. You hear all sorts about those Somersets. They're a weird bunch,' said Peter.

'You don't even know them, either of you. You're just jealous because I'm friends with Mr Benjamin now. I'm not listening to another word from either of you,' I said, and ran off.

Beside her sat another lady with the same bold expression.

12

MR BENJAMIN MOVED INTO THE MANOR on the last Saturday in June. I spent ages making him a welcome card. I pinched a sheet of good white paper from the stationery cupboard when Miss Nelson wasn't looking, and when I got home I folded it carefully and drew Mr Benjamin's drawing room on the front. I found it difficult to make the armchairs face the right way, and the sofa ended up several inches above the rug, but I had to leave it floating because I'd already done so many rubbings out that the paper was starting to look furry. I drew the picture of the naked man too, but only suggested his outline because Aunty was hovering nearby.

The card looked very boringly grey, while Mr Benjamin's drawing room was so colourful, so I had a go at painting it. I only had a small paint box (a gift from Lady Somerset's Christmas party two years previously). The Crimson Lake wouldn't make the right shade of pink, no matter how much I watered it down, and the Prussian Blue was nothing like that soft forget-me-not blue of the armchairs, but I did my best. It was hard working with such watery shades, and I couldn't stop some of the colours running.

'Oh dear,' said Aunty. 'You're going over the lines, Mona.'

'I can't help it!' I wailed.

'I think you'd better start again.'

'But I've only got one sheet of paper. It doesn't look *too* bad, does it, Aunty?'

'Well,' she said, and that was all.

I waited until the paint dried, and then I opened my card up and wrote in my very best handwriting:

Welcome to your New Home,
Mr Benjamin.

With love from Mona xxx

'But it's not Mr Benjamin's *new* home,' said Aunty, inspecting what I'd written. 'It's his ancestral home, where he grew up. And you shouldn't put *love*, that's far too forward. You should write something like *Yours respectfully*, and you should never put kisses on a gentleman's card.'

'Well, I have, so there,' I said mutinously.

I knew that she was probably right, and I had half a mind to tear the card up there and then, but I badly wanted an excuse to go up to the manor – I still couldn't believe I was welcome to drop in any time I cared to. So on Sunday morning I ran off, hoping that he might be dancing through the grass in his nightshirt again – but this time he was up and dressed.

He wore a navy smock with a little red checked scarf tied at the neck and workman's trousers, though he still managed to look stylish. He was standing by a row of removal vans, among real workmen who were trudging backwards and forwards with great tea chests, while a fair-haired man in overalls directed them here and there. He was the man who had accompanied Mr Benjamin to Lady Somerset's funeral. I suddenly wondered if he was the naked man in the portrait and came over all shy.

'Mona! Welcome! Ambrose, this is my special little friend Mona. Mona, Ambrose is my dearest friend, and an interior designer with exquisite taste to boot,' Mr Benjamin exclaimed.

Ambrose nodded briefly, not particularly interested in me, but Mr Benjamin still gave me his full attention.

'We are just about to break for cups of much-needed strong tea, because we've been toiling like beavers since eight this morning. You must join us. I dare say Cook can magic up some cake too. What's that you've got in your hand?'

'Oh, it's nothing,' I said foolishly, hiding the card behind my back. It seemed incredibly childish now and I wished I hadn't brought it.

'Nothing?' said Mr Benjamin, and suddenly pounced. 'Aha!'

He took the card and peered at it in seeming delight. 'Oh, Mona, did you do this yourself?'

'I'm sorry it's so smudgy,' I mumbled. 'And the shapes are all weird.'

'It's utterly perfect – practically a Cézanne!'

I had no idea who Cézanne was, but it seemed to be a compliment, and I beamed in relief.

Ella brought Mr Benjamin, Ambrose and me a big pot of tea and plum cake, and ferried the workmen off to the kitchen for their own refreshments. She glanced at me as if I should be scurrying along with the men.

Mr Benjamin chuckled. 'Oh, Mona, if looks could kill!' he whispered.

'She thinks I should know my place,' I said.

'Isn't Mona one of your many nieces?' Ambrose drawled, picking the fruit out of his cake like a little child.

'As good as,' said Mr Benjamin, putting his arm round me, while I glowed.

'This is absolutely scrumptious cake,' I said, with my mouth full.

'Yes, I totally agree. I gave dear Cook a hefty pay rise and fitted out her kitchen, so she's going the extra mile for me. I shall need an entire new wardrobe if I keep stuffing myself like this. I think I might be getting a little paunch already,' said Mr Benjamin, patting the entirely flat stomach under his smock.

Ambrose simply yawned. I frowned at him. He didn't seem a nice enough friend for Mr Benjamin, for all his looks.

'You must pop up for tea too, Mona,' Mr Benjamin continued. 'Rumour has it that chocolate cake is on the menu!'

'You're such a child, Benjy,' said Ambrose.

'And why not? It's utterly lovely being a child – isn't it, Mona?'

I wasn't sure I agreed with him, but I nodded emphatically.

'I had such a wonderful time playing here before I was sent off to that ghastly school,' said Mr Benjamin. 'My brothers were all much bigger than me, too old for childish games, but I didn't care a jot. I was perfectly happy playing by myself. I dressed up in all sorts – I became a pirate and a lion tamer and an acrobat and—'

'A fairy queen?' Ambrose interrupted rudely.

'Now, now,' said Mr Benjamin. 'As a matter of fact, I'd lie down in the meadow and watch for hours, hoping for just one glimpse of a real fairy.'

'I have a tiny doll called Farthing, and sometimes I pretend *she's* a fairy. Well, I did when I was little,' I confided.

Ambrose rolled his eyes, but Mr Benjamin seemed enchanted. 'Do you still have this tiny doll?' he asked. 'Oh, bring her here. Would she fit in a doll's house? Wait till mine is unpacked!'

I was surprised to find a man owning a doll's house, albeit an eccentric one like Mr Benjamin, but it made him even more interesting.

'I've always wanted my own doll's house,' I said. 'There was one in Mr Berner's shop last Christmas, but it was much too expensive.'

'As soon as the workmen find the crate in which it's

packed, I'll invite you over and we can arrange all the miniature furniture together. And you will come back for tea this afternoon, won't you? Do you like chocolate cake?' Mr Benjamin asked.

'It's my favourite!'

'Then you shall have a big slice. And bring your aunt with you. I'm sure she'd like to see the house – though I doubt she'll be as enthusiastic as you, Mona!'

I danced back home and talked non-stop to Aunty, recounting every word of our conversation.

'And chocolate cake, Aunty. He promised!' I said, licking my lips.

'You can't have cake twice in one day – it'll heat up your blood,' said Aunty. 'And, anyway, Mr Benjamin was only being kind, I'm sure. He doesn't really want you pestering him.'

'Yes he does, Aunty. He was insistent. And he invited you too.'

'Well, I'm certainly not poking my nose in when he's just moved here,' said Aunty. 'Perhaps we might call in when he's got everything sorted, in a week or so.'

'He said today! Aunty, we *have* to go! Mr Benjamin asked us and it would be very rude not to turn up,' I said.

This made her waver. I went on nagging all through lunch – not quite a joint this time, but we had roast potatoes and cabbage, and shared a big pork chop, and Aunty let me have the half with the kidney.

'We're not going up to the manor,' she insisted, but when I asked if there was pudding she said there was no point filling ourselves up with jam tart and custard if we were going to be gorging on chocolate cake later.

I kept quiet then, and did the washing-up, even scrubbing the greasy chop pan until it shone, while Aunty got back to her sewing. Then I lay on my bed for an hour or so, reading 'Cinderella' in my fairy-tale book. At half past three Aunty turned herself into a fairy godmother and appeared at my bedroom door in her best black beaded dress and her string of pearls (they weren't real – they came from Woolworths – but they still looked very impressive).

'Look at you, lolling on your bed, getting your dress crumpled. Brush yourself down, wash your hands and face, and let me retie those messy plaits. You'd better wear your best satin ribbons – these are a bit frayed.'

I tidied myself up as quickly as I could, scared she might suddenly change her mind. Then we set off hand in hand, both of us wearing little white gloves. As we approached the manor, Aunty's stride lost its purpose. The furniture vans were still there, along with a couple of cars – Mr Benjamin's Lagonda, and another shiny black one with a chauffeur polishing the hubcaps energetically. He nodded at Aunty and she blushed.

'Whose car is that, then?' she hissed to me.

'It'll be that Ambrose's. You know, Mr Benjamin's friend, the good-looking one,' I said.

'I'm not sure we should call in,' Aunty said. 'Let's just go home, Mona.'

'No! Come on,' I said, pulling her towards the front door.

'We can't go in the front! That's for gentry,' she hissed. 'I always went round the back when I did a fitting for Lady Somerset.'

'If we're Mr Benjamin's friends and we've been specially invited, we count as gentry,' I told her.

'Anyone would think you'd swallowed a bally book of etiquette,' she said, giving me a little shake, but she summoned up her courage, marched up to the front door and knocked.

Ella answered the door in afternoon black silk, with a spotless fresh cap and apron. Her face contorted. 'Come in . . . madam,' she said.

'Oh, don't, Ella,' said Aunty. 'I'm all in a tizz. Mona said that Mr Benjamin specially invited us both. Did he?'

'How would I know?' she said, sniffing. 'Wait here in the hall, please.'

I squeezed Aunty's hand and we stepped inside. She peered around in astonishment. 'It's all so different!' she said, craning her head to see the huge sun light fitting properly.

'It's lovely, isn't it?' I said.

'Well,' said Aunty, not at all sure.

Ella returned. 'Come with me,' she said curtly.

'We are expected?' asked Aunty.

Ella nodded, but as she ushered us into the drawing room she said, 'He's got other company too.'

It was too late for Aunty to turn tail and run for it. Mr Benjamin was standing beaming at us, making welcoming gestures, while Ambrose reclined on a sofa, not even bothering to turn round. There were three other people sitting on the blue armchairs, all complete strangers. They *were* strange too – excessively so.

There was a tall thin man with spectacles and a wispy beard, wearing a green shirt and orange corduroy trousers. His brown boots had surely never been polished. He looked as if he could do with a good scrub himself. His long narrow hands ended in dirty fingernails. I'd have thought him one of the workmen, but the thin reedy voice telling some anecdote was quite definitely upper class.

Then there was a lady who seemed very young at first, but when I looked closely I saw that she was actually about Aunty's age, or even older. She had astonishingly short black hair, and wore a brief green dress showing a great deal of her legs. Her arms were bare, apart from clanking silver bangles, and she had silver shoes to match, with fancy buckles. She was very striking and her face was pretty, but there was a sharpness about her. I didn't like the way she was looking at Aunty and me.

Beside her sat another lady with the same bold expression and dark bobbed hair, but she really *was* young, though she wore a lot of face paint. Her thin lips were crimson, which made her teeth look very white. She wasn't wearing a dress at all – instead she wore a striped jersey and *trousers*, fitting tightly over her hips but with very baggy legs, like a sailor's. She was smoking a cigarette in a long ebony holder.

Aunty and I stood there, shifting awkwardly from foot to foot while Mr Benjamin waited for the tall grubby man to finish his story. In the end he had to interrupt.

'Excuse me a moment, Alistair. These are my delightful neighbours, Miss Watson and her niece, Mona. Do let me introduce you to my friends! They've driven down from London to help me move in. This is Lady Arabella Dooley.' The older lady gave us a little nod and adjusted the hem of her green dress. 'And her daughter, the Honourable Desiree Dooley.' She waved her cigarette at us. 'And my dear friend Alistair Michael – the artist, you know.'

We nodded, though we'd never heard of him. Aunty gave a stiff little bow. I dithered, not sure whether to curtsy or not.

'No formalities, my dears. Come and sit with me,' said Mr Benjamin, patting the empty sofa. 'Ella, I think we're ready for our tea. And chocolate cake.' He gave me a little nudge.

I smiled at him gratefully. Mr Michael carried on talking, not including Aunty or me in the conversation, which was rude but rather a relief. I saw that Aunty was feeling awfully out of place and felt bad for making her come. Desiree offered her a cigarette, and she squeaked a refusal. I couldn't help staring at Desiree. At first I thought her short hair quite dreadful, but it wasn't as stark-looking as her mother's, and when she moved it danced about her head and shone like silk. Perhaps it looked all right after all. Her trousers were certainly a shock, but then she stood up to stub out her cigarette, and I loved the way they fell fluidly down to her instep. I saw Aunty eyeing them too.

'Those two clearly find your trousers appalling,' Lady Arabella said to her daughter, amused. Her voice was sharp, and her accent cut-glass.

'I like them,' I said.

'Do you really?' said Desiree.

'Oh, Mona has impeccably *avant-garde* taste,' Mr Benjamin told her.

'But no doubt *you* find them shocking,' Desiree said to Aunty.

'I find them interesting,' she murmured.

'You're observing the cut of the trousers, aren't you, Miss Watson?' said Mr Benjamin. 'You should see the pyjamas Miss Watson has made for me! Oh, how you'll envy me them, Desiree. Purple silk, ultra exotic.'

'Perhaps you might care to make me a pair too . . .' said Desiree.

'Perhaps,' Aunty said. 'Perhaps not,' she added, which made Mr Benjamin laugh.

'Really, Desiree, you do obsess over your thousand and one outfits, fetching though they are,' said Mr Michael. 'When will you realize that it's the inner you that matters? I don't care a jot what *I* wear. In fact, I frequently fling on the same thing day after day without even noticing.'

He might not notice, but it was perfectly obvious to everyone else that his jersey and trousers had been flung on too many times without a good wash. And how could he say that he didn't care what clothes he wore? He must have gone out of his way to find a pair of trousers in that shade of orange. I glanced at Aunty and I could tell she was thinking the same thing.

'So you're a seamstress, are you, Miss Watson?' Lady Arabella asked.

'A dressmaker,' Aunty mumbled.

'A dress designer par excellence,' Mr Benjamin insisted. 'Miss Watson used to make all my mother's outfits, and they couldn't have been more elaborate.'

'I can imagine,' said Lady Arabella. 'So you specialize

in clothes for the *older* lady, do you, Miss Watson?' She clearly didn't mean herself.

I hated the way she was looking at Aunty.

'She makes clothes for every kind of lady – and children too,' I piped up. 'Her children's range is sold in Harrods, and that's the finest shop in the whole country, so there!'

'Mona!' said Aunty, mortified, but Mr Benjamin was delighted.

'That's it, Mona, you put Lady Arabella in her place,' he said.

Ella brought in the tea and an enormous glossy chocolate cake. She divided it expertly with a cake slice, and offered it first to Lady Arabella, who pulled a silly face.

'Oh no, I have to think of my figure,' she said.

Desiree would take only the weeniest slice, and then toyed with it, licking the chocolate icing with her pink tongue in an affected way. Mr Michael refused the cake as if it was poisonous, and told us we would all be much healthier if we avoided sugar and became vegetarians. Aunty and I had existed largely on potatoes and onions and carrots, and we hadn't felt particularly healthy then, just starving hungry. However, even Aunty shook her head when Ella offered her a slice.

Ambrose had dozed off and, though Ella cleared her throat and murmured his name, he chose to keep his eyes shut.

'Well, well, Mona. It's up to you and me,' said Mr Benjamin. 'Please don't let me down. I can't have the cake going back to the kitchen barely touched – poor Cook will be offended.'

'I'd like a very, very large slice, please, Ella,' I said, and started eating it very quickly in case Aunty protested. I washed it down with my tea, which tasted surprisingly flowery.

The conversation moved on to the cakes on offer at the Café Royal, which seemed to be a place in London, and sounded nothing like my idea of a café.

'Can we go there when I come up to Harrods in the holidays?' I asked.

'I'm not sure it sounds very suitable,' Aunty murmured, which made them laugh, even Mr Benjamin.

Then Lady Arabella started raving about some art exhibition she'd just seen, and Mr Michael began discussing people I'd never heard of.

'Do you care for the Vorticist movement, Miss Watson?' Lady Arabella asked.

'I couldn't say, I'm sure,' said Aunty.

I tried to remember how Mr Benjamin had described my home-made card. 'We prefer Cézanne,' I said.

Mr Benjamin clapped and, surprisingly, Desiree said, 'Bravo!'

'I think we'd better be going, Mr Benjamin,' Aunty mumbled. 'We didn't mean to intrude. We didn't realize you had guests.'

'You and your niece are my guests, Miss Watson,' Mr Benjamin insisted, but Aunty stood up, determined to escape.

I had to cram half my chocolate cake into my mouth at once, which meant I could scarcely say goodbye. I choked when I tried, and chocolate crumbs shot out of my mouth.

'Mona!' Aunty dragged me out of the drawing room so quickly that my feet scarcely touched the floor.

We weren't quite quick enough though. We both heard Lady Arabella say, 'Benjamin, darling, why on earth are you making such a fuss of that sad old spinster and the pert little girl?'

Ella heard her too, because she was hovering outside. I thought she might look triumphant, but she just shook her head pityingly. It made it even worse somehow.

We didn't say anything – nor did we talk to each other as we hurried back to the cottage. I didn't even glance at Aunty until we reached the front door – and then I saw that her eyes were brimming with tears.

'Oh, Aunty, I'm sorry I let you down,' I said, starting to cry myself. I wasn't sure what *pert* meant, but it didn't sound nice.

'You were very rude,' said Aunty. 'But I'm glad. That Lady Arabella is no lady. She just wanted to make a fool of me – and she succeeded too.' She fumbled in her pocket for her handkerchief, and took off her spectacles to give her eyes a dab. She looked so vulnerable without them – I could see the little pink marks on either side of her nose where they pinched.

'No she didn't. *She* looked the fool. When she crossed her legs I saw her knickers,' I said. I picked up Sixpence, who was mewling happily, welcoming us back. 'She's hungry – I'll give her some milk. And I'll make us a cup of tea, shall I, Aunty?'

'We've only just *had* tea,' she said, but we shared a pot even so. It was comforting – so much nicer than the strange sort served at the manor. I nibbled a reassuring digestive biscuit, even though I was full of chocolate cake.

'I hope Mr Benjamin won't keep on inviting his horrid friends. Do you think he *likes* that Desiree?'

'I think it's her mother who's setting her cap at Mr Benjamin, flashing those great white legs all the time,' said Aunty. 'Unless that display was for Mr Michael's benefit.'

We both snorted at the idea.

'Or maybe they like Mr Ambrose. Now, he really *was* rude, ignoring everyone,' I said.

'Yes, he was.' Aunty shook her head. 'Whatever would Lady Somerset say if she could see that arty rabble in her drawing room? I'm shocked at Mr Benjamin, for all he was kind to us. I wouldn't go up to the manor again, even if he came and begged me.'

'Nor me,' I said, wanting to sound loyal. I hated them looking down on poor Aunty and thinking her a sad old spinster. She couldn't help it if no one had wanted to marry her. Or had they? Had Aunty had a sweetheart who died in the war? I wondered if I dared ask her. But perhaps that would be pert.

I didn't mean it when I said I wouldn't go up to the manor again. Of course I would. I loved Mr Benjamin. I couldn't bear not to see him any more. I wished he could be *my* sweetheart when I grew up.

'Poor you!' said Maggie.

13

PETER ROBINSON STILL WANTED TO BE MY
sweetheart, even though we'd had words about
Mr Benjamin. Maggie was cool with me for a couple of
days, but then we made friends again too. Every day we
compared notes about our kittens. We even started up a
Kitten Club, Maggie and Peter and me. I made badges
out of thick cardboard and safety pins borrowed from
Aunty. I was the best at drawing, so I did a ginger kitten
on Peter's, a black kitten with a white face on Maggie's,
and a beautiful black kitten on mine. I added a pink
tongue on Sixpence's portrait to give it a bit of colour,
but it reminded me of Desiree, so I scribbled over it with
black crayon.

We invented a kitten game too – a variation of tag,

where we had to mew loudly if we were caught. It was a bit pointless really, but it meant that the three of us could play together without falling out.

Then, one morning at Prayers, Miss Nelson announced to everyone that the school inspector was coming at the end of the week. There were groans. Miss Nelson hushed us and said we were being silly, but she didn't look too happy either. The school inspector was a wizened old man called Mr Riley. All the boys, and most of the girls, in our class were taller than him – and yet the moment he stomped into the hall there was total silence. If you fidgeted or yawned he'd throw blackboard chalk at you. He once even threw the wooden blackboard eraser and made a boy's head bleed.

He'd ask us terrifying questions. The little ones only had to recite their two times table and chant their way through the alphabet, but when it was our turn we had to parse a sentence and do complicated multiplication sums in our heads and answer his general knowledge questions. They were nearly all of a religious nature: *Which is the shortest book in the Holy Bible? Spell Deuteronomy! Give three examples of Our Lord's miracles*. And finally he would pick an older child at random and command them to recite Psalm 121 or Corinthians 13, and if they weren't word perfect he would berate them as if his small frame contained the wrath of God itself.

Over the next few days Miss Nelson did her best to prepare us, but everyone became so anxious they couldn't concentrate. She snapped at us and said we'd get her into trouble. But it wasn't Mr Riley who turned up on Friday! Since his last visit he had retired, and the board sent a new school inspector. When we filed into the school, he was standing at the front, a smiley man in a checked shirt and corduroys and a knitted tie. He was young enough to be Mr Riley's son – maybe even his grandson.

'Good morning, children. Settle down now!' Miss Nelson twittered, pink in the face. 'This is the new school inspector, Mr White. Say good morning!'

'Good morn-ing, Mis-ter White,' we droned obediently.

'Good morning, children. And isn't it a lovely morning too! Tell me what you noticed on the way to school today. Who saw a bird or a butterfly? How many types of wild flowers did you see by the wayside? Who saw an oak or an elm tree? Where are you likely to spot a yew? I saw several magnificent specimens as I walked through the village this morning.'

We all blinked at this new type of question. We were country children. We'd never had a nature study lesson in our lives, but we'd grown up knowing and naming the flora and fauna all around us. I knew less than most because Aunty was town born and bred, and thought most birds were sparrows and most flowers dandelions, and wouldn't have known the difference between an oak and an elm.

Still, I'd become an expert on the things that grew in churchyards, and I knew that the huge trees with very dark green leaves and twisted roots were yews, so I put my hand up along with all the others.

'Yes, the girl with the black plaits,' said Mr White.

'You find yews in our churchyard, sir. They're very old, as if they've been there hundreds of years,' I said.

'And they often have too! Some people reckon that the yews were planted long before the churches were built. Why do you think that would be?'

Maggie waved her hand, not wanting to be outdone. 'Because folk in the old days liked yew trees?'

'Yes, they liked them in a special place. Why would this place be special, do you think?'

'It was where they buried their loved ones,' I said.

'I think you're absolutely right. Yews are poisonous to many animals, so they don't come trampling around disturbing graveyards. They are left in peace.'

'I don't like graveyards – you get ghosties there!' one of the little girls piped up, and her friends started shrieking.

'There are no such things as ghosts,' Miss Nelson said firmly. 'Mona, don't shake your head like that!'

'I think there *are* ghosts, Miss Nelson. And if you listen very carefully they whisper to you,' I said.

'Do they?' asked Mr White, looking interested.

'Nonsense!' said Miss Nelson. 'Mr White, would you like to test the children on their arithmetic now?'

Mr White opened up a suitcase full of brightly coloured toy blocks and tumbled them out onto the floor. He set the little ones counting each brick, seeing who could make the tallest tower. I rather hoped he might let us older ones join in. I ached to make a tower. I had Farthing tucked in my pocket. She would make a beautiful Rapunzel.

'Now, while the little ones are busy constructing their towers, shall we try a spot of mental arithmetic?' Mr White asked. 'Let's pretend I'm going to give each of you two shillings,' he started.

There were multiple squeals of joy. I had to press my lips together to stop myself saying I'd actually held two *pound notes* in my hand.

'Children! Don't get overexcited now! Mr White isn't *really* going to give you two shillings.' Miss Nelson was starting to look exasperated.

'I want you to imagine going to the shops in the village and buying whatever you want. You can be virtuous, and spend most of it on groceries for your families. Or you can be very greedy, and spend it on sweets for yourself. You can buy a top or a boat or a little doll in the toyshop. You can buy whatever you wish, but you must add all the prices up in your head and then tell me how much change you get from your two shillings,' said Mr White.

There was an excited general discussion as everyone said what they wanted to do with the money.

Miss Nelson clapped her hands. 'Children! This is mental arithmetic. That means *silence* – doesn't it, Mr White?'

'I suppose it does, though it's fun to let the children express themselves,' he said, smiling.

Miss Nelson looked at him as if *he* was mental – though I thought he was wonderful. I knew which toys I wanted to buy, but I couldn't keep track of all the money in my head. I tried counting on my fingers, but the sums disappeared into thin air. I found arithmetic such a struggle that I sometimes resorted to squinting at Maggie's notebook and copying, but I couldn't squint inside her head.

When Mr White asked for answers I didn't put my hand up. Some of the children got their sums right, some got them wrong, but at least they all had answers.

'What about you, Mona?' Mr White asked, looking directly at me. 'How much change do you have from your two shillings?'

Sudden inspiration struck. 'I bought the biggest doll in Mr Berner's toyshop. She cost one shilling and eleven pence. I'm sorry I've been so extravagant. I've only got one penny left.' Any fool could work that out, even me.

'That's cheating, Mona,' said Miss Nelson.

'I think it's a rather clever reply,' said Mr White. 'Especially as I expect mental arithmetic isn't Mona's strong point. Now, let's see which infant has constructed the tallest tower. Shall we all count the bricks out loud?'

When every tower was counted and the tallest builder given a pat on the back, Mr White said, 'Now, let's set those towers a-tumbling!'

There was a wonderful crash as the bricks scattered. Miss Nelson put her hands over her ears.

'Marvellous,' said Mr White. 'You will all make wonderful demolition men when you grow up. Now, one last task, ladies and gentlemen. Little ones at the front, I'd like you to draw me a splendid picture of your home. The rest of you, please write me an essay on the same subject, but you can embellish your work with a drawing at the end if you have time. Right, everyone get started!'

'I'm not sure there will be enough paper to go round,' said Miss Nelson anxiously. 'The little ones usually use slates.'

'Oh, Miss Nelson, where's the joy in that? They should be using huge sheets of paper and big pots of paint,' Mr White insisted. 'Ah well, they will have to make do with these.' He found a drawing pad in his suitcase, tore out several pages and handed them round, along with some packets of big, bright wax crayons. I looked at them longingly, but we older children had to make do with our own scrubby notebooks and brown ink.

I sat down beside Maggie, wondering how to start. She had begun already.

There are ten people who live in My House.
Mum and Dad and Johnnie and Mabel and
Sarah-Jane and Johnnie and Bertie and
Bertha and baby Sam and Mittens and
me. Mum and Dad are my parents. They
are kind. Tom and Johnnie and Bertie are
my brothers. They are norty. Mabel and
Sarah-Jane and Bertha are my sisters.
Mabel and Sarah-Jane are mean but
Bertha is swete. Sam isn't anything much
becos he is a baby. Mittens is my kitten.
She is very swete.

She saw me peering. 'What? You haven't even started and I'm halfway down the page already,' she said smugly. She started listing every item of furniture in her home.

I yawned and dipped my pen into the inkwell. Someone had stuffed it with little pieces of blotting paper that stuck to the nib. I made an enormous blot writing *My Home* at the top of my page.

'Uh-oh!' said Maggie. 'You'll get a black mark for making a mess.'

'I don't care,' I said, but I did care dreadfully. I wanted to impress Mr White.

I carefully tore out the page with the blot and started again, using Maggie's inkwell this time. I wrote the title again, very carefully. I didn't want to write about the two people in my home – three including Sixpence. I didn't want to list our few possessions.

> I recently inherited my dear mother's enormous manor house. I have completely refurnished it. Mother had very old-fashioned taste, bless her. I am extremely avongard.

'You fibber!' Maggie whispered indignantly. 'And what does that silly word mean?'

'It means modern,' I said. 'And I am. Now you get on with your essay and I'll get on with mine.'

Now I'd started I couldn't stop. I wrote about the light that looked like a sun in the hall, and said I sometimes lay down beneath it in my bathing suit, which made the servants shriek. I described my favourite drawing room in loving detail. I decided not to describe my large portrait of a naked man, and substituted several Cézannes instead. I described my daily tea parties, with an entire chocolate cake for each guest. I described the guests in detail too: my tall, thin artist friend often got cake crumbs in his beard, my smart lady friend wore skirts that showed legs as white as lard, my young lady friend clinked her bangles, and my lazy designer friend sprawled on the sofa and fell fast asleep.

When all my eccentric guests had left (the sleeping designer removed in a wheelbarrow), I held another tea party for the cook and the maid and the very special dressmaking lady, which was much more fun, and we all danced the Charleston until midnight.

'What on earth are you going on about?' said Maggie, squinting at my writing. 'It's a pack of lies!'

'It's a *story*,' I said, but I was starting to worry.

'Time's up, children!' Mr White called. 'Hand in your work please.'

I decided it might be better *not* to hand mine in, but before I could slip my notebook into my desk Mr White snatched it up and added it to his pile, while Miss Nelson gathered up the little children's drawings. Many of them were random scribbles, and she shook her head mournfully at the waste of paper.

Mr White examined all the pictures and then read our essays. He was taking quite a while getting through everyone's work, so we had extra playtime. I peered through the window, trying to work out which of the dun-covered notebooks was mine. Sometimes Mr White simply glanced at a page and shut the notebook with a sigh. I hoped he wouldn't do that to mine.

The Kitten Club gathered in a corner, but we didn't talk about our pets. We discussed Mr White. Maggie said he looked like a film star, though she thought his knitted tie silly. Peter liked him because he didn't shout or throw chalk around.

'*I* like him because he does everything differently,' I said. 'He's very *avant garde*, like Mr Benjamin.'

'Oh, you and your fancy words,' said Maggie. 'Mr White's not a bit like your precious Mr Benjamin. Mr White's a real man, not a silly twerp.'

I felt my face going red, especially when Peter sniggered. 'You button your lip, Maggie Higgins. And take that smirk off your face, Peter Robinson. Don't you dare say another word about Mr Benjamin,' I said.

'Look at her, Peter! She's gone all moony-eyed,' said Maggie. 'She's really sweet on him!'

'That's plain daft,' said Peter, looking peeved.

At last the bell went for us to file back into school. Mr White was standing there smiling, the drawings neatly stashed on one side, the notebooks on the other. He dealt with the little ones first, praising each child extravagantly, even if they'd just done a lopsided square and a family of blobs.

'You're being very kind, Mr White, but I don't think we'd better turn their heads,' Miss Nelson murmured.

'On the contrary, Miss Nelson, I feel that every child needs encouragement – and I truly think they've done some excellent, colourful work. I hope you're going to pin their efforts up,' he replied.

Miss Nelson looked appalled. The classroom boasted a picture of Jesus in a white gown holding a lantern, an alphabet frieze and several times tables charts, all neatly displayed and held in place with gold drawing pins. I could see she was thinking that fifteen or twenty scribbles would ruin the effect.

'Now for the essays!' said Mr White.

I felt my tummy clench. He started handing them out one by one, saying kind things to everyone. He even praised Daft Dougie, who could barely print his own name.

'Well done, lad. I can see you've made a great effort. Perhaps Miss Nelson might see fit to give you a little extra tuition in spare moments, to get you up to speed,' he said.

'I think that might be a waste of time, Mr White. Dougie's a little simple, poor lad, and can't learn like the others,' Miss Nelson told him.

'You must never give up on a child, Miss Nelson,' he corrected her.

'When you've been teaching as long as I have, Mr White, you realize that there are some youngsters who are hopeless cases,' she said crisply. 'Your predecessor, Mr Riley, didn't expect miracles.'

'Oh, I've met Mr Riley. A principled man, but rather a dinosaur,' Mr White said breezily.

I had a sudden vision of Mr Riley as a wizened grey dinosaur, and I had to hold my nose to stop myself snorting with laughter.

'What are you doing, Mona Smith?' Miss Nelson snapped.

'Nothing, Miss Nelson,' I said, practically choking.

'Ah, Mona Smith!' Mr White drew my notebook from underneath the pile. 'I was keeping your effort till last. Now tell me, Mona, do you really live in a palatial manor with real Cézannes on the wall?'

The children gasped, and Miss Nelson was angry with me.

'Honestly, Mona! What nonsense have you been writing? I'm so sorry, Mr White. The child lives in a little cottage with her maiden aunt. It's all lies.'

I hung my head. Half the children were sniggering now, and Mr White was mocking me. I couldn't bear it. I shut my eyes tight to stop my tears.

'On the contrary, Miss Nelson, I think Mona has written an imaginative masterpiece,' said Mr White.

I peeped at him with one eye. He didn't mean it, did he?

'Yes, Mona, I never expected such a stylish and convincing essay, and you're so bang up to the minute with your modern artistic taste. You have such a sharp satirical eye. What books have you been reading?'

'Fairy tales, sir. And *A Little Princess*.'

He shook his head. 'Then your vision is all your own, and all the more dazzling for that. How old are you, Mona?'

'I'm ten, sir.'

'Clearly advanced for your age. I take it you've put the child in for a scholarship, Miss Nelson?'

'Our children don't sit any outside examinations, Mr White. There's no call for it,' said Miss Nelson.

'Well, *I'm* calling for it! There's a special second-chance examination at Hailbury High School for Girls this very Saturday – tomorrow! It's for bright children who missed the scholarship exam in the spring. Can you get your aunt to take you there for ten o'clock, Mona? Bring a pen and a pencil and your birth certificate to prove who you are. I'm certain you will pass the exam with flying colours.'

I stared at him. His voice suddenly sounded muffled. He divided into two Mr Whites, and then went so blurry I couldn't see him properly. I felt prickles of sweat all over me. And then I fainted dead away.

I came to in the little stationery room. It wasn't much more than a cupboard, but it was the only place Miss Nelson could think of. I was lying on the floor with her folded cardigan under my head. It smelled faintly of coal-tar soap and peppermint.

'Oh my goodness, Mona, you gave us all a fright! Whatever did you do that for?' she demanded, as if I'd fainted on purpose.

'I don't know,' I said, trying to sit up.

'Better stay lying down for a few minutes!' said Mr White, peering over Miss Nelson's shoulder. 'Sorry, dear, I didn't mean to get you in a state. You will take the examination tomorrow though, won't you? I'll send the adjudicators a message to say I've authorized it. And you will remember your birth certificate? We've had thirteen- and fourteen-year-olds trying to pass themselves off as Juniors before now. You don't have to be frightened – you'll probably enjoy it enormously. Just write them another essay like the one you wrote today!'

I kept nodding, though I was still only taking in half of what he was saying. I'd suddenly stopped being weird Mona, the girl who didn't belong. Now I was clever Mona, imaginative Mona, intelligent Mona. I imagined going to the girls' school in Hailbury, wearing that smart navy uniform, the tunic with the tassel, the gold-edged blazer, the straw boater. Aunty would be so proud of me!

'That's it, you've got some colour in your cheeks now,' said Mr White. 'Well, I'd better be on my way. I've caused enough havoc in your school for one morning, Miss Nelson, haven't I?' He winked at me. 'Chin up then, Mona. Good luck tomorrow.'

When he'd gone, Miss Nelson said I'd better stay lying down. She left the door open and told me to call out if I felt faint again or needed to visit the lavvy. I lay there feeling special. After about ten minutes Peter Robinson came to see me.

'I told Miss Nelson I needed a new pencil, but I don't really. I just wanted to see if you were all right,' he whispered.

'That's nice of you, Peter.'

'And are you? All right, I mean?'

I nodded.

'That's good,' he said, and gave my hand a quick squeeze.

'Peter Robinson, don't you go disturbing Mona now!' Miss Nelson called.

'I'm not, Miss Nelson, promise.' He reluctantly let go

of my hand. 'I'm going to walk you all the way home, and I don't care what Maggie says,' he insisted.

He did just that, telling Maggie I needed to be accompanied because I might faint again, and hit my head, and lie unconscious for hours. They marched on either side of me, telling me how weird I'd looked when I fainted.

'Your eyes went right up into the back of your head. Talk about creepy!' said Maggie.

'And you were all floppy, as if you didn't have any bones inside you any more,' said Peter.

'For goodness' sake!' I snapped. 'Stop going on about me fainting. *That's* not the important bit. What about Mr White saying I must take the scholarship exam?'

'Yes, poor you!' said Maggie. 'But he can't make you, can he?'

'*Poor* me?'

'Well, how awful for you, having to do exams on a Saturday! They'll be very hard too, especially the arithmetic, and you won't have me to copy off, will you?'

'I don't always copy,' I said.

'Yes you do. You're hopeless at sums, you always have been. You'll probably come bottom in the exam and then feel bad about it,' said Maggie.

'But Mr White thinks she's ever so clever,' said Peter loyally. 'Especially with her writing. He kept going on about it, didn't he?'

'He just liked it because she was pretending to be posh and daft like her precious Mr Benjamin. If Mona had written about her real home, he wouldn't have cared tuppence about her essay.'

'He said I had vision,' I said fiercely, because his praise had meant so much and I couldn't let Maggie spoil it for me. 'He said my work was an imaginative masterpiece.'

She rolled her eyes. 'Yes, and he said Daft Dougie had done well too,' she reminded me. 'He can't even spell his own name right.'

'You keep quiet, Maggie. I bet she'll do brilliantly in the examinations. I think she'll come top!' Peter said.

'Well, what if she does? You wouldn't really want to go to that awful high school with all the posh girls, would you, Mona? I bet it's called a high school because they talk in awful high-pitched voices that make your head ring. And they'll look down on you because they live in big posh houses and you're just a village girl, sort of.'

I shivered. Was Maggie right? I wondered.

'But imagine going to a proper school where you learn all sorts,' I said. 'Teachers who really know stuff, not like silly old Miss Nelson. Then I could – I could—'

'You could what?' said Maggie.

'I could be someone important. I could get a good job if I had qualifications,' I said.

'But don't you want to marry?' Peter asked. 'Ladies don't work once they're married. My mother doesn't work. She can do whatever she likes. It's a shame your aunty isn't married – she has to work so hard at her sewing.'

'Yes, but I might find it a bit boring, just sitting at home all day doing nothing much,' I said.

'You'll have babies to look after,' said Maggie.

I thought about it. I liked little Bertha, but I didn't think I wanted to play with her all day long, let alone feed her and change her and rock her to sleep.

'I might prefer to have a good job,' I said. 'I might be an interior designer, for instance.'

'What on earth's that?' asked Maggie.

'You decide how rooms are going to look, and choose the colours and the curtains and the furniture,' I said.

'Well, that's pretty easy. You whitewash the walls and stick the table and chairs and beds in and it's all done.'

'Then I might be an artist,' I went on. 'No I won't. I know, I'll be a writer,' I said, and I felt a sudden burst of joy. Of course! Mr White had been impressed by my essay. I loved reading books. I could write my own books when I was grown up – clever, imaginative books, very modern and daring and *avant garde*.

I suddenly leaped into the air and then skipped along with sheer happiness.

'You don't half look daft, Waggle-Bum,' Maggie said sourly.

I turned round and stuck my tongue out at her. 'You're just jealous,' I said.

'I am *not*! I told you, I wouldn't want to go to no high school, not in a million years,' said Maggie, but her voice wobbled and she suddenly looked as if she might start crying.

I slowed to a stop. Maggie hardly ever cried, not even when one of the big lads punched her in the stomach – she punched him right back, and kicked him in a rude place too.

'What's the matter, Mags?' I asked.

'It's because *you* want to go,' she said, tears starting to roll down her cheeks.

'But *you* don't want to – you just said.'

'She'll miss you,' said Peter, screwing up his face at me as if he couldn't believe I was being so stupid. 'And so will I. And you're acting as if you don't care tuppence.'

I stared at them both, stricken. 'But we'll still stay friends and have the Kitten Club and everything,' I said.

'No we won't!' Maggie sobbed. 'How could we meet up? You'll have to travel all the way to Hailbury and back each day. We won't be able to play together on the way home, and you won't be calling in at mine for your bread and dripping.'

'Or mine,' said Peter mournfully, forgetting to be discreet.

Maggie was too distracted to notice. 'And I won't *have* anyone to sit next to me or play with at break time. It will be so lonely!'

'Oh, Maggie, I'm sorry,' I said, trying to put my arms round her, but she pushed me away. 'I'll always be your best friend.'

'No you won't. You'll swagger about like Lady Muck in your posh school uniform and start talking in a silly high voice and look down on me,' said Maggie.

'And you won't want to be my sweetheart any more,' said Peter. 'You've never really wanted to be anyway. You'll make friends with someone posh like that sissy Mr Benjamin.'

'Don't call him names!'

'There you go. You stick up for him through thick and thin, no matter what. You'd care if you couldn't see Mr Blooming Benjamin any more. It's all his fault.

He's given you ideas above your station, that's what Mother says,' Maggie told me.

I was really hurt. I loved kind Mrs Higgins. I couldn't bear the idea that she was discussing me like that behind my back. I felt bad about Maggie and Peter. I knew I'd been horribly tactless, but they were both being so mean to me now, spoiling everything.

'Just shut up, will you? I'm sick of you both. If I get into the high school, I won't miss you one little bit,' I said, and I flounced off by myself.

I turned the little gold key in the lock.

14

IT WAS AUNTY'S DAY AT HARRODS. I WAS
supposed to go to Mrs Higgins for my tea, but that
seemed impossible now. I was glad that Sixpence was
big enough to be left at home. She'd have to wait a bit
longer to see me because I needed to visit the graveyard.
I stroked the rough bark of the yew trees, and then lay
down carefully on top of Mother.

'You don't think I've got ideas above my station, do
you, Mother?' I whispered down to her through the
tickling grass.

Mother said that it was a good thing to be ambitious.

I told her all the lovely things Mr White had said to
me, word for word, and Mother said she was very, very
proud of me.

I glowed all over, though the grass was damp and my

dress was getting wet. I stayed until I started to shiver, and then I pressed a fond kiss right into the earth and trailed home.

Sixpence greeted me with enthusiastic mews, and I picked her up and made a fuss of her, rubbing my cheek against her soft head. It was still lonely without Aunty there, even though she was always in her workroom. She wasn't expecting me to be home for tea, so there was nothing much in the larder. I looked at a tin of sardines, wrinkled my nose, and mashed half of them up for Sixpence instead. I made do with the heel of a loaf and some jam, and then wandered around the cottage, unable to settle to anything.

I thought about running up to the manor, but Mr Benjamin was having visitors for the weekend, and they usually arrived on the Friday evening. I hated the thought of encountering them, especially Lady Arabella. I stayed in my room and picked up my book, but soon tossed it aside and started another.

I couldn't even get lost in an old favourite like *A Little Princess*. It made me worry that the high school might be like Miss Minchin's seminary. Even if it was, I still wanted to go there. It was my chance to better myself. I didn't want to slave all day and half the night sewing a sparkly dress for a young lady. I wanted to *be* the young lady. There wasn't much chance of my becoming a dressmaker like Aunty anyway. She'd taught me how to sew but she fretted at my incompetence.

Nor did I want to wear an apron and cap and call people Madam when I served the tea, like Ella. I wanted to *be* the Madam, and wear an outrageously short frock and smoke a cigarette in a long holder while my bangles slid up and down my bare arm. I would be a clever young woman of good education, a famous writer of witty modern novels, the talk of literary London. All Mr Benjamin's guests would *beg* him to invite me to his weekend parties because I was so bright and famous.

I thought about the examination tomorrow. I didn't have too many qualms about the essay. No matter what the subject, I would simply pretend to be a Somerset. But what about the arithmetic? Maggie was right: I was hopeless at it. Perhaps I'd better practise.

I tried setting myself sums in an old notebook. I could do adding and subtracting and multiplication and short division. I wavered a bit over long division, and went to pieces whenever I attempted a fraction. I could never unravel those terrifying problems where five men are asked to dig a field thirty-two yards wide and sixty-four yards long. I'd always go into a daydream, wondering why they were digging the wretched field. Were they going to plant cabbages or keep donkeys? Were they creating a lido so that all the village children would have a pool to splash in? Did they need a communal burial ground after a sudden outbreak of the Black Death?

I tapped my head to make myself concentrate. It was so hard and so incredibly boring. I didn't even know if I was managing to get any right answers because I'd set the sums myself. What on earth was I going to do tomorrow, when the arithmetic might be even harder?

Perhaps there would be lots of clever girls taking the examination and our desks would be close enough for me to copy from one. I knew this was cheating and we were supposed to despise cheats but, if I was going to pass this exam, it didn't look as if I had any alternative.

Maybe Mr White would put in a good word, seeing as he'd taken such a shine to me. I was thrilled that he'd singled me out. Mr Benjamin made a big fuss of me too. Even Peter wanted me to be his sweetheart – he'd seemed personally affronted when I said I didn't want to get married. When I peered in the looking glass I still looked very thin and scrappy and ordinary. Maybe when I was older I could cut off my plaits and wear rouge and lipstick, and look like a film star?

I threw my notebook on the floor and started dancing the Charleston, striking attitudes and stamping my feet.

'My, someone's gone a bit la-la!' said Aunty, peering round my bedroom door.

'Oh, Aunty, I didn't even hear you come in,' I said, and then I gave her such a big hug I nearly toppled her off her feet.

'Hey, hey, what's all this about?' she asked. 'Why weren't you with Mrs Higgins? Maggie said you'd just run off by yourself. That was very rude of you. Mrs Higgins was worried.'

'Maggie was being horrid to me,' I said. 'I don't think I want to be her friend any more.'

'Well, I always hoped you might find a more suitable friend. Maggie's a bit rough and ready,' said Aunty.

'I might make new friends sooner than you think!' I told her. 'Oh, Aunty, you'll never, ever guess what!'

'*You'll* never guess what, Mona! Sir Burbidge called me into his office today, and said he was very pleased with me. My children's clothes are proving to be a big success!'

'Well done, Aunty! But listen—'

'He wants me to make older girls' garments too. He'll give me a couple of Harrods' own seamstresses to do all the basics – seams and hems and whatnots – while I design each dress and do all the smocking and embroidery and fancy work myself. And, best of all, he'll add a pound to my wages, Mona. A whole pound! It'll make such a difference. I'll be able to afford all sorts of treats for us. Who's got a clever old aunty then?'

'*I* have! And who's got a clever little niece?' I said as we went downstairs to the kitchen.

'I have too,' said Aunty, opening the oven to light it. 'I bought a Harrods mutton pie for my tea – half price to staff because it's been around for a few days, though it's still perfectly good to eat and a really good size. I'll warm it up and we'll share it.'

'Aunty, do listen! I might be going to the girls' high school in Hailbury after the summer!'

She banged the oven door shut and whipped round to look at me. 'What was that?'

'The high school! We had a new school inspector today – Mr White – and he's ever so lovely, not a bit fierce. He set us older ones an essay, and he said mine was an imaginative masterpiece!'

'He never!'

'He did – he said all sorts of nice things, and thinks I'm very *avant garde*,' I boasted.

'What's that when it's at home?'

'Ever so modern. It's like Mr Benjamin's art and furniture. I think it's French,' I said airily.

Aunty looked at me as if I was actually talking French. 'Well I never,' she said weakly.

'So he says I should take the scholarship examination – tomorrow, in Hailbury.'

'But you've not been entered for it, have you?' Aunty asked.

'He says he'll make sure that my name is on the list. I have to be there at ten o'clock.'

'Oh Lord! I can't think straight! How many others are going to sit it?'

'I'm the only one from our school.'

'The only one! I knew you were bright, but I didn't think your school work was *that* good! I thought you were near the bottom in arithmetic,' said Aunty.

'Yes, but Mr White does different sorts of lessons from Miss Nelson. Modern stuff,' I explained.

'Avant-whatsits?' said Aunty. 'Well, Mona, I'm very proud of you.'

'So can I go on the bus tomorrow? I've just got to take a pen and a pencil with me— Oh, and my birth certificate.'

Aunty stared. 'Birth certificate?' she said. 'What do they want that for?'

'Oh, to check I'm really me and I'm ten. What's the matter, Aunty? I have *got* a birth certificate, haven't I?'

'Yes, of course you have, somewhere or other. But hold on – let's think this through. It's all very well this Mr White saying you're the bees' knees, but he doesn't really know you, does he? I don't want you getting over-excited about going to the high school and then not passing. That wouldn't do at all, would it? Maybe you're better off not bothering with this examination. I don't want you upset.'

I blinked at Aunty. Why had she suddenly changed her tune?

'I won't be upset,' I said, trying to reassure her. 'I'd just like to have a go, that's all. Mr White thinks I'll pass with flying colours.'

'Well, this Mr White isn't God Almighty, is he? And, anyway, even if you *do* pass, I'm not sure the high school is the right place for you, Mona. Do you really want to take the bus all the way there and all the way back every single day? You'll get exhausted. And what would we do about the fancy uniform? That'll cost a pretty penny. How are we going to afford it?'

'But you've just told me you'll be earning more at Harrods! And I could run errands for folk on Saturdays. And we could use Lady Somerset's money!' I finished triumphantly.

'You're not touching that, not till you're grown up. You'll need it then, you mark my words. Life's very hard for young women nowadays. I'm not having you starving in a garret,' said Aunty.

'But if I go to the high school and pass matriculation, I'll be able to get all kinds of jobs. I could have a proper career, Aunty! I wouldn't have to work for other people all the time like you.' The words came flying out of my mouth before I could stop them.

Aunty's head jerked as if I'd slapped her.

'I didn't mean it like that! I mean, you do wonderful work, you're the best dressmaker ever – it's just—'

'That's enough, Mona. I can see this Mr White has turned your head already. Well, you're not sitting this examination and that's that. Now set the table for tea.

There's a lovely crust on the mutton pie, better than I could ever manage.'

I stared at Aunty. She was trampling on all my hopes and dreams and talking about the wretched pie-crust as if it was of equal importance!

'I can't believe you could be so mean! What's the matter with you? I could understand Maggie being nasty. She's just jealous. Surely you're not jealous too, because you didn't have the chance to go to high school when you were young!' I shouted.

Aunty went white. 'How dare you speak to me like that! Go to your room this instant. And you're not getting any supper until you apologize.'

'I don't want any of your horrid mutton pie, so see if I care,' I yelled, and stamped off to my room.

I threw myself on the bed and had a good cry. After a while I fell asleep, fully dressed. I didn't wake up until Aunty came in much later, on her way to bed.

'Mona?' Her voice sounded thick, as if she'd been crying too.

I buried my head in the pillow.

'Mona, you're crumpling your dress, you silly girl,' said Aunty. 'Get undressed properly. Are you ready to say sorry now?'

'I'm not the slightest bit sorry,' I mumbled into the pillow.

Aunty sighed miserably and went out again.

I pulled off my clothes, put on my nightgown and got under the sheets. I wasn't at all sleepy now. I tossed and turned, still raging at Aunty and fretting about the examination tomorrow. Then I dozed a little, dreaming about Mr White. He was shaking his head sorrowfully and turning away from me.

I woke up very early, still burning with indignation. Then I suddenly jumped out of bed. I didn't care what Aunty said. I'd go to Hailbury by myself – if I could only find the bus fare . . .

I pulled on yesterday's dress, creased as it was, because I didn't want to risk waking Aunty by clinking coat hangers on my clothes rail. I knew my socks were grubby, but it couldn't be helped. I silently brushed and plaited my hair, wishing I had a quick and easy bob like Desiree. Then I clutched my pencil case and crept downstairs, carefully avoiding the steps that creaked.

Sixpence was curled up in her basket in the kitchen, but she leaped up when she saw me, clearly hoping it was morning already. I gave her a little milk, and then nursed her on my knee until she started dozing.

The mutton pie was untouched, its pie crust pristine. I felt a little twinge of guilt – Aunty had been looking forward to it so much. She'd been so happy about her wages. Still, she shouldn't have dashed all *my* chances of happiness.

I gently popped Sixpence back in her bed and looked at Aunty's purse, which was lying on the table beside the pie. It was half open, almost invitingly. I took a handful of coins and dropped them into my pocket quickly, as if they were red hot. I felt bad enough for yelling at Aunty. It was even worse to steal her money. But I couldn't help it. I'd never have this chance again.

Now I just had to find this birth certificate. I didn't even know if I would recognize it, but I knew where to look. Aunty had a large cash box hidden behind the good embroidered tablecloth in the sideboard. She didn't keep cash in it, because we had none going spare. It was where she kept all our precious things.

I drew it out carefully, set it on the table beside the pie and turned the little gold key in the lock. I'd already peeped inside when I was on my own in the cottage, and knew what to expect. I found my baby teeth in a little pink sachet, and a lock of fine baby hair, black as a crow's feather even then. There was a gold locket: the first time I came across it I hoped it might have a portrait of Mother inside. I prised it open again, just in case, but there was no picture at all. There was a pair of enamelled cuff links, which might have belonged to my father. I picked them up now, trying to imagine them attached to white cuffs, with masculine hands below. A soldier's hands, with the nails cut short, not carefully shaped and buffed to a shine like Mr Benjamin's.

I wondered what sort of father he would have been. Would he have been stern and strict – or would he have made a fuss of me and swept me up in his arms when he came home from work? There were no photos of him either.

I sifted through the documents at the bottom, which had never interested me before. There were receipts for our few sticks of furniture, old bills ticked and paid long ago, including doctor's bills for my bouts of measles and whooping cough, and dentist's bills for extracting one of my teeth and half a dozen of Aunty's. There were my report cards from school, with lukewarm comments from Miss Nelson this year: *Mona is a diligent pupil*; *Mona knows her times tables but struggles with arithmetic; Mona is quite good at English; Mona speaks nicely but sometimes talks out of turn.* Judging from these reports, I certainly wouldn't be considered high school material.

I found Aunty's school leaving certificate too, which was surprisingly glowing: *Florence has been a joy to teach. She has an excellent grasp of all subjects, as her examination results bear out. Her needlework is outstanding. We wish her well in the future.*

Why didn't Aunty want to go to a high school and continue excellently grasping all subjects? If she'd been considered bright but hadn't been able to carry on studying, why didn't she want me to have the chance?

I wished I had Mother's school reports. I was certain she'd been even cleverer than Aunty. *She'd* want me to go to the high school. All I had to do now was find the wretched birth certificate.

I flicked through all the documents, and then found a folded piece of paper at the bottom. I undid it and saw the words *Birth Certificate* in fancy italic writing. At last! But I couldn't see my name. This certificate recorded the birth of Florence Gertrude Watson, daughter of Ivy Enid Watson, market stallholder, and Albert Watson, docker. So this was Aunty's birth certificate, and Ivy and Albert were my grandparents.

Aunty had told me that they were long dead – but she had also said they'd had their own draper's store. I'd imagined them being as prim and proper as Aunty, my grandma in a long black frock and spotless apron, my grandpa in a black suit with a high white collar. I couldn't imagine this genteel couple calling out to prospective buyers in a market or clambering on and off boats in a dockyard.

So where was *my* birth certificate? I went through all the documents again, taking each one out and double checking. It wasn't there. I wondered about taking Aunty's, in the vain hope that the examiner might just give it a casual glance. If they queried it, I could pretend there had been a mix-up and I'd simply brought the wrong one. But I couldn't convince myself that I'd get away with it. I thought of the humiliation of being turned away, all the other girls staring at me. I needed *my* certificate and it wasn't there.

I put the cash box back and searched elsewhere. I rifled through the rest of the sideboard, the cutlery drawer, inside the Queen Victoria tea caddy. I opened Aunty's recipe book and her ladies dressmaking book and her old fashion books, flicking through every page, and found the odd shopping list or bus ticket, but no birth certificate.

The only other place I could think of was Aunty's wardrobe, but I couldn't search it while she was asleep. So I gave up and for waited an hour or so, feeling more and more desperate. Then I made a cup of tea and took it up to Aunty. Sixpence followed, having recently learned to climb the stairs.

'Oh, that's very kind of you,' said Aunty, her voice muffled because her teeth were in the glass on the bedside table. She covered her face with her hand and popped them into place as daintily as she could. She gave me an apologetic smile, then put on her glasses and settled back on her pillows, looking relieved that I'd stopped sulking.

'You're up early, dear,' she asked.

'Yes. I've been looking for my birth certificate,' I said.

She sighed. 'Oh, Mona. Don't start all that again, please. Just forget about it.'

'I can't forget. I have to take the examination. All right, I might not pass, but I have to try – can't you understand? But I need the birth certificate. Where have you hidden it? It's not in the cash box.'

'Have you been going through it then? Mona, you know you mustn't poke your nose where it doesn't belong. I won't have it!' Aunty's hands were trembling and she spilled her tea.

'Then give me my certificate!' I shouted. 'Where is it? Is it in here?' I went to her wardrobe and started flicking through her clothes.

'Mona Smith, how *dare* you!' Aunty leaped out of bed and tried to pull me away. 'Look, you can search for ever but you'll never find it – it was lost long ago.'

'What? How can it be lost?'

'It was lost when we moved here. Things often get lost when you move,' said Aunty.

'You're lying, I know you are!'

'How can you be so wicked as to call me a liar?'

'Because you *are* a liar! You said my grandparents had a draper's shop, but my grandma worked in a market and my grandpa was a docker – it's written on your birth certificate.'

'You *mustn't* go snooping around like this! You deserve a good whipping!' Aunty shouted.

There was a sudden frenetic barking outside the cottage, then eager thumps as something hurled itself against our front door. The old latch gave way and the something bounded inside and up our stairs.

'Nigel! Come back! How dare you, sir!' came from below.

'Oh my Lord, it's Mr Benjamin!' said Aunty, grabbing her old dressing gown in a panic.

A cream puppy careered around her bedroom, charging at poor Sixpence. She yowled and climbed up the curtains for safety.

'Don't just stand there looking gormless, Mona! Grab the puppy!' said Aunty. 'Take it downstairs. Don't let Mr Benjamin up here, for pity's sake.'

I did as I was told, hanging onto the squirming little puppy as best I could.

'That's it. Take it downstairs. Make Mr Benjamin a cup of tea while I make myself decent.'

I held the puppy tight against my chest and hurtled downstairs.

'You clever girl!' said Mr Benjamin. 'I'm desperately sorry. I was so keen to show off my new puppy that I lost all sense of time – and decorum. Your aunt must be horrified.'

'She says I must make you a cup of tea. She'll be down in a minute,' I said, handing the puppy over and putting the kettle on.

'I feel simply dreadful. Hang your little head in shame, Nigel,' said Mr Benjamin. He beckoned me nearer. 'Do excuse my mentioning it, Mona, but I couldn't help hearing your aunt threatening you with a whipping.'

I hung my head.

'I couldn't believe it. You and your aunt always seem devoted to each other. Whatever's up? I heard your aunt shouting, and I thought, *I'm not having my little Mona whipped, no matter what she's done.'*

I felt thrilled that he'd acted like a knight in shining armour, and I was still furious with Aunty, but I couldn't let him believe she would do that.

'She wouldn't really have whipped me,' I said. 'But she's very, very cross with me.'

'Why? What have you done?' Mr Benjamin asked, all agog. He wrestled with Nigel, who had smelled the mutton pie and was drooling.

I told him everything, my words tumbling over each other as I hurried through the story, keeping my voice down so that Aunty couldn't hear. Mr Benjamin was a wonderful audience, going, 'Oh, my!' every now and then. He mimed clapping when I told him that Mr White thought I could pass the high school examination, and shook his head sadly when I said that Aunty was against the whole idea. When I told him about the birth certificate he was suddenly serious, so absorbed that Nigel wriggled his head free and attempted to take a mouthful of pie.

'No, Nigel! You bad, thieving pup! How dare you try to purloin the ladies' lunch!' said Mr Benjamin sternly.

'He's more than welcome to it,' said Aunty, coming into the kitchen fully dressed, though she'd forgotten she still had a curler above each ear. 'It comes from Harrods, so it will be very high quality.'

'I wouldn't dream of depriving you of it, Miss Watson,' said Mr Benjamin. 'I am so very sorry that I came bursting in on you in such a thoughtless and ill-mannered way. I am not myself – it's lack of sleep. I think Nigel is missing his mother. He has the cosiest dog basket in the world, but he wouldn't settle and howled miserably most of the night. I ended up taking him into my own bed to comfort him, but then he wanted to play games, and there's a limit to the number of times I wish to play tag at two o'clock in the morning. I seriously considered curling up in his dog basket myself, simply for a bit of peace.'

'Naughty boy,' I said, stroking Nigel.

'And I believe Mona has been a naughty girl, Miss Watson . . .' said Mr Benjamin.

Aunty glared at me. 'I hope you haven't been troubling Mr Benjamin with our private affairs, Mona!'

'Oh, I prised it out of her, Miss Watson. I believe she wants to take the examination to get into Hailbury High School for Girls?'

'And I have forbidden it,' said Aunty, pinch-faced.

'I quite understand. The high school is the stuffiest of institutions, intent on turning carefree little girls into earnest young bluestockings. And the uniform is a total fright! Those gymslips! A lady who makes such exquisite clothing could never clothe her precious niece in such a hideous garment.'

'I know you're being facetious, Mr Benjamin, but you're not going to make me change my mind. I doubt Mona would pass the examination in any case, and then she'd be distraught. I don't want her upset,' said Aunty. She pressed her handkerchief to her mouth as if she had toothache. 'I know you mean well, but you don't understand.'

'I think perhaps I do, dear Miss Watson,' Mr Benjamin murmured. 'Why don't you let me drive her over to

Hailbury this morning? I already have connections with the school. My mother endowed an entire new wing, so the governors think kindly of the Somersets, as well they might. If I take little Mona into the school, they will treat her kindly too, and I will personally vouch for her. I'm sure there won't be any problem with her birth certificate. How about that?'

Aunty looked at him, her eyes brimming with tears. 'Would you really do that?'

'Of course I would.' He looked at his gold pocket watch. 'We still have a little time. Mona, why don't you come and take Nigel for a five-minute walk with me, and help me start his training. Then you can come back and get changed into a fresh dress and tidy your pigtails. Is that all right with you, Miss Watson?'

I looked at Aunty, who had taken off her glasses to dab her eyes. She nodded. I hugged her – and then I hugged Mr Benjamin too.

'Mona!' said Aunty. 'Mr Benjamin doesn't want you hugging him!'

'Oh, yes I do, Miss Watson. I'm very fond of Mona. I like to think I'm her token uncle now.'

I skipped off with Mr Benjamin and Nigel. The puppy gambolled in delight at the end of his lead, running round and round us so that sometimes we were tied together, helpless with laughter. Mr Benjamin kept issuing fierce instructions, telling Nigel to get down, to walk to heel, to stop rolling in the grass. Nigel took no notice whatsoever, but when I patted my hip, barely knowing I was doing it, he came running over and trotted along beside me.

'My goodness, Mona, you're a miracle worker! What

a magnificent animal trainer! Perhaps you don't need to get yourself properly educated. A career in the circus beckons. Madame Mona and her troupe of wild wolves, her trained tigers, her courageous camels, her elegant elephants . . .'

I burst out laughing as his suggestions became more and more ridiculous, and yet I suddenly saw myself in a circus ring wearing a spangled dress and ballet pumps. I flung out my arms as if inviting applause, and Mr Benjamin understood and clapped heartily, his diamond rings flashing. I swept him a curtsy, holding out the skirts of my creased dress, and he curtsied back gracefully.

'If I'm going to be an animal trainer, you can be a ballet dancer,' I said.

'There's nothing I'd like better! Oh, to be the principal dancer in a Diaghilev ballet! How I'd leap and twirl!' He demonstrated, and Nigel leaped up, barking excitedly, thinking it a grand game.

'Well, my dear, I suppose we'd better get you back to your aunt's and then whisk you off to the school,' said Mr Benjamin.

'I hope she hasn't changed her mind,' I said.

'Just so long as you haven't changed *your* mind . . .'

'Not at all.'

'I'm sure you'll do extremely well – you're an astonishingly intelligent child. God bless Mr White for discovering this himself. But just supposing everything goes wrong and you fail the examination – it's easily done, because I've failed many an exam in my time – then promise me you won't brood about it and go into a nervous decline as your aunt fears,' he said, sounding serious for once.

'I promise,' I said.

'Nothing in life should be taken too seriously, my dear. Don't waste your time striving for wealth or possessions or power, it rots the soul. Enjoy each day, and live for art and culture and beauty – and sheer glorious fun!' he said, taking my hand and twirling me round.

I thought that was a bit rich, seeing as he already had great wealth and a huge house full of beautiful possessions, and possibly enough power to enable me to sit the entrance exam without the appropriate documents – but I nodded and solemnly repeated his last sentence word for word.

'That's my girl,' he said, and then we ran back to the cottage, Mr Benjamin, Nigel and me.

The lady with the clipboard came chasing after us.

15

AUNTY HAD IRONED MY DAISY DRESS AND polished my shoes until they looked like new.

I ran upstairs to get changed. When I was ready, Aunty unravelled my straggly plaits, brushed my hair vigorously, and parted it with the pointed end of her comb. When she'd finished both plaits she added neat satin bows, and then inspected me gravely.

'There! I think you'll do,' she said. Then she suddenly kissed me on both cheeks. 'Good luck, dear,' she said.

I swallowed. 'I'm sorry I was rude to you, Aunty,' I muttered.

'And I'm sorry that you felt I was standing in your way, Mona. Please believe I only want the best for you,' she said.

Mr Benjamin beamed at both of us and then held out his hand to me. 'Come along then, my dear.'

We walked up the long driveway to the manor, and round the back to the stables, now converted into a garage twice the size of our cottage. The chauffeur and the gardener were sitting at an old ironwork table playing cards, but both jumped to attention when they heard Nigel's eager barks and Mr Benjamin's black-and-white brogues crunching on the gravel.

'Playing Poker first thing in the morning! How very dissolute, gentlemen,' said Mr Benjamin.

'Sorry, sir. I'm just teaching the lad the intricacies of the game,' said the chauffeur. 'We're still on our breakfast break, sir.'

'Ah, breakfast! Have you eaten breakfast, Mona?'

'I'm not really hungry, Mr Benjamin.'

'But you must eat all the same! You can't sit an important examination on an empty stomach, you'll faint dead away. We've got plenty of time. Come and have a little bite first,' he said persuasively.

That breakfast! It was three times the size of the breakfast I'd had before. Mr Benjamin lifted the lid of each silver tureen in turn to show me the contents: scrambled eggs, bacon, sausages, mushrooms, tomatoes, fried potatoes, a strange rice dish with smoked haddock and eggs . . . enough to feed half the village.

'Have you got many guests staying with you this weekend, Mr Benjamin?' I asked, my tummy going tight at the thought of another encounter with all those strange sharp-tongued people, especially Lady Arabella.

'No one in particular. Ambrose is here – he seems to have taken up permanent residence now that his London flat is being renovated. But he won't be down for breakfast. He frequently doesn't surface until lunchtime,' said Mr Benjamin. 'He's turning into a serious rival to Rip Van Winkle.'

'Who's Rip Van Winkle?' I asked. 'Is he another painter?'

'No, my dear, he's an American folk character who slept for twenty years,' said Mr Benjamin, piling bacon on a plate.

'Sleeping Beauty slept for a *hundred* years,' I said.

'Oh, you read fairy tales too, Mona! How delightful. I must show you my library some time. I have an entire bookshelf of fairy tales. I tried to interest Barbara's brood, but Esmeralda and Roland declared they were too old for fairy tales, Marcella took a polite interest but preferred *Dr Dolittle*, and Bruno turned the pages himself and tore one in the process. Here, Nigel, lovely bacon! Do you think he'd like a sausage too, Mona?'

'I think he'd love one, but perhaps only a tiny bit? And just one piece of bacon, chopped up. He's still a puppy,' I said. 'He might be sick otherwise.'

'How sensible you are!' said Mr Benjamin, adjusting Nigel's breakfast. 'And what about you? Might you be sick if you eat a few rashers of bacon and a sausage?'

'I don't think so,' I said, watching him give the dog his portion on beautiful pink china edged with gold. 'I don't think you should give Nigel his breakfast on that plate either.'

'Yes, it is pretty hideous, isn't it? Mother did have such conventional taste. Don't you prefer my marvellous rustic peasant-ware from Portugal?' Mr Benjamin asked. 'Help yourself then, Mona.'

'I don't know which to choose,' I said, dithering.

'Then take a little of everything and see which tastes best,' he said.

I never knew if he was serious or not, but I did as he suggested. He just took a few modest spoonfuls of the rice dish, which he said was called kedgeree. I wasn't too sure about it myself, but everything else was delicious. I had toast too, with a special little pat of butter in the shape of a flower.

No one else appeared while we were breakfasting.

'Do you think the servants eat the leftovers?' I asked.

Mr Benjamin put his head on one side. 'Possibly, though I think they're eating their own breakfast right this minute down in the servants' quarters.'

'So what on earth happens to all this food?' I asked.

'Perhaps it's put in a pig bin?' he suggested.

'Then you must have a herd of absolutely massive pigs!'

'What a glorious thought. Oh, I do hope I have! I shall listen out for ravenous gruntings as they fight over it at their trough.' Mr Benjamin saw my incredulous look. 'I'm sorry, Mona. I'll stop this ridiculous whimsy. Ambrose says I can be sickeningly fey at times.'

I wasn't sure what *fey* meant, but I thought it was probably rude. 'I don't think you should take any notice of Ambrose. He seems sickened by everyone,' I said.

Mr Benjamin laughed. 'A spot-on observation! I do enjoy your company so. Could you possibly come and have breakfast with me every morning?'

'If I eat this much every morning, then *I'll* be the one who gets absolutely huge,' I said. 'And then you'll wish you'd never invited me.'

'I shouldn't mind at all,' he said. 'The more Mona the better. I should simply ask Ambrose to source a massive armchair so you could take the weight off your gigantic legs.'

I laughed.

'There, that worried little frown has disappeared,' said Mr Benjamin. 'Well, my dear, our chariot awaits. Perhaps you'd like to wash your hands in the ladies' powder room and then meet me in the hall in a couple of minutes . . .'

It was at least five minutes because I was so enchanted by the lavatory. The room was deep blue, the sink gleaming white with silver taps and a little dish of bluebell soap. The lavatory was white, with a blue willow-pattern design in the pan. It was very like sitting on a throne. I enjoyed putting my hand on the plunger set into the mahogany fittings and watching the flush mechanism.

Aunty and I didn't have a lavatory in our house, just a dark earth closet in a shed at the back, and I hated using it because there were spiders.

Mr Benjamin was looking a little anxious when I joined him in the hall at last. 'Are you all right, Mona? Are you feeling nervous? You haven't been sick, have you?' he asked.

'I'm not nervous at all, and I haven't been sick, I promise,' I reassured him.

But sitting in the back of the Lagonda on the way

to Hailbury, I rather wished I hadn't eaten so much breakfast. I tried saying my times tables in my head to distract myself, managing the twos and threes and fours and fives, though I had difficulty after that, and my nine times table defeated me altogether. I'd definitely fail arithmetic.

I wasn't even confident about English now. I prayed that *My Home* would be one of the options for the composition, and then I could simply repeat the story that had so impressed Mr White. But what exactly *had* I written? I knew I'd pretended that I lived in the manor – but how had I started? Which rooms had I described? And how had I finished?

By the time we reached Hailbury High School for Girls I was a wreck, though I was faintly cheered to be driving up in such style. The other girls and their mothers stared at Mr Benjamin and his car, though I wasn't worth a second glance, even in my best frock with my plaits tied tightly into place.

The other girls were in smart school uniforms, green and blue and navy, with straw hats. Some had their hair plaited, but in one fat pigtail hanging down their backs like a bell rope, tied with a big bow. They spoke in clear, confident voices, though one girl was clutching her mother and another was as white as a sheet and near tears.

'You'll wipe the floor with them,' Mr Benjamin whispered in my ear.

The parents kissed their children's cheeks (one stern father shook his daughter's hand) and sent them into the playground by themselves, but Mr Benjamin strolled in beside me, his hand resting lightly on my shoulder. He didn't hesitate when we reached the door – he marched right in. The girls were standing in an obedient queue on the left-hand side of the corridor, while an officious lady with a clipboard checked them in.

'We'll turn right,' said Mr Benjamin.

'Sir! Excuse me, sir!' The lady with the clipboard came chasing after us, her shoes squeaking on the polished floor. 'I'm afraid you can't come in with your daughter. All girls must report to me and show me their birth certificate, and then go straight to the examination room.'

'I wish my little charge, Mona, to meet your headmistress first. I am Mr Benjamin Somerset. My mother, Lady Somerset, was a benefactress of this school,' Mr Benjamin said grandly.

'Oh my goodness, I do apologize, Mr Somerset,' she said, dropping her pen in her confusion. 'Miss Eliot is in her study – first right along the corridor. I had no idea she was expecting you.'

Mr Benjamin smiled imperiously and swept us past.

Miss Eliot was a very large lady, but tightly corseted. She looked as if she was wearing armour instead of underwear. I thought she would object to our bursting in on her, but she seemed thrilled to see Mr Benjamin.

'This is a very pleasant surprise. I'm so pleased you're keeping up the very special Somerset association with the school. And this is . . . ?'

'My charge, Mona Smith, a delightful girl who shows

considerable promise. I've brought her here to sit the examination today.'

'Ah, so you're Mona! Mr White sent a report about you, child. He was very impressed when he visited your school,' said Miss Eliot. 'So you have *two* gentlemen champions!'

I blushed, feeling thrilled but foolish.

'And you want to attend Hailbury High School for Girls, Mona?' she asked.

'Yes please,' I murmured.

'And why is that?'

I didn't know what the right answer was. I hadn't even thought of it until yesterday, but I didn't think that would go down well.

'It's always been my dream,' I said earnestly. 'I want to learn lots of things, because I'm going to be a writer when I'm grown up.'

This was another ambition less than twenty-four hours old, but Miss Eliot seemed impressed, and Mr Benjamin nodded at me fondly.

'May I deliver the budding authoress to the examination room, Miss Eliot?'

'Of course, of course,' she said. 'Can I offer you a quick cup of coffee, Mr Somerset, before I give the girls a few words of encouragement?'

'Thank you so much, Miss Eliot, but I wouldn't dream of imposing at such a time. I'll hurry Mona along while you prepare yourself,' he replied.

He waited until we were halfway down the corridor before saying, 'Phew! A narrow escape! I'm planning a pot of coffee and a plate of pastries at The Crown, and then I'll take a little stroll around the town in the sunshine. You scribble away and do your best, my dear. I'll be waiting in the car from noon onwards. Good luck!' And he breezed past the lady with the clipboard, who was checking in the last of the entrants. This time she didn't try to see my birth certificate, and Mr Benjamin escorted me to the door of the examination room.

He gently pressed the tip of my nose, blew me a kiss and waved his fingers.

'Is that your father?' a girl whispered.

I glared at her because Mr Benjamin wasn't anywhere near old enough. 'He's my *uncle*,' I said.

'He looks a bit weird, doesn't he?' she said, unimpressed. 'Poor you.'

I stuck my nose in the air. 'He's extremely modern and artistic – and comes from a very grand family,' I said. '*Lucky* me.'

'No talking, girls!' said the clipboard lady. 'Sit down at the first available desk, and then set out your pens and pencils and sit up straight. If any girl is caught so much as whispering once the examination papers are handed out, she will be sent out of the room immediately.'

I'd thought Miss Nelson was strict! I sat down and had a quick glance left and right. The desks were in rows, so far apart that I'd need eagle eyes to copy off anyone. I scrabbled in my pencil case, and my sharpener fell out and landed with a clatter on the floor. A couple of girls laughed nervously.

The clipboard lady glared. 'If that happens during the

examination, you will be sent out too – and I don't care who you are,' she said.

I felt myself going red, but pretended she couldn't scare me. Some of the girls looked terrified now, and one started sniffing. I peered round and saw there were tears rolling down her cheeks. I tried to give her a sympathetic smile but she looked away, dabbing at her face with her hankie.

'Calm down now,' said the lady. 'There's nothing to cry about.'

Miss Eliot swept into the room, her huge bosom sailing before her. 'Welcome to Hailbury High School, girls. We're holding this extra examination as some of you couldn't attend the one in the spring due to the outbreak of influenza. And I believe one or two of you suffered with nerves and were sadly in no fit state to take the exam.' She looked pointedly at the tearful girl behind me. 'There is absolutely no need for any of you to be nervous. You must simply try to answer all the questions and do your very best – that's all we ask of you. Now, if anyone is having a little weep, just wipe your eyes and give your nose a good blow. I want all of you to take three very deep breaths: i-n-n-n and o-u-t-t-t, i-n-n-n and o-u-t-t-t, i-n-n-n and o-u-t-t-t.'

Someone accidentally snorted loudly on her last i-n-n-n, and caused a chorus of smothered giggles.

'Stop that!' The lady had abandoned her clipboard now, and was handing out two documents, putting both face down on each desk.

One girl touched hers, probably just straightening

them, but she received a loud telling off: 'No one is to turn their papers over until I blow my whistle!'

'I wish you all good luck, girls,' said Miss Eliot.

She nodded, the other lady blew her whistle, and we were off. I turned the first paper over. *ARITHMETIC TEST.*

The first few questions weren't too terrible – simple adding up and taking away, the sort of sums I'd done when I was six. My hand stopped shaking. Maybe this was all you had to do to get into the high school. We did much harder sums with Miss Nelson. I felt suddenly superior.

Then I turned the page, and my heart started beating a little faster. Multiplication and long division were harder, and I knew I was prone to make silly mistakes. Still, I carried on steadily, checking my workings. The next page was fractions and decimals, much trickier. And then problems. Terrible complex problems. My head ached just reading the questions. I couldn't answer a single one.

I flicked through the rest. Some of the questions had odd pictures of triangles and rectangles. Others had sums that didn't even make sense, with letters of the alphabet mixed in with plus and minus and equals signs.

The girl behind me was sniffing again. It took all my willpower not to burst into tears myself. It was no use just sitting staring at these new sums. Instead I wrote at the bottom of the page, in my neatest handwriting:

I'm terribly sorry but I haven't ever been taught how to do these sums.

I wrote it at the bottom of all of them, even the page of problems, which was a downright lie. Still, they *might* just blame my teacher instead of me. I put the arithmetic test to one side and opened the English test.

I expected a list of titles and a lot of blank paper, but there were several other tasks to complete first. Some were quite interesting, like puzzles, where you had to fill in the missing word. I rather liked doing them. But the next page brought me up short, because we had to underline and identify all the adjectives, nouns and adverbs in a set of ten sentences. Miss Nelson occasionally droned on about grammar, but I'd never listened properly because it was so boring. I knew I didn't have much hope of getting any of them right, so I wrote my *terribly sorry* excuse, and turned the page.

This *still* wasn't the composition. It looked like a poem. I cheered up a little. Miss Nelson was fond of poetry and often chalked a poem on the blackboard for us to learn by heart. I nearly always learned it first, much to Maggie's annoyance, and recited it with great expression. I had particularly loved proclaiming *My Mother*, even though it made the boys giggle. I once set myself the task of learning the whole of *Hiawatha*, but I got sick of it halfway through.

This poem wasn't that sort of story poem though. It was a description of a bank of wild flowers where some lady called Titania was sleeping. There were questions afterwards. How many types of flower were on this bank? That seemed easy enough. I dithered over *eglantine*, because I'd never heard of it. I thought it might be some kind of tree and wouldn't count it as a flower. They asked what we thought her dreams were about. Dances were mentioned, and I wanted to impress with my contemporary knowledge, so I suggested she might have been dancing the Charleston. Then we had to describe Titania, though we didn't have much to go on. I thought she might look like Desiree. I couldn't work out why she was lying down outdoors instead of sleeping in her bed, so I suggested she was eccentric. Then, at long last, I got to the essay titles – but there wasn't a choice. There was just one title, and it wasn't *My Home*, even though I shut my eyes and opened them again several times, trying to will the right words onto the page. The title didn't change. *The Market Place.*

I didn't want to write about a market place! I wasn't remotely interested in markets. I couldn't give a boring Maggie-type list: there's a stall of red apples, a stall of yellow pears, a stall of green cabbages . . . I wanted to make my composition *interesting*.

Then I remembered Aunty's birth certificate. Ivy Enid Watson, stallholder. What was she like, this unknown grandmother? What did it feel like to be her?

Oh, I am so sick and tired of weighing out all these red apples, all these yellow pears. I polish the fruit at the front of my stall until it gleams to attract the crowds, and woe betide any interfering customer who picks out these choice fruits.

"No, madam, let me pick out your Coxes. We don't want the whole arrangement tumbling down, now do we?" I say hastily, and then quickly fill their paper bag from the bruised apples tucked away at the back.

It's not dishonesty. They're still apples, aren't they? I have to make a living, though it's always meagre. I get no support from my husband, off down the docks. I'm the one who feeds and clothes our little daughter. She's the love of my life – such a bright little girl and so nimble with her needlework. She won't have to slave at a market stall from dawn to dusk. She won't have rough red hands that smell of rotting fruit and copper pennies. She'll have dainty white lady's hands as she sews a fine seam…

'Time's up, girls! Put your pens and pencils down!'

I couldn't believe it! I was just getting into my stride. I'd only written three paragraphs, and yet I knew that my composition was my best hope of passing this wretched examination. I tried scribbling another sentence or two to explain my story, but clipboard lady shrieked at me.

'You, girl! Don't you have ears? Put that pencil down this minute or I shall tear up your papers!'

I flung my pencil down so quickly that the lead broke. We sat in silence while she went up and down, collecting our tests. She sniffed at me when she took mine.

At last everyone's papers were in neat piles on the front desk. Miss Eliot came back into the room. 'There now, girls. You can relax!'

There was a little hiss of whispers, even a giggle or two. I peered round and saw that the crying girl was actually dry-eyed and smiling.

'It wasn't such an ordeal, was it?' Miss Eliot said, and they all shook their heads. I shook mine too, because I didn't want them to see how I'd struggled. 'It will be nearly the end of term before we've processed your papers and discussed your merits. Then we will write to your parents. You can run and find them now. Well done!'

She smiled at us, and most of the girls smiled back. Several even chorused, 'Thank you.' The crying girl actually skipped off down the corridor. 'Mummy, Mummy, it wasn't too bad at all!' she called when she reached the playground. 'I think I've passed!'

Several other girls were calling out too. They sounded eager and excited.

Mr Benjamin was waiting, splendid in his stylish suit. 'Hello, Mona. Do you think *you've* passed?'

'I – I'm not sure,' I said.

'Well, I'm sure you have, my dear. Shall we go and have lunch to celebrate? I'm sure The Crown can rustle up something decent – or we can drive back and have lunch at the manor, how about that? Perhaps that would be better – your aunt will be on tenterhooks.'

I nodded. For once I wasn't at all hungry. I was going over all the questions in my head, and starting to get really worried. I remembered the sums I hadn't even attempted. If the clipboard lady was marking them, she'd never accept my *terribly sorry* excuses in a million years. I could only get half marks for arithmetic. Not even that. And perhaps the easy sums at the beginning barely counted. There was no getting away from it.

'I think I might have failed my arithmetic paper,' I confided to Mr Benjamin in a tiny voice, not wanting the chauffeur to hear.

'Never mind! I'm sure it won't matter in the least. My goodness, who cares about silly old sums!' he said. 'It's the English paper that's the important one. It was your composition that impressed your school inspector.'

'Yes, but I didn't have time to write much,' I said. My voice was starting to wobble.

Mr Benjamin reached out and held my hand, sensing my panic. 'You're not expected to write pages and pages, not in an exam,' he said.

'Yes, but I didn't even manage *one* page,' I said. 'There was all this other stuff – grammar things – and I've never been able to do them.'

'Oh, I totally agree. I found grammar incredibly tedious when I was at school,' said Mr Benjamin. 'Don't worry about it, Mona.'

But I *was* worrying, though I was pretty certain I'd got all the word puzzles right. And the poem questions.

'Eglantine is a tree, isn't it, Mr Benjamin?' I asked.

'Hmm. I rather think it's another word for *honeysuckle*, and that's a flower,' he said. 'I have honeysuckle and jasmine climbing up the walls of my rose bower. They all smell heavenly, especially at night.'

'Who's Titania?' I asked.

'She's the Queen of the Fairies,' said Mr Benjamin. 'She's in *A Midsummer Night's Dream* by William Shakespeare. Oh, I've just had the most tremendous idea! I think I will organize a performance of the Dream in my rose bower! It would be so beautiful! Would you like a part, Mona? You could be one of the fairies! Would you like that?'

I ducked my head, unable to answer. I couldn't stop the tears rolling down my cheeks. I knew I had failed the examination.

'What's the matter, eh?' Ella asked.

16

I WISHED WITH ALL MY HEART THAT I'D NEVER taken the wretched exam.

'I told you so,' said Aunty, though she was kind to me all the same. 'Never mind, chickie. Just forget about it.'

I couldn't forget.

'How did you get on doing that silly exam then?' Maggie asked on Monday morning.

I shrugged in an exaggerated way. 'I don't know, and I don't care. Not sure I want to go to that school anyway. The teacher was an absolute dragon,' I said.

Maggie was no fool. 'You mucked it up, didn't you?' she said. 'Not so bright as you thought you were, eh?'

'Maybe,' I said humbly. 'Shall we play Treasures today?' I put my arm round her, wanting us to be friends again, but Maggie wasn't having it.

She shied away from me. 'Oh, you're all smarmy now, but you acted like you didn't give two hoots about me before. You can't chop and change with people, Mona Smith. I don't see why I should be friends with you any more. I've gone off you, if you really want to know.'

We'd had enough arguments in our time. We'd once stopped speaking for three whole days. But this was different. Maggie didn't look like she'd ever be friends with me again. It was all my fault. Now I'd not only lost Maggie, I'd lost Mrs Higgins too, and even little Bertha would probably turn her nose up at me.

However, I thought, I still had Peter. He cared about me. He was desperate to be my friend. He acted like a sweetheart.

But not any more. He took scarcely any notice of me at school and didn't wait for me afterwards. The next day I went up to him in the playground.

'Hey, Peter. Would you like to come round to my house tonight?' I asked.

'No thank you,' he said.

'We could have cake,' I said. 'And play with the kittens.'

'Maggie's asked if I want to bring Ginger round to see Mittens.'

I stared at him, feeling utterly betrayed. 'All right, see if I care,' I said, though I cared enormously.

I cared even more the next morning. Maggie looked triumphant, Peter bashfully proud.

'*We're* sweethearts now,' she announced when we bumped into each other in the girls' toilets. 'Peter and me.'

'But you don't even like him,' I said.

'Well, I do now,' she said.

I didn't know if they were doing it to spite me or because they really *had* made friends. It didn't matter. They made it plain they didn't want me hanging around with them in the playground. Maggie scarcely spoke to me in class, even though we still sat next to each other. Whenever we had arithmetic she put her hand up, guarding her page as she wrote her answers so I couldn't copy.

Miss Nelson told me off in no uncertain terms. 'You've always been bad at arithmetic, but now your work is utterly appalling. You've got nought out of ten twice running. Fat chance *you've* got of getting into Hailbury High School, Mona Smith,' she said.

'I don't think I want to go there any more,' I mumbled.

'I'm not surprised. You certainly had your head turned by that Mr White, with all his fancy modern ideas. He'll change his tune when he's had a bit more experience. I've been teaching all my adult life. He'll learn,' she said smugly.

I had to learn too. It was very painful.

'Cheer up, Mona,' Aunty encouraged me. 'Don't act like this is the end of the world. *I* never went on to high school, and yet look at me now, doing so well at the finest department store in the country, Lady This and Mrs Hyphen-That begging me to make clothes for their children.'

'Yes, but I bet your mother wanted you to go to high school. That's why she worked so hard on her market stall,' I said. After writing those three paragraphs, my version of my grandmother had become so real that I felt as if I'd actually known her.

Aunty looked at me as if I was quite mad. 'Market stall?' she repeated.

'It said that's what she did. On your birth certificate. I saw it written there,' I insisted.

'You shouldn't have been prying. And, anyway, you're wrong. She might have worked in a market once, but not when I knew her,' said Aunty, going red. 'Never.'

'Oh, Aunty, there's no need to feel ashamed. There are lots of lovely people working in the market. Mrs Higgins sometimes sells eggs there,' I said.

'I know that, Miss Cocky. I also know that when I was growing up my mother worked in a factory – a filthy noisy place, and she was too, filthy and noisy,' Aunty said vehemently.

'You can't say that about your *mother*!' I said, shocked.

'You can if it's true. My mother didn't want me to better myself. She wanted me to join her in the factory. She was furious when I got myself apprenticed to a dressmaker because I'd have earned two shillings more in that wretched factory. More for her to waste on drink.'

'Drink!' Aunty *had* to be making it up. This was my grandmother! *Mother's* mother, and she was perfect in every single way.

'She didn't want Mother to go into the factory, did she?' I asked urgently.

Aunty sighed. 'Never mind about your mother. Don't go on about it, Mona. There's no point dwelling on the past. Now listen, I want the very best for you. I'm thrilled you have your own money in the bank. You won't need to go out to work at all now. You can get married and have babies, and I'll make all their pretty little clothes.'

'I'm not getting married and I'm not having babies,'

I declared. 'I'm going to be a writer even if I don't go to high school. I'm going to write stories all summer.'

I had to have a plan for the summer holidays. Maggie and Peter would be playing together, and I didn't have any other friends. Mr Benjamin would probably lose interest in me when the examination results came out.

I hadn't heard a thing yet. How everyone at school would gloat when they knew I'd failed – Miss Nelson most of all.

On the last Friday of term she was all smiles. Perhaps she was looking forward to the holidays as much as us. I imagined her paddling at the seaside, her long skirts bunched up, her plaited earphones let loose so that her hair waved wildly in the sea breeze.

We didn't have proper lessons. We did a nature quiz, following Mr White's example, for all that Miss Nelson despised his new-fangled teaching. She even repeated Mr White's question about the tree often found in churchyards. Maggie didn't bother to guard her notebook, and I saw she'd spelled it *you*. I raised my eyebrows, and she stuck her tongue out at me and waggled it. She could be so tiresome at times. Perhaps I was glad we weren't friends any more.

Then Miss Nelson cut sheets of sugar paper into quarters – we all wanted to help her use the slicing machine because it made such an exciting sound. She chose Peter Robinson, and he swaggered up to the front. His mother had given him another severe haircut: the back of his neck looked raw and his ears stuck out painfully. I didn't want him for my sweetheart any more.

Miss Nelson told us all to draw and colour a summer nature scene, though there weren't enough coloured crayons to go round. I ended up with an orange and a red and a brown, which were useless unless I attempted a raging forest fire. I decided to use the brown crayon and my black pencil for a sepia effect. I drew the graveyard at night, with the great shadowy yew and the gravestones grey in the moonlight. I drew Mother rising up from her grave, like Jesus ascending into heaven.

'Is that a *ghost*?' Maggie hissed. 'You're not supposed to be drawing anything creepy, you should be doing flowers and birds.'

'You get all kinds of nature in a graveyard,' I said, drawing ivy and deadly nightshade and a lot of big black crows.

Miss Nelson came round and inspected our drawings. She was particularly gushing about Maggie's brightly coloured flowers (she had commandeered my orange crayon for her marigolds). She didn't say a word about my night-time graveyard scene. She just shook her head and sighed.

We were allowed home at lunchtime on our last day. Aunty would be in London and I'd be so lonely with just Sixpence for company. Perhaps I should attempt to make friends with Maggie and Peter again. I could invite them both home with me and offer Maggie a go on Aunty's sewing machine, and get Peter to help me construct a kitten climbing tower from the wooden offcuts Mr Benjamin's workmen had given me.

But before I could hurry out with them Miss Nelson called me back.

'Mona Smith! Stay behind, please. I want a word with you.'

I was tempted to pretend I hadn't heard and make a run for it, but the other children nudged me.

'Mona! Miss Nelson wants you!' they chanted, glad she didn't want *them*.

I had to make my way back into the classroom and stand meekly while Miss Nelson fussed around putting pens and books in her carpet bag and stowing all the clutter on her desk in a cupboard. I shuffled from one foot to the other, getting irritated.

'Do you still want me, Miss Nelson?' I said at last.

'Of course I do, Mona. Be patient just a little longer,' she said, starting to unpin the times tables from the walls. 'In fact, you can help me take these down – only be very careful to pull the drawing pins out first. We don't want to tear any of them, do we?'

She'd ignored Mr White's advice about putting the little ones' scribbly drawings on the wall. Jesus reigned supreme, holding a lantern. I'd always thought it a wonderful painting, so realistic that Jesus seemed ready to clamber down into the classroom, though he'd only reach up to our waists. But when I thought of the bright slapdash picture of the naked man hanging in Mr Benjamin's drawing room, the schoolroom artwork seemed very old hat.

However, I rolled Jesus up carefully and stored him in the stationery cupboard.

'That's a good girl,' said Miss Nelson, unpinning the last times-table chart.

'Why are you taking everything down, Miss Nelson?

Can't you leave them on the wall during the holidays?'

'Mr White has recommended the whole school be painted. He feels it's too dark and gloomy,' she said. 'Though personally I disagree.' She ran her hand lightly over the green and brown wall.

'What colour is it going to be?'

'Daffodil yellow,' said Miss Nelson, shaking her head. 'He says it will make everywhere look sunny. I suspect it will make the children feel bilious, but then what do I know? I've only had thirty-five years' experience.'

'I think daffodil yellow will look lovely,' I said.

'Yes, I dare say you do. But you won't be here to see it, will you?'

I stared at her. 'Why not?' I suddenly thought she might be expelling me. She'd expelled Mad Jethro because he'd grabbed her cane and tried to hit her back when she was punishing him. I'd never done anything as terrible, but I knew she didn't like me.

She sighed. 'Really, Mona, I thought you were supposed to be bright! Why on earth do you *think* you won't be here? You've passed the examination to go to Hailbury High School.'

'I've *passed*?' I thought of the arithmetic test, the grammar, the eglantine and Titania fiasco, and the lamentably scrappy story. How on earth could I have passed? 'I haven't had word from the school, Miss Nelson,' I said.

'No, they sent the letter to me last week.' She took it out of her desk and handed it to me. I skimmed it quickly, scarcely able to believe it. The typewritten words on the page wavered up and down, but I could just about make out my name and the wondrous phrase *passed the examination*.

'Why didn't you *tell* me?' I asked.

'I'm telling you now. I didn't say anything previously because I didn't want you showing off and unsettling the others,' said Miss Nelson. 'I know you, Mona Smith.'

'You don't know me at all, Miss Nelson,' I said. 'Please may I go now?'

She nodded. I couldn't even bring myself to say goodbye to her. For an entire week she'd known that I'd passed and yet she hadn't said a word, watching me trail around miserably, convinced I'd failed. *How* had I passed when I knew I'd done so badly?

But it didn't matter! I'd passed! The letter said so.

I ran down the street, all the way to the churchyard, and burst through the lychgate. I capered wildly around the old yew, crying, 'I've passed, I've passed, I've blooming well passed!'

Then I flung myself down on Mother's grave. 'I've passed the high school exam, Mother! I'm going to be properly educated! You'll be so proud of me!' I waited for a reply, straining my ears. At first all I could hear was the pulse of my own blood, but then Mother said, 'Well done, my darling, clever girl.'

I ran home, leaping and singing.

'I've passed the exam, Aunty,' I shouted, running into her workroom, though I knew perfectly well that she wasn't there. Unfinished dresses and romper suits hung from hangers all around the room. I imagined rosy-cheeked heads poking out of the little white collars, chubby arms thrusting through the short sleeves, pink legs kicking below the tacked hems. 'I've passed, I've passed, I've passed,' I told them.

Sixpence emerged from a little nest in the basket of satin ribbons, stretching luxuriously.

'I've passed, Sixpence,' I said, picking her up and giving her a cuddle.

She mewed at me loudly, but I think she was only asking for food.

I gave her some leftover fish that was on a plate in the pantry, hoping that Aunty wasn't planning to make it into a fish pie. Then I ran upstairs to my bedroom and told my reflection in the mirror. I saw that my face needed a good wash. My knees were gritty too, and my dress covered in grass stains. I had an all-over wash, and put on clean socks and knickers and my daisy dress. I rubbed my scuffed shoes with my grubby socks, undid my plaits, brushed out my hair, and did my best to tie it into one fat pigtail at the back. Then I walked up to the manor, telling every tree and bush that I'd passed.

I went to the front door and Ella opened it for me. She sighed at the sight of me. 'You're meant to go round the back, Mona. I've got better things to do than run to open doors for you, like you're Lady Muck,' she said.

'I've passed, Ella!'

'You what?'

'I've passed the examination to Hailbury High School!'

'Well, you're a clever little miss, aren't you,' said Ella grudgingly. 'Come on in then. I suppose you're here to show off to Mr Benjamin . . .'

'Has he got company?' I asked her anxiously.

'Shedloads are expected tomorrow, worst luck, but

right now there's only that waste-of-space Mr Ambrose. He's more an unwanted pet than a proper person. A cat! He only wakes up to be fed, and he's got fingernails like claws,' she said. 'He gives me the creeps. My, things haven't half changed since Lady Somerset passed away. I'm forever on the brink of handing in my notice, but Mr Benjamin's got such a way with him you find yourself forgiving any imposition.'

'Is he in the drawing room?' I asked.

'I think so,' said Ella.

I didn't wait for her to take me. I burst in, not even bothering to knock. Mr Benjamin was sitting cross-legged on the rug, absorbed in a big fat book.

'Oh, Mr Benjamin, I've passed the exam!' I cried, and flew at him to give him a hug. I very nearly tipped him over, but he only laughed merrily.

'Well done, Mona! You clever child! I just knew you'd pass, didn't I? What did your aunt say?'

'I haven't told her yet. She's at Harrods today. My teacher only just told me,' I said breathlessly, sitting down cross-legged beside him.

'And was she pleased for you?'

'Not in the slightest! She doesn't like me much.'

'Well, I like you a great deal, Mona, and I'm very happy for you. We must have a celebratory lunch! It will be served any minute now. And meanwhile you can help me peruse this excellent book, though you might find it a little difficult,' said Mr Benjamin, putting it in my lap.

'I can read even the hardest books,' I said, a little indignantly, but when I looked at the page I realized he was teasing. It was written in an entirely foreign language. It wasn't a story, more like a long list – and there was a black-and-white picture of a big pot of some kind of stew.

'I can so read it!' I said. 'It's a recipe for beef stew!'

'Oh my Lord, there's no flies on you, Mona Smith. It is indeed – *boeuf bourguignon*. Cook says she's no idea how to make it, so I'm trying to work it out myself so I can show her. I'm planning it for dinner tomorrow. When you're a little older you must come to one of my dinner parties, Mona.'

I wasn't sure I'd ever want to eat foreign food with a funny name, and I hadn't liked Mr Benjamin's choice of guests so far, but I thanked him anyway.

'Though I think I'd like it best if it was just you and me, Mr Benjamin,' I said daringly.

'Your wish is my command,' he said. 'Ambrose has actually bestirred himself this morning and is out in the garden consulting with a team of builders. He is encouraging me to build a little lido. It will be such a lark to have my own pool! I'm not sure when he'll be joining us.'

The door opened, and the new butler announced that lunch was indeed served.

'Thank you so much, Harold. As you can see, I have a little guest. Could you rustle up another plate, please, and I hope Cook has got a pudding. Mona has a very sweet tooth.'

'Certainly, sir.' Harold smiled at me. 'I have a very sweet tooth too, Miss Mona. Wait till you sample Cook's raspberry meringue!' He was much friendlier than old Mr Marchant, who had looked at me as if I was something the cat had brought in.

The meal was superb. We had asparagus soup to start with. I'd never even heard of such a vegetable, and looked at the green liquid anxiously, but it was extremely tasty. Then we had fish, but it wasn't anything like the fish that Aunty and I ate. It was sole – a sliver of a fish that tasted delicately delicious, with tiny garden peas and weeny potatoes to go with it. Everything was so doll-sized that I still felt hungry, so I was looking forward to the raspberry meringue. It looked like a magnificent white-gold crown studded with rubies. My mouth watered as Harold cut me a very big slice.

Just then Ambrose came ambling into the dining room, and Mr Benjamin asked Harold to bring him soup and fish.

'No, no, I can't be bothered. I'll just fill up on dessert,' said Ambrose, barely looking up. He'd come to the table in a smock and corduroys, both flecked with earth, and as he ate (not one but two enormous portions of pudding) he sketched out a drawing on his pad.

He kept interrupting Mr Benjamin and me while we were having a most interesting conversation about fairy stories. I'd decided that 'Cinderella' was my absolute favourite, and Mr Benjamin agreed that it was a very satisfying story, and said he'd always hankered after glass slippers, which made me laugh.

'I've had a most brilliant idea, Benjy!' Ambrose said suddenly. 'I think a pool in the shape of a crescent moon would be divine, with marble tiles giving off a pearly effect, imagine!'

'That sounds beautiful, Ambrose. I wonder what marble slippers would be like, Mona? Perhaps a little clumpy, but very useful if you wanted to stamp on someone. Now, have you ever read *The Happy Prince*?'

'However, the wretched builders insist the tiles would all have to be specially cut in Italy, and we'd have to wait months, and of course we want to be swimming as soon as possible, don't we?' Ambrose continued.

I said I didn't know *The Happy Prince*, and Mr Benjamin said it always moved him to tears.

'That was another one of my ideas – a pool in the shape of a teardrop! But the workmen keep recommending a conventional rectangle, which I think would be very boring, don't you?'

'Perhaps you could design a pattern of tiles around the edge to give it some character, Ambrose. I must lend you my copy of *The Happy Prince*, Mona – I know you'll love it too, even though it's sad.'

'I suppose the art deco look is all the rage. Jade-green tiles, perhaps? And maybe jade steps leading down into the pool. I *could* design a mosaic of a mermaid on the pool floor, but might that be a little obvious?'

'I love "The Little Mermaid", and *that's* sad,' I said.

'I always think of her when I wear my black patent boots. They're utterly beautiful, but total agony to wear,' said Mr Benjamin.

'For God's sake, Benjy, stop prattling on about fairy tales and shoes with this grubby child and concentrate on the pool!' said Ambrose.

I was incensed. Mr Benjamin and I had started our conversation first. And how dare me call me grubby when I'd had a thorough wash and was wearing clean clothes! He himself was truly filthy – I don't think he'd even bothered to wash his hands. *And* he'd taken yet another helping of raspberry meringue, not cutting it cleanly, so the whole meringue crumbled and the red juice splashed all over the pristine white.

'It's all right, I'm going now. Please may I get down?' I said icily.

'Ambrose, you've offended poor Mona! Take no notice, dear. Ambrose can't help being rather a boor, it's simply part of his nature,' said Mr Benjamin. 'Do you really have to go so soon?'

I didn't have to go anywhere at all, but my pride made me pretend I did. Mr Benjamin expressed regret, but didn't absolutely insist I stay. And he'd forgotten about his *Happy Prince* book. It might have looked too forward if I reminded him, so I said goodbye – ignoring Ambrose – and marched out of the dining room, with Mr Benjamin congratulating me yet again.

I shut the door, but then lurked outside, wanting to hear what they said about me.

'I'm cross with you, Ambrose. Mona's a very sensitive child,' said Mr Benjamin.

My heart beat faster when I heard him taking my side and calling me sensitive into the bargain.

'You and that queer little girl! I don't know why you encourage her. You're treating her like an infant phenomenon – but didn't the headmistress of that wretched girls' school say she'd failed the exam?'

I put my hand over my mouth.

'She couldn't help it, poor lamb. She's hardly learned a thing at the village school. And Miss Eliot did agree that she was very good at writing. It was easy enough to persuade her to take Mona by making a donation towards the school roof fund. It's such fun to be truly wealthy!' said Mr Benjamin. 'And I have a very soft spot for Mona, for all sorts of reasons.'

'Well, don't get attached to too many other waifs and strays or you'll find yourself running out of cash,' said Ambrose. 'Now listen, Benjy – about the pool . . .'

I crept away, my head reeling.

Ella was in the hall. 'You off home now?' she said. 'Wait a minute, you've got red all round your mouth! You've never been experimenting with lip rouge, have you?'

I wiped the raspberry stain fiercely with the back of my hand.

'What's the matter, eh?' Ella asked, more softly. 'You look as if you're going to burst into tears.'

'I'm not,' I said, blinking hard. 'I have to go now.'

'Has that Mr Ambrose been horrid to you? Don't take any notice, Mona. He's a nasty piece of work. I heard him suggesting to Mr Benjamin that he give me the sack and employ someone more decorative! I came to work at the manor when I was just a slip of a girl and I've given loyal service all these years – and that lazy toad wants rid of me because I'm a decent, old-fashioned woman. What does he want me to do – bob my hair and wear my skirts above my knees?'

I left her ranting and walked slowly back to the cottage. So I *hadn't* passed. Well, of course I hadn't. I *knew* I'd made a mess of the exam. I wasn't clever at all. Those other girls had probably passed with flying colours, even the crying one. I had failed.

But no one need *know* that Mr Benjamin had

persuaded the headmistress to let me go to her precious school. He was my champion. My spirits soared. I didn't care if I was stupid and ignorant. Mr Benjamin cared about me so much he'd fought my case and bribed the school into taking me on! Oh, I loved him with all my heart! What did it matter if I couldn't do arithmetic or grammar, and didn't know about wild flowers and fairy queens? I could write good stories – they all agreed on that!

I was skipping now. When I got home I went to my room and started writing a story about a Prince Benjamin who had the knack of making everyone happy, happy, happy.

When Aunty came home at last, tired out and worried that I'd had to spend so long by myself, I told her that I'd passed the examination after all. I didn't tell her that I was only going to the high school because Mr Benjamin had spoken up for me. I wanted Aunty to go on thinking I was clever.

'I could take you down to the village,' I said.

17

ON SATURDAY MORNING I CARRIED ON WITH my story, though I was distracted every time a car passed the cottage. Some of Mr Benjamin's guests had come last night, and more were arriving this morning. I kept rushing to the window, wanting to see if Barbara and her artist and their four children were coming for the weekend, but the cars swept on up the driveway before I could have a proper look.

Aunty was busy in her workroom. She had so many new orders she was worried she wouldn't get them done in time, even with the Harrods dressmakers doing all the donkey work.

'I have to watch them like a hawk. They don't always keep their stitches small enough, and one of them puckered a whole hem. It's not good enough, not when it's bespoke. My customers expect perfection. As it is, I can't trust them to iron them properly and have to do it myself. The younger one's such a flighty piece too, answering back whenever I correct her. If only I could train up my own girl!' Aunty looked at me wistfully.

'Is that why you didn't want me to sit the exam at first, Aunty? Did you want *me* to be your apprentice?' I asked.

'I can tell that your heart wouldn't be in it, so there's no point, is there?' said Aunty.

'Did Mother like sewing?' I wondered.

She shook her head and changed the subject, asking me to go and make her a cup of tea.

'So I take after her then?' I said as I put the tea down carefully beside her. She was always terrified I'd spill it over the fine materials.

Aunty shrugged, reluctant as always to talk about Mother. But then she said, 'You're your own person, Mona. You go your own way.'

I rather liked that. I hung about Aunty, hoping that she might tell me more. I tried fashioning a little hat for Sixpence out of a strip of green satin ribbon and a couple of crimson cloth roses. She looked incredibly sweet when I put it on her, but she clawed it off indignantly and ran out of the room, going her own way too – though she rushed back eagerly when she smelled the sardines on toast we were having for lunch.

I wished I was up at the manor eating green soup and white fish and raspberry-red meringue. Mr Benjamin had told me to visit him whenever I fancied, but that wasn't quite the same as a specific invitation. Besides, I didn't want to run into any of his house guests – unless they were Esmeralda and Roland and Marcella. I could live without seeing Bruno.

'Do you think Mr Benjamin will have invited Barbara and her family?'

'That's the second time you've asked me that,' said Aunty. 'How do I know?'

'They *might* be here as it's the start of the summer holidays,' I said hopefully. 'Mr Benjamin said he'd asked them to stay.'

'I don't know why you're so keen to see them. I think it's a disgrace, the way they're allowed to run wild. They looked like a bunch of ragamuffins at the funeral. Lady Somerset would have been mortified,' said Aunty.

'Perhaps she was peeping out of a crack in her coffin and glaring at them,' I suggested.

'Mona! It's not nice to talk like that,' said Aunty.

'Why?'

'Well, it's morbid, for a start, making out the dead have feelings.' Aunty shivered.

I wondered what she would say if she knew I had long conversations with Mother. Then I paused, suddenly anxious. How was I going to visit her regularly when I no longer went to the village school? And how could I lie full length to talk to her properly when I was wearing that expensive blue uniform? Aunty would kill me if I got it dirty.

I sighed, and Aunty shook her head at me.

'There now, you've gone and upset yourself, silly. Don't sit there with a long face. Why don't you go for a little walk in the grounds and see if the Somerset children are there?' she suggested.

I was suddenly overcome with shyness. What if they groaned when they saw me coming? What if they thought I was odd or pert? So I stayed in the cottage, wandering around restlessly, unable to settle.

Then I heard a bark – the high-pitched bark of a bouncy puppy.

'Nigel!' I said. I scooped Sixpence up and shut her in my bedroom for safety. (Hours later I found her curled up cosily against my pillow, as if it was her mother.) Then I ran to the door.

Nigel leaped up to greet me, tossing his head until his ears flapped – but Mr Benjamin wasn't holding his lead. It was a girl with tousled hair wearing a strange blue embroidered smock, bright red socks and brown sandals.

'Hello, do you remember me? I'm Marcella. We met when my grandmother died. And this is Nigel, though I think he knows you already,' she said. 'I'm taking him for a walk and I wondered if you'd like to come too . . .'

'I'd love to,' I said. 'Aunty? Aunty!'

She came out of her workroom tutting, and then stood still, staring at Marcella, clearly taken aback by her odd outfit. But she composed herself quickly and said, 'How do you do, Miss Marcella.'

I didn't like Aunty calling her Miss – after all, Marcella was only a little girl, a year or so younger than me. Goodness, was I supposed to call her Miss too? Well, I wasn't going to!

'Can I take Nigel for a walk with Marcella, please, Aunty?' I gabbled.

'I suppose so, dear. Don't get in the way now,' said Aunty anxiously. She came nearer. 'And mind your manners!' she whispered.

I went out quickly, before she could embarrass me any more.

'Your aunty's very strict, isn't she?' said Marcella. 'A bit like my grandmother. She was always telling us to mind our manners. I don't miss her a bit. Do you think that's awful of me?'

'Not really,' I said, looking around hopefully for Esmeralda and Roland.

'The others aren't here,' said Marcella. 'Roland and Bruno are helping the workmen with Uncle Benjamin's swimming pool. Esmeralda is messing around with Desiree. She's showing her how to dance the Black Bottom.'

'The what?'

'I know, it's ridiculous, isn't it? I tried, but I kept tripping and they laughed at me.'

'I think it's a silly name for a dance. I prefer the Charleston,' I said, showing off. I was pleased when Marcella looked impressed.

'I don't expect that's any easier,' she said. 'Anyway, Uncle Benjamin suggested I take Nigel for a walk. He said I should come and find you because you're an excellent dog handler.'

'I'm not really. He's just being kind,' I said.

'He *is* kind, isn't he? I think I love him almost as much as my mother. Certainly much, much more than my stepfather, Stanley. Where shall we walk to then?'

'I could take you down to the village,' I said.

'Oh *yes*,' said Marcella, clapping her hands as if this was a great treat. She dropped Nigel's lead as she did so, which was a mistake.

It was ten minutes before we managed to catch him, but this meant he'd worn himself out so much that he walked down the street in a reasonably docile fashion, not pulling on his lead.

'You really are good with dogs,' said Marcella.

'Do you have a dog of your own?'

'No, worst luck. Stanley doesn't like dogs because he once got bitten. He's pathetic. I can't understand what Barbara sees in him. She acts as if he's the greatest artist ever. I like *her* paintings better than his, and yet ghastly Stanley says they're only decorative, and don't count. Isn't that ridiculous?'

'I think he sounds very rude,' I said. 'Your mother looks very artistic. Do you always call her by her first name? Doesn't she mind?'

'No, she likes it,' said Marcella.

'I wonder if I should call my mother Sylvia?' I'd spoken out loud without really meaning to.

'I didn't know you had a mother,' said Marcella. 'I thought you lived with your aunt.'

'I do.'

'So where's your mother then?'

'In the graveyard.'

Marcella blinked. Then she realized. 'You mean she's dead. Oh, I'm sorry.'

'It's all right. I still talk to her,' I said.

'Do you?' She sounded very interested.

'Almost every day.'

'Goodness. But isn't that a bit lonely when she can't talk back?'

'She *does* talk back when I want her to.' Marcella

stared at me. 'Do you think I'm weird?'

'Oh, people always think *I'm* weird. And stupid,' said Marcella cheerfully. 'Esmeralda got fed up with me following her around – she said I was like an eager puppy dog. I felt a bit hurt, but I pretended I was pleased and went *woof-woof*. So then she said I was actually turning into a puppy, and she slid her hand down my back and touched this little bony bit right at the bottom and said it was my tail starting to grow.

'Well, I knew she was just teasing me, but I started to worry all the same. I kept feeling the bone, and it did seem to be getting bigger, almost as if it was going to burst right through my skin and start wagging, and that night I had a bad dream that I'd really turned into a dog all over, with fur and paws and everything, and I started crying. Barbara came and I sobbed it all out – though I didn't say it was Es who had shown me the tail bit on my spine because I'm not a sneak. But she told the boys and they thought it ever so funny, and they kept calling me The Dog and throwing sticks for me to fetch.'

'That's really mean,' I said indignantly. I knew I didn't like Bruno, but I was surprised to hear that Esmeralda could be so horrid.

'Oh, it's just teasing,' said Marcella. 'You know what sisters and brothers are like.'

I didn't know. I'd always longed to be part of a big family, but now I was almost glad that I was an only child. Perhaps it was better to be an older sister rather than a younger one. I didn't think I'd ever want to tease Marcella though. I was starting to like her very much.

We were approaching the church now. Marcella

peered at it with interest. 'This is the church where my grandmother's buried. Is it where your mother is too? Will you show me?'

'If you like,' I said. 'Only you won't laugh or anything, will you?'

'Absolutely not!'

We went in through the lychgate. I steered Marcella past her grandmother's tomb, not wanting her to be upset, but she noticed anyway and didn't seem to mind.

'It's very grand, isn't it?' she said. 'But I don't like it much. I do hope they won't put me in there.'

'There wouldn't be room, not if your uncles are in there too,' I said.

'I don't think my grandmother would like it in there either. She'd hate being shut away, not able to boss anyone around. She was always nagging me. *Oh, Marcella, what a shame you're not going to be a beauty like your sister. Can't you do something with that wild hair? And do stop biting your nails or I'll paint them with bitter aloes.* She did too, on all of us, because we all bite our nails, even Esmeralda. That was our nickname for Grandmother – Bitter Aloes!' Marcella giggled. 'Go on, then. Show me your mother's grave.'

I took her round the back of the church, leading her along the row until we came to Mother's mound. I had put a jam jar of ox-eye daisies at her head, and added an edging of white pebbles.

'Oh, it's so pretty,' said Marcella. 'Where's her headstone?'

'She doesn't have one. I don't think Aunty had enough money for one.' I suddenly remembered my secret savings in the bank. 'When I'm grown up I shall buy her a splendid one – and give her a big white angel too.'

'Oh, that would look lovely! So her name's Sylvia?'

'Sylvia Mona Smith. I'm named after her.'

Marcella gently patted the grass over Mother. 'Hello, Sylvia Smith. I'm here with your daughter Mona. Will you talk to me?'

'I don't think so. She only talks to me. And then not always,' I said quickly.

'Oh!' Marcella looked very disappointed.

'But I'll talk to her if you like,' I offered. I lay right down on top of Mother, feeling self-conscious. 'Hello, Mother. I've brought a new friend with me today. Marcella thinks your grave is pretty.'

I knew perfectly well that Mother wouldn't say a word in these circumstances, but I pretended to listen. Marcella crouched lower, straining to hear.

'I think she might have said hello, very faintly,' I said. 'But perhaps you didn't catch it.'

'I *might* have heard it.' Marcella patted the grave again. 'Thank you!'

We stayed still for several minutes, but all we could hear was a blackbird in a nearby tree.

'Shall we go to the village shops now?' I suggested.

'Oh, yes please,' said Marcella.

We walked past the Higginses' cottage. Maggie was in the garden minding the baby in his tumbledown pram, the handle hanging crookedly and the wheels at odd angles after supporting so many Higgins babies. Little Bertha was tied to the handle with the long washing line, which gave her room to roam among the flowers.

I wanted Maggie to see that I had other friends now.

She'd know Marcella was a Somerset. I hoped she'd be impressed – though Marcella did look very strange in her smock and sandals.

Maggie stared at us.

'Hello, Maggie,' I said tentatively.

She didn't answer, but Bertha waved her fat little arms and came as near as she could.

'Oh, she's a darling!' said Marcella.

'That's Bertha. I used to play with her,' I said, waving back at the toddler.

Maggie still said nothing, but Mrs Higgins came to the open front door and peered out.

'Why, Mona!' she said. 'How lovely to see you, dearie. We've missed you recently! And who's your friend?'

'This is Marcella,' I said. 'Marcella, this is Mrs Higgins.'

'Pleased to meet you,' said Mrs Higgins, beaming. 'Would you both like to come in for a bite to eat?'

My tummy tightened. I loved Mrs Higgins's bread and dripping, though I knew Marcella was used to far daintier food. But then I saw that she was nodding happily.

'Yes please, Mrs Higgins,' she said.

I caught Maggie's eye, and for a moment we were united again, both wondering if Marcella was going to sweep around like a duchess, looking down her nose at everything in the cottage. But Marcella behaved beautifully, admiring the colourful rag rug on the floor and the pair of china dogs on either side of the mantel clock. Nigel was less well-behaved and made a little puddle in the corner, but Mrs Higgins simply laughed and mopped it up.

She didn't offer us bread and dripping this time. She'd

baked some shortbread and gave us each a slice. She offered the tin to Maggie and her brothers and sisters playing with the pig in the back garden. They all took a slice, but Maggie shook her head stubbornly. Bertha yelled frantically until Mrs Higgins put half a slice into her fat little fist.

It was delicious shortbread, very light and dusted with sugar, but I was finding it hard to swallow mine. I felt embarrassed and guilty, even though it was Maggie who had broken up with me.

Marcella seemed happy to stay all afternoon, especially when Johnnie took her to meet the pig. He was called Porker. All the Higginses' pigs were called Porker. They made a great fuss of him, and he responded happily, grunting with pleasure when scratched, especially behind the ears. Marcella insisted on climbing into his pen to scratch him properly, though her sandals got very mucky.

'Who cares?' she said light-heartedly. 'Oh, you're so lucky to have a pig for a pet. I love the way he squeals!'

'He squeals even louder when it's time to stick him,' said Maggie.

'What do you mean? You don't hit him with a stick, do you?' Marcella asked.

'No – once he's got big and fat enough, we kill him,' said Maggie, and laughed at Marcella's face.

'You're teasing,' she said uncertainly. 'You couldn't kill your pet!'

'Maggie!' Mrs Higgins remonstrated. 'There's no need to upset the child.'

'Well, she's daft,' said Maggie. 'Any fool knows a pig isn't a pet, he's food for the winter. Bacon and pork belly and loin and sausages and black pudding and chitterlings.'

'Oh yes. Of course,' said Marcella. 'But how awful to kill him when you've got to know him.' She knelt down and patted the pig sympathetically.

'Best stand up, dear, or you'll get your pretty dress all dirty,' said Mrs Higgins.

'It's not pretty at all – it's like a shepherd's smock and it looks stupid,' said Maggie.

'If you can't keep a civil tongue in your head you'd better go upstairs, Maggie!' said Mrs Higgins.

'Come on, Marcella,' I said, pulling her to her feet. 'We should be on our way now.'

'Well, it's been lovely to see you, Mona – and to meet you, Marcella. Do come again soon,' said Mrs Higgins.

I suddenly blurted out, 'I have missed you, Mrs Higgins.'

'We've missed you too, haven't we, Maggie?' she said.

'No,' said Maggie, but she looked wistful.

'So she's your friend?' said Marcella as we carried on down the lane. We had to drag Nigel, who had loved the cottage and the children and the pig and the shortbread biscuit he'd stolen on the sly.

'Maggie used to be my friend,' I said. 'But not any more. I'm leaving the village school, you see, and going to Hailbury High School in September.'

'Oh, poor you,' said Marcella.

'Why poor me? It's meant to be a very good school. Mr Benjamin took me there to sit the scholarship examination.'

'Yes, but why would you want to go to a stuffy old high school? Esmeralda was sent to one and she positively hated it. She said all the teachers were mean and shouted all the time. Esmeralda was forever getting detentions because she stood up for herself. And she said the lessons were all beastly boring,' said Marcella. 'You don't *have* to go, do you?'

'I *want* to go,' I insisted, though I wasn't quite so sure now. 'So where does Esmeralda go to school now?'

'She doesn't go to school at all, and neither do Bruno or I. Roland was supposed to go away to school this September, but he made such a fuss that Barbara's getting him a tutor instead. And Esmeralda and Bruno and I have Mademoiselle Bernice every morning – she's our governess. We tease her dreadfully. She lets us read most of the time we should be having lessons,' said Marcella.

'But you need to have a proper education,' I said.

'Why?'

'So you can get a good job if you don't get married,' I said, and then realized I was being stupid. Of course a Somerset girl would never need to earn her living.

'I can see that's a good idea,' Marcella said, however. 'What job do you want then, Mona?'

'I rather think I'd like to be a writer.'

'Oh yes. Uncle Benjamin said you were good at writing stories.'

'*Did* he?'

'I'm not keen on writing though. It makes my hand ache and I can't always think what to write,' said Marcella. 'So what could I do? I'm not very good at anything, though I like helping people.'

'*I* know! You could be a nurse like Florence Nightingale. I've read about her in a book. She went around with a little lamp, comforting wounded soldiers,' I said.

'I'd rather like to do that,' said Marcella, pleased.

'My aunty's called Florence,' I told her, 'but I don't think she ever wanted to be a nurse, just a dressmaker.'

'Barbara makes our dresses, but they always look odd. Maggie was right, my dress *is* weird,' she said.

'I think it looks very modern,' I lied. *'Avant garde.'*

'You must be crazy,' Marcella told me.

Some of the village folk were staring at her. Old Molly clutched at her grubby apron with her gnarled, shaky fingers.

'My, who's this you've got with you, Mona Smith? She looks a fright in that dress,' she said loudly.

'This is Old Molly,' I said to Marcella, embarrassed.

'How do you do, Old Molly. I'm Marcella. And I think you look rather a fright too,' she said.

Old Molly cackled with laughter. 'My, you're a rum 'un. You're a Somerset girl, aren't you? You tell that fancy uncle of yours to open an account at my shop. You get all the finest local produce here – he don't need to send to London for his grub.'

'I'll tell him,' said Marcella, looking doubtfully inside the dark shop, where the flies were buzzing around a wheel of cheese. It made the whole shop smell.

'Come and see Mr Berner's shop – you might like it,' I said, taking Marcella's arm.

I thought she might already have a whole room full of toys: a street of doll's houses and a menagerie of stuffed animals. Mr Berner's shop might seem dull by comparison – but Marcella loved it. She didn't put her nose to the window and peer in, playing the what-shall-I-buy? game. She went straight in and wandered around, touching everything on display, even asking Mr Berner to take one of the dolls out of the glass cabinet.

Marcella didn't actually buy anything. In the end, embarrassed, I fumbled for the bent penny in my pocket and bought two tiny china dolls no bigger than my thumb. They were called Frozen Charlottes, and were rather dull because they couldn't move their limbs. You couldn't dress them and they didn't have proper hair like Farthing, just painted black curls – but at least they were a purchase.

'Thank you, Mr Berner,' I said politely, and walked out.

'I wish I had some money. They're such lovely little dolls,' said Marcella. 'You can pretend they're twins.'

'I bought one for you,' I said, pressing it into her hand.

'Really? Oh, that's so lovely of you! And it's not fair at all, because I know you're very poor – Barbara said.'

'We're not poor any more, actually,' I said, stung. 'Aunty has a special contract with Harrods in London. And I've got my very own bank account.'

'I think you're fibbing,' said Marcella, cradling her doll in her hand.

'No, truly. I'm not allowed to spend it yet though.'

'I'm not allowed to spend *anything*. Barbara and Stanley are so stingy. We've got hardly any toys. The only person who buys us lovely things at Christmas is Uncle Benjamin. Can we visit all the other shops too?'

Marcella was interested in them all, but thought Mr Berner's by far the best. Nigel liked the butcher's shop, and dragged Marcella inside.

'Oh dear, I'm so sorry,' she said as he scrabbled eagerly in the sawdust, trying to jump up at the hanging rabbits.

'Come on the scrounge for a bone or two, have you?' said Mr Samson, looking at me.

I blushed, but Marcella didn't understand. 'Oh, yes please, I think Nigel would love a bone! Thank you very much.'

Mr Samson shook his head at us, but gave Marcella a parcel of bones, all with quite a lot of meat on them. They would have made Aunty and me a stew to last all week.

'I do like this village,' said Marcella happily. 'It's going to be absolute heaven staying here this summer. We can play together again, can't we, Mona?'

'Yes, of course,' I said.

We headed homewards. When we passed the Higginses' cottage Bertha was still tethered to the pram, but Maggie was indoors, which was a relief. Aunty asked Marcella in for a cup of tea. 'But hang on tight to Nigel. I've got a kitten,' I said proudly.

'Oh, you lucky thing!' said Marcella. 'Please let me see it, I simply love kittens.'

We left Nigel in Aunty's care while I took Marcella up to my bedroom. Aunty didn't look very thrilled about it, but didn't object.

Sixpence was curled up dozing in the middle of my pillow.

'Oh, she's adorable!' said Marcella. 'I'd swap Nigel for her any day of the week.'

Sixpence yawned and stretched and purred, delighted to have company. We played with her until Aunty called to say the tea was ready. We went running down. Aunty had set the good china out neatly and opened a packet of Petit Beurre biscuits too, laying them in a little fan on the best bluebird plate.

'What lovely dainty biscuits,' said Marcella. 'Oh, they've got French writing on them. It says they're "little butter" biscuits!'

I hadn't known that *petit beurre* meant 'little butter'. I don't think Aunty knew either, but we both nodded. A cup of tea and a biscuit was hardly a feast, but Marcella was very complimentary.

'It's such fun eating in your kitchen,' she said.

'We don't have a parlour because Aunty has a special workroom,' I explained.

'Can I see it?' Marcella asked.

Aunty hesitated, looking doubtfully at Nigel. She was worried he'd jump up at the clothes hanging neatly from their racks.

We left him tied to the kitchen table leg while Aunty led Marcella into her workroom. I watched from the doorway as she wandered around, staring at all the dresses. She looked awed, as if she was tiptoeing around a church. She asked questions in a whisper, examining the tiny stiches, the lace collars, the embroidery.

'Do you always make your dresses in very small sizes, Miss Watson?' she wondered.

'I make my dresses in ages two, four and six,' said Aunty.

'I'm nine,' said Marcella dolefully.

Aunty didn't even hesitate. 'I'll make you a dress in your size, if you like, Miss Marcella.'

'Really? But I dare say they're very expensive. I'm not sure Barbara would want to pay a lot,' she said.

'I wouldn't dream of asking for payment,' said Aunty. 'I'll make it as a present.'

'I can't believe you'd make such a lovely kind offer!

I expect I should say no you mustn't, but I'm going to say yes please!' said Marcella, clasping her hands against her blue-smocked chest. 'Oh, I should just die of happiness if I could wear a frock like that.'

'This particular design? With the rainbow smocking?' Aunty asked.

'Actually, I'd rather not have the smocking – maybe just a plain bodice? I'm rather sick of smocking, though you do it so beautifully. Barbara always makes it pucker unevenly,' she said, plucking at her own dress.

'I think she does it very well,' said Aunty, plainly fibbing. 'Of course, she's not a trained dressmaker.'

Marcella blew upwards through her fringe to indicate her agreement. 'Could the dress be a lot shorter too? This one keeps bunching up around my legs and getting in the way.'

'Of course. Knee length? Maybe just above the knees?' Aunty suggested.

'Oh yes!'

'Then we'd better include matching knickers.'

'Oh goodness! Look at the ones I'm wearing.' Marcella hitched up her coarse blue smock to show an ancient pair of white drawers – now an unattractive grey, with a distressing droop. 'They weren't even new when Esmeralda had them. They were cut down from a pair of Barbara's, can you imagine!' she said.

I'd have died rather than show off such a pair, but Marcella seemed to be enjoying herself. Aunty clucked sympathetically and got out her tape measure. 'I'll just jot down a few measurements, Miss Marcella, but you seem a pretty standard size to me.'

'How soon do you think you could make my dress, Miss Watson? By teatime?' she asked hopefully.

I knew that this was ridiculous. It would take Aunty much, much longer, and she had all her Harrods orders to get through first. Marcella would be lucky to have her dress made in a week – *several* weeks.

'Pop back *tomorrow* teatime, dear, and let's hope for the best,' said Aunty.

'Oh, you're a positive angel,' said Marcella. She gave Aunty a hug, and to my astonishment Aunty hugged her right back, pink in the face. I felt a strange twinge. She was trying to please Marcella much more than she ever had me.

Marcella went skipping off, holding up her dress so that she wouldn't trip over it.

'How on earth will you get her dress ready by tomorrow, Aunty?' I asked.

'Oh, it won't be the first time I've stayed up all night stitching,' she said cheerfully.

'I know you did for Lady Somerset, but at least she paid you for it.'

'Goodness, Mona. I thought you'd be thrilled that I was putting myself out for your new friend,' said Aunty. 'What's the matter with you?'

'Nothing's the matter,' I said. 'And I *am* pleased Marcella wants to be friends. I just don't see why you're being so nice to her. You never offered to make Maggie a dress, and she's been my friend for ages.'

'Well, *Maggie*!' said Aunty, in a need-I-say-more kind of way. 'Marcella's different. She's a Somerset.'

'Hello, Mona.' He'd remembered my name!

18

MARCELLA WAS THRILLED WITH HER NEW frock. Aunty chose a pale green muslin with a slight silver shimmer. She'd fashioned perfect puffed sleeves, and two pockets edged with darker green lace. There were knickers to match, as promised, and they had green lace too, three layers. Aunty had even cut a satin hair ribbon in the same shade of green.

'Oh, Miss Watson, you're the most heavenly angel ever!' said Marcella, dancing around her. 'I love you to bits!'

'Now, now, Miss Marcella, no need to get carried away,' said Aunty, but her eyes shone behind her glasses.

I couldn't help wondering whether Marcella would ever come calling again now that she'd got her pretty green frock – but she knocked on our door nearly every day. Bruno came too. He managed to mutter a polite greeting to Aunty.

'Hello, Fishface,' he said to me.

'Don't tell me you're after a new frock too,' I said.

Bruno pulled a hideous face. 'Don't be stupid! I want to see the big pig in someone's back garden.'

'You could eat six puddings a day, and in a week or two *you* could be the pig in your uncle's back garden,' I said.

'Mona! Watch your tongue! Don't talk to Master Bruno like that,' said Aunty, shocked.

'Yes, don't talk to me like that,' Bruno echoed.

I didn't want to take him to the Higginses' cottage, but when Marcella and I wandered down to the village arm in arm Bruno tagged after us, even though we kept telling him to go away.

Bertha was once again tied to the baby's pram outside the cottage, and Johnnie and Bertie were making mud pies, but Maggie was nowhere in sight. I grabbed Marcella's hand and we ran past, but Bruno wasn't fooled.

'Is this the pig cottage? It is, it is! I want to see the pig!' He raised his voice and bellowed, 'I WANT TO SEE THE PIG!'

'Mum! Our mum! There's a strange boy with Mona wanting to see Porker!' the brothers yelled, running into the cottage.

'Hello, dears,' said Mrs Higgins, coming out with a rolling pin in one hand, up to her elbows in flour.

'He's not with me,' I insisted.

'We've never even seen him before,' said Marcella.

Mrs Higgins shook her head at us. 'You're a pair of fibbers,' she said, amused. 'Why are you teasing him?'

'TAKE ME TO SEE YOUR PIG AT ONCE!' Bruno boomed.

'I beg your pardon?' said Mrs Higgins. 'Who do you think you are, young man?'

'I'm Bruno Somerset,' he said.

Mrs Higgins didn't seem impressed. 'I thought you were. Well, watch your tongue, child. You don't give orders here, no matter who you are. But if you was to say nicely, *Please may I have a peep at your pig, Mrs Higgins*, then I might decide to say yes.'

Bruno knew when he was beaten. His urge to see the pig was too much for him. 'Please may I have a peep at your pig, Mrs Higgins?' he parroted.

'Of course you can, my dear. Bertie, take Master Bruno to see Porker, there's a good boy,' said Mrs Higgins. 'Are you girls going to see him too?'

'Not today thank you, Mrs Higgins. I don't want to risk getting my new frock dirty,' said Marcella. She held out her skirt. 'Do you like it?'

'I think it's truly pretty. You look a picture. I think I know who made it for you too!'

I went hot all over, because Aunty had never offered to make Maggie one, but Mrs Higgins was too kind to bear a grudge. She even pretended that Maggie would be sorry she'd missed me.

'She's gone to have her tea with a friend,' she told me.

'*Boy*friend,' said Bertie.

I knew who that was. I decided I didn't care. I liked Peter, but Maggie was welcome to him. I liked Roland much better. I wished he wanted to see Porker too.

'How's your other brother?' I asked Marcella as

casually as I could as we strolled back, Bruno trailing behind us making snorty pig noises.

'Roland? He's still hanging around with the workmen,' she said. 'He even likes to share their lunch outside. Which is just as well, because he gets terribly dirty helping them dig and then forgets the state of his clothes. He flopped down on one of Uncle Benjamin's new blue chairs the other day, and that silly Ambrose went demented because he left marks on the velvet. Uncle Benjamin was a jolly good sport and said you mustn't blame a chap for sitting on a chair, because surely that was their sole purpose. Ambrose has been in a sulk ever since.'

'And is Esmeralda still friends with Desiree?'

'Desiree has gone to London for the week, so Esmeralda's at a bit of a loose end. She tried painting with Barbara but got terribly bored. I think she'd really like to come with me, but she won't because she's too proud. She absolutely loves my new dress but doesn't want it to look as if she's asking for one for herself,' said Marcella.

'I think my aunty would be happy to make her one too,' I said.

'Yes, but we don't really want her to come, do we?' Marcella said. 'She'd only start bossing us about. You have no idea how lucky you are not to have an elder sister, Mona.'

I wasn't sure I agreed. I was thrilled when we spotted Esmeralda drifting listlessly around the cottage when we got back from the village. She saw us, and started walking rapidly back towards the manor.

'Esmeralda! Esmeralda, come back!' I called.

'Oh, don't,' said Marcella.

'Can't we just be nice to her?'

'She's not nice to me!'

Nigel was straining on his leash, obviously wanting to see Esmeralda too. He pulled so hard that Marcella lost her grip on the lead and he went tearing off.

'Oh, rats,' she said. 'Stupid dog!'

Nigel was leaping up at Esmeralda, licking her bare legs and barking a love song to her. She couldn't move for Nigel whirling around her.

'Can't you control the silly animal?' she shouted to Marcella, but she bent down and fondled Nigel, tickling him behind his floppy ears. He rolled over onto his back so that she could tickle his tummy too. 'Honestly!' she said, but she obliged, her long golden hair falling over him like a curtain.

She was wearing a Barbara-sewn blue smock too, but somehow it didn't look hideous on her. The bulky material emphasized the slenderness of her wrists and legs, and the tight smocked chest showed she was starting to get a figure. I stared at her enviously.

'Don't tickle him like that!' said Marcella. 'If he gets too excited he wets himself. You'll get dog wee all over your smock.'

'Good,' said Esmeralda. 'I hate it. I'd like him to tear it to shreds.'

'Would you like a dress like Marcella's? My aunty made it for her – she could make you one too. If you'd like it, that is,' I said.

Esmeralda looked up from Nigel. 'That's very kind of you, but I don't think so,' she said.

'It would be no trouble at all,' I insisted, though Aunty had red-rimmed eyes and a splitting headache after working on Marcella's green dress by lamplight.

'Go on, Esmeralda. You know you'd love a dress like this,' said Marcella, stroking her shimmery skirts.

'I wouldn't, actually,' she replied lightly. 'It's tremendously pretty and beautifully sewn, and you're very lucky that Mona's aunt has been so kind – but it's far too babyish for me.'

'I'm sure Aunty could make you something more grown up,' I said, a little hurt.

'A dress like Desiree's?'

'Well, not exactly like that,' I said. Aunty disapproved of Desiree's dress: she said it was downright disgusting, fit only for a woman of the night – whatever that was.

'That's what I'd like,' said Esmeralda. 'Desiree's going to bring me several of her old dresses when she comes back from London.'

'They'll look stupid on you. You're only a little girl,' said Marcella.

Esmeralda raised her eyebrows. 'You're just jealous because *you're* the little girl,' she said, and walked off.

Nigel whimpered, feeling rejected. Marcella clutched his lead. 'No, Nigel. You don't want to go to her. She's a silly stuck-up beast. And she'll look totally ridiculous in one of Desiree's dresses, won't she, Mona?'

I nodded, but privately I thought that Esmeralda would look amazing in a short spangled dress. She didn't come near the cottage again, and Bruno tired of seeing the pig and stayed away too. I'd hoped I might spend the summer playing with all four children – but

I was glad that I had Marcella as a friend.

Late one afternoon Aunty sent me scurrying down to the village because we'd run out of flour and she wanted to make a pie. When I came out of Old Molly's, clutching my paper bag, I bumped straight into Roland!

'Hello!' I said, praying I wasn't blushing.

'Hello, Mona.' He'd remembered my name! He was tanned, his hair bleached even fairer, his eyes very blue. I couldn't quite look him in the eye.

He peered into Old Molly's shop. It was very dark inside, which was probably just as well. I sometimes heard a scuttling in the corners, and once we'd found mouse dirt in our sack of porridge oats. The cheese smell was worse than usual because it had been a very hot day. Roland wrinkled his nose, hesitating in the doorway.

'Well, come in or go out, make up your mind,' Old Molly called out of the gloom.

Roland looked startled. 'I was wondering if you might sell cigarettes,' he said.

'Oh my Lord!' she shrieked. 'Cigarettes, is it, young master? Your poor dead grandma would be turning in her grave. As if I'm going to sell cigarettes to a little boy, even if he *is* a Somerset!'

'The cigarettes aren't for me,' said Roland.

'What kind of a fool do you take me for? Be off with you!'

Roland's cheeks were flushed.

'She *is* an old fool,' I whispered. 'And she doesn't sell cigarettes anyway. But I know where you can get some.'

'What's that you're muttering, Mona Smith? If you're off buying cigarettes, I'll tell that stuck-up aunt of yours and she'll give you the whipping you deserve!' Old Molly threatened.

I poked my tongue out at her and then backed away.

Roland came with me. 'What an old witch,' he said.

'Yes, she is. And she smells as bad as her shop. You have to be careful.' I opened my paper bag and peered at the flour. 'You have to check for weevils.'

'Good God!' said Roland, taken aback.

I hoped to find something wriggling about just to show him, but for once the flour was white and undisturbed.

'Does your aunt really whip you?' he asked.

'She used to smack me sometimes, but it didn't really hurt. And she doesn't do it any more – I'm too big.'

'Barbara's never, ever smacked us. My father wouldn't have laid a finger on us, but Stanley once beat me because I smeared his paints all over the wall,' said Roland.

'Deliberately?'

'Of course.'

'Goodness!' I said. I was pretty sure that Aunty would beat me if I ever took it into my head to do something similar.

'He wanted to make me cry but I didn't. My mother cried a great deal, though she didn't stop him. So that night I ran away and I wasn't found till the next day. Barbara vowed then that I would never be beaten again, no matter what I did,' said Roland. 'So I won in the end.'

It didn't sound to me as if he'd won at all, but I didn't argue.

'I know where you can get cigarettes,' I said. 'Mr Berner sells them in his toyshop. And he sells sweets and all sorts. Do you really smoke, Roland?'

'No, I want to buy a present for each of the four workmen building the swimming pool. They've been awfully decent to me, showing me how to do things, and we rag each other. It's so jolly,' said Roland. 'They're not a bit like the workmen in France, who call me *Petit Choux.*'

'That's little something,' I said.

Roland looked faintly impressed. 'Do you speak French then?'

'Not really, but I'd like to. They have all the best words. So what does *choux* mean? Is it very rude?'

'It means "cabbage". It's actually a term of endearment, but they mean it in a nasty way. They tease me because of my hair and my clothes and the way I talk French. But I don't care a jot,' said Roland, though he clearly did.

'I get teased at the village school, but I'm going to the Girls' High School in Hailbury in September,' I said, hoping he would be more impressed than his sister.

He was barely listening. 'So where's this shop then?'

'It's over the road,' I explained, pointing. I went with him, because he didn't seem comfortable with shopping. Maybe he'd never had to do it before.

He didn't give the toys a second glance, and he wasn't even interested in the sweet jars. He went straight up to the counter and said in his posh voice, 'I say, do you have any cigarettes?'

Mr Berner folded his arms over his brown overall. He shook his head. 'You're too young for cigarettes, laddie – unless you fancy the sweetie sort,' he said, chuckling at his suggestion.

Roland glared at him.

'He's buying them as a present for some workmen up at the manor,' I said quickly.

'He could say he's buying them for the Queen of Sheba – he's still too young, Mona,' said Mr Berner, but I could tell he was wavering. He was the nicest of the shopkeepers, and he was always very polite to Aunty. In fact, one Sunday we met him out in the street, and he took his hat off to Aunty and she went pink. When he'd gone past I'd teased her, saying that Mr Berner was sweet on her.

'I don't think there's a Mrs Berner, is there? Maybe you two should start courting,' I'd suggested. I was only joking, but I rather liked the idea because Mr Berner was a nice, mild man and I'd have an endless supply of sweets.

However, Aunty had sniffed disdainfully. 'I'm not having anyone courting me – especially Mr Berner,' she said firmly.

'My aunty will vouch for Roland, Mr Berner. He's from the manor,' I said now, because he still seemed keen on Aunty, even if she didn't return his regard.

'I know very well who he is,' said Mr Berner, but he had his head on one side, staring at Roland appraisingly. 'What brand of cigarettes were you looking for, laddie?'

Roland looked nonplussed, but after a few seconds he said, 'The ones with the sailor on the front. I've seen them smoking that sort.'

'Very well then. A packet of twenty is it, young sir?'

'No, I think one each. Five packets then – a hundred cigarettes,' said Roland.

Mr Berner raised his eyebrows. 'Are you sure you've got enough bunce, lad?'

'"Bunce" means money,' I hissed, because Roland looked baffled.

He took a pound note out of his pocket with a grand gesture. 'This should cover it,' he said. 'Keep the change.'

Mr Berner blinked. He looked tempted, but after he'd put five packets of cigarettes in a bag and rung up the money on his till, he insisted on giving Roland his change. 'Don't want your grandmother to haunt me, now, do I?' he said.

'You knew my grandmother?' said Roland, looking surprised. 'Did she come here to buy sweets?'

'I didn't *know* her, lad, but I knew *of* her. The whole village knows the Somersets. So think on,' he said.

When we were outside I looked at Roland. 'You said there were four workmen. And yet you've bought five packets of Players.'

'You're so sharp you'll cut yourself,' he said. 'That's what Nanny says.'

'You have a nanny?' I asked.

'Not any more. I miss her dreadfully. We all do. Bruno's got far worse since she went. She was the only one who could make him do as he was told. Well, most of the time.'

'So who looks after him now? Your mother?'

'Barbara's hopeless. She says she wants us to run wild and enjoy our childhood – but she just can't be bothered with us now that she's taken up with that awful Stanley,' said Roland. 'The other packet is for me, silly. I'll give you a cigarette if you like.'

'All right,' I said, though I knew that Aunty would faint if she thought I'd smoked a cigarette.

'Where can we go that's private then?' Roland asked. 'Doubtless some busybody will stop us if we light up in the street.'

'I know the perfect place,' I told him.

I took him to the graveyard. I steered him away from his grandmother and Mother. It would be disrespectful to smoke anywhere near them. We went right to the back, by the old brick wall, and squatted down in a clear patch amongst the nettles and ivy. I hoped Roland would suddenly realize that we didn't have any matches – I was a bit scared of smoking in case I couldn't do it properly. However, he brought out a box of Bryant & May's.

'I filched them from the kitchen,' he said, shaking them.

'Why didn't you filch Mr Benjamin's cigarettes too? I've seen Ambrose helping himself from that silver box,' I said as he opened one of the packets.

'He would,' he replied scornfully. 'As if I'd ever steal from my uncle!'

I nodded and accepted the cigarette he offered me, pouting my lips in readiness.

'Not like that – you're not supposed to get the end wet,' he said. 'Now, when I light it, suck hard.'

I did my best. The hot smoke tasted horrid and I choked. Smoking was worse than I'd feared.

'It's all right, everyone coughs a bit at first,' said Roland. 'Try again.'

He smoked with style, assuming the right appreciative expression. He didn't hold his cigarette aloft like Desiree. He held it cupped in his hand.

'This is the way all the workmen smoke,' he said.

'They're such decent chaps – they have such a laugh together. They call me their apprentice. I wish *I* could be a workman.'

'Can't you be anything you want?' I asked, taking a cautious puff. It still tasted as bad and burned the back of my throat, but I managed not to choke this time.

'I suppose I could command the workmen to let me join in if I was paying their wages, but it would be very strange. I don't think they'd like it then. It would be as if we were all play-acting,' said Roland. He looked at me. 'Are you getting the hang of it now?'

'Sort of,' I said. 'I don't like it much. Does Esmeralda smoke?'

'She's tried with Desiree. She says she likes the idea of women smoking, but she just doesn't personally care for it. She smoked in front of Barbara, rather hoping she'd be shocked, but she pretended not to notice.'

'Aunty wouldn't pretend not to notice if she caught me puffing away,' I said, trying to tap the ash off the end of my cigarette. 'She would really lose her rag. She definitely doesn't approve of women smoking.'

'Marcella thinks the world of your aunt because she's made her that green dress. She looks quite pretty in it – better than in those smock things,' said Roland. 'She thinks the world of you too, Mona. She's so happy to have a friend at last. You won't suddenly turn against her, will you?'

'As if I'd do that!' I said indignantly. 'I like playing with her.'

I took a deep breath, ignoring my cigarette now. 'I'd like to play with all of you,' I mumbled.

'Well, you can, when I'm not busy helping the men. And we can always come here and smoke together,' said Roland.

'Yes, I'm starting to like smoking now,' I lied.

'You've brought Marcella here, haven't you? She said you showed her your mother's grave. She insisted that your mother *spoke* sometimes.'

'Well, she does. Privately, to me.' I prayed Roland wouldn't mock, but he just looked interested.

'I'll show you her grave,' I said when we'd both stubbed out our cigarettes.

Roland stared at her grassy mound between the grey graves covered with lichen. He looked puzzled.

'She hasn't got a headstone, but I'm going to get one for her when I'm grown up. Her name's Sylvia: Sylvia Mona Smith,' I said.

'*Who is Silvia?*' Roland asked.

'My mother!'

'No, it's a quotation. It says she's wise and holy and fair.'

'Oh yes! That's a perfect way to describe Mother!' I said happily. 'Who said it?'

'It's in a Shakespeare play.'

'Oh. I don't think I like Shakespeare,' I said. 'He wrote a play about Titania and eglantine, didn't he?'

Roland was touching all the little white stones. 'Did you put them here? You've made it look very pretty,' he said.

'Your grandmother's tomb is much grander,' I said. 'I suppose you'll be put in that tomb too when you die.'

'I can't imagine anything worse. I'm not being stuck in

the dark with ancient Somerset bones. I'd much sooner be buried in some distant battlefield.'

'That's where my father is – in France,' I said.

'Mine would have wanted to die there too instead of a dreadful hospital,' said Roland. 'It seems so unfair that he fought bravely all through the wretched war and then had to die of influenza.'

'Still, at least you're not an orphan like me,' I pointed out.

'That's true,' said Roland awkwardly. 'Are you going to talk to your mother then?'

I stood up, suddenly feeling shy. 'Not in front of you,' I said, brushing my skirt down.

'All right. I understand. Anyway, I'd better get back to give the chaps their present before they knock off work,' said Roland. 'Let's meet up again though. Come up to the manor tomorrow and I'll show you how the pool is getting on. Would you like that?'

'Yes, I would!' I said.

'Stop staring at me,' Esmeralda said.

19

A FTER THAT I SPENT EVERY DAY UP AT
the manor. I almost felt like a fifth Somerset child.
I always had lunch with them – often a picnic by the pool
or up in the treehouse. If it rained we took the picnic
up to the attics, and sprawled on Lady Somerset's cast-
off chairs. Roland lay on her chaise longue with a shawl
round his shoulders, pretending to be his grandmother.
He imitated her imperious voice while we spluttered
into our ginger beer.

No matter what the weather we had afternoon tea
with Mr Benjamin. We splashed our hands and faces and
tidied ourselves first. Bruno had to strip off altogether
and dunk himself under the garden tap, because he loved
to play moles in the mounds of earth by the swimming
pool.

Mr Benjamin often had company, most frequently Ambrose and Mr Michael and Lady Arabella and Desiree. Desiree's hair was bobbed even shorter now, and she wore carmine lip rouge that made her teeth look very bright and sharp, as if she might take a bite out of someone. There were sometimes new guests too, who wore odd clothes and talked in high-pitched voices and shrieked with laughter.

We liked it best when Mr Benjamin had no company at all. Then we sat beside his chair like faithful dogs, and ate little bridge rolls and jam tarts and iced biscuits and big slices of cake. He talked to each of us in turn. He discussed the development of the swimming pool with Roland, he asked Esmeralda's advice on the decoration of the spare bedrooms, he talked about Nigel's training with Marcella, and he told Bruno silly jokes that made him roll around on the carpet, laughing.

Mr Benjamin often talked books with me. He lent me his copy of *The Happy Prince* and I confessed that it made me cry.

'Me too, me too,' he said. I shyly showed him my own version of the story, and he said that Oscar Wilde himself would be impressed.

On Aunty's Harrods Fridays, after dashing back home to feed Sixpence, I stayed for dinner too, and once actually spent the night at Somerset Manor. Marcella and Bruno weren't considered old enough to dine with the adults, and had eggy toast and a glass of milk in their nightgowns, supervised by Ella. Barbara thought that I should join them, but Mr Benjamin insisted I was practically middle-aged and must be treated as such.

I was pleased to be joining the others for their evening meal, but it was rather an ordeal. I hadn't realized that posh people changed their clothes for dinner, even Roland and Esmeralda. He wore a white shirt and long dark trousers, with a spotted neckerchief instead of a tie. She wore a long silk kimono patterned with purple flowers. It was faded and the hem was torn, but she still looked amazing. She wore a string of amethyst beads on her golden hair like a crown, and a silver snake bangle on one thin white wrist.

I felt like a little girl in my crumpled daisy dress and my schoolgirl plaits, but Mr Benjamin took a pink rosebud from the vase to match my best pink ribbons and tucked it over my ear.

'There, you look beautiful!' he said, and insisted I sit beside him. I think Esmeralda usually sat there because she glared at me throughout the meal.

Mr Benjamin chatted to me as if I was an adult, discussing his future plans for the manor and seeking my opinion. He asked me about Aunty and her experiences at Harrods. He seemed delighted that she was still doing so well and had regular work.

'I wish she'd take me up to London again. It was wonderful,' I said, sipping my lemonade, pretending it was wine.

'I knew you'd appreciate London,' said Mr Benjamin. 'I shall have to take you to see the great galleries and museums.'

I was actually thinking of Harrods and its glorious confectionery department, but I nodded enthusiastically when he told me about the Italian paintings in the National Gallery, and the Egyptian mummies in the British Museum, and the Oriental galleries in the Victoria and Albert.

'Such treasures from all over the world,' he said. 'Oh, I must, must, must take you to the big exhibition at Wembley! I went with Ambrose when it opened, but they say it's even better this year. Would you like to come, Mona?'

'Yes please!' I said, so excited that I tilted my glass and lemonade dribbled down my front. 'Oh dear!' I exclaimed, mortified.

'Dab yourself with this, darling!' said Mr Benjamin, passing me his immaculate napkin. 'Oh Lord, the times I spill things down my shirt! My poor washerwoman must be fed up with scrubbing out my stains. Do you know, one evening at the Eiffel Club I managed to spill an entire bottle of red wine all over myself, and I was wearing a brand-new white suit!'

'Can I come to the exhibition, Uncle Benjamin?' Esmeralda asked, twisting a long strand of golden hair around her finger.

I so hoped he would say no, but naturally he didn't.

'Of course you must come too, Esmeralda, and Roland, if he can bear to spend a day away from all his workman chums,' said Mr Benjamin. 'And we mustn't forget Marcella and Bruno.'

'Oh Lord, not Bruno,' said Esmeralda. 'He'd keep dashing off. We'd lose him altogether.'

'Then you must absolutely promise to take him,' said Stanley, who didn't seem to like any of his stepchildren, Bruno least of all.

'Shame on you, Stanley!' said Barbara, shaking her head fondly at him.

'But he's such a little beast. He daubed an extremely rude appendage to my painting of the statue by the new pool.'

'Oh, sweetheart, I'm so sorry,' Barbara chuckled, nuzzling her head into the crook of his neck.

I stared at her. Esmeralda was staring too, her nose wrinkled. I caught her eye and we had a moment of shared disgust.

I hoped that this might make us friends, especially as Barbara suggested we share a bedroom. Marcella and Bruno were sharing the old nursery.

Esmeralda's room was white and gold. There was a pink lustre jug filled with ox-eye daisies on the window sill and a painting of angels above the mantelpiece. I thought I'd be sharing her pretty white bed, but Ella trundled an old canvas camp bed into the room for me. It spoiled the whole effect.

'It makes your lovely room look ugly now,' I said apologetically.

'Oh well, it's just for one night,' said Esmeralda, sighing.

She slipped out of her kimono and sat at her dressing table in her skimpy petticoat. Unwinding the beads from her hair, she started brushing it vigorously. It made an amazing crackling sound, as if it was alive.

'Stop staring at me,' she said.

'Sorry,' I said, but how could I *help* watching her? I took off my own frock, feeling very self-conscious, and quickly pulled my white nightie over my head. It was freshly starched, and Aunty always used Reckitt's Blue in the wash so that it shone eerily white in the lamplight.

'If I wake in the night I shall think you're a ghost,' said Esmeralda.

'Maybe I'll make weird moaning noises and frighten you silly,' I said, climbing into the camp bed. 'But then you can put that snake on your arm so you can make it hiss at me and frighten me back.'

'You're such a weird girl.' She picked up the snake bangle she had laid on her dressing table. 'Do you like it? Desiree gave it to me. She's very generous. She gave me this kimono too.' She picked it up and rubbed it against her cheek. 'It's silk,' she said.

'I know. Silk feels lovely,' I said.

'The other evening Alistair Michael tried to stroke it,' she told me.

'Oh, how horrible!'

'Yes, he's positively disgusting. I can't understand why Uncle Benjamin keeps inviting him here. I suppose he thinks he's clever because he drones on and on about boring things like philosophy and politics. I think he's simply tedious. So does Desiree,' said Esmeralda. 'She's rather marvellous, isn't she?'

'I suppose,' I said doubtfully. 'What do you think of her mother?'

'I can't stand Lady Arabella. She's incredibly spiteful.'

'Yes, isn't she? She called me a pert little nobody,' I said, wincing.

'That's nothing. I heard her telling Barbara to keep an eye on me because I was a little trollop in the making, the way I was flaunting myself.' Esmeralda tried to laugh to show she didn't care, but her voice wobbled.

'That's hateful,' I said.

'Poor Desiree, it must be vile to have her as a mother. Barbara's bad enough because she forgets we're here half the time. When Bruno was little she left him in his perambulator under a tree and wandered off to paint. She didn't remember him for hours, and when she ambled back at the end of the afternoon he was shrieking his head off. She thought it was *funny*.'

I was shocked to hear that she was such a bad mother. 'I'm so lucky – my mother was wonderful, even though she's dead now,' I said.

'*Dead, dead, and never called me Mother!*' Esmeralda declared.

I blinked at her.

'It's a quote, silly. From a play,' she told me.

'Mr Benjamin said he wanted to put on a play in the garden,' I said. 'I think it was going to be *A Midsummer Night's Dream*. You'll probably be Titania. She's Queen of the Fairies.'

'I know,' said Esmeralda, laying down her silver hairbrush, switching off the lamp and climbing into bed.

'I'm not sure the villagers will like it, not if it's full of fancy words they can't understand,' I said. 'I know Mr Benjamin thinks it will be a lovely treat, but they might laugh.'

'I'm sure they'd positively hate it. And I'd hate it too if I had to act in it. It's such a bore to learn lines. I think Uncle's gone off the idea now anyway. He's planning to have a ball to celebrate the opening of the new swimming pool,' said Esmeralda.

'A ball!' I exclaimed, thinking of 'Cinderella'.

'He's going to erect a huge marquee beside the pool, and we all have to dress up as sea creatures,' said Esmeralda.

I'd have preferred a proper ballroom and beautiful gowns and glass slippers, but it still sounded wonderful.

'Mr Benjamin has such amazing ideas,' I said.

'Why do you always call my uncle Mr Benjamin? It sounds so funny.'

'Well, I can't call him Uncle, because he isn't.'

'Why not just call him Benjamin?'

'I couldn't!'

'I call my mother Barbara. And Stanley Stanley. Along with a lot of worse names. We all hate him. He doesn't think much of us either. He's always moaning that he left his own brats to run off with Barbara, and now he's saddled himself with a worse lot.'

'He says that to your faces?'

'All the time. He's not so bad with Marcella and me, but he's positively beastly to the boys. He hits them sometimes. How I wish I could hit him back,' said Esmeralda, punching her pillow.

'Isn't it strange that people with children are often so mean to them, when someone like Mr – like Benjamin – is always so kind and courteous and treats us like grown-ups,' I said.

'Mm,' said Esmeralda.

I thought she might have resented my saying *us* as if I was part of the family. Or maybe she was simply going to sleep, because in a minute or two I heard her breathing heavily. She didn't snore though. Perhaps

Esmeralda was too dainty to do such a coarse thing.

I feared I might snore terribly. Aunty often said I did. 'Wakey wakey! Stop snorting like a warthog! You're a little girl!' she often cried when she tried to get me up. I thought she was teasing – but what if it was true? I decided to stay awake as long as possible.

I have no idea if I snored or not during the night. I woke very early, and was about to creep along the corridor to the water closet. I'd have died rather than use the chamber pot under Esmeralda's bed in case she woke up and saw me. Someone was outside the door, pushing at it urgently. I peeped out anxiously, but it was only Nigel, escaped from his basket in the basement. He licked my bare feet, giving little barks of joy.

I knelt down to pet him, but he seemed very fidgety, desperate to go out. I was decently covered because my nightie came down to my ankles – and Mr Benjamin didn't give a fig about wandering the grounds in his own nightgown.

'Come on then,' I said to Nigel, and he pattered happily along the corridor, waited while I visited the water closet, and accompanied me downstairs.

It was very quiet and still. None of the servants seemed to be up – though perhaps they were down in the kitchen. I found Nigel's leash on the hall table and attached it to his collar. I couldn't manage the complicated bolts on the front door, but the back door was easier.

Nigel pulled on his lead and we shot out into the bright early morning air. I didn't have any shoes on and the gravel path hurt my bare feet, so I kept to the grass. Nigel and I ran together. His nose quivered as he smelled rabbits and his ears twitched whenever a bird flew past. He had a jaunty air, seeming to know that all this land belonged to him because he was a Somerset dog.

I wondered what it would be like to be a Somerset child. I pictured myself as Esmeralda, gliding along, my Rapunzel hair warm on my shoulders. I wished I was her – and yet *she* wished she was Desiree. Roland simply longed to be one of the workmen constructing the pool.

The only person I knew who seemed really happy in himself was Mr Benjamin. I hoped he was taking another early walk today. We could do a stately dance together in our nightgowns! But there was no sign of him – no sign of anyone.

'So Somerset Manor and all the grounds belong just to me now,' I said.

It was a dizzying idea. I wandered around, touching trees and shrubs and flowers, whispering, 'Mine! Mine! Mine!' I headed for the pool and marvelled at the pearly tiles and the green coping stones that blended with the grass. Ambrose had ordered palm trees in great terra-cotta pots, a cluster of three here, two there. I couldn't stand Ambrose, but I had to admit that he was good at design. The trees gave the pool a tropical feel. I hoped parrots might come and roost there, while monkeys swung from the branches.

The workmen had been busy levelling a very large area of grass, presumably for the marquee. I held out the imaginary skirt of a ball gown and waltzed around in a circle. No, they'd have modern dances at Mr Benjamin's ball. I stepped out, waving my arms, trying to remember the Charleston. I worried that the workmen might arrive early and think me a fool, prancing about in my nightgown.

'Come on, Nigel, time to go home,' I said.

He was very reluctant, so I had to drag him back and then carry him down to the kitchen. Cook was there, cracking eggs into a big bowl, and an anxious kitchen maid was scurrying backwards and forwards. The new butler, Harold, was there too, eating a bacon sandwich in his shirtsleeves. I blushed and bent my knees so that my nightgown covered more of me.

'Excuse me, sir,' I murmured.

Mr Marchant would have told me off, but Harold nodded to me in a friendly fashion. 'We were wondering where the dog had got to! Here, boy!' He held out a rasher of bacon from his sandwich.

Nigel jumped out of my arms and ran over to him eagerly. My mouth watered at the smell of the bacon and I looked hopefully at Cook, but she carried on beating her eggs, and when Ella bustled into the kitchen, her cap pulled down to her eyebrows, she shooed me away.

'You go back to bed for another half-hour, Mona, there's a good girl. You're too old to be wandering around in your night things,' she said. 'What would your aunty say?'

'Don't tell her, will you?' I asked. Aunty had been doubtful about letting me stay the night – she'd made me promise to mind my manners and not let her down.

'As if I've got time for telling tales!' said Ella. 'I'm run off my feet, what with extra guests and now this blooming ball to prepare for. We're getting girls in from the village to help out, but it's still going to be an ordeal – most of the staff are brand-new and not used to the house or each other. They keep saying, *Where's the best tea set, Ella?* and *Where do we put the leftovers, Ella?* and *When should we change the sheets, Ella?'* She moaned on and on, but I could tell she was pleased with the extra responsibility. And she'd boasted to Aunty that Mr Benjamin had doubled her wages.

I tiptoed back to the bedroom. Esmeralda murmured sleepily, 'Where have you been?'

'Just the W,' I said. I'd heard Esmeralda and Marcella calling it that, and was careful to use the right term. 'Go back to sleep, it's not time to get up yet.'

Esmeralda was asleep again in seconds, but I was still wide awake when another new maid knocked on the door and brought in a tray with two cups and two glasses.

'Morning, miss, morning, miss,' she said. 'Cook wasn't sure whether you'd prefer a cup of tea or a glass of milk so I've brought both. And there's biscuits too.'

I sat up and drank my tea *and* my milk. There were five ginger biscuits on the plate, which was awkward. I ate two and politely left three for Esmeralda, though I did wonder about snapping one in half so I could have my full share. They were home-made biscuits, fatter than the shop sort, and very tasty. I knew Aunty would like them, and I tried to save one biscuit for her, but greed overcame me.

Esmeralda didn't stir for another five minutes, and then leaned up on one elbow to take two sips of her tea. She didn't bother with any of her biscuits, so while she was brushing her hair I quickly snatched them off the plate, wrapping them in my handkerchief, and stuffing them in my shabby carpet bag.

I didn't have another best dress, so Aunty had packed my school frock. I knew I looked very young in it. Esmeralda put on her blue smock, adding a long white petticoat and a pair of old-fashioned kid boots she'd found in a trunk in the attic. She looked quaint but beautiful.

When we went down for breakfast Mr Benjamin was already in earnest discussion with Ambrose about the decoration of the marquee. Esmeralda ran ahead and sat down beside her uncle, joining in their conversation.

The other children were sitting further down the table. Roland was by himself, reading as he ate. I wanted to sit with him, but I was worried about disturbing him, so after dithering for a few seconds I plumped myself down next to Marcella. Bruno was pouring syrup onto his bowl of porridge. The syrup went all over his hands too, but he licked it off with relish.

'Bruno, darling!' Barbara murmured, but then turned to discuss costumes with Stanley.

'I'm not dressing up like a clown,' he said disagreeably.

'I'm not asking you to be a clown, my love – just a sea god. I see you in a toga, with a seaweed crown,' Barbara said in her throaty voice. 'You will look magnificent.'

'What's a toga?' Marcella asked.

'It's a short dress thing that Romans used to wear,' said Roland, his eyes still on his book.

Marcella grinned, and Bruno spluttered into his porridge bowl.

'Why does your mother want him to dress up?' I whispered to Marcella.

'It's for the ball,' she said. 'It will be such fun. I can't wait to see Stanley in a dress!'

'He will look sooo stupid,' Bruno murmured, pouring out yet more syrup. '*I'm* not wearing a girly dress!'

'Well, you're not wearing anything at all, so you'll look stupid too,' said Marcella. '*I'm* wearing the beautiful pale green dress your aunt made for me, Mona. Barbara's stitching wings onto the back and I'm going to be a sea fairy.'

She flapped her arms excitedly and knocked over her glass of milk.

'Can't you control your brats, Barbara?' Stanley said irritably, pushing his chair back. He stalked out of the breakfast room, a slice of toast in his hand.

Barbara tutted. 'You two! Poor Stanley. I'd better go and calm him down.' She swept off, scarves trailing, her hem coming undone.

'Are you really going to the ball?' I asked Marcella and Bruno.

I hadn't dreamed that children would be going. I'd got out my fairy-tale book and pored over the picture of Cinderella dancing with the Prince, but there were no children peeping out from behind the marble pillars or sitting on the little gilt chairs.

'Of course we are,' said Marcella.

'I'm going as a water baby,' said Bruno. 'Barbara says I will look enchanting. I'm not even going to be wearing drawers!'

'How alarming,' I said weakly. I'd helped myself to a large plate of bacon and eggs, but now I suddenly wasn't hungry. I *felt* like Cinderella, left behind to sweep up the ashes.

'What are you going to wear, Roland?' I asked timidly.

He was still deep in his book. For a moment I thought he hadn't heard me. Then he murmured, 'Robinson Crusoe.'

'He's silly. He's not a sea creature, he's in a storybook,' said Bruno.

'He was shipwrecked. His boat sank in the *sea*. And I can make my own costume – I just have to rip up a shirt and my old cricket flannels. Simple,' said Roland. 'I'm not parading around like an ass.'

'So what will you wear, Mona?' Marcella asked.

'I haven't been invited,' I said in a tiny voice.

Mr Benjamin was in the middle of a discussion on Chinese lanterns, but he must have heard me. He waved his fork in the air as if it was a wand.

'Abracadabra. I am your fairy godfather, Mona, and I say you *shall* go to the ball. Of course you're coming – and you must persuade your good aunt to come too. I haven't bothered to send you a formal invitation because you're practically family. And, to be absolutely honest, I'm a little embarrassed. Barbara has taken it upon herself to organize the family costumes, when I did very much hope your ultra-talented aunt would do the honours. Barbara is extremely artistic, but I'm not sure stitching is her forte. Her costumes are likely to fall apart in the middle of a dance.'

'It won't matter to me, because I'm not wearing a stitch,' said Bruno, and roared with laughter at his joke, syrup dribbling down his chin.

'Is Barbara designing your costume too, Mr Benjamin?' I asked.

'Uncle's no fool,' said Esmeralda. 'He's ordered his

from a special costumier in London. And Desiree is helping me with mine. I'm going as a mermaid. She's got an old green beaded evening dress that will make a wonderful tail.'

Esmeralda would make a splendid mermaid. She already looked like one with her long golden hair. I sighed. If I really was going to this Sea Creatures Ball, I would have loved to be a mermaid too.

'Do you think your aunt would be kind enough to run up a costume for you?' asked Mr Benjamin. 'And, of course, one for herself.'

'If not, Mona can be a water baby like me,' said Bruno.

'And Mona's aunt could be . . . a tadpole!' said Marcella. 'Because she's little and she always wears black.'

I knew she was simply trying to be helpful but the others all burst out laughing. I didn't like to think that they might be mocking Aunty. I had been planning to stay on after breakfast but I felt the sudden need to go home.

Sixpence ran to greet me as I walked in the front door. I picked her up, cuddled her close, and then gave her a drink. Her little pink tongue lapped hard, though she was careful not to get her whiskers wet.

Aunty was in her workroom, getting started on her new orders. 'Hello, dear! Did you have a lovely time at the manor? It was just as well they invited you, because after the shop shut I had a meeting with the two girls who sew for me, and then the train was delayed and I didn't get home till nearly ten o'clock,' she said. 'I'd have been so worried about you if you were all on your own. So, come on, tell me all about it.

Were they nice to you? Did they make you feel welcome?'

I nodded, shuffling very close to Aunty until I was actually leaning on her.

'Hey, give me room to sew! What's the matter? You look a bit droopy. Did you and Marcella stay up half the night talking?'

'I had to share with Esmeralda,' I said.

'She's a bit of a madam, that girl,' said Aunty. 'Far too grown up for her age. I hope she didn't put any ideas into your head.'

'She was all right,' I said. 'Mr Benjamin is going to throw a Sea Creatures Ball, and Esmeralda's going as a mermaid.'

Aunty snorted. 'I can imagine,' she said. 'What's she going to wear on her front?'

'I don't know. Desiree is helping her with her costume.'

'Oh well, that says it all!' said Aunty. 'What's her mother thinking of?'

'Barbara's letting Bruno be a water baby, completely bare,' I said.

'She's never! He's not a baby, he's a proper little boy. It's not decent!' said Aunty. 'She's never making poor little Marcella go around starkers too?'

'Marcella's wearing the frock you made her. She's going to be a fairy.'

'And she'll look very pretty, even if I say so myself. So I suppose Mr Benjamin wants me to help with the rest of the costumes . . . I'm up to my eyes in work for Harrods, but I'll do my best, though I can't work miracles.'

'Well, actually, I think Barbara's doing their costumes,' I said awkwardly.

'Barbara! But she can't even sew straight!'

'Yes, I know.'

'We can't have her making poor Mr Benjamin look ridiculous. I can at least make *his* costume,' said Aunty.

I took a deep breath. 'He's gone to a dressmaker in London,' I said in a rush.

Aunty frowned. '*I'm* a dressmaker in London. In Harrods. The best department store in Britain,' she pointed out.

'Yes, but I think this other person is French. You know how fancy people think anything French is better – they even cook their beef the French way and give it a funny name,' I said. 'Don't be upset, Aunty. You wouldn't have time to make heaps of costumes, not with all your other work.'

Aunty sniffed. 'Have they invited you to this ball, Mona?'

'Yes, but I'm not sure I want to go. It sounds a bit silly. I wish it was a proper ball like in "Cinderella",' I said.

'Well, that wouldn't be Mr Benjamin's way, would it?' It was the nearest Aunty had ever come to criticizing him. 'I'll make *your* costume, Mona. What would you like to go as?'

'Well, I'd have liked to be a mermaid, but Esmeralda's going to be one,' I said, sighing.

'You can be one too,' said Aunty.

'Yes, but I won't look nearly as good. She's got much longer, thicker hair than me, and Desiree is giving her a green beaded dress for a tail.'

'I'll make you a better mermaid costume, just you wait and see,' said Aunty, her chin up.

'Will you really?' I asked. 'And what will you go as?'

'Don't be ridiculous,' she said, starting to sketch a design.

'You're invited. Mr Benjamin said you must come,' I said.

'Oh, he did, did he? Well, Mr Benjamin's very kind, but I'm declining. You shall go though, Mona. And you'll be wearing the best costume of the lot, you just wait and see.'

Mr Benjamin bowed and took her hand.

20

S HE MADE ME THE MOST BEAUTIFUL MERMAID costume. The top half was pale pink silk, so that it looked like flesh – 'But you're still perfectly respectable,' she said. Then I had a wide green satin sash around my waist, with chain-stitched cockle shells all around it. I wasn't too sure about the mermaid tail though. Aunty had fashioned a Turkish bloomers affair out of more green satin, and she'd covered my old slippers in satin too.

'But it's not a proper tail, Aunty, it's trousers,' I said.

'If you stand with your legs together and your feet turned out, it makes a perfect tail, but you'll be able to move about. You can't wear an actual tail, silly, or you'll just have to lie there like a log all evening, not joining in,' she told me.

'I don't think I'll be joining in anyway,' I said. 'I don't know what you do at a ball. And I won't know many people there. I won't belong.'

'Yes you will!' said Aunty fiercely. 'You know how fond Mr Benjamin is of you. And you're great friends with Marcella too. You stick with her. You'll have the time of your life. There'll be lovely food. Ella said that in Lady Somerset's day they had meringues and ice cream and strawberries and the finest champagne.'

'Can I have champagne?'

'Don't be so silly, of course not! You'll have lovely lemonade or some such.' Aunty paused. 'Unless they take you for a real mermaid and feed you a bucket of herrings.'

I knew it was a beautiful costume, even though I wasn't sure about the bloomers, but I wished *I* looked more beautiful in it. I kept thinking of curvy Esmeralda and her long golden hair. I'd look so small and skimpy beside her, and although my hair grew down to my shoulder blades it was as straight as a poker.

'I know what we'll do,' said Aunty, the morning of the ball. She washed my hair and then plaited it into twenty thin braids, breathing hard with concentration.

'But I look weird, Aunty,' I wailed, peering into the mirror. 'You can see my scalp now!'

'You won't look weird when I brush your plaits out later,' she said. 'Trust me, Mona.'

'But what if someone sees me like this?' I worried that Roland might appear.

'No one's going to come. They'll all be busy preparing for the ball. You stay home with me and read your books. You can always help me with a bit of sewing if you get restless.'

It was a very long day. I couldn't concentrate on any of my favourite stories, and the book I'd borrowed from Old Molly's library was a silly mystery story with the last pages torn out. I tacked a few hems for Aunty, keeping close to her pins, but the flimsy material bunched up in my hands and she had to pull out all my thread and start again herself. I played with Sixpence, throwing her toy mouse again and again so that she could pounce on it, but eventually she tired of the game. In the afternoon we curled up on my bed together and went to sleep.

Aunty woke me at six with a cup of tea and a biscuit. 'Here now, have a little sip and nibble. You won't need a proper supper – you'll be eating all sorts of fancy things at the ball. Wash your face and clean your teeth after, and then we'll get you into your costume and sort out your hair,' she said.

I did as I was told, and then sat on a stool while Aunty patiently unplaited my hair and then started brushing it out.

'There!' she said at last, standing back and peering at me, her head on one side. 'Go and look in the mirror and see what you think now.'

I had a knot in my stomach, terrified I'd look ridiculous, but when I saw myself I caught my breath. My hair had been transformed into a thick, curly cloud.

'Oh, Aunty, it's magic!' I whispered. 'I look pretty!'

'Now don't start getting big-headed!' she said, but she looked pleased. 'Right then, my girl. Off you go. Have a lovely time. You can stay till ten. Keep an eye on the time now. I'm sure Mr Benjamin will make sure someone sees you home in the dark.'

She gave me a kiss on the cheek and went to the door with me. As I set off she waved, and I waved back, striding out in my strange green tail-feet – but the nearer I got to the manor, the slower I walked. Cars full of strangers were chugging up the driveway. I could hear the guests chattering and laughing through their open windows. There was distant music coming from the marquee. It was lit by Chinese lanterns – rose pink and blue and crimson and jade. I could see silhouettes inside, all prancing about to the music.

It was a warm summer evening but I started shivering. I hated the sound of the guests' high, hard voices – among them Lady Arabella's ringing tones. No doubt she'd say something crushing when she saw me. Mr Benjamin would be busy with his guests. I doubted he'd even spot me in the crowd.

I couldn't see Roland or Esmeralda or Marcella. I'd have even run to join Bruno, but I couldn't see him either. I never quite knew where I was with the Somerset children. I felt a sudden pang when I thought of my old friendship with Maggie. We might have fallen out from time to time, but I had never felt awkward or uncomfortable with her. If she was here now, she'd take my arm and say, *Come on, scaredy cat. Let's go and have a laugh at all these posh nobs*.

I tried whispering it to myself, but it didn't work. I just couldn't make myself go into that marquee. I turned round and ran all the way back to the cottage.

Aunty leaped up from her chair when she saw me. 'What's up, Mona? What's happened? Has someone been horrible to you? Why have you come back?'

I tried to think of any number of excuses. I started making up a story about Lady Arabella saying something insulting – but then I simply told the truth.

'I was too shy to go in.'

'Oh, Mona!' said Aunty, shaking her head. 'How can you be such a ninny?'

'You get scared of them too, I know you do,' I retorted.

'Of course I don't,' she fibbed.

'Well, you come too then.' I reached out a hand to her. 'Please!'

'A great girl your age!' said Aunty, but she squeezed my hand back. 'All right, I'll walk up and see you in. We don't want to waste that lovely costume, do we?'

'Oh, thank you, Aunty, thank you!' I said fervently.

She tidied her hair and brushed the cotton threads off her black dress. 'Come on then.'

We walked up towards the manor together.

'Oh, my!' Aunty murmured when she saw the marquee and heard the music. 'Lady Somerset never put on a do like this! Trust Mr Benjamin!'

We walked a little nearer, and watched the guests sauntering up to the marquee. A woman with a seashell necklace right down to her waist held the arm of a man wearing an elaborate waistcoat, angel fish embroidered on sea-green velvet.

'Look at the work in that,' Aunty whispered.

Another man was actually dressed as a fish, with a huge silver-scaled head and pop eyes, and silvery trousers to match.

'But they don't look like a tail,' Aunty said. 'I've made a much better job of *your* tail, Mona. Ah, look! Is that

Mr Benjamin standing by the entrance? It *is*! Whatever does he *look* like?'

He looked incredible. He was wearing a pink outfit covered in pearls and twigs of coral, with a matching pointy pink clown hat bearing a large gold star. He had another star on each arm, and two more on either leg.

'Oh, Aunty, don't you see what he is?' I cried. 'He's a starfish! How clever!'

I forget to keep my voice down, and Mr Benjamin had very sharp ears. He looked round and spotted us standing under the trees.

'Mona! My, what a marvellous little mermaid you are! Well done, Miss Watson! Come along, ladies! This way!' he called, waving to us with a starry arm.

'There you go, dear. Quickly!' said Aunty, giving me a little push forward. She turned to go, but Mr Benjamin darted forward, his stars glinting.

'Not so fast! You're invited too, Miss Watson!'

'That's very kind of you, sir, but I'm far too old for balls!' said Aunty.

'That's nonsense. Try saying that to Lady Arabella!' said Mr Benjamin. 'You *must* come. You can study all the costumes.'

'But I'm not in *any* kind of costume, sir!'

'Don't you *sir* me when we've become such good friends. Now, let's see – how can we make you an instant costume?' He put his head on one side, looking at Aunty in her old black dress.

My stomach turned over. I was terrified he was going to suggest she should be a tadpole.

'Look, Aunty, you can have my sash,' I said, untying it quickly.

'Excellent thinking, Mona,' said Mr Benjamin, clapping his hands. 'It will look very regal worn over the shoulder. And I'll give you one of my gold stars to wear in your hair, Miss Watson. You can be Queen of the Sea.'

'No, no, you mustn't spoil your beautiful costume!' Aunty protested.

But he ripped one of the stars off without hesitation and carefully wove the points into Aunty's hair.

'There! Utterly splendid. Now come along, both of you.' He took our hands and led us through the entrance. Harold the butler was standing to attention, wearing silver livery, and a great silver pendant in the shape of a fish. Mr Benjamin had clearly enjoyed kitting him out too.

'Oh, my!' Aunty whispered again.

'May I have your name, madam?' Harold asked.

'No, please don't announce us!' said Aunty, but he insisted.

'Miss Florence Watson, and Miss Mona Smith,' he called to the tent at large. Thank goodness hardly anyone turned to look at us.

'Harold, find Miss Watson and Mona a seat and serve them some refreshments, please,' said Mr Benjamin. 'A Coral Cocktail for Miss Mona.' He saw Aunty's face. 'Don't worry, Miss Watson, it's a harmless strawberry cordial. And can I tempt you with a Seaweed Sizzler? Are you partial to a little crème de menthe?'

'Oh no, no cocktail for me!' Aunty looked over at the array of drinks and saw a large silver bowl with a ladle. 'Is that a fruit cup? I'd like that, please.'

'Certainly, madam,' said Harold. 'Excellent choice.'

'Enjoy yourselves, my dears,' said Mr Benjamin as a fresh cluster of guests came into the marquee. 'I shall come and find you later.'

Harold started to lead us to a table near the band, but Aunty shook her head. 'Could we sit at the back, please?' she begged.

'Certainly,' he said, finding us a quieter spot. 'I'll fetch your drinks. If you need anything at all, don't hesitate to call me over.'

'He's so much nicer than old Mr Marchant,' I said as he went off.

Aunty was fingering the star in her hair. 'Do I look a complete fool, Mona?' she whispered.

'No, you look lovely,' I insisted, though poor flustered Aunty *did* look a little strange, the bright star and the sash contrasting with her shabby dress. 'Do you think that star's real gold, Aunty?'

'It couldn't possibly be – could it? They've certainly spent a fortune on their outfits. And they'll probably never wear them again! At Lady Somerset's balls they wore proper evening dress. I made her a beautiful beaded silk, with a high neckline and long sleeves suitable for an older lady. She never wore anything revealing. She'd faint if she could see some of these young women. Oh my Lord, look what Desiree's wearing!'

She was barely wearing anything at all – just a wisp of white chiffon artfully wound about her bare body. I've no idea how it stayed in place. She had a few fronds of seaweed green dangling here and there, and wore a matching green turban on her bobbed hair, with a silver brooch in the shape of a seahorse.

She was dancing all by herself, bangles jangling as she lifted her arms. Around her, admiring men clapped to the rhythm of the music.

'She looks like she's doing the Dance of the Seven Veils – and there's only one to go!' Aunty sniffed, taking a gulp of the fruit cup Harold had brought her.

I sipped my own strawberry cordial, savouring it on my tongue. 'This is heavenly, Aunty. Is your fruit cup nice?' I asked.

'Well, it tastes a little strange. There's some funny flavouring in there, but it's very refreshing,' she said.

I turned and gasped: Lady Arabella and Mr Michael had taken to the dance floor. Lady Arabella looked extraordinary, with a snake headdress on her glossy hair. Her face was powdered chalk white and her eyes heavily outlined with black. Over her white dress was a golden corset affair that hitched up her bosoms, and her skirts clung to her legs.

'Who does she think she is, the Queen of Sheba?' said Aunty.

Two young gentlemen in matching orange suits – goldfish? – heard her and guffawed.

'No, my dear, she's the Queen of the *Nile*,' one young man explained. 'Trust Arabella to go as Cleopatra!'

We learned our geography parrot-fashion at school, a paragraph on each country.

'I thought the Nile was a river, not the sea,' I said. 'This is meant to be a Sea Creatures Ball, not River Creatures.'

'Ooh, you're a pedantic little miss,' said one of the men.

'But quite right. You must tell Arabella!'

'Don't you dare!' said Aunty.

'Is Mr Michael the King of the Nile?' I asked, because he was wearing a crown.

'No, child – look at the trident he's lugging around the dance floor with him. I hope he doesn't do Arabella a mischief! He's Neptune, God of the Sea, bless him.'

They waved goodbye to us and started dancing together. Aunty and I blinked at them.

'I didn't know gentlemen could dance together!' I said.

'I think we should go now, Mona,' said Aunty.

'But we've only just got here! And Mr Benjamin gave you his gold star. It would look rude if we went now,' I pointed out.

'I don't think this ball is suitable for you. None of the children seem to be here,' said Aunty.

'Yes they are!' I said, spotting them marching out of the house, helping the staff carry great platters of food over to the long trestle tables. Roland looked dashing as Robinson Crusoe, his hair tousled, his shirt open, his white trousers frayed. Marcella looked very pretty in her shimmery green dress, though Aunty gasped when she saw that her paper wings had been clumsily attached with big safety pins.

'They'll rip the material! What's that woman thinking of?' she muttered.

Bruno capered about behind them, spilling half the plate of prawns he was carrying. He was painted pale green all over, only wearing tiny knickers. People pointed, giggling. Bruno smiled broadly, playing up to his audience.

'That boy needs a good slap,' Aunty murmured. 'And that green paint will rub off all over his sheets tonight.'

'Where's Esmeralda?' I asked.

'There she is!' said Aunty, pointing.

She wasn't carrying anything. She herself was being carried, held aloft by two men in bathing costumes. She looked stunning. Her long fair hair hung over her shoulders like a curtain. She wasn't wearing a pink silk vest like me – it looked as if she was bare to the waist. I couldn't actually see her chest, but it still seemed incredibly daring. Her tail was magnificent, the green beads gleaming under the Chinese lanterns. It swept down gracefully and then divided into two sharp points. Her legs and feet were invisible inside, but she must have been gently kicking, because the tail rippled convincingly.

There was a spontaneous round of applause as she was carried over to a special chaise longue.

'Doesn't she look beautiful, Aunty?' I sighed.

'She looks indecent, if you ask me,' she sniffed. 'What's her mother thinking of, letting her show herself off like that! That's not a proper costume. They've turned the child into a statue. How is she going to join in the fun and have a dance if she can't move her legs?'

I supposed I was free to join in, but I was too shy, even when Marcella spotted us at the back of the tent and came running over.

'Mona! Miss Watson! I didn't think you were here! Doesn't Esmeralda look splendid? Can you see her over there on the green chaise longue?'

'We could hardly miss her,' said Aunty.

'Doesn't she make a splendid mermaid?' said Marcella.

'You make a splendid fairy or whatever you are. But turn round and hold still a moment. Let me pin your wings on properly for you. You should have told me you wanted wings. I'd have made you some proper ones.' She tutted, seeing that one was bent and the other was starting to tear.

'Barbara made them for me,' Marcella told us unnecessarily. 'Look, she's over there.'

She was supervising Ella and the other maids as they set out yet more platters of food. Aunty and I stared. Barbara wore a cobbled-together patchwork dress in red and yellow and blue and green – and a very large black false nose. I didn't dare look at Aunty. I had to press my lips together to stop myself bursting out laughing.

'Can you guess what she is?' Marcella asked.

We struggled. 'Is she the Pied Piper?' I suggested, because the dress was predominantly red and yellow.

'No! Why would she be wearing a beak if she was the Pied Piper?' asked Marcella. 'She's a parrot!'

'Of course she is,' said Aunty weakly.

'But parrots aren't sea creatures,' I said.

'Yes they are, if they're on a pirate's shoulder,' Marcella said triumphantly. 'See Stanley over there? He's Long John Silver.'

He was helping himself to oyster patties, making a mess of the careful arrangement. He wore his ordinary paint-stained smock and trousers, but sported a scarf knotted around his head and a patch over one eye.

'Barbara begged him to tie one leg up behind him, but Stanley said he wasn't going to stump around looking like an idiot all night. He's such a bad sport,' said Marcella, shaking her head.

All at once the band struck up a lively new tune.

'Oh, it's a polka,' she said. 'I love the polka! Come and dance with me, Mona.'

'I don't know how!'

'It's ever so easy. Even Bruno can do it. One-two-three-hop! That's all it is,' said Marcella, demonstrating. She did it very daintily, picking up her skirts and pointing her toes. I was sure I'd look silly beside her in my green bloomers.

'I don't like dancing,' I lied.

'Oh, meanie!' Marcella pouted. 'Please, Mona!'

'Go on, dear,' Aunty urged.

I shook my head.

'All right, I'll go and find Bruno,' said Marcella, and ran off.

'Why did you say no, you silly girl?' Aunty hissed to me. 'You *do* like dancing! You're forever prancing around the house.'

'I don't like this kind of dancing,' I said obstinately.

I thought Bruno would look ridiculous dancing naked, but he seemed entirely unselfconscious. He whirled around merrily with Marcella, and the guests cheered.

I looked across at Esmeralda, wondering if she was feeling hampered by her beautiful tail, but several young men had deserted Desiree and now lounged at her side, plying her with drinks and plates of food.

Desiree herself was dancing with Mr Benjamin, her white chiffon in danger of falling off altogether. Lady Arabella was dancing with the silver fish. He was tall, so I thought he might be Ambrose, but then I spotted Ambrose himself drifting about in white gauze with long dangling tentacles, the white turban on his head wobbling like a jelly.

I spluttered into my strawberry cordial. Harold was keeping Aunty and me regularly supplied with drink. He brought us wonderful food too – gigantic prawns, tiny portions of fried fish in crispy batter, smoked salmon and oyster patties. I liked the desserts even better. I tried lime posset, pale green blancmange, and little blue fairy cakes studded with pearly sweets.

I ate and drank with gusto – until I spotted Roland dancing with a fair-haired girl in a sea-green dress. A little later he was dancing with a redhead in a midnight-blue costume. Neither seemed to be wearing fancy dress, but they both looked very pretty. I wished I wasn't wearing my baggy bloomers. Roland glanced at me once or twice, but he didn't come and ask *me* to dance.

Aunty saw me looking. 'It's your own fault, dear. Marcella probably told him you didn't like dancing.' She reached out and squeezed my hand, nearly knocking my glass of cordial over. 'Whoops!' she said. 'Silly old Aunty!' She seemed to be enjoying herself, which was quite a surprise.

I turned and saw Ella scurrying past, lugging another bowl of fruit cup. She scowled at us. 'It's all right for some,' she hissed.

'Poor Ella,' Aunty murmured.

Then I spotted Mr Benjamin threading his way through the dancers towards us.

'Here's your chance, Mona!' said Aunty. 'I think he's

going to ask you to dance. Don't be shy this time! It doesn't matter if you don't know the dance – you just have to follow the gentleman's lead. Oh, my, I still think we're dreaming! Imagine us, at a Somerset ball.'

Aunty was right. Mr Benjamin bowed formally to me. 'May I have the pleasure of this dance, Miss Mona?' he asked politely, eyes sparkling.

I took a deep breath. 'Yes, you may,' I said.

I felt very shy but very proud as I took to the dance floor, Mr Benjamin holding my hand. I repeated *one-two-three-hop* in my head as the band struck up the new tune. But it wasn't a jolly polka! It was a slow and stately waltz and I didn't have a clue what I was doing.

I tried to follow Mr Benjamin's lead, but kept stepping forward instead of back and treading on his toes.

'I'm sorry! So sorry! Oh dear, I'm so clumsy,' I muttered.

I was horribly aware that people were staring at us. Lady Arabella swirled past us, bending and swaying with some young man, and Desiree raised her eyebrows as she danced with horrible Stanley, who was holding her far too closely. Barbara was dancing with Marcella while Bruno capered around them. All three were making up their own dance rather than sticking to the waltz, but at least they weren't stumbling about like me. I saw Esmeralda watching from her chaise longue, shaking her head in a superior fashion. I was sure she was shaking it at *me*.

Mr Benjamin kept up the conversation, doing his best to put me at my ease. I prayed for the dance to finish, but it seemed to go on and on and on, until it seemed I was wearing fairy-tale red shoes, doomed to dance for ever.

'You look as if you're in absolute agony, Mona,' said Mr Benjamin.

'You're the one who must be in agony – I've stepped on your toes so often,' I said despairingly. 'I just can't remember which foot I should be using.'

'Tell you what, why don't you step up onto my feet and then I'll guide you along. You won't hurt me, a little scrap like you,' he said. 'Come on, climb up!'

So I stood on his beautiful sparkly shoes and we progressed more smoothly around the floor, though I was sure his feet would be black with bruises in the morning. At last the waltz finished and I jumped off immediately.

'Not so fast, little mermaid. Shall we try another dance now that you're getting used to it?' Mr Benjamin suggested. 'Ah, listen to the introduction! This sounds much livelier!'

I hoped for another polka – but it was something wild and jazzy. Mr Benjamin's guests cheered and started prancing about, kicking their legs out at odd angles. It was the Charleston!

'Oh goodness!' I said. Maggie had taught me the steps. Maybe I'd manage better this time.

'Perhaps we'd better have a little rest now.' Mr Benjamin was trying to be tactful in case I made a fool of myself again, so I let him walk me back to our table.

Aunty had drained another glass of fruit cup and was tapping her fingers on the mosaic table and nodding her head to the music, the gold star in her hair glinting.

'There you are, Mona! Did you have a lovely dance with Mr Benjamin?' she asked. 'What a lucky girl you are.'

'I don't think Mona cares for dancing – but perhaps you do, Miss Watson?' said Mr Benjamin. 'Would you come and do the Charleston with me?' He was joking, in the nicest way possible.

Aunty looked at him, realizing that he wasn't serious. Then her chin jutted. 'I *do* like dancing,' she said, standing up. 'Thank you very much.'

Mr Benjamin bowed and took her hand, looking amused.

I went hot with horror. 'Aunty! Stop it! You'll make a fool of yourself!' I hissed, trying to grab her old dress, but she shook me off.

'Ssh, Mona!' she said, and she walked a little unsteadily to the middle of the dance floor with Mr Benjamin.

I waited, clasping my hands tightly, willing Aunty to lose her nerve at the last minute. This couldn't be happening. My aunty would never, ever do such a thing! I heard the people in front of me murmuring.

'Who is that old duck with Benjamin?'

'Perhaps she's the children's nanny.'

'She looks a bit squiffy, if you ask me. Too much fruit cup!'

Aunty, Aunty, Aunty, I shrieked inside my head, horrified to see her making such a show of herself. I saw her as they did – a gaunt little woman with a lopsided star in her hair, wearing a worn dress and down-at-heel shoes.

Mr Benjamin put his arm round Aunty protectively – he seemed to be asking if she was sure she wanted to dance. Aunty nodded determinedly, shaking her star loose. Mr Benjamin gently reattached it and then took her hand.

Aunty smiled and stood up straight, her whole stance suddenly altering. She followed Mr Benjamin for a minute or so, stepping with pinpoint precision exactly when he did, her toes swivelling as she did so, her whole body bobbing to the rhythm – and then, when he tried gently spinning her round, she held out her arms and kicked her legs sideways.

He grinned in delight and tried more spins, more twists, Aunty equal to them all, whipping round and round, sometimes holding her arms in the air, sometimes stepping to the side and showing him her profile, dancing like an Egyptian. The other dancers stared and then stood up, starting to clap. They weren't mocking. They were astonished and amused, but genuinely admiring.

The band went on playing, acknowledging the star dancer, while Aunty tapped and twirled. She lost half her hairpins so that her hair escaped its tight bun and flew about her shoulders. Her long skirt hitched up to her knees as she kicked, showing surprisingly shapely legs. I hardly recognized her now.

I saw Desiree watching. Then she ran right across the dance floor, over the grass towards the new swimming pool, and unwound her wisp of white chiffon.

'It's too hot for dancing! Let's christen the pool!' she shouted, and dived into the water while everyone squealed and shouted.

Someone started singing, *'For she's a jolly good fellow,'* and the band stopped playing jazz and joined in. Aunty was left in mid-twirl, looking dazed. She shook her head, and the gold star fell out and skidded across the floor. Mr Benjamin went to retrieve it for her, but

Aunty stared around wildly. She clapped her hands to her mouth, and then suddenly bolted off the dance floor, running towards the shrubbery.

I ran after her and found her there, bent over, being horribly sick.

We perched on the little rocky bit.

21

I HELPED AUNTY HOME IN THE DARK. SHE WAS
crying.

'It's all right, Aunty. Nobody saw, I promise. They
were all rushing to gawp at that awful Desiree. It was
obvious why she threw herself in the swimming pool.
She couldn't bear to see everyone staring at you,' I said.

Aunty gave a little whimper.

'No, they were *admiring* you! You're an amazing
dancer! How ever did you learn to dance like that? You
were incredible!' I said, but she wouldn't be comforted.

I had to hold onto her tightly or she would have
fallen. I knew the grounds so well that I could find my
way home easily in the moonlight. When we reached the
cottage I put the kettle on, hoping that Aunty might feel
better for a cup of tea and a biscuit, but she didn't seem

to want to drink or eat. She slumped down on a kitchen chair, her hands over her face as if she were trying to hide from me. Sixpence came and mewed at her.

'Shall I help you to bed?' I asked anxiously.

Aunty tried to stop me, but she needed a hand going up the stairs, and didn't even seem capable of taking off her clothes. I had to undress her like a baby and then tuck her into bed. She wept all the while, and I began to get really worried.

'You seem so ill, Aunty. Do you think I should go and get the doctor?' I asked.

'No, no. I'm not ill. Just . . . stupid. *Stupid!* I feel so ashamed!'

'You're not stupid at all. You were magnificent, dancing like that!' I said.

Aunty buried her face in her pillow and fell asleep in seconds. I patted her back awkwardly and then crept to my room. I opened my window wide and heard distant music and laughter – and splashes too. It sounded as if half the guests were joining Desiree in the pool.

I lay down in bed, pulled the covers over my head and tried to sleep, but it was impossible. Even when I was dreaming at last, I seemed to be at the ball: all the guests were real sea creatures, wet and menacing, and the food was alive, wriggling on the plate.

I slept late and jumped out of bed, wondering why Aunty hadn't called me. I went downstairs, but she wasn't in her workroom. It was half past nine! Aunty was always up before seven, stitching away.

I ran upstairs and went into her room. She lay huddled up, her hands over her head. She groaned softly.

'Aunty! Oh, Aunty, you're still ill!' I cried.

'Not ill,' she murmured. She tried to sit up, her eyes little slits in the sunlight. She held her forehead, rubbing her fingers across her eyebrows. 'My head!'

'Have you got a very bad headache?'

She nodded, and groaned again.

'Shall I bring you a damp flannel?'

'Yes please,' Aunty said, her voice cracking.

'You don't sound right at all,' I said.

'I'm just a little thirsty.' She looked at her alarm clock and gave a cry. 'So late! And I have to start work on that christening dress!'

'You stay in bed for a while. You can't work in this state. That's what's wrong with you. You've been working far too hard,' I told her.

I ran downstairs and put the kettle on. I made a pot of tea and some toast, and dowsed Aunty's flannel in cold water. I carried everything upstairs and helped her sit up in bed. She looked terrible, her face grey, her eyes bloodshot. I laid the flannel on her forehead and she patted my arm limply.

'Thank you, dear. That feels lovely,' she muttered.

'And I've made you breakfast, see!'

'It's very kind of you,' she said, putting on her glasses. She sipped her tea gingerly but screwed up her face when I offered her the buttered toast.

'Do you still feel sick?'

'A little.' Aunty took another sip of tea and then lay down again, holding the cold flannel to her forehead.

'I think I *had* better send for the doctor,' I said.

'You mustn't!' she said in alarm.

'I know it will cost a lot, but we've got money now.'

'I'm not having any doctor seeing me in this state,' said Aunty. 'Don't you understand, Mona? I had too much to drink!'

'No, you didn't,' I said, staring stupidly at her full cup of tea.

'Last night. I was drunk,' Aunty said, and tears started rolling down her cheeks. 'How could I have been such a fool?'

'But you didn't touch the cocktails. You just had fruit cup!'

'It must have been laced with something,' said Aunty, shuddering.

'But you weren't to know. I remember you saying the fruit tasted funny. It wasn't your fault it made you drunk,' I insisted.

'I realized soon enough. And I kept on drinking it. Then I made a complete fool of myself, prancing about like an ancient chorus girl! Oh dear Lord, how will I ever face Mr Benjamin again? What must he have thought?'

'He thought you danced beautifully,' I said.

'And what sort of example am I to you?' Aunty groaned. 'Leave me alone, Mona. I can't bear you seeing me like this.'

So I crept away. I hoped Aunty would get better soon. I still couldn't quite believe it. Ladies like Aunty didn't get drunk! And they didn't dance so wildly and wonderfully either. I suddenly remembered the sparkly pink dress that had once hung in the back of her wardrobe. Did *she* go out drinking and dancing long ago, before she looked after me?

It didn't seem possible. She was *Aunty*!

I ate her toast and drank some tea, and then washed and dressed, feeling out of sorts myself. My head felt as if it was bursting, trying to make sense of everything. The cottage seemed smaller than usual, the walls closing in on me. In spite of my long sleep I felt tired, and yet far too restless to go back to bed.

Then I heard a dog barking. Marcella must be taking Nigel for a walk. I ran to the door – and then, as I flung it open, I suddenly thought it might be Mr Benjamin. I couldn't face seeing him just yet, even though he'd been so kind last night. But it wasn't Mr Benjamin and it wasn't Marcella. Roland was standing there, with Nigel straining at his lead. The dog leaped up at me, licking my hands and my bare legs.

'I'm sorry,' said Roland. 'I thought I'd take him for a walk as no one else seems to be up this morning. I wanted to go up that big hill over there, but Nigel had other ideas. He dragged me down here. You're obviously his favourite person.'

'I'm sure I'm not really,' I said, tremendously pleased. I bent down to hide my blush and made a great fuss of Nigel. He hurled himself against me so enthusiastically he nearly knocked me over.

'You could make Nigel's day and come for a walk with us – though I expect you're busy,' said Roland.

'No I'm not,' I said. 'I'd love to come.' I closed the front door behind me.

'Shouldn't you tell your aunt where you're going?'

'She's asleep,' I said.

'They're all asleep back at the manor,' said Roland. 'I was the only one down for breakfast. Even Bruno's still conked out. They all ended up having a midnight swim. And most of the grown-ups drank and drank after that. They were making such fools of themselves, playing the giddy goat. When the band went home they got out the gramophone and did all the new dances. Idiots!'

'Aunty danced, but she's not an idiot,' I said.

'I know! She danced beautifully. Everyone said so,' Roland agreed. 'Where shall we go then? Can we get to that big hill, the one with all the bushes? It's difficult to gauge how far away it is.'

'That's Blackberry Hill. I know the way. It's about an hour and a half,' I said. 'Aunty and I go in the autumn to pick the berries for jam and pies and crumbles, but they won't be ripe just yet.'

'Never mind. I'd like to go. You don't mind walking that far?'

'That's not far,' I said, though I always moaned when Aunty dragged me along, our bowls and basins clanking at our sides.

We strode down the driveway towards the gates. There were several cars parked there, one with a dishevelled-looking couple snoring loudly on the back seat.

'Idiots,' Roland said again.

'It's like "The Sleeping Beauty",' I said. 'They've all been enchanted and must now sleep for a hundred years.'

'I shall never, ever give balls when I'm grown up,' said Roland emphatically. He shook his head and then shut his eyes briefly.

'What's the matter?'

'I've got a bit of a headache,' said Roland. 'It's my own fault. I drank a couple of those cocktails last night.'

❀ 364 ❀

'You didn't!'

'They tasted disgusting too. Still, I think Esmeralda drank more. She didn't have anything else to do but drink, stuck in that ridiculous mermaid costume.'

'I was a mermaid too,' I said.

'Yes, but you had enough sense to make sure you could walk around properly, and dance if you felt like it,' said Roland.

'You didn't ask me to dance!' My mouth said it before I could stop myself.

'I was going to, but Marcella said you didn't want to.'

I felt a little flare of happiness in my chest. 'I'm a hopeless dancer anyway,' I said. 'But you're quite good at it.'

'Barbara forced us to have dancing lessons when we were little. Luckily there aren't any dancing teachers near us in France,' said Roland.

'Do you like it there?' I asked.

He shrugged. 'I do, rather. But they were going to send me to school back here in September. Stanley's idea. He just wants to get rid of me. But then Uncle Benjamin said that English public schools were worse than prison and that Barbara was mad to send me, and he made her have second thoughts. She's always been very fond of Uncle Benjamin.'

'*Everyone's* fond of him,' I said. 'Even the villagers like him, though they think he dresses funny.'

We walked down to Rook Green, Nigel springing about with joy at the end of his lead, his ears flapping up and down. I hoped Maggie might be around, wanting her to be impressed, but her cottage was quiet. Maybe they were all at church. I saw a few families going to church in their Sunday best: Peter Robinson was walking along between his mother and father, looking very pink and scrubbed in his high white collar and Sunday suit. I nodded at him and he nodded back, though his mother tossed her head at me.

'Do you know that boy?' Roland asked.

'Yes, we're in the same class at school.'

'He looks as if he likes you.'

'He used to, but we're not really friends any more,' I said.

We walked all the way through the village and along to the crossroads.

'They hang people here,' I said.

'What?' said Roland.

'Not nowadays. Back in the past. They once hanged a woman for witchcraft,' I told him.

'What did she do?' He sounded fascinated.

'I don't think she did anything very much. They just didn't like her, and blamed her when things went wrong. I used to wonder if I might be a witch,' I said.

'Really? Did you boil up a magic potion and cast evil spells? Eye of toad and toe of newt and all that stuff?'

'I just put some herbs in a bottle of vinegar. I was going to sprinkle it on the children who teased me, but then I made friends with Maggie, and she bashed them for me. She can be very fierce,' I said.

'So can you,' said Roland.

I felt proud. At first it felt strange to be chatting to Roland without the others around, but it was a help having Nigel with us. If ever there was a break in the conversation we talked to him: *'Hey, Nigel!' 'Here, boy!' 'Nigel, stop doing that! Come back! Bad boy!'*

Nigel took no notice, not caring whether we thought him good or bad. When we left the village he strained at his lead so much that I let him off, which was a big mistake, because he immediately dashed off after a rabbit and disappeared entirely. We spent an anxious ten minutes calling and whistling, to no avail.

'What if he never comes back?' I said. 'He might have gone right down a rabbit hole and got stuck. I was the one who let him off the lead. It's all my fault!'

'Of course he'll come back. I'm sure he's perfectly all right. And it was just as much my fault as yours. If anything *has* happened, I'll say I was the one who let him go,' Roland said.

I was very touched, but insisted we both take the blame. And then Nigel suddenly reappeared, cutting a swathe through the long grass and dashing back to us.

'There! See? I told you he'd be all right,' said Roland, but he looked relieved, and quickly slipped the lead on him again.

'He can pull us along when we get to the really hilly part,' I said.

By the time we got to the top we were both hot and breathless. We perched on the little rocky bit. Roland rolled up his shirtsleeves and I peeled off my socks and rubbed my feet. I saw him glance down at my shoes, looking at the soles where they were worn thin. I hid them quickly.

'We often have holes in our shoes too,' he said. 'Barbara forgets that sort of thing. I think that's why she makes the girls wear those hideous sandals. They're practically indestructible. I refused to wear them, and Bruno copied me, much to Barbara's annoyance. She made us go barefoot for a while.'

'She's a bit weird, your mother,' I said.

'She's trying so hard to be Bohemian. It's because Stanley's an artist. She was never like that when my father was alive. I wish, wish, wish he hadn't died,' said Roland.

'I wonder if my father and your father knew each other,' I said. 'Perhaps they fought in the same regiment . . . Though I suppose your father would have been a colonel or something and mine would have been just an ordinary soldier,' I said.

'My father was a captain,' said Roland.

'Will you be a soldier too?'

Roland peered down at the yellow and green and brown fields below us. 'I fancy growing things. And I love animals. I shall rear the most tremendous pigs like the one in the village.'

'I don't think you'd like to do the killing part if you love animals,' I said. 'I heard Mrs Higgins's last pig having its throat cut and it was simply terrible. I still dream about that squealing sometimes.'

'You're right, I'd hate that part,' said Roland. 'I think I'll just rear pigs because they're comical and delightful. And I'll keep sheep for their wool. I'd never turn the young ones into lamb. And I won't kill cows for beef, I'd just have them milked.'

'But that's upsetting too, when they take the calves away. The cows moo for days, missing them.'

'You're relentless, Mona,' said Roland, giving me a

little push. 'Maybe Bruno will have to run the farm too. He can be very tough. Marcella's soft, so she can help rear the baby animals and feed the chickens.'

'What about Esmeralda?'

'She wants to live in London, especially now she's chummed up with Desiree. She's no fun any more. She just fusses about her hair and her clothes all the time.'

'Her hair's so beautiful,' I said, and then blushed because I sounded soppy.

'Esmeralda doesn't think so. She hates it – she says long hair is old-fashioned. I didn't know hair could go in and out of fashion, but there you are.' Roland shook his head.

'Does she want to put it up?'

'No, she wants to have it all cut off.'

'She mustn't do that!' I said, horrified.

'She keeps begging Barbara to let her go to Desiree's hairdresser, but Barbara won't hear of it. So now she's threatening to cut it off herself,' said Roland.

'Well, it's a good job she didn't do it yesterday. She'd have looked like a very odd mermaid without any hair and we'd have seen her chest!' I said.

Roland chuckled. 'Gosh, I'm starving. We should have brought a picnic. You haven't got anything to eat, have you? Let's go through our pockets.'

My dress didn't have real pockets, just pretend slits, because Aunty thought they'd spoil the design. Luckily Roland had deep pockets, and after a lot of rummaging he found a couple of dog biscuits in the shape of bones, and half a sandwich he'd forgotten about. He examined it carefully.

'I think it's only a couple of days old. The cheese

hasn't gone mouldy. Would you like it?' he said, offering it to me.

'I can't take your sandwich,' I said.

'We'll split it.' He tore it in half, and we munched it while Nigel crunched his biscuits and then begged for crusts.

'He's a very greedy dog,' said Roland. 'It's Uncle Benjamin's fault. He's hopelessly soft with him and feeds him all kinds of titbits. He does the same with us actually. He once let Bruno eat an entire box of chocolates. You can imagine what happened afterwards, on one of his Persian rugs. But Uncle just laughed, and Bruno thought it worth being sick to have had such an amazing experience. He boasted about it for months.'

'Mr Benjamin always gives me cake,' I said. 'He's the kindest man ever. I'm so glad he's living in Somerset Manor and not your uncle George.'

'We all are! Apparently he invited Uncle George and Aunt Mary and Cedric and Ada to the Sea Creatures Ball, but they wouldn't come. Such a shame. Imagine what a splendid walrus Uncle George would have made with his whiskers. And I'm sure Aunt Mary could have grown some too,' said Roland.

I burst out laughing. 'They were horrid to Aunty,' I said.

'They're beastly to everyone. At my grandmother's funeral Aunt Mary made Barbara cry. She said we looked like a bunch of ragamuffins and we'd all end up degenerates,' said Roland.

'That's terrible!' I pretended to be shocked, although half the village had muttered the same thing, Aunty included.

'Uncle Benjamin said I was far more likely to become

a degenerate if they forced me to go to boarding school,' said Roland.

I wasn't sure what a degenerate was, but I nodded sympathetically.

'Anyway, if they do send me, I shall run away at the first opportunity. I've already started saving my pocket money for train fares, and I'll take my pocket knife. I'll need rations too. Maybe a packet of biscuits or that mint cake explorers take on voyages. And matches.'

'For smoking?'

'That's a good idea – I've developed a real craving for it now I've made friends with the workmen. But I meant for a fire, in case I have to lie low somewhere. I've got it all planned out,' said Roland proudly.

'But how will you get all the way to France? Wouldn't a boat cost much more than pocket money?'

'I'm not going home! What would be the point? Stanley would probably give me a thrashing and then send me straight back. I'll come here instead. Uncle Benjamin would take me in like a shot. I know he'd let me live with him. And I'd probably learn heaps more than if I went to some lousy school. Uncle's got so many books. I could browse in the library all morning and work on the farm in the afternoon to earn my keep.'

I was starting to wonder why I'd been so keen to get into Hailbury High School. 'That sounds like bliss,' I said.

'And we could take Nigel for walks,' said Roland.

I grinned happily at him. We sat there talking for a very long time. Neither of us had a watch, and neither of us wanted to suggest going home. Eventually hunger got the better of us.

'My stomach's rumbling dreadfully. I think it must be lunchtime by now, maybe even later,' said Roland. 'Perhaps we'd better start back. Your aunt will be worrying about you. And I dare say my people will be making a fuss – if they've surfaced yet. Come on.' He stood up and held out his hand. I seized it and he pulled me up.

It seemed a very long way. I was sure I had blisters on my feet. Roland strode out manfully but he was starting to look tired too, and his hair kept flopping in his eyes, irritating him.

'Maybe you're the one who should get his hair bobbed,' I said.

He laughed. 'No fear!' Then he hesitated. 'Do you think it looks stupid this long then?'

'No, I think it looks lovely,' I said.

By the time we got to the village we were exhausted, and painfully thirsty.

'Tell you what, let's get a drink,' said Roland, looking at the Plough and Harrow Inn on the corner.

'We can't go in there! Children aren't allowed to drink beer.'

'We're not going to drink beer, silly.' Roland was counting the change in his pockets. 'I think that's enough.'

'But isn't that your running-away money?'

'I've got heaps more. Don't worry. You'd better stay outside and wait for me,' he said. 'Hold Nigel's lead.'

I knew Mr Pogson who owned the Plough and Harrow. He was a big, red-faced man with shoulders wider than most doors. I was worried he'd send Roland packing. I waited there, all of a dither, but Roland came strolling out with a pint of lemonade in either hand.

'Oh my goodness!' I said, impressed. 'What did you say to him?'

'I just asked for some lemonade and put my money on the counter. Easy,' said Roland.

Everything was easy if you were a Somerset. I gulped down my drink, though I wasn't sure it was wise. I was already aching to use the lavatory. On a long walk I usually went behind a bush, but with Roland there I was too embarrassed.

The last stretch back to the manor seemed to go on for ever, and I had a bad pain in my tummy. I envied Nigel, who simply cocked his leg whenever he felt like it.

'Thank you so much for the walk and the lemonade, Roland. I've had such a lovely time,' I said when we got to the cottage.

Then I scooted inside quick sharp before I wet myself.

I wanted to go to India.

22

AUNTY WAS UP AND DRESSED, HER HAIR IN
a neat bun, but she still looked terrible.

'Where have you been, Mona?' She sounded terrible too.

'I'm sorry, Aunty. I've been for a walk with Roland.
I should have left you a note,' I said. 'How do you feel now?'

Aunty ducked her head. 'I'm fine, thank you,' she lied.

'You were amazing last night,' I started, trying to
make her feel better, but she shook her head.

'I don't want to talk about last night,' she said.

'I never knew you could dance like that!' I persisted.

'Mona, please! Stop it now. Have you had any lunch?'

'No. I'm absolutely starving. We walked right up
Blackberry Hill together, Roland and me,' I told her.

'Roland and I,' she corrected automatically. 'Right, I'll
fix you something.'

She hadn't started on our Sunday roast lunch. She cooked me an omelette instead. She didn't eat anything herself. She didn't have anything at teatime either – just a cup of tea, not even a biscuit. Most of the time she was in her workroom, but when I looked in on her to see if she was all right, she wasn't sewing. She was clasping her head in her hands, her eyes shut.

On Monday she was mercifully back to normal, working hard, but she still wouldn't talk about the Sea Creatures Ball, not even to Mr Benjamin. He came calling on Monday morning, with Nigel.

'Good morning, Miss Watson. Good morning, Mona. I do hope you enjoyed yourself on Saturday night,' he said cheerily.

'Oh yes, Mr Benjamin. It was amazing,' I said.

'Thank you, sir,' Aunty murmured.

'We danced up a storm!' Mr Benjamin started, but stopped short when he saw Aunty's face. He quickly changed the subject. 'Nearly all my visitors have gone now, but the children are having a swim. I wondered if Mona would like to join them . . .'

'Oh, yes please!' I said, but Aunty was shaking her head.

'She doesn't know how to swim, sir. And she doesn't have a proper bathing costume,' she said.

'Oh, she'll soon pick it up from the others – they swim like little fishes. Esmeralda has gone to stay with Arabella and Desiree in London for a couple of days, so Mona can borrow her costume. I'll get Barbara to look it out. And what about you, Miss Watson? Can I tempt you away from your work? You could lounge by the pool while keeping an eye on young Mona.'

'I'm afraid I can't, Mr Benjamin,' Aunty said firmly, but she let me go, telling me not to go out of my depth and begging me to be careful.

Mr Benjamin promised that he would watch me like a hawk. 'I am only a moderately competent swimmer myself, but Ambrose got a swimming certificate at school, so he is our resident lifeguard,' he assured her.

I felt guilty at leaving Aunty again, but I didn't want to miss this chance. As we walked up to the manor, Mr Benjamin chatted about the ball.

'I hope you really *did* enjoy it, Mona. I'm afraid it got a little wild, but I think you and your aunt had left by then. I didn't get to bed until dawn, and then the spirit of my mother hovered over me, admonishing me for the decadent behaviour in her house. I found myself apologizing abjectly. I was always a little afraid of her, the dear old duck.'

When we arrived, everyone was in the pool. Roland waved to me, and Marcella jumped up and down excitedly and said, 'Come and join us, Mona!' Bruno started splashing me, but Roland seized hold of him and dunked him.

Barbara heaved herself out of the water and went to find me a swimming costume. Her own blue knitted outfit was embarrassingly clingy, with several moth holes. I hoped Esmeralda's costume would be less revealing. Luckily it was made of stiff navy material, with legs that came right down to my knees. It was much too big, but at least I was decently covered.

Barbara found me a lifebelt ring to wear about my waist. 'Bruno doesn't need it any more. It will help you enormously, Mona. And see here – you kick your legs like this and move your arms at the same time. Keep your chin up! That's the spirit,' she said encouragingly.

The pool was so shockingly cold that for a few minutes I could barely think, let alone listen to instructions, but I found if I jumped up and down I stopped shivering quite so violently. I tried a few strokes as Barbara suggested.

I hoped I would pick it up straight away and swim up and down the pool as easily as the others, but I kept getting mouthfuls of water and I panicked whenever I took my feet off the bottom. Marcella bobbed along, trying to show me, while Bruno dived in, doing his best to put me off.

'I'll teach you, Mona,' said Roland. 'I'll tow you around. I won't let you go under, I promise. Trust me.'

I did trust him, so I let him put his hand under my chin while he gently tugged me away from the side of the pool. I kicked my legs a little, and waved my arms around too. I'm not sure I was actually swimming, but it felt as if I was.

Stanley was thrashing up and down, making great waves, and Ambrose swam lazily but stylishly for several lengths. Mr Benjamin *looked* stylish in his black-and-white-striped costume, but his breaststroke was timid and he held his head well out of the water at all times. His black curls stayed bone-dry. When we got out of the pool, he was the only one who didn't look like an otter.

Ella brought a huge pile of fluffy towels so we could dry ourselves. 'Quite one of the family now, aren't you, Mona?' she murmured to me.

'Do feel free to use the pool yourself, Ella,' said Mr

Benjamin, dabbing himself dry. 'I know young Harold dives in at every opportunity.'

'I've got better things to do with my time than fling myself into cold water, sir,' she said crisply.

She went to help catch Bruno, who was running away from his mother.

'Come back, you silly boy – you can't stay soaking wet,' she called.

'I don't want to get dry. I want to go in the pool again. And again. And again. I have to have lots of swims before we go home. I don't want to go home!' Bruno wailed as Ella caught him and bundled him under her arm to give him back to his mother.

'When are you going home?' I asked Marcella.

'Stanley says we have to go on Saturday as he wants to get back to his studio. We can't see why he doesn't go back by himself and let us stay till the end of the summer. Or stay for ever. We love it here,' she said, shivering.

'I love having you here, chickie,' said Mr Benjamin, wrapping himself in a white towelling robe. 'Can't they stay, Barbara?'

She sighed and shook her head. 'Poor Stanley needs to get back. He says he can't paint here. It's the wrong atmosphere. And we mustn't split up the family.'

'Uncle Benjamin is proper family,' said Roland, towelling his wild hair. 'Not that oaf over there,' he muttered, nodding at Stanley, who was performing callisthenics by the pool.

'Roland, stop this, please,' said Barbara, looking wretched.

'If you really do have to go on Saturday, then we

must make the most of the time we have left. Swimming. Picnics. Outings. Yes, when Esmeralda's back we'll have a grand outing. How about Friday? Mona will be with us anyway while her aunt is in London,' said Mr Benjamin.

'Where will we go?' Bruno asked eagerly, allowing himself to be caught and dried. 'What's the furthest place we can go, so it will take up the most time? How about Timbuktu?'

'Excellent idea, Bruno. I'm sure we can go there, and perhaps we'll stop by Egypt on the way and see the pyramids . . . And I've heard the Taj Mahal is a sight worth seeing, so we'll put that on our itinerary too. And I've always had a yearning to cross the Rocky Mountains. We're going to have the most exciting trip in the world,' said Mr Benjamin.

'Don't, Benjamin, he believes every word you say,' Barbara remonstrated.

'I shall keep my word, I swear it,' he said, smiling.

'I know where we're going!' said Roland. 'We're going to the big Empire Exhibition at Wembley!'

'We are indeed,' said Mr Benjamin.

'Well, count me out,' said Stanley rudely. 'I'm not going anywhere near all those gawping crowds.'

'No one's asking you to, old chap,' said Mr Benjamin. 'Why don't you and Barbara have a day to yourselves. Lie by the pool and relax. I'll take the children.'

'That would be heaven,' said Barbara, 'but you can't possibly cope with five children, especially when one of them is Bruno.'

'I won't be by myself. Ambrose will be coming too,' said Mr Benjamin.

'Oh no I'm not,' said Ambrose, appalled. 'I'm not looking after a parcel of brats. Besides, I went to the exhibition last year. I've seen it all.'

'It's even bigger and better this year, and there's a new section on interior design, dear chap – right up your street,' said Mr Benjamin.

Ambrose didn't look convinced, but when I went running up to the manor early on Friday morning, he was standing beside the motorcar, yawning and stretching, wearing a green shirt, mustard-yellow jacket and blue trousers. Mr Benjamin was resplendent in an embroidered Indian tunic. Roland wore a blue shirt and grey trousers, with Mr Benjamin's cream jumper knotted casually around his shoulders. Marcella wore her shimmery green dress, while Bruno was in a striped Breton top, and shorts that showed the scabs on his knees. Then I saw a strange young woman in a very short dress and buttoned satin shoes with spindly heels. She had a brutally bobbed haircut.

'Hurry up, you're late. We've been waiting for you,' she said.

It was Esmeralda! She looked so different without her wonderful long fair hair. Her face seemed too big without it – much longer, with too much nose and chin, though her eyes were still blue and beautiful. They were glaring at me now.

'Don't just stand there gawping,' she snapped.

'You didn't recognize Esmeralda at first, did you, Mona?' said Marcella, jumping up and down. 'Doesn't she look grown up? *I* want a bob too, but Barbara says over her dead body. She practically exploded when she saw Es, and then she rang up Desiree and was *so* angry.'

'No wonder. Her hair looks awful!' said Bruno.

'As if I care what you think, scruffy infant,' said Esmeralda.

'But it does. Don't you think it looks awful, Mona?' he asked.

I swallowed. 'No, I think it looks very . . . *avant garde*.'

'Exactly,' said Mr Benjamin. 'I can't believe I have such a grown-up niece. I feel I should curtsy to you now, Esmeralda, and call you Madam.'

'Men don't *curtsy*, Uncle Benjamin!' Bruno squealed.

'Let's all get in the blasted car,' Ambrose said curtly, clearly fed up with children already.

It was a struggle fitting us all in. Bruno begged to travel in the luggage rack but was forced into the back with the rest of us. Nigel had been left with Harold, so Bruno insisted that he was now Nigel, and he scrabbled and barked and lay down on top of our feet.

'Get off!' Esmeralda cried, kicking at him with her pointy shoes.

'Come and sit on my lap, little doggie Bruno, and I'll feed you a chocolate titbit,' said Mr Benjamin.

It was still a squash. Marcella chattered on about Esmeralda's adventures in London with Desiree, and how some young man at a party had thought her at least eighteen.

'Don't you think *I'll* look older if I get my hair bobbed?' she said.

'I dare say you'll look at least fifty, and very beautiful into the bargain, Marcella darling, but do you think you could stay looking like a little girl for a few years?' said

Mr Benjamin. 'And don't you go getting any fancy ideas either, Mona.'

'No, don't,' said Roland.

'It wouldn't suit her,' said Esmeralda.

'It doesn't suit you either,' Bruno muttered.

She sat up straight, patting her hair, and ignored us for the rest of the journey to Hailbury. We left the Lagonda outside the railway station, Mr Benjamin tipping the porter to keep an eye on it while we were in London.

Esmeralda walked up the platform and pretended she was on her own. Two young men whistled at her and she stuck her chin in the air, but she looked pleased.

We travelled up to town in a first-class carriage. It was very comfortable, and the seats didn't itch my bare legs at all. Ambrose sat and read his newspaper, but Mr Benjamin talked to us, organizing games of I-Spy and Famous People. No one could guess Marcella's famous person.

'It's Mona's mother!' she said triumphantly when we'd all given up.

'Marcella!' said Roland uncomfortably, glancing at me.

'You can choose dead people as well as people who are alive, it's in the rules,' said Marcella. 'And Mona doesn't mind – do you?'

'Not at all,' I said, pleased that she considered my mother famous. I felt guilty too – I'd been so taken up with the Somersets that I hadn't talked to Mother recently. I decided to go and see her first thing tomorrow.

I'd neglected Aunty as well. She'd been so quiet and withdrawn since the Sea Creatures Ball.

'How could I have made such a spectacle of myself?'

she kept muttering, clutching her head as if a tiny cinema screen was shining there, showing her dancing and dancing and dancing. I felt sorry for her, but I wished she'd just forget about it. I'd avoided her as much as possible.

This morning she'd braided my plaits very tightly so they'd stay neat, and given me three sixpences wrapped in tissue paper to keep safe in my knickers pocket.

'You must offer to pay for your train fare and the entrance to the exhibition. Promise me you will,' she said.

I'd nodded, but I hadn't actually offered: I'd have been so embarrassed fumbling under my dress in front of everyone. None of the others had tried to pay for their ticket at the station.

When we got off the train at last, we had black smuts on our faces from the open carriage window, and Bruno had chocolate all round his mouth, so we went to the public washrooms.

'This is such an adventure!' said Marcella, rubbing soap between her hands until she had enough froth to blow bubbles.

I copied her, while Esmeralda gazed into the looking glass above the washbasins and rubbed rouge on her lips.

'You're not old enough to wear face paint,' said Marcella.

'Oh yes I am,' she said. She patted her hair, looking left and right to catch herself from every angle. I wondered if she was regretting the loss of her beautiful long locks.

I saw that a lady washing her hands beside us was staring at her. 'Oh my dear, what a beautiful cut!' she exclaimed. 'Where did you have it done?'

Esmeralda smiled. 'I went to Peter of Mayfair, but I'm

afraid he's booked up for weeks. He only did my hair because my friend Desiree goes to his salon regularly,' she said, giving her bob another pat.

When the lady had gone, Marcella and I raised our eyebrows.

'*Oh my dear, where did you get your lovely hairstyle?*' Marcella whispered, twiddling one of my plaits and getting it soapy.

'*Oh my dear, I go to Aunty of Gatekeeper's Cottage, and she cuts an inch off every three months with her dressmaking scissors,*' I replied, and we both burst out laughing.

'Silly little fools,' said Esmeralda. She yawned affectedly. 'It's going to be so boring having you two trailing around with me all day.'

However, even Esmeralda got excited when we took a Metropolitan line train all the way to Wembley. None of the Somersets had been on the Underground before. We set off down the stairs, Bruno taking the steps two at a time.

'Bruno, don't run, for pity's sake!' shouted Mr Benjamin. 'Grab his collar, Ambrose.'

'Dear God, is it going to be like this all day long? I feel like a sheepdog herding sheep,' Ambrose complained.

While we waited on the platform I told them about the Underground train. 'It's all dark outside, and there's a great roar and a rattle, and we'll hardly be able to hear ourselves talk.'

'So don't let's talk,' said Ambrose.

'Lighten up, old pal,' said Mr Benjamin, punching him playfully on the chest.

Ambrose rolled his eyes in protest, but he cheered up when we piled out at Wembley Park Station and started walking towards the exhibition. Our train had been crowded, and now many more people joined the eager stream, hurrying as they approached the entrance. We had to queue for quite a while. When we got to the front, I saw Mr Benjamin take out his wallet.

'Aunty says I must pay for myself, Mr Benjamin,' I whispered. 'I can't quite get at my money right this minute, but I'll be able to give it to you when I next visit the ladies' room.'

'Thank you so much for the offer, but I wouldn't dream of accepting it. You only cost ninepence, dear! It's my pleasure to treat you,' he said.

He bought a programme and told us all about the different palaces and pavilions inside.

'Can't we have lunch first?' Bruno begged. 'I'm absolutely starving.'

He'd eaten enough chocolate for ten boys, and it was only mid-morning, but Mr Benjamin decided we might as well enjoy a little snack while we got our bearings.

'I believe the Wembley Garden Club Restaurant isn't too far from this entrance,' said Ambrose, peering at the map. 'It's meant to be delightful.'

'I'm not sure it's quite the right place to take children,' said Mr Benjamin.

We went to the first restaurant we found – the Colonnade Quick-Lunch, which was certainly delightful, and we all had cups of tea and helped ourselves from a big plate of iced buns.

'We might as well be in an ABC caff,' said Ambrose snootily, but he ate *two* buns.

Then we set off down the wide tree-lined path towards the lake, holding hands so we didn't get separated in the jostling crowd. The exhibition was all so much bigger than I'd imagined, spreading as far as I could see, with more domes and turrets on the skyline. We walked and walked and walked, and at last we reached the lake.

'Let's go on one of those boats!' Bruno cried.

'Yes, let's,' said Esmeralda, slipping one shoe off and rubbing her heel.

'I don't know why you wore such silly shoes,' said Roland. 'You'd have been much better off in your sandals like Marcella.'

Esmeralda simply snorted derisively.

The boat was a splendid idea. We chugged up and down the long lake while Mr Benjamin pointed out the different pavilions.

'What fun to float past Canada and Australia, with India's white domes in the distance, all in a matter of minutes!' he said.

Even Ambrose was charmed, and they started a conversation using all the different accents.

'Which country shall we visit first?' Mr Benjamin asked, consulting his programme. 'Shall we go to Australia and see the Sydney Harbour Bridge, with real water and boats? There's even a sheep-shearing shed!'

I wanted to go to India – it looked like a pearly fairy palace with its towers and minarets, and Mr Benjamin told us that there was a bazaar selling ivory and jewels and silver and embroidered silks. I wondered if the wrapped coins in my knickers pocket would stretch to half a yard of Indian silk for Aunty.

Canada looked much plainer, and sounded too much like a geography lesson, with its forestry and paper industry and water power – but when we heard that there was a life-size figure of the Prince of Wales sculpted in butter in the dairy section, everyone clamoured to see him.

We had to wait patiently to get a proper view. This was beyond Bruno, who whined and pushed until Mr Benjamin heaved him up onto his shoulders.

'I can see him! He's bright yellow, all of him! Is he really butter? Can I lick him?' Bruno squealed, making the crowd of people laugh.

'Imagine if Queen Victoria was still alive! She was such a fatty they'd have needed thousands of pounds of butter to make *her*,' said Mr Benjamin.

After that we went to the Indian bazaar, where the jewels were breathtaking. There were cheaper trinkets too. You could buy three little glass bangles for sixpence. I clasped my hands over my tummy, feeling the hard shapes of the coins in my knickers. With my three sixpenny pieces I could buy three bangles for me, and three for Marcella, because she loved them too. I supposed I'd have to buy some for Esmeralda, though she wasn't being very nice to me.

But then I wouldn't have any money left to buy a piece of silk for Aunty. They had some beautiful bolt-end bargains for a shilling. I found one large piece – pink with silver thread and little decorative black bead flowers. It reminded me of the beautiful frock at the back of Aunty's wardrobe. She could turn it into a bodice or a little blouse.

I couldn't buy three lots of bangles *and* the material. If I bought one set of bangles, Marcella and Esmeralda and I could have one each – but the whole point of the bangles was having three sliding up and down your arm and jingling.

I could buy the silk and one set of bangles for Marcella, because she was the kindest of the Somerset children and we were officially best friends. I didn't think Esmeralda would care that much if I didn't buy her any. Desiree had already given her some bangles from her own jewellery box.

However, *I* cared. I wanted the bangles desperately. There were different colours, with a tiny pattern inside the glass. I wanted a pink one, a purple one and a green one. I clasped my hands over the sixpences in my pocket, unable to decide.

Mr Benjamin came and stood beside me. 'Do you have a tummy ache, Mona?' he whispered.

I shook my head.

'Perhaps you need to pay a little visit?' he asked delicately. 'I'm sure there will be a place nearby. Esmeralda will go with you.'

'No, I don't need to, thank you,' I said, blushing.

'Then what's the matter, my dear?' He bent nearer. 'Whisper!'

I found myself telling him my problem, and he burst out laughing, which made me blush. I didn't want him to think me ridiculous – or selfish.

'Dear Mona! Do you know something? I was just about to select a handful of bangles for you three girls, so you can stop worrying about that. But if you'd like to buy the little present for your aunt, I'm sure she'd be delighted. Then you'll still have sixpence, just in case there's anything else that takes your fancy.'

I gave him a hug because he was so understanding and generous. I chose my three, and Marcella copied me. Esmeralda chose different shades of blue: sky and royal and navy.

'It's not fair! *I* want bangles too!' Bruno wailed.

Mr Benjamin bought Bruno and Roland little pocket knives instead, the handles studded with rubies. They weren't real rubies of course, they were just red glass, but they looked lovely all the same.

I bought the pink silk for Aunty, and a lady in a sari tucked it into an embroidered bag. I was thrilled with the extra present.

By this time Ambrose was thoroughly bored, yawning and cracking his knuckles.

'So what am I going to buy *you* to cheer you up, Ambrose?' Mr Benjamin joked. 'Aha! I know where you might like to go for a proper lunch. You're always going on about your stint in the Indian Army, and the curries you ate. Let's go to the Indian restaurant and give the children a taste of the exotic.'

Ambrose *did* cheer up. He ate a very large yellow Indian curry and drank a large yellow Indian beer. I thought both smelled utterly disgusting. Mr Benjamin chose mild curries for Roland and Bruno, and they said they actually liked them. Esmeralda and Marcella and I had chicken and vegetables, but they tasted very odd.

'It was quite nice, I suppose, but now my mouth is all hot and burny,' said Marcella, drinking a whole glass of water in one go.

'Then I think we need to give your mouth a little sweet treat,' said Mr Benjamin. 'We'll tackle the Palace of Industry next.'

We walked through vast halls of wool and pottery and household things until we came to the Food Village. We strolled down Biscuit Avenue, where we were offered samples of butter puffs, and arrowroot and Petit-Beurre biscuits – Aunty's favourite. I turned my back and discreetly tucked one into my hidden pocket, along with the remaining sixpence.

There were also biscuits I'd never seen before. I wished Old Molly stocked Iced Stars – tiny biscuits with icing rosettes in white, pink and yellow. We ate a lot of those, the sugar soothing our spicy mouths.

'There now, you've all sweetened up considerably,' said Mr Benjamin. 'Where next?'

'How about seeing this modern dining room in the Palace of Arts?' said Ambrose. 'I bet it's not a patch on yours, Benjy.'

Roland looked impatient. 'That's not fair – we went to the Indian restaurant for you, Ambrose, and we went to the Indian Pavilion for the girls, and Canada for Bruno.'

'So where would *you* like to go, Roland?' Mr Benjamin asked.

'I'd like to go to Australia to see the sheep shearing,' he said.

'For pity's sake,' said Ambrose. 'You can watch wretched sheep being shorn any old time.'

'You can look at boring old dining rooms any old time,' Roland retorted.

'But the Australian Pavilion is back the way we've come,' Ambrose pointed out, consulting the programme. 'And we're right beside the Palace of Arts – look!'

'Then let's have a vote,' said Mr Benjamin. 'Who wants to go to the Palace of Arts?'

Ambrose put up his hand. So did Esmeralda and Marcella. Mr Benjamin raised his own hand, looking at Roland apologetically.

Bruno wavered. 'I don't want to go to either of them. I want to see the Butter Man again,' he said.

Everyone sighed and looked at me. I longed to go to the Palace of Arts and see the paintings. I even wanted to see if the dining room was *avant garde*. But I could see how much Roland wanted to go the Australian Pavilion.

'I vote for Australia,' I said.

Roland's face lit up. 'There, then! Tell you what, Mona and I will go to Australia, and you can all go to the namby-pamby Palace of Arts. We'll meet up later, by the lake.'

'Oh, yes, yes, yes, then we can have another boat ride!' said Bruno.

'Oh, no, no, no!' said Mr Benjamin. 'We must stick together! I'm not having you getting lost!'

'We won't get lost, I promise,' said Roland. 'Please, Uncle Benjamin. I'll look after Mona. Trust me.'

Mr Benjamin looked helpless. Then he consulted

his watch. 'Very well. Be back at the boating lake in an hour. If you're not there, I'll have to jump in the lake and drown myself rather than return home to tell your mother and aunt that I've lost you,' he declared.

'Thanks so much, Uncle,' said Roland. Then he gave me a beaming smile. 'Come on then, Mona!'

I absolutely loved the Palace of Beauty.

23

'YOU'RE AN ABSOLUTE SPORT,' ROLAND TOLD me. 'I don't think you really wanted to see Australia.'

'Yes I did,' I said. 'Let's find the sheep. You want to see them because you want to be a farmer, don't you?'

'That's exactly it!' he said.

I wondered if we'd missed the sheep shearing. After all, they couldn't keep shearing the same sheep again and again. But when we got there at last, we heard an announcement on the loudspeaker: the sheep shearing would take place in ten minutes' time.

Roland and I ran through the crowd, hoping we were going the right way. There were masses of people around the sheep-shearing pen, but we were both skinny and Roland had sharp elbows. We were soon breathing in the woolly smell of the sheep and the sweat of the shearers.

A man in a cowboy hat and checked shirt held a crackly microphone and did the commentary while the shearers took it in turns to hoist a huge sheep over their shoulders and start shearing off the thick wool in one long fleece. Each time they held the shorn wool aloft the crowd gave a great cheer.

I worried about the sheep – they looked so naked without their wool – but they hurried off into the next pen, a little surprised, but none the worse for their experience.

'I wonder if they sheared Esmeralda like that,' said Roland, making me laugh.

We watched until all twelve sheep had been shorn, and then looked at the dioramas, the first showing the countryside looking really wild, and then a few years later, properly cultivated.

'There – I wish I could show this to the gardener back at the Manor.' Roland seemed very interested, and was thrilled by the samples of soil and seed that were handed out.

The biggest diorama was of Sydney Harbour Bridge, with real water in front of it. I had hoped for real boats like the ones on the lake, but these were only big toy replicas of ocean liners, ferry boats and yachts. All the same they were much better than the toy boats in Mr Berner's shop. I wished I had Farthing in my pocket so I could give her a sail.

Neither Roland nor I had a watch, and I started to get a little anxious about the time.

'Don't fuss, Mona, we've got ages left,' said Roland. 'Aren't you having fun?'

'I'm having tremendous fun,' I replied truthfully.

It was wonderful having this tall, good-looking boy smiling at me, telling me jokes, treating me like a sister. No, not quite like a sister, almost like a sweetheart.

I stopped listening to the jolly, cockney-like tones of the Australian man talking about the harbour, and watched a personal diorama play out inside my head. Every holiday Roland would come to Somerset Manor, and we'd meet up and go off by ourselves to his treehouse. It was still just a few planks nailed across two broad branches, but I hoped that one day it might be a proper little alpine chalet.

When Roland and I were too old to climb trees, he'd make us our own summer house by the pool, and after our swim we'd sit there, wrapped in thick towels. He would put his arms round me to warm me up, and then he'd bend his head and kiss me.

I knew that my fantasy was as silly as the love stories in Old Molly's library, but I couldn't help myself . . .

Roland was smiling at me. 'Maybe some time in the future, when I'm eighteen or so . . .' he began.

'Yes?' I said, hardly able to breathe.

'I could go on one of those big ocean liners and sail all the way to Australia and see their farming methods first hand,' he said.

'Yes, you could,' I said. 'Roland, I'm sure we've been here for more than an hour. We'd better go.'

When I'd dragged him back to the lake at last, we weren't sure exactly where to meet the others. We'd both assumed it was the place we'd taken the boat from – but now we realized that there were several boat stations.

'Tell you what, let's split up. You look this way and I'll look that,' Roland suggested.

'No! Let's not get separated too!' I said, clutching him.

'All right, don't get so het up! We'll stick together then. Look, we'll go all the way along this bank first, and then cross over one of the bridges and come back on the other side.'

'But what if we can't find them?'

'Don't worry, of course we'll find them,' said Roland.

Five minutes later we spotted them on the other bank, waving and calling to us.

'Don't tell Esmeralda about my farming plans,' said Roland. 'She'll only mock. You know what she's like.'

'I won't tell, I promise,' I said.

'Come *on*, you two!' Bruno bellowed, using his hands as a trumpet. 'We've been waiting for *ages*.'

He was hopping up and down. Esmeralda was sitting on the grass: she'd taken off her pointy shoes and was massaging her feet. Marcella was lying limply on her back like a rag doll. Ambrose was sitting smoking, taking up almost a whole bench. Even Mr Benjamin looked tired, but he gave us both a lovely welcoming smile.

'I'm so very glad to see you, my dears. I was starting to get just a teeny bit anxious, but here you are, and we're one big jolly family again. In need of further refreshments, I feel. How about ice cream and lemonade?'

We went up to the third floor of the big Boathouse restaurant, and ate and drank enthusiastically. Almost immediately Bruno darted off to the window to peer out over the exhibition.

'There are hundreds and thousands and millions and

billions of people here,' he said, 'and I'm up above all of them, like God!'

'You're the most delightful chap, Bruno, but you don't seem at all God-like to me,' said Mr Benjamin. 'Don't lean out of the window like that – you're worrying me.'

Bruno leaned out further and then exclaimed in astonishment. 'I'm not the highest! There are people on some amazing swoopy thing in the sky, going up and down, up and down!'

'Ah! The Giant Switchback!'

'Can we go on it? Oh, please let's!' Bruno begged.

'Let me see!' Marcella ran to stand beside him and then gave a little squeak. 'Oh my goodness! There *are* people on that thing! It's so high up too. I bet you could reach up and touch the sky!'

'Count me out,' said Ambrose faintly.

'My heart isn't leaping either,' said Mr Benjamin. 'And I'm not sure it's a good idea to go on the switchback when we've just had our fill of ice cream and lemonade.'

'And it looks miles and miles away. I can't walk another step,' said Esmeralda.

I agreed, but Roland was craning his neck to see it, as excited as Bruno.

'Do let's! It would be such fun!' I said. I wanted him to think me a happy-go-lucky sort of girl, up for anything.

So we made our way towards the Amusement Park, and because we all had aching feet Mr Benjamin hired an electric Railodok bus.

'It's not a proper bus, it's just like a luggage trolley,' Ambrose complained, but it was still a marvellous way of getting around. Bruno pretended he was a bus conductor, calling, '*Tickets please, ladies and gents,*' again and again.

The Railodok took us all the way to the switchback. We had to queue for quite a while. We peered up at the carriages rattling along the narrow metal tracks, climbing slowly up and up and up, and then tipping over and swooping down in a terrifying rush that set everyone screaming.

'I really don't think I can bear to go on this infernal machine,' said Ambrose. He'd gone very pale. 'Can't the children go on it by themselves, Benjy?'

'Don't talk nonsense, Ambrose,' said Mr Benjamin. 'We have to hold onto them!'

'Then they'll struggle and we'll all fall to our deaths,' he replied.

'Oh dear Lord, why are you always so full of gloom and doom?' said Mr Benjamin, losing patience at last. 'Pull yourself together, dear boy. This is *fun!*'

He was insistent, though he looked very pale himself, and I saw little beads of sweat on his brow. When we clambered into the carriage, he sat at the front, between Bruno and Marcella, his arms round them, holding them tightly. Roland grabbed my hand and pulled me into the back with him. Esmeralda and Ambrose had to sit in the middle, keeping well apart.

'Fun!' said Mr Benjamin as we started the slow, juddery ascent. 'Repeat after me: *Fun, fun, fun!*'

We chanted it obediently, but when we started the first swoop downwards we screamed at the top of our lungs. I hung on to my hat with one hand, and clutched hold of Roland with the other, feeling as if my head was being ripped off my shoulders.

'It's all right, I've got you!' he yelled at me, but he was clinging too, his fingers digging into my arms.

Even Esmeralda and Ambrose were desperately holding onto each other.

Then we started climbing again, and there was another swoop down, and soon there was scarcely time to draw breath, and we screamed and screamed, and the ride seemed to go on for ever, and when at last we juddered to a halt we were barely able to speak, and wobbled when we got off.

'Again! Again! Oh, please, Uncle Benjamin, can we go on the switchback again?' Bruno begged.

'I think we might disgrace ourselves if we repeated the experience immediately,' said Mr Benjamin.

Ambrose was moaning, his eyes shut, relying on Esmeralda to steer him. Her sleek bob was standing up on end and she'd smeared lip rouge down her chin.

'Oh, Es, you do look a fright!' Bruno declared.

Mr Benjamin tactfully lent her his tortoiseshell comb and one of his beautiful white handkerchiefs.

'I still feel so giddy!' Marcella whirled round and round, her full skirts flying.

'Whirl the other way then, silly,' said Roland, turning her.

'But I like the feeling,' said Marcella, and begged to go on a ride called Whirl of the World.

'Why not? Perhaps we've all had enough instruction for one day. Let us give ourselves up to amusement.' Mr Benjamin patted Ambrose on the back. 'Brace yourself, old thing.'

We went on the Witching Waves, and Jack and Jill, and the Joy Wheel, and Over the Falls, the real waterfall splashing us all. We even went on the Ice Toboggan Slide, which was just as terrifying as the Giant Switchback.

Ambrose dug his heels in and utterly refused to join us. 'For heaven's sake, I'm exhausted. Can't we do something *peaceful*?'

'There's Pears' Palace of Beauty over there,' said Mr Benjamin. 'It sounds just the ticket. You'd like that, wouldn't you, girls? According to the programme it boasts beguiling ladies representing ten famous beauties of the past. You might like it, Roland!'

'*I* don't want to go to a sissy Palace of Beauty,' Bruno protested.

'Maybe they'll spruce you up a little, you grubby little ragamuffin,' said Esmeralda, smoothing his hair and dabbing at his grimy face with Mr Benjamin's handkerchief.

Bruno took her seriously, and batted her hands away. 'I don't want my hair cut and I don't want nasty red stuff on my face!' he yelled. 'I don't want to be turned into a beauty!'

'Well, we'll try and find you a Dungeon of Ugly,' said Mr Benjamin. 'But give this one a try. I promise the ladies inside won't attack you with scissors and face paint, young man.'

I absolutely loved the Palace of Beauty. It was just like a fairy-tale palace, pure and white and beautiful, with two curved staircases leading to a domed gazebo. It smelled heavenly, and girls in white robes handed out free Pears' soaps in special souvenir boxes. We were each given one, even Bruno, though he held it at arm's length, not wanting to smell fragrant.

We came to a room with ten glass-fronted booths containing the ten historical ladies: Helen of Troy, Cleopatra, Scheherazade, Dante's Beatrice, Elizabeth Woodville, Mary Queen of Scots, Nell Gwyn, Madame de Pompadour, Mrs Siddons and Queen Elizabeth. I wasn't sure who half of them were, but they had name cards at their feet.

'Are they real or are they big dolls?' Bruno demanded.

'Maybe they're wax models,' said Marcella. 'They're not moving.'

All ten stayed as still as statues – though I saw one blink. Then I noticed Helen of Troy wriggle her toes in her gold sandals, and watched Nell Gwyn's bosom rise gently up and down as she breathed.

It felt strange to be staring so intently at real women. They stared back, which made me feel uncomfortable. A raucous crowd of young men were rating them. They jeered and made rude remarks, and I hoped the historical beauties couldn't hear behind the glass.

'Which do you like best?' Marcella asked. 'I like the one with the great big silver hair and the flouncy pink gown – the Madam Pompey lady.'

'I like the one who's showing all her bosoms,' said Bruno, staring.

'Grubby little tyke,' said Roland, cuffing him – though he had been staring at Nell Gwyn too.

'I don't think any of them are particularly beautiful. They should show modern beauties like film stars,' said

Esmeralda. 'Some of them aren't even young. Cleopatra's quite old. And look at Queen Elizabeth – she's *ancient*!'

'That's the point, my dear. To show that all women can be beautiful, whatever their age,' said Mr Benjamin. 'Their beauty comes from within.'

'So long as they use Pears' soap *without*,' said Ambrose, and laughed at his joke.

I stared at Queen Elizabeth. She was a much older lady and she wasn't actually pretty, but I liked her pale face and blue eyes and bright red hair. She was the smallest of all the beauties, but she held herself very erect. Perhaps she had to, because if she'd bent her head her pleated ruff would have dug into her chin. Her costume was very elaborate. It must have taken some poor dressmaker ages to embroider those wide skirts with gold thread and sew on all the pearls. Queen Elizabeth also wore several strings of pearls around her neck, and big rings on her little white fingers.

Her hands were clasped in front of her, but when I looked closely I saw that she was twiddling her thumbs. Her heavy skirts were swaying slightly, as if she was shifting from one foot to the other. I thought it must be so tedious standing there hour after hour with all these people gawping at her.

I stared at her sympathetically, and she stared back – and then suddenly winked. She wasn't blinking. It was a deliberate wink, her blue eyes sparkling mischievously. I tried to wink back, but I'd never quite mastered the technique, and it was more of a grimace. I saw her mouth twitch.

'I think Queen Elizabeth is by far the best beauty,'

I said, enunciating the words very distinctly and hoping she could lip-read.

'Yes, well, you're hardly an expert,' said Esmeralda. 'Come on, I think they're giving out shampoo over there.'

She turned her back – and Queen Elizabeth's pink tongue suddenly poked out and waggled in Esmeralda's direction. If the glass window hadn't divided us, I'd have hugged her. I waved goodbye to her reluctantly, and she wiggled her fingers at me for a second.

'Well, my chicks, time's getting on. I think we'd better have a quick tea and then go and get the Underground train. We've got a long journey home,' said Mr Benjamin.

'No, no, I want to stay here for ever!' said Bruno. 'This is the best place in the whole world.'

'And Uncle Benjamin is the best uncle in the whole world, isn't he?' said Marcella. 'Three cheers for Uncle Benjamin! *Hip hip hooray!*'

I joined in, even though he wasn't *my* uncle. Ambrose raised his eyebrows and sighed, but he brightened when Mr Benjamin ordered Empire Cocktails in the Grand Restaurant. They were pink, and their silver swizzle sticks had little lions on the end. I'd have loved one myself because they looked so pretty. Mr Benjamin and Ambrose ate Devils on Horseback, which were prunes wrapped in bacon. They didn't look very nice at all. We had fruit salad and cream, and iced walnut cake, and chocolate biscuits, all washed down with ginger beer.

The restaurant overlooked a special children's playground with the name *Treasure Island* in sparkly lights. The minute he'd finished his tea Bruno begged to go in.

'No, darling boy, it's too late. It'll be getting dark soon. We must get you home,' said Mr Benjamin.

'Why do we have to go home when all those children in the playground are allowed to stay and have fun?' asked Bruno.

'It looks ever so nice in the playground,' said Marcella, climbing on Mr Benjamin's knee. 'Do you think they have real treasure there? Couldn't we just have a *little* look?'

'Stop being so artful, poppet,' he said. 'You're wasting your charms. I've developed a heart of stone. In five minutes' time we will be making our way to the Underground station.'

In five minutes' time the seven of us were standing in front of Treasure Island, Marcella dancing and Bruno whooping triumphantly.

'Come and visit Treasure Island, me hearties,' said the man at the entrance. He was dressed as a pirate, with a splendid tricorne hat and a hook instead of a hand.

'Captain Hook!' Marcella said, a little fearfully. 'Are you going to capture us?'

'I've repented of my wicked ways, little missy. I'm here to show you my island delights. Do you want to explore Wendy's little house? Or come and see some dear little puppies and kittens?'

'Oh, both please!' said Marcella.

'And what about you, young sir? Sir Francis Drake wants you to board his splendid vessel the *Golden Hind*. And Mr and Mrs Noah would like to show off their animals, two of each kind,' he continued, capering about.

'But it's all mixed up,' I said. 'Long John Silver's in *Treasure Island* and Captain Hook is in *Peter Pan*. They're just made up, but Sir Francis Drake was a real man.'

'And Mr and Mrs Noah are in the Bible. We know that, Mona. No need to show off,' said Esmeralda sharply. 'It's just for babies.'

'But Marcella and Bruno will love it,' said Mr Benjamin. 'All right, my chicks. We'll have half an hour in Treasure Island, and then we really must go home.'

Marcella and Bruno jumped up and down and cheered. Esmeralda sighed sulkily. Roland looked enthusiastic, which was a relief. I badly wanted to see the puppies and kittens and the Wendy house.

'I think it all sounds very jolly indeed,' said Mr Benjamin, taking Marcella and Bruno by the hand. 'We'd like to come and see your Treasure Island, Captain Hook.'

''Tis against the rules, splendid sir. Indeed, it's Treasure Island's only rule: no adults allowed. This is a private land reserved for boys and girls. You want to have fun all by yourselves, don't you, my dearies?' he said, gesturing to Bruno and Marcella.

'Yes, yes, yes!' said Bruno, but Marcella looked uncertain, and flinched as he flung out his hook – though it was clearly pretend, and you could see he'd tucked his real hand up his sleeve.

'You'll come too, won't you, Mona?' she asked.

'I'm not sure I should let any of you go,' said Mr Benjamin, looking worried. 'I don't think our Bruno's safe to be let out on his own!'

'We'll look after the young gentlemen and ladies, sir. Peter Pan himself patrols the island, and Wendy is very motherly if any little tot gets upset,' said Captain Hook.

'Excellent!' said Ambrose. 'They can all go off and have fun while we have another cocktail, Benjy.'

'I'm too old to traipse around a little kiddies' island,' said Esmeralda indignantly.

'Nonsense, you're still a little girl in spite of your bob,' said Ambrose, and he ruffled her hair.

Esmeralda pulled away from him, furious.

'Don't worry, Uncle Benjamin, I'll look after them all,' said Roland.

'You're a regular trooper, my boy. Bless you,' he replied. 'Well, off you go then. Ambrose and I will be back in the restaurant if you need us. Just half an hour now. We'll come and wait at the entrance.'

'Can't I come to the restaurant too? My shoes are pinching me so. I can hardly walk another step,' said Esmeralda.

'No, I'd be much happier if you kept an eye on Mona and Marcella. Roland will have his hands full keeping Bruno under control,' said Mr Benjamin. 'Cheer up, sweet girl.'

'You can pretend you're a real mermaid like the one in the fairy tale, and every step on land is like walking on knives,' I suggested.

I was trying to be helpful, but Esmeralda rolled her eyes at the suggestion. She refused to join in any of the Treasure Island activities. She wouldn't even hunt for treasure in Aladdin's Cave. Roland was much more fun: he played pirates on the replica ship and climbed up and down the 'Canadian Rockies' with Bruno. Esmeralda took off her shoes and sat on the sandy 'beach' by herself.

However, even she was enchanted by the puppies and kittens. They were kept in a special enclosure in a tent presided over by a grown-up lady dressed like a little girl.

'I am Miss Pretty Pet,' she said in a silly voice. 'You may play with my dear little doggies and kittens, but please be very gentle.'

I fell in love with a little cream kitten with big blue eyes, though I felt disloyal to Sixpence. Marcella sat with two cocker spaniel puppies wriggling around on her lap, a huge smile on her face. Bruno tried to teach a little Alsatian how to sit up and beg. Roland nursed a collie pup, fondling his black-and-white fur. And Esmeralda picked up a tiny Pomeranian and rubbed her cheek against his pale orange fluff.

A boy sitting cross-legged next to Marcella was teasing a marmalade kitten, putting it down on the ground and then immediately snatching it up so that it couldn't run away. The kitten got frustrated and thrust out a paw.

'Ow! It scratched me! Little beast!' he complained. I stared at him. His slicked-down hair and beady eyes seemed somehow familiar. He wore a fussy little sailor suit, and his socks were dazzling white.

'He doesn't want to play,' said Marcella, 'but you can have one of my little spaniels if you like. I think this one's a boy. Would you like to play with him instead?'

The boy was staring at her. He had a little sister with him, her hair in ringlets. She was wearing a fancy dress with smocking, obviously expensive but not Aunty-standard – and I suddenly recognized her.

Meanwhile the boy was blinking at Marcella. 'You're my cousin!'

She stared back. 'Oh goodness! Cedric. And Ada. How lovely!' she said, trying to sound pleased.

Esmeralda didn't bother. 'Oh Lord, it's the spoiled brats,' she muttered to Roland.

'Hello, you two,' he said. 'What a coincidence.'

Bruno was eyeing up Cedric. 'We had a fight last time we met, and I won, remember?' he said.

'I'm not allowed to fight any more,' said Cedric. 'Especially not with you. Daddy says you're too rough.'

'Don't worry, Cedric, we all agree with your daddy,' said Roland. 'Mind how you're holding that kitten now – you're squeezing him too tightly.'

'I don't care, he's stupid anyway,' said Cedric, loosening his grip, and the kitten darted away thankfully.

'I've got a kitten too,' said Ada. 'I think she's a girl but she's not very pretty. I like the one that girl's got, the little cream one. Will you swap?'

Ada was only little, and I knew I should probably hand over my kitten. We had to leave soon anyway, but I badly wanted one last cuddle. I sighed, and then reluctantly held her out to Ada.

'No! You don't want that one!' Cedric shouted, making us all jump. 'Not after *she's* been holding it.'

'Don't be silly,' said Marcella. 'It's Mona! She's my best friend!'

Cedric wrinkled his nose. 'You can't have *her* for a friend!' he said.

'We're *all* friends with Mona,' said Roland. 'Don't be so rude, Cedric.'

'She's the one who's rude. Daddy says she's disgusting!' He held his nose, as if I smelled.

'I'm *not*!' I said indignantly.

'Right, I'm going to fight you again,' said Bruno.

'Children, children, calm down,' said Miss Pretty Pet. 'You must go outside if you're going to squabble. You'll upset all my little puppies and kittens.'

'Right, we'll leave, Ada,' Cedric commanded. 'Come on. Mummy and Daddy would be ever so cross if they knew we were talking to our cousins.'

'Clear off then,' said Roland.

'Yes, disappear, tiresome little kiddies,' added Esmeralda.

'I'm still going to fight you,' Bruno threatened.

'Yes, you're not being at all nice, and you've been positively horrid to my friend Mona,' said Marcella.

'You're the ones who are beastly. And you're mad being friends with that girl. Mummy and Daddy say it's a positive disgrace that her and her awful mother are still allowed to live in the cottage,' said Cedric.

'Oh, shut up, you loathsome worm,' I said. 'I don't live with my *mother*. I live with my aunty. My mother died when I was born.'

'No she didn't.' Cedric had a horrible gleam in his eyes.

'She did so,' said Marcella. 'Stop being nasty to poor Mona. She still misses her mother dreadfully and goes to talk to her in the graveyard. I've seen her grave. You have too, Roland, haven't you?' She tugged on his arm.

He nodded. 'Yes, I have,' he said, but he didn't quite meet my eye.

'I heard Mummy and Daddy talking!' Cedric said importantly. 'Ada did too. They said that lady she calls her aunty is really her mother.'

'How could that possibly be?' I said. 'You're talking wicked nonsense. Of course Aunty's my aunt. She doesn't have *any* children. She's never even been married.'

'I know that.' Cedric squared up to me. 'Daddy says she set her cap at my uncle and had his baby to try and make him marry her.'

'*Mr Benjamin?*' I said, and the idea was so ridiculous that I couldn't even take offence. 'You must be off your head.'

'No, my uncle Eric,' said Cedric. 'My daddy's dead brother.'

'Frederick?' I said, totally bewildered. My head was reeling. None of his words seemed to make sense. I didn't know what he meant about Aunty setting her cap at him. She'd never wear a common cap, only a proper lady's hat. And she didn't even know an Eric.

'There was Uncle Frederick first, and then Uncle Eric, and then my daddy, and then Uncle Benjamin,' said Cedric, counting them off on his fingers.

Now I remembered that there had been a second Somerset brother, though no one ever mentioned him. How on earth could Aunty have known him?

'You're a very stupid, wicked boy,' I said stoutly. 'You're making all this up just to be spiteful, because Mr Benjamin likes Aunty and me.'

'Daddy says Uncle Benjamin's a ninny. And he says your so-called aunty is a scheming hussy,' said Cedric.

I was so outraged I slapped his face as hard as I could. He was nearly knocked off his feet. He staggered, his cheek flushing deep red. Tears seeped out of his beady eyes.

'I'm telling!' he sobbed. 'I'm going to tell my daddy, and he'll have you locked up in the workhouse, where you and your mother belong.'

Ada started snivelling too. Cedric grabbed her hand and they ran out of the tent, almost tripping over the puppies and kittens.

'Oh, children, you're being very naughty!' said Miss Pretty Pet. 'Out you go, all of you!'

We put down our pets and stumbled out of the tent. I saw Cedric running off, pulling Ada behind him.

'What a pig,' I said, scarcely able to breathe.

'Uncle George won't *really* lock Mona up in the workhouse, will he?' Marcella asked anxiously.

'Of course not. She just slapped Cedric – and he totally deserved it,' said Roland. 'Don't be upset, Mona.'

'I'm not the slightest bit upset,' I lied. 'But why would he tell such terrible lies? And about Aunty, of all people? He should go to hell for making up such a wicked story.'

'So it isn't true then?' asked Bruno.

'Of course it's not,' said Marcella.

'That's right. Let's just forget all about it. We'd better

push off before Uncle George comes steaming back, looking for trouble,' said Roland.

'It's all terrible lies,' I repeated, struggling not to cry.

'Yes, of course it is,' said Roland, and he put his arm round me.

'Well . . .' said Esmeralda.

I felt Roland tense. 'Don't, Es,' he said.

'I don't know why you're pretending. You know the truth about Mona as well as I do. It was *you* who told *me*, after you asked Uncle Benjamin,' she said.

'Will you just shut up!' said Roland furiously.

'It's a wonder Mona hasn't worked it out for herself by now, seeing as she's supposed to be so bright,' said Esmeralda.

'What do you mean?' I asked shakily.

'Don't be horrid, Es,' said Marcella.

'How could you be taken in by that old grave? Roland said it was just a grassy mound amongst the really ancient graves. It's obviously been there for hundreds of years. It couldn't possibly belong to Mona's mother,' she said.

I felt the ground tipping beneath my feet. All the huge concrete buildings in the exhibition seemed to be falling on top of me. Roland had to hang onto me to keep me upright.

'Now look what you've done,' he said. 'How could you be so cruel, Es?'

'Look, it doesn't *matter*. We don't care if Mona's mother pretends to be her aunt because she's not married. We're not old-fashioned fuddy-duddies like Uncle George and

Aunt Mary,' said Esmeralda. 'I don't know why everyone's getting in such a tizz about it.'

I pulled away from Roland so that I could see his face. 'She's saying that Aunty is actually my mother?' I whispered.

'Yes, but we don't mind in the slightest,' he told me.

'*I* mind!' I cried.

I pushed him hard, and then I started running.

I cried and cried, until at last the sobs slowed down.

24

I RAN RIGHT OUT OF THE AMUSEMENT PARK.
I saw Mr Benjamin waiting with Ambrose, but Mr
George and his wife were there too. He was shouting
angrily, and she had her arms round Cedric and Ada,
who were still bawling.

They didn't even see me. I ran in the opposite direction,
past the restaurants, through the trees, crying so hard
I couldn't see where I was going. I didn't care. I'd lost
Mother. I'd loved her more than anyone in the world, and
she'd never even existed. I'd been talking to a complete
stranger who had long since crumbled into dust.

She had *surely* spoken to me. Had I been imagining
it? She wasn't Sylvia at all, pure and wise and fair.
She wasn't Mother. I didn't *have* a mother, only Aunty.

How could she have lied to me all these years?

She *couldn't* be my mother. She wasn't soft and sweet and comforting. She was as prickly as her pins, and never cuddled or kissed me. She never acted as if she really loved me – she looked after me because it was her duty.

Well, I didn't love *her*. I *hated* her for pretending all these years. I'd longed to have a mother, and she'd been there all the time – the *wrong* mother.

And people *knew*. I couldn't bear the thought of the Somersets whispering about me. Was Cedric right? Was my father a Somerset? That seemed even more impossible. Even with dear, friendly Mr Benjamin, Aunty was forever bobbing her head and stammering. I thought of Maggie's crude description of how babies were made. I couldn't imagine Aunty even kissing a man, let alone doing *that*.

It *couldn't* be true. Maybe it was all a terrible dream . . . I tried opening my eyes as wide as I could, wanting to wake up into my own old life, with Mother safe in her grassy bed under the yew tree and Aunty sewing in her workroom.

Families were jostling their way towards the exit, keen to get the children home before bedtime. So many families, all with a mother and a father, and they seemed to be staring at me, pointing, sneering, holding their noses in disgust like Cedric.

I was desperate to get away. I tried pushing through the crowd, and bumped into a child, nearly knocking it over. The father seized hold of me and shouted, his face red and angry. I couldn't make sense of what he was saying and only cried harder.

He let me go, and I staggered into a little clump of bushes and sank down, hiding from everyone, my head in my hands.

'Hey there, what's the matter?' Someone was scrabbling their way through the bushes after me.

I tried to get up and toppled over.

'I should just sit still and have a good cry, dear.' It was a woman's voice. She sounded soft and warm, like Mother – which made me sob even more.

'There now,' she said, and she settled herself down beside me, patting my back as if I was her child.

I cried and cried, until at last the sobs slowed down. I sniffed hard and tried to wipe my face.

'Here.' The woman handed me a handkerchief and I mopped my face.

'Thank you,' I said, my voice croaky. 'Why did you come after me?'

'Because you looked pretty desperate. I know how that feels,' she told me.

I looked at her, blinking through my tears. She was small and thin and quite old, but her hair was bright red, and her blue eyes were beautiful.

'Sometimes it helps to have a really good cry,' she said. 'But sometimes it makes no difference. You cry and cry, and nothing changes, and you've just given yourself a splitting headache on top of all your woes.'

'Yes,' I said, sniffling.

'You haven't hurt yourself, have you?'

'No.'

'It's just hurting inside?'

I nodded.

'That's the worst sort of hurt,' she said. 'What's your name, my love?'

'Mona.'

'Pretty.' She peered at me. 'You came to have a peep at me, didn't you? You were with that snooty miss with the bobbed hair. I stuck my tongue out at her.'

I stared at her. 'Oh my goodness, you're Queen Elizabeth!' I gasped. She looked so different in her short green dress and jacket, cut in the latest fashion.

'Yes, I am, and it's the worst job in the world, standing still like that for hour after hour, with only ten-minute breaks. When will I ever learn? I once had a job as a mermaid in a seaside carnival, and that was bad enough, but at least I was lying down.'

'I dressed up as a mermaid for a ball! So did Esmeralda, but she looked much better than me. She's the snooty miss,' I said.

'Is she a friend or a sister?'

'Neither, really.'

'Won't she be wondering where you've got to?'

'She won't care. She doesn't like me much,' I said, my voice wobbling. 'So if you're here, are there only nine beauties left?'

'My friend Diamond's doing the evening shift – I'm meeting someone in the West End. She *is* a diamond too: she's blonde and has to wear a red wig – it must make her itch like crazy in that hot glass cage. The ruff makes you itch too. I come out in a rash and have to powder my neck to disguise it.'

'I'm sorry I'm holding you up,' I said.

'Oh, never mind. He can wait. I'm not sure I should be

meeting him anyway. You'd think I'd know better at my age. I'm not lucky in love. Sometimes I think I've made all the wrong choices. Maybe I should have followed Queen Elizabeth's example and kept men at bay. Still, she had a good career. It must be grand work being Queen.' She chuckled.

'Have you always worked as a model then?' I asked.

'I've done all sorts. I was actually on the stage at one time. You're too young to have heard of me, but I was quite famous once. But then age caught up with me and the parts fizzled out. Perhaps I'll be in demand again soon. A casting director will ponder, *Now, who would be perfect to play the part of an ancient old crone? I know, send for Emerald Star!*'

'Is that your name? It's beautiful,' I said.

'Well, I chose it carefully. I've had several names in my time. My friends call me Hetty Feather, my foundling name.' She shrugged. 'I think it's pretty hideous, but I'm stuck with it now.' She rummaged in her bag and found a tin of fruit drops. 'Here, have a sweetie, Mona. My throat always hurts when I've been crying.'

I took one gratefully. 'What do you mean, your foundling name?'

'Mama couldn't keep me, so she was forced to put me in the Foundling Hospital. It was a horrible place, with the meanest matron in the world. We were brought up very strictly, and trained to be servant girls. Never be a servant, dear, it's a dog's life. Get yourself a good education if you possibly can,' Hetty said, taking a fruit drop and sucking it with gusto.

'I'm going to a girls' high school in September,' I told her.

'Well, good for you! I knew you were a bright girl. Are you looking forward to it?'

'I suppose so,' I said. I hugged my knees. 'Only everything's turned upside down now.' I swallowed hard to stop myself crying and nearly choked on my fruit drop.

'Goodness, choke up, chicken,' said Hetty, thumping me on the back. 'So what's gone wrong then?'

'I've been brought up by my aunt. It's always been just Aunty and me. She's a dressmaker,' I said, wiping my eyes again.

'Ah, I'm not surprised. I've been admiring your pretty frock, dear. I've always made my own clothes, and I like to think I cut quite a dash, but I haven't got that professional touch.' She picked up the hem of my dress and clucked appreciatively. 'Such tiny even stitches! She's a brilliant dressmaker, your aunt.'

'But I've just found out that she's not really my aunt. All these years she's been lying to me. She told me that my mother died when I was born, but now they tell me that *she's* my mother,' I said in a rush.

'Who's "they"? The snooty girl with the bob?'

'Yes, her, and her cousin. Cedric said my aunty was a hussy and it was disgusting. He said *I* was disgusting, and held his nose as if I smelled,' I said, shuddering.

'Well, he sounds a right charmer. Do you think he's telling the truth?' Hetty asked, putting her arm round me.

'Roland said it was true, and I know he wouldn't lie,' I said. 'I never thought *Aunty* would lie. She was always so cross with me if I told the tiniest fib, but now I find out that she's been lying all along. She's a hateful hypocrite,' I muttered.

'Hey, hey, don't be so fierce,' said Hetty, and she gave me a little shake. 'Why do you think she's been lying all this time?'

'I don't know.'

'Of course you do! It was to protect you. Some folk can be very mean to children whose parents aren't married. *I* should know. All us children in the Foundling Hospital had unwed mothers, and it was considered shameful. People pointed and sneered at us whenever we were allowed outside. Your mother didn't want that to happen to you. She obviously wanted you brought up respectable. So she told a harmless little lie.'

'It was a big, big, big lie,' I insisted.

'So she could keep you and bring you up herself. Don't look so sorry for yourself, you silly girl. I'd give anything to have been brought up by my mother. For years and years I didn't know who she was – and then I lost her, the person I loved most in the world.' She shook her head. 'You'll have *me* in tears soon.'

'But Aunty's not a bit like a real mother. I was so sure I knew what Mother was like. I used to go and talk to her in the graveyard, and she talked back, I'm sure she did,' I whispered.

'My saints, *I* did that after my dear mama passed away. Still do, if truth be told. You and me, Mona, we've got a lot in common. I ran away once too, when I was just about your age. And this wonderful circus lady looked after me and gave me cake! Then another kind lady took me back to the Foundling Hospital, because London's no place for a little girl on her own. Now it's my turn to be a wonderful kind lady! Let's reunite you with your friends.'

'I don't want to be reunited!'

'Well, you can't wander around all on your own, it's not safe, especially now it's starting to get dark. Come on, poppet, up you get,' she said.

Hetty pulled me up and led me out onto the path. I looked around at the crowds – they stretched as far as I could see.

'How will I ever find them?' I said, starting to panic.

'I'll take you to the children's crèche. That's where all the lost children end up. Don't worry, I'm sure you'll find them there. But listen just a second.' Hetty put her hands on my shoulders and looked at me steadily. 'You give your mother a big hug when you see her. She's hung onto you and brought you up with care – I can see that. You cherish her while you can. And keep your chin up. You're as good as anyone else. Likely better! That dreadful old matron at the hospital said that I was a child of Satan and would never amount to anything. Ha! I'm only Queen of all England now!'

We set off along the path, and suddenly the twilight shone with thousands of coloured lights. The big concrete pavilions and palaces were outlined, and above the great stadium a rainbow of searchlights lit the entire sky. Everyone gasped and shouted and marvelled, and Hetty Feather whirled me round and round until I was breathless.

Then she took me to the children's crèche, reassuring me all the way.

'But what if they're *not* there?' I asked. 'What if they've given up and caught the Underground train?'

'Then you'll come with me, and we'll meet up with

my gentleman friend and he'll take us to Rules, which is very grand but not too frightening for girls like us, and I'll have champagne and oysters, and you'll have a tiny sip and a nibble if you promise not to be ill. Then you and I will go back to my rooms and we'll tuck you up in my bed for the night, though heaven knows how I'm going to get you home in the morning.'

'I don't want to go home! Can't I stay with you, Hetty Feather? Please can I? I won't be any trouble, I promise,' I begged.

But suddenly Mr Benjamin was there, running towards me, his curls awry, his jacket unbuttoned, his collar undone.

'Mona!' he cried, and swept me up in his arms. 'I've been going simply demented! I can't believe I've got you safe at last!' I could feel his heart thumping beneath his shirt.

Behind him I saw the others come running too.

'Oh, Mona, we thought we'd never find you,' said Roland, and he hugged me as well.

'I didn't mean to upset you so,' said Esmeralda. She actually looked as if she'd been crying!

'I thought I'd never see you again, and I felt absolutely dreadful because you're my best friend,' said Marcella.

'Golly, you've been missing for *ages*,' said Bruno.

'Why ever *did* you run away?' Ambrose asked. 'Poor Benjy here went utterly berserk when he found you were missing. And what did you do to make those dreadful relations froth at the mouth?'

'Don't let's even talk about them now,' said Mr Benjamin firmly. He turned to Hetty Feather. 'Madam,

I am entirely in your debt. How can I ever repay you for restoring this little girl to us?'

'Think nothing of it,' she told him cheerfully. 'Mona and I have taken a real shine to each other. We have a lot in common.'

'Good heavens, I think I recognize you!' he said.

'She's the model who dressed up as Queen Elizabeth,' said Esmeralda, looking a little shame-faced.

'You are far more than a model, madam,' said Mr Benjamin. 'I think you are actually Miss Emerald Star!'

'I am indeed,' said Hetty happily.

'I saw you when I was a little boy!' he declared.

'My goodness, so did I!' said Ambrose. 'You were magnificent.'

'Oh yes, I've been around a long, long while,' said Hetty.

'And now you are clearly enjoying your heyday,' said Mr Benjamin gallantly. 'I do hope you can accompany us on the Underground. There are so many things I'd like to ask you. Perhaps you might even be kind enough to give us your autograph . . .'

On the train they sat on either side of her, though Mr Benjamin also kept a firm hold of my hand, as if he feared I might make a bolt for it. Marcella held my other hand, though she looked exhausted and her eyes kept closing. Bruno was already fast asleep on Esmeralda's lap, crumpling her dress. Roland peered along the row every so often, nodding at me reassuringly.

They were all being so kind to me. They weren't even angry that I'd run away and worried them so much. And they didn't seem to care that Aunty was really my mother, even though Mr George and his family thought it so terrible.

When we got out at the railway station, Mr Benjamin asked for Hetty's address so that he could send her some flowers. She seemed happy to oblige – and when she gave me a goodbye hug she asked if I'd write to her.

'Maybe you and I could go to Rules together one day. I'd love to hear how you're getting on, my dear,' she said. 'You *will* give your mother a big hug when you get home, won't you?'

I nodded, although I had no intention of doing any such thing. I was dreading seeing Aunty. I couldn't possibly start thinking of her as Mother yet – I was still too angry with her. I decided I'd try not to shout or cry. I'd be coldly dignified but unforgiving. I didn't see how we could ever be close again.

I practised what I was going to say to her in my head, but on the train back to Hailbury I fell fast asleep, and barely woke to climb into the back of the car. When we reached Gatekeeper's Cottage, Mr Benjamin roused me gently and helped me out.

'Would you like me to come in with you and talk to – to Miss Watson?' he asked.

'No thank you.'

'I'm sorry Cedric was so unpleasant. It must have been a terrible shock. We need never speak of the matter again if you'd sooner not. But I'd just like to say one thing, Mona. I'm so glad you're my niece, my dear,' he whispered.

Then the cottage door burst open, and there was Aunty, still dressed. She was weeping.

'Oh, thank the Lord! You're so late! I thought you must have been in a terrible accident,' she sobbed.

'A thousand apologies, dear Miss Watson,' said Mr Benjamin. 'We had a little mishap – but I promise we are all safe and sound. Goodnight now. Mona probably needs to go straight to bed – she's very tired.'

Aunty took hold of me and pulled me indoors. She was shivering. 'What mishap? Whatever happened? Oh, Mona, I've been beside myself. I've been waiting hour after hour. I didn't know what to do! But thank heaven you're back safe now!' She made to embrace me, but I pulled away sharply.

'What's the matter? Why are you acting so strange? Have you done something wrong? Come on, own up! Tell me the truth!' she cried.

All my plans for acting with cold dignity disappeared in a flash.

'How dare you order *me* to tell the truth!' I shouted. 'What sort of a mother are you?'

She flinched, then closed her eyes and clutched her chest for a moment. Finally she shook her head. 'I don't know what you're talking about, Mona. Why on earth are you calling me a mother?'

'Because I know you *are* my mother. Lots of other people know too. All this time they must have been mocking me behind my back! And there I was, going, *my aunty this, my aunty that*, when you're not my aunty and you never have been.' I clenched my fists, trembling with rage.

'Who's been saying that?' she asked hoarsely, leaning against the wall.

'All the Somersets for a start,' I said.

'Mr Benjamin?' she whispered, shaking her head in disbelief.

'No, not Mr Benjamin. He knows all about me – they all do now – but it was Cedric who told me. He said horrid things. He even held his nose,' I said.

'Mr Benjamin took him to the exhibition too?'

'No – we met him and Ada by chance. He said he wasn't allowed to talk to me because I was disgusting,' I said. 'And he said you were a hussy.'

Aunty covered her face and hunched over, silent now. I thought she might be crying. My stomach churned. I wanted her to keep denying it or to slap me for my cheek. I didn't want her to stay bent over like a little old woman.

'Are you crying?' I asked, my voice wobbling.

She still didn't say anything.

'Perhaps Cedric was making it up,' I said in a very small voice.

Aunty sniffed. 'No, he was telling the truth,' she said. She sounded broken. She slid slowly down the wall and sat in a little heap on the floor.

'Aunty?'

She shook her head. I didn't know what to do. I wished I'd held my tongue. I stood there, towering over her.

'Aunty, please!' I remembered the bottle in the sideboard. I ran to get it and then thrust it at her. 'It's the medicinal brandy. Take a sip. It'll make you feel better,' I said.

'I'm not taking to drink!' said Aunty, sounding more like herself, but she took the top off the bottle and had a couple of sips. The taste made her shudder, but then she took a deep breath and sat up straighter.

'Yes, I am your mother, Mona. But I was never a hussy, even though I'm not married.' She rubbed the third finger of her left hand. 'And I'm not stupid – I don't suppose your father would ever have married me, but he was a caring man all the same, and he did his best for me. For us.'

'Tell me,' I said, sitting down cross-legged beside her.

'There's not much to tell. I was lonely. My own mother wasn't a good woman, and my father was a stern, strict man. I had to get away. I was always skilled with my needle, so I got a job at a dressmaker's in Hailbury – Madame Orwell's Fine Gowns. She was kind enough, I suppose, but she never treated me like one of the family, and just gave me a tiny room in the attic to sleep in. I stayed there year after year. I always hoped I might find myself a young man and start walking out with him, but I never met anyone. If any of the lads whistled at me in the street, I always scuttled away, too shy to let them talk to me.' Aunty shook her head.

I shuffled a little nearer.

'Then there was all this talk of war. It changed people – somehow livened them up, even me. They started holding Saturday-night dances in Hailbury Town Hall, and somehow I plucked up the courage to go along by myself. I got into the habit of going every week, and got to know some of the girls there. I found I was quite good at dancing, heaven knows why, so I had my fair share of partners. Lads started coming along in their stiff new uniforms, with pink faces and short hair. The other girls considered them handsome, but I didn't think much of the new look. They couldn't dance properly in their great clumping boots either. Then one night your father came to the dance.'

'And he was handsome,' I said.

'No, I can't tell a lie,' said Aunty, then sniffed. 'Though you're right, I've been lying all your life. But I need to tell you how it really was. It wasn't a love match. We didn't look at each other across a crowded room like the people in Old Molly's romantic novels. He didn't look up at all – he was so shy, even shyer than me.'

'But I thought he was a Somerset. The Somersets aren't shy,' I protested.

'Eric was, dreadfully. He sat there, staring down at his brand-new boots, a fish out of water. I had no idea he came from a grand family. I thought he was just some poor country bumpkin. I waited to see if he asked anyone to dance. Once or twice he shifted in his seat, but he always seemed to lose his nerve. Somehow it made me feel fond of him. When the Ladies' Choice was announced, I waited a minute or two, not wanting to look too bold, and then I hurried across the floor and asked if he'd like to trip the light fantastic with me. He went scarlet, but he said yes. He had such a surprisingly plummy voice I rather wished I hadn't asked him after all. I was scared he'd look down on me, but he seemed to like me, although he didn't say much. We danced every dance, and then he walked me home. He didn't even kiss my cheek, but he asked if I'd come to the big fundraiser ball for the war effort the next Saturday.

'I was taken aback. I didn't have anything to wear for a ball. For the village dances I wore my best summer dress, but I could see that wouldn't do. So I spent my week's wages on yards and yards of pink silk and made my own dress, sewing on hundreds of beads to make it sparkle.'

'The dress that was in the back of your wardrobe!'

'That's right. I've hidden it away in an old pillowcase. I didn't want you asking any more questions about it,' said Aunty. 'So I went to the ball with him, and he chatted a bit, and it turned out that he was being sent off to fight in France the very next day. When he said that, he got a bit choked up. His elder brother, Frederick, was an officer and had had proper army training. Eric was just an ordinary soldier, and he admitted that he was terrified of what waited for him in France. He didn't want to go, but he knew that it was expected. Then he said he'd been looking for a special girl to remember when he was in the trenches.'

'So you were his special girl?'

'I felt sorry for the poor beggar. I let him take me to this hotel. When we checked in I felt everyone staring at me. I'm sure they knew we weren't married. I was terrified too, to be truthful. I'd always been a good girl and kept myself to myself. But there it was. I stayed the night, and then he went off to fight, and I went on working at Madame Orwell's, and after a couple of months I realized that you were on the way and I didn't know what to do. Eric had sent me a postcard with the address of his regiment, so I wrote to him. And he wrote back, bless him. It wasn't a very lovey-dovey letter – that wasn't his style – but he said he'd written to his mother begging her to make sure the baby and I were provided for if he was killed. Then I didn't hear any more until I got a terrible letter from one of his pals telling me that he had died in action. Apparently he didn't suffer at all, but I wondered if that was true. Then, when I got nearer my time, Madame Orwell said I couldn't possibly continue to work for her and threw me out.

'I had nowhere to go. I couldn't go back to my father – he'd have thrown me out too. A church charity for unwed mothers took me in, and when you were born they planned to give you to some good God-fearing couple. But as soon as I held you in my arms I knew I couldn't go through with it.'

'Why?' I breathed.

'I couldn't give you up because you were my own little baby. I loved you. The charity people said I was being terribly selfish. I was condemning you to a life of poverty and shame. I wouldn't listen. I packed my bag and took you in my arms and went to Somerset Manor to see her ladyship.'

'That was brave!' I was sitting so near Aunty now that we were nearly touching.

'At first she was furious. I knew she wanted to send me packing, but she'd had a soft spot for Eric and was grieving terribly. She felt she had to help me out for his sake. I had to promise her that I'd keep the circumstances of your birth a secret. I didn't just have to keep quiet about your father: I had to say that I was your aunt, and make up a cock-and-bull story to keep everything respectable. It seemed to make sense at the time. I'd had enough of people pointing at me.

'Her ladyship's gatekeeper had gone to join up, along with most of the other men, so she said I could live in the cottage rent free,' Aunty went on. 'I made her a gown in gratitude, and she was so pleased she had me make more, and recommended me to her friends. The gatekeeper was killed in the war, and I made just enough money to support us both. I kept myself to myself and did my best to bring you up like a little lady. I think some of the villagers suspected the truth. I thought you'd start asking questions when you went to school, so I found an old grave without a headstone and said that your mother was buried there.'

'And I've been visiting her all these years! I believed in her! I've talked to her, and she talked back to me. But it was all pretending,' I said, the tears rolling down my cheeks. 'She was so real to me, Aunty.'

'I'm sorry, Mona, so very sorry.'

'But you must have realized that I'd find out the truth *some* day.'

'I just hoped we could carry on the way we were. Lady Somerset seemed to be in robust health. I thought she might live on into her eighties or nineties. It was such a shock when she died. I thought we were done for then. It was such a wonderful relief to find she'd left everything to young Mr Benjamin,' said Aunty.

'So he's known all along?' I asked.

'He was not much more than a child when I came to live here. Such a pretty boy, with those wonderful dark curls. He was always so sweet with me, fascinated by my sewing basket, playing with the silks and ribbons while I discussed materials with his mother. I don't think he knew my circumstances then. He was never one to judge anyway,' said Aunty.

'So he really *is* my uncle,' I said. 'I still can't quite take it in. Do you think that's why he was so keen for me to go to the high school?'

'Perhaps.'

'But you didn't want me to.'

'Of course I did, you noodle. But they wanted the wretched birth certificate. I haven't lost it, I've got it hidden away, but we can never show it to anyone because there's a blank where your father's name should be. It was part of my deal with Lady Somerset. I had to keep the circumstances of your birth secret. She would never change her mind, not even when she was dying.' Aunty took a deep shuddering breath. 'I hated her. Sometimes I've hated the whole lot of them.'

'So why did you stay? Couldn't you have found another dressmaking job?'

'I stayed because of you. I hoped that in time they might accept you. You're a Somerset, Mona.'

'I still can't take it in. Mr Eric was my father. Mr Benjamin and Mr George are my uncles, Barbara is my aunt, and the children are my cousins.'

'Yes, you're part of the family, Mona,' said Aunty.

I looked at her pale, careworn face, the lines across her forehead, her stooped shoulders, her swollen fingers. All my life she'd stitched every day and half the night so that she could keep me.

'I'm part of *our* family too,' I said. 'You and me.'

Aunty was nothing like the mother I'd imagined, but it didn't matter. I knew she loved me. And I loved her. I reached out and we hugged each other tight.

ABOUT THE ILLUSTRATOR

NICK SHARRATT has written and illustrated many
books for children and won numerous awards for his
picture books, including the Children's Book Award
and the Educational Writers' Award. He has also
enjoyed great success illustrating Jacqueline Wilson's
books. Nick lives in Brighton.

HOW TO DANCE THE CHARLESTON

This is a fast-moving, energetic dance. Give it a go!

1. Step forward with your right foot, while pivoting both feet. Keep your arms apart by your sides and swing them to the right.

2. Step backwards with your right foot and swivel your feet, while swinging your arms to the left.

3. Step backwards with your left foot and swivel your feet, while swinging your arms to the right.

4. Step forward with your left foot and swivel your feet, while swinging your arms to the left. Keep going!

5. Now you can experiment and freestyle! Add some knee shuffles and kicks in time to the music. Anything goes!

TOP TIP: move on to the balls of your feet to make swivelling easier!

THE ROARING TWENTIES

Mona's story takes place in the 1920s. Read on to find out more about this amazing period of history . . .

The 1920s was a decade of relative peace and comfort between the First World War and the Great Depression.

In 1928 all women in Britain over the age of twenty-one were granted the right to vote! Women, particularly wealthy ones, had a lot more freedom in society. In the First World War men were conscripted into the army, leaving their jobs vacant at home. New avenues of work also opened up in industries like munition manufacturing, making weapons for the war. Women were employed to fill empty jobs and many started to earn their own money, like Mona's aunt.

Mona loves writing stories. There were lots of wonderful female writers in the 1920s who made their living from storytelling. Agatha Christie, known for her ingenious murder mysteries, was one of them. She is still one of the bestselling authors of all time!

A popular fashion in the 1920s was the flapper style. Women would cut their long hair into a bob and wear

shorter skirts and even trousers, like Desiree Dooley. This was considered very fashionable but quite scandalous compared to the long dresses and hair of the Edwardian era!

Men were also experimenting with fashion in the late 1920s. The height of fashion was finely cut suits, influenced by Hollywood and jazz clubs, and exquisite party outfits, worn by socialites like Mr Benjamin. People were desperate to keep up to date with trends and couldn't bear to look old fashioned!

Many children in the 1920s were living in poverty but, unlike the Victorians, they had to go to school until they were fourteen. School was still strict and focused on reading, writing and arithmetic. In the 1920s for the first time it became common for poorer children to wear uniform to school.

ALSO AVAILABLE

Jacqueline has written lots of other brilliant stories
inspired by history. Have you read them all?

Find out more about Jacqueline and her books at
www.jacquelinewilson.co.uk